ion Both
2025

ABOUT CHARLIE

J M LANGAN

CASTLE PRIORY PRESS

First published in Great Britain in 2024 by Castle Priory Press, Brightlingsea

978-1-915970-24-4

Copyright © JM Langan, 2024

The moral right of the author has been asserted.

All characters and events in this publication, other than those in the public domain, are fictitious and any resemblance to real persons, living or dead, is purely coincidental.

What am I, if I am not yours?

1993

His lips are on mine, soft, warm, familiar. He's smiling, his green eyes are smiling. My fingers tangle in the dark hairs on his chest.

Bang.

Bang.

Bang.

Is that the door? No. His arms are holding me tight.

Bang.

Bang...

He's undoing the buttons on my blouse.

Bang...

'Wake up Em. Em! Em!'

Someone's shaking me. My head hurts, my eyes dry, sleep cracks as I open them. 'Jas...?'

'Em, for fuck's sake. Stand up. Shit.'

'Don't wanna...'

'Stand up!'

Jason has his hands under my armpits, he's lifting me. My head lolls, Artex swirls on the ceiling. Charlie and I painted it... I remember. Why am I moving?

'I don't...'

'No? Well, tough shit. You're getting in the shower.'

'Please... no... Jas'

'Come on.'

We're in my bathroom, I sit on the floor as Jason turns the water on. I want to go back to sleep. He pulls me up again, taking off my clothes.

'Why, are we gonna...' I put my hand on his cheek and grab my breast.

'No. Em. We're definitely not. You smell really bad.'

'Oh...'

'You have sick all down you. I thought you were fucking dead. Now go on, get in.' He bundles me up, pushes me. His hands are on the top of my arms.

'I...beyond nothing...Me...I can do it.' I tug my arm away and stumble forward, hitting my head on the tiles. I crumple.

Jason whispers, 'Fuck.'

With one eye open I watch him undress. He's in the shower with me, lifting me, holding me around the waist. My head flops forward. Neck not working. So heavy. Who's washing my hair? Turning around, using him as a prop. His mouth is a line. I don't like it. My finger is on his lips.

'Where's your smile?'

'You took it Em.'

'No, I... remember... Charlie... Oh no... I don't wanna... Jason, what happened?'

'Not now Em. I need to straighten you out. This is going to be cold, are you ready?'

I scream. It's fucking freezing. Why's Jason doing this to me? Why's he in my shower?

'Jason?'

'It's OK Em, it's OK.'

I'm in bed, it smells clean. I smell clean. How did I get clean?

'Hey, you're awake.' Jason sits on the chair in the corner of the bedroom, he's sketching. The bedroom looks tidier than it has for months. Harold Lloyd is purring, curled up by my feet.

'Jason? Why're you here?'

'Because you're not doing so well.'

'I'm fine.'

'Em, you're not fine. You and Harold Lloyd are going to come and stay with me for a while.'

'No. Need to be here.'

'No Em, you don't. It's time to get up and dressed. I've packed a bag for you and put out some clothes.'

'OK. Just need to go and get some things.' As I move to climb out of bed, it suddenly feels massive, my bare feet dangle miles away from the floor. Slowly, I slide off the side waiting for my feet to hit carpet. My legs are jelly, my knees go and I'm on the floor. Giggling. I grin as I say, 'Upsy-daisy.' I'm back on my feet but only because Jason has his arm around me. I say, 'You smell nice. I need the stuff in the lounge.'

'What stuff?'

'My stuff, my... er... medicine and cigarettes.'

'I'll get your cigarettes. The other stuff, we're not bringing.'

'I need it.'

'No.' I try to push him away; I'm a feather hitting stone.

Not my bed? There's a smell of turps. I'm in Jason's bed. Why am I in Jason's bed? I'm sweating, I need to pee. I fall out of bed. I'm crawling to his ensuite. Oh, the tiles are cold and nice. My cheek is on the floor as the rest of my body follows it. Harold Lloyd is meowing.

'Em, what're you doing?'

'I'm cold.'

'I'm not surprised.' He scoops me up, I'm an ice cream.

'I need to pee.'

'OK. I'll help you.' He takes down my pants and sits me on the toilet, holding me under my arms.

'I can sit on my own... I can sit... let go.' I wiggle.

'Em, sit st... for fuck's sake. Em. Stop it.'

Why's Jason shouting at me? I'm crying again. I need to throw up. Oh, all over the bathroom floor. Can't stop retching. It hurts, my whole body hurts. Cold, shivering, itching. Jason has a cold flannel on the back of my neck. He wipes between my legs with toilet tissue and pulls me and my pants back up. The sound of the water flushing. He carries me back to his bed. Why am I in Jason's bed? I'm sweaty again, but I'm cold. I'm shaking and scratching my skin. A million tiny ants are crawling underneath it? Fuck. My teeth are chattering.

It's dark. Someone's breath touches my face. A body is on top of the covers, I'm underneath. The covers are tight around me, I don't like it. It's too tight, cocooned, I can feel pine needles on my knees, panic rising. I tug at the covers to loosen them. Panting with exertion, my chest is wheezing, it's exhausting.

'Hey, what're you doing?'

I'm in Jason's bed. His eyes have opened, they're black in the dark.

'I'm trapped, I don't like it. Jas. What's happening, why am I here? I don't understand, my knees hurt.'

His hands touch my knees, they don't hurt now. His hands are warm, 'They're OK Em, go back to sleep.'

Jason climbs under the covers, holding me tight. It's nice. His heartbeat slowly drums my back, rocking me to sleep. I close my eyes and Charlie is smiling.

I wake up with Jason next to me. Did we? My mouth feels like it's been stuck together. I need my stuff, it's all coming in, I'm remembering. I don't want that. Why is everything so heavy? I tap Jason's arm.

'I need to go get my stuff.'

'Emma... No.' He yawns, maybe if I...?

'Em, what the fuck, stop it...'

'Baby... I thought you wanted to, wanted me... If I just do this, you'll let me...' His hand is on mine, taking it off his cock. He scowls at me.

'Em. I'm not getting your stuff. And I don't want you,' he says, then under his breath, 'Not like this.'

I'm shaking... 'Jas...' My eyes roll back in my head.

'Fuck...'

A different man is talking, I don't recognise his voice, 'She's alright, it was a seizure. A combination of dehydration and withdrawal. Try and get some fluids into her. If she has another one, we'll take her in.'

'OK thanks, Doctor.'

Why are they talking about me as if I'm not here? 'I don't wanna...go.'

'It's alright, you're not going anywhere, but I need to get you to drink.' Jason rubs my shoulder, his face towards me, his eyes are black. His eyes were black before. Why are his eyes black?

'OK. A nice glass of wine, please.'

'Ha, funny.'

Why am I here? The smell of turps, Jason's bed? I'm in Jason's bed. Jason is holding a glass with a straw. He's sat me up, his arm around my back.

'Drink it, come on Em.'

'OK.' I sip on the straw, Vimto, my favourite. I sip again.

'Slowly, not too quick.'

'OK. It's good. Thank you. Why am I here?'

'Oh Em.' Jason looks down; he can't look at me. Why can't he look at me? Where's Charlie? Oh. I remember. I don't want to drink any more. 'Come on Em. Keep sipping.'

I curl up but don't go to sleep, I'm in my head. Charlie was so thin. His beautiful face reminded me of those photos of children in Auschwitz. I told him to keep fighting, he fought so hard for me. He tried so hard. I lay next to him on the thin bed and held him tight, curled up together, but then he had to go. He couldn't hold on. Jason had to come and unwrap me from him, I wouldn't let go. The doctors and nurses didn't know what to do with me. Jason took me away from him.

I whisper, 'I hate you.'

'I know, you've told me, many times.'

'You took me away from him.'

'He was gone. He wouldn't have wanted this. He wanted you to move on, to live.'

'Let me go, Jason.'

'No. I made a promise to him.'

'I need my stuff.'

'No.'

'I hate you.'

———

'Time to shower. Come on.'

'No.'

'Yes, don't make me get in there with you again.'

He's walking me, holding my elbow. My stomach is hollow and my ribs visible. I ate soup yesterday. I need my stuff. Harold Lloyd weaves between our legs.

'You should look in the mirror today, Em.'

'No. What's the point?'

'Just do it, open your eyes.' I sigh. A woman stands in front of me, she's all skin and bone. She has dark hollows for eye sockets, her hair is long and straggly around her face. Her lips are full but cracked, she has a scab around one side of her mouth. I put my fingers to my mouth and touch the scab. I'd pick it but my nails are bitten to the quick. The woman's skin shines with tears.

'I don't want to look at her anymore.'

'That's you Em.'

'No.'

Jason is taking me towards the shower. He turns it on. I sit down underneath the water, wrapping my arms around my knees.

'Are you going to wash?' The water is pounding my head. When it pounds my head, I don't have to think about the other thing. Jason's hands wash my hair, my body, making me stand up. He has a towel around me, we're going back to his bed. Maybe if I...

'No. Em, you have to stop. Nothing you do will make me get your stuff. It's not happening, do you understand?'

I turn my back on him in the bed.

'Can I have a cigarette?' I don't know how long I've been in Jason's bed. Is it minutes, years, always?

'Not in bed, come and sit in the kitchen, get dressed and you can have one there.'

He walks away from me and goes out of the door. Looking around the room, I spot my suitcase in the corner. Arranging myself from horizontal to vertical is a slow affair. Gravity is not my friend. It takes, what feels like days to put on leggings, a baggy T-shirt and a cardigan. As I walk, I keep my hand on the wall. My legs are old and unused. In the kitchen, there's a cup of coffee, a packet of cigarettes and my Zippo on the table. I half sit, half fall into the chair in front of them. Lighting a cigarette, I place my other hand on the mug of coffee, it's still too hot. I notice Jason is sitting down opposite me watching me. His mouth is a line. Where did his smile go?

'Hello.'

'Hello.'

'How long have I been here?'

'Nearly three weeks.'

'How bad was it?'

'Bad.'

I nod and look down. Take a drag on the cigarette, inhale and then blow out the smoke. My hand is on the table, my fingers look thin, my wedding ring, loose. Harold Lloyd jumps onto the table and comes towards me; I scratch behind his ear.

'I'm sorry. Was I awful?'

'Yes.'

I nod again, another drag. I let the smoke come out through my nose, I'm getting a head rush. I relax and embrace it, knowing it won't last. Harold Lloyd has jumped down and gone towards Jason.

'I'm better now, I want to go home.'

'Not yet.'

'Jas. Come on.'

'No. I made a promise. I'm not letting you go home and repeat this. I should have caught you sooner. I took my eye off the ball and look what happened. You're not going home.'

'I will not be your prisoner.' I stub out the cigarette in the ashtray and stand up too quickly. I grab the table and hold on. It takes a moment for the spinning to stop.

Jason says, 'You're not. But I will have you committed if you try to leave. I'll tell them you were suicidal; I'll tell them everything.'

'Ah!' I push the chair behind me with the backs of my legs, it hardly moves just making a tiny scraping sound, 'It's not fair. I can't... It's too much.'

Jason stands up and comes towards me. His arms are around me. I don't know how I'm crying again. Where do all the tears come from, surely there's a limit?

'Please make it stop. I don't want to feel like this anymore. How could he leave me? I'm so angry with him.'

'It's OK, Em. I'm pissed off with him too.'

———

Jason makes me get up every morning. He makes me dress and eat. He gives me books to read. I don't want to read. He makes me sit in his studio. He paints, he's always painted. He's painting a sad, hollow-eyed girl with straggly hair, she has a cat on her lap and her thin fingers are stroking its head. His painting is beautiful and sad. I go to bed. He sleeps next to me. Sometimes, he curls around me and holds me tight because of the crying. Jason gives me a pad and pen. It sits on the kitchen table. One day, maybe six weeks after he brought me to his flat, 'Come on, put your coat on. We're going for a walk.'

'OK.' I'm compliant. I know Jason won't let me go home until he's sure I'll be safe. But ghosts are living in the flat.

When we're outside, it's Autumn. I don't remember spring and summer happening, but they must have. The leaves are shades of red, orange and brown. They crunch under my feet. Jason takes us to a small urban park; finds a bench and we sit down. I'm tired, we've walked for ten minutes. My body doesn't work very well anymore. Children are throwing leaves, their parents smile and people walk past quickly going somewhere important to them. I've nowhere to go. Nowhere to be. My eyes leak tears like the leaves. Jason's arm is around me; we walk back to his studio.

1992

We are seeing the New Year in with Jason and his current girlfriend, Shannon, in Trafalgar Square.

We're inside an incredibly crowded pub where moving involves pushing through a crowd of sweaty, drunk, happy people. Jas and I have volunteered to go into the fray to get the next round in. When we finally make it to the bar and order I say, 'She's lovely Jas, are you going to keep this one?'

'Haha, very funny.'

'Just saying.'

We've never bothered with the touristy Trafalgar Square thing before, but we thought a drug-free, drink-fuelled, new year would make a pleasant change. We continue to go from pub to pub, clambering through masses of people to get to bars and paying a small fortune for each round. We're tipsy but joyful as the clock chimes twelve. Charlie and I kiss, as people knock against us.

'I could kiss you until the end of days Mrs Richards?'

'Then why did you stop, Mr Richards?' That smile, his lips, drawing me to him, 'When can we go home?'

'Now. Let's go home now.' Looking up Charlie spots Jason and Shannon and lifts his arm, they are about ten people deep away from us. We make the sign that we are going home and Jason nods and comes back towards us. I kiss Jason full on the lips. He folds me into him putting his fingers in my hair. I taste Shannon's lipstick, it's sweet like cherries.

'Enough, you two. We've talked about this.' Charlie gently yanks me away, as I grin at Jason.

'I'll see you in a couple of days. Love ya!'

He grins back and says, 'Love you too.'

'Bye Shannon, nice to meet you.' Shannon is looking at me as if I'm the devil's spawn. I smirk and wave goodbye.

Charlie squeezes my hand and says, 'You're naughty, he'll never keep a girlfriend if you keep snogging him in front of them.'

'It wasn't a snog, it was a friendly kiss goodbye, standard New Year's fayre.'

'It's a good thing I know and love you both.'

'It is, but you love me more than him, right?'

'Maybe a smidge.'

Charlie puts his hand up and hails a taxi. We kiss all the way home. We make it upstairs to the bedroom, then take our time with each other. Afterwards, we're both sweating. I whisper, 'Happy New Year.'

'Happy New Year to you. I love you, but I'm exhausted.' Charlie switches off the bedside lamp and throws an arm over me, I hear his breathing change almost immediately.

We were married on Christmas Eve 1990. I'd just finished my masters and Charlie had opened his photography studio and was taking commissions from some top fashion houses. He was in demand and making good money, enough for the deposit on our little ground-floor flat in Barnes. I'd been able to contribute a little to the deposit by working as a waiter at a posh restaurant, where I made more in tips than they paid me. The downside was the gropey old blokes who thought squeezing my arse was part of dinner. In the daytime, I would write while he'd either work in his studio or go out to jobs.

After New Year everything changed. Charlie kept coming home exhausted from work. He'd fall asleep in his chair before we could eat. By the end of January, we were in his oncologist's office.

He'd already been given a bone marrow biopsy plus blood tests and an MRI.

'It's not good news Charlie, I'll get straight to the point, it's back.'

I say, 'No, but he was in remission. I've read all the blurb. It doesn't come back after a couple of years.'

I squeeze Charlie's hand too tightly, leaning forward with loads of pieces of paper I've collected with information about Hodgkin's Lymphoma.

The doctor looks at me, 'It's rare to come back, but it can and it has. Aggressively.'

Charlie looks at our entwined fingers, blinks slowly and then looks up, 'How aggressively?'

'Very. We could try a cocktail of chemo and radiation and remove as much as we can but Hodgkin's at this stage... It's in your marrow this time, as well as your lymph nodes, Charlie.'

Charlie nods once.

'No, but he had those removed.'

'He had a couple removed, there're about six hundred lymph nodes in the body and several of Charlies are under attack.'

Charlie has switched off; he's staring into space.

I say, 'So, when can he start treatment?'

'Straight away, but Charlie...' The doctor takes off his glasses, his expression sombre, 'Get your house in order. I will get you a bed for the day after tomorrow.'

Charlie says, 'I understand, thank you, Dr Benjamin, come on Em.'

He stands up and we walk out of the doctor's office into the tangle of hospital corridors that smell of shit, piss and sterilising fluid. Everyone walking by is silent, their faces either resolute or panicked. No one smiles in hospital corridors.

In the car, as I'm driving us home, Charlie says, 'I need to speak to a solicitor.'

'No, no... You don't. There's no need, you can beat this. You'll be fine, you're young and strong.'

He sounds weary, 'No Em. I'm not sure I can. Please find one for me, I'm knackered. I need to sleep.'

'OK.' I'm trying so hard not to cry. Charlie lays his head against the headrest and closes his eyes.

On our last night in the flat together, before Charlie goes into hospital, we make love, slowly, carefully. I'm on top; he can't manage it any other way anymore. As he finishes, he says, 'This is what I'll remember. Us connected. We're one person, Em. Just you and me.'

'Just you and me. I love you, Charlie.' He's already asleep.

———

Over the coming weeks, Charlie disappears, his flesh, his hair, his spirit. A soul slowly leaving a body. I'm in the hospital as much as they'll let me. I hold his hand as they fill him with huge doses of chemotherapy, pumping poison into him. The nurses try to find a vein that doesn't collapse the minute the needle goes in. He has ulcers in his mouth, he can hardly speak. I wear a mask so I don't infect him with anything, I can't kiss him or touch him.

Nothing works. Then they tell me I don't need the mask or the scrubs anymore when I visit. They tell me to say goodbye. For three days, I lie on the bed next to him. I hold him, whisper to him, kiss his hair, his ears, his neck, his fingers. I try to remember every plane of his face, every tiny scar, every mole. It's a rainy Monday at the end of March when he breathes out for the last time. I feel it, his whole body is suddenly limp.

Jason arrives and wrenches me away as I keen for my lost love. I punch him twice, once in the nose and once in the stomach before he manages to hold my arms by my sides. Half carrying me, half dragging me as I scream. 'I hate you. I hate you. I hate you.'

He takes me back to our flat and puts me in our bed where the smell of Charlie remains strong. I inhale his pillow and hold onto it like a life raft.

Jason sleeps on the sofa and brings me coffee and sandwiches. I refuse to eat or drink. Eventually, he makes me. It becomes clear, I need Jason to believe I'm OK so I can stop all this. So, I eat. I drink. I try not to cry all the time. I'm on automatic. Jason helps arrange the funeral. Charlie's parents and brother Robert arrive. I hold onto Charlie's mum as we weep. Jason helps me write a eulogy. I read it in the crematorium. Charlie didn't want a religious funeral. I say words and read a poem he liked. I talk to people and shake hands, let them hug me. Jason stands by me throughout. Watching. I must keep up the pretence. I must. My parents come, I smile, I cry. They all leave. Everybody leaves. Jason thinks he can leave too. He promises to visit. I tell him I'll be fine. I'm lying, I'm as far from fine as a person can be.

As soon as the flat is empty, I phone Dean, put in an order and arrange to meet.

We do the deal outside a pub in Hammersmith, my cash for his drugs. I take an E straight away and as soon as I'm home I snort two thick lines of coke. I take the 2nd E before the first rush. By the time the second E hits me, I'm off my head, where's Charlie, why isn't he here with me? I take a third E and snort some more coke. I decide to go for a walk.

I end up in a pub. I order a Diet Coke and sit in a corner, jiggling my leg to the music. A man disturbs me, he's saying something. I don't understand what, but he seems nice. We go outside, he gives me some speed. I snort it off my hand as he fucks me from behind against a wall. I don't remember agreeing to that.

'Stop it. No.'

I twist away but my body is pathetic. He doesn't stop, it doesn't matter. My body doesn't matter. I walk away. Where am I? Then I'm sitting down next to a homeless person and they offer to share their sleeping bag with me. I didn't know I was cold. I've forgotten my coat, it's dark.

Shivering, I wake up, the homeless person has gone, along with my bag and all my drugs. I walk the two miles home along the Thames towpath as the sun is coming up. The river looks pretty in the orange light. When I'm home, I find the spare key above the front door. I phone Dean. I need something stronger.

Charlie's office is a mess, all his photos are all over the floor. Why didn't I take more photos of him? Most of the photos here are of me or tall skinny models. They're beautiful. He managed to make me look beautiful, even though I'm shorter and curvier than the models he usually works with. Where's Charlie, shouldn't he be home?

My arm hurts, I look at it and untie the ligature around it. The needle, spoon and lighter are all sitting on Charlie's desk. Charlie wouldn't want them here. In the living room, Harold Lloyd stands on the back of a comfy chair meowing at me. I feed him. Not fair to let him starve. Back to the sofa, curled up at Charlie's end, holding the cushions, my nose deep, trying to smell the remnants of him. On the coffee table, cigarettes are ripped up to make joints, pills are scattered about or crushed to snort... I lean forward, pressing one nostril in with my forefinger as I sniff up some residue from the table. What was that? E, speed, coke or something else? I can't remember, it feels good. I lie back for a bit. The black and white film of our wedding plays in my mind. Jason was best man, Kaz was my maid of honour and little Gracie was a bridesmaid. I wore a white lace dress that came to my knees, it hugged my body. The men wore dark single-breasted suits, what colour were they? Blue because they had cornflowers for buttonholes, I remember. My bouquet was all cornflowers and I had them sewn into my hair which was made to look like it could tumble down at any moment. Kaz wore a satin blue dress cut on the bias, she looked amazing. Gracie wore the same colour but with a twirly dress because she loves to dance, like me.

We all went to an Italian restaurant after, Jason made a toast that had everyone crying with laughter. Kaz insisted on doing a toast as well, including loads of embarrassing stories of when we were small. My dad said lovely things and talked about how proud my gran would be. I cried. I remember. Is that smoke? Somethings burning. Forcing my eyelids open, there's a cigarette burning in the ashtray, a scrunched-up Rizla is alight. It's OK, nothing to worry about. Nothing to worry about. Eyes closed. I'm on my knees, the smell of pine sap and dirt fills my nose. My knees hurt. I don't wanna... They make me. Kevin makes me... No. I don't wanna. My knees. Hand on knee, it's fine. I'm OK I just need to... I find the piece of rubber tubing and wrap it around my arm. I pop an E into my mouth and swallow it, then focus on warming the smack into liquid so it'll go into the needle. My arms look like Charlie's did, they were bruised and sore. I want to be with Charlie. I find a working vein and push the needle in.

1987

Jason has found us a flat to share that's only about three-quarters of a mile away from my college. It's inside an impressive-looking Victorian house in a posh suburban street about halfway between college and Putney High Street. It's a prime location and I can't believe I've got so lucky. We have the top flat on the third floor. The stairs on the ground floor are fairly wide, but soon become thin and creaky as they reach the third, we're in the roof space of the house. When I check out the three bedrooms they all have slanting beams which make each room fairly unique in shape. The beams are still higher than me, but Jason can only stand upright in the very centre of his room. Jason has the first room on the left as you go in, next to him is Charlie's, the other person sharing with us and opposite there's mine. It's the smallest one as I'm the last one to join the flat share. The bedrooms, kitchen and bathroom all come off a tiny hall, where a phone perches on a stool between the doors of the two larger bedrooms. The bathroom is tiny but somehow a massive roll-top Victorian bath with lion's feet sits in pride of place. My new flatmates are surprised at how happy I am with the room; it's bigger than halls and my room overlooks an overgrown mature garden with a magnolia tree in its centre. The two larger rooms look out onto the street. I immediately get on with unpacking and making it feel like home, Blu Tack at the ready.

Charlie is a year older than Jason and me, he took a year out before starting Uni. Jason doesn't know what he did that year, but he has told me not to pry as Charlie can be 'a bit funny.' I asked Jason what that meant, and he said, maybe Charlie had depression or something, but knew nothing for sure. Jason said he didn't know him that well, they didn't socialise. Jason is studying fine art, whereas Charlie is studying photography. But, Jason said, 'He pays his rent on time, he's clean and keeps himself to himself. Compared to some of the other horror stories you hear about, he's a dream flatmate.'

I grimaced at Jason and said he sounded like a serial killer, but if Jason vouched for him, I was OK with it.

When I finally meet Charlie, my first impression isn't great. Jason decides to make some tea and introduce us properly on the day we all move in. We're around the tiny kitchen table next to the equally tiny window that looks out into the garden. I sit opposite Charlie with Jason next to me. Charlie is tall, so when we sit down, mine and his knees touch under the table, we awkwardly apologise and try to find a way to sit so none of our body parts are touching. In the end, one of my knees is between his legs. I'm glad I'm in leggings.

Jason is rambling on to us about how he met each of us, filling the silence with his usual happy chat. I'm looking at Jason and smiling then looking at Charlie, who is not. He's staring at me. I start to wonder if he ever blinks. Jason is completely oblivious and still talking. When he finally stops and I'm about to excuse myself, Charlie says, 'You look like Zoe Lund.'

'Oh?'

I don't know who that is.

'Except she has longer hair.'

Charlie has clearly said everything he's going to say, our knees bang together as he stands up - more mumbled sorrys. Once he's left the kitchen and his bedroom door is closed, I turn slowly to look at Jason with wide eyes and whisper, 'What the fuck?'

'Like I said, he can be a bit intense.'

'And who's Zoe Lund?'

'No idea, mate.

'Have you ever seen him around girls, with a girlfriend or maybe blink?'

'He sometimes photographs girls.'

'Jason!'

'What?'

'You've moved me in with a frigging psycho.'

'Nah, he's fine. I've never once seen him murder anyone, or to my knowledge have sex.'

Jason is seeing the funny side and I can't help but smile. Still, the man gives me the creeps.

'Fucking hell.' I sigh.

1993

They're talking, they think they're being quiet.

'How is she?'

'Not good. I don't know what else to do.'

'She needs time. That's all. We just have to wait for her to come back to us. She's strong, she'll be … Oh.'

'I'll be what?'

'OK.' Kaz's arms are around me, Dave is watching me. I'm a bird trapped in a cage that everyone has come to see.

'Yeah, I'll be OK.' When hell freezes over.

'Well, hello you.' Kaz holds me at arm's length and looks me up and down. Her mouth smiles but her eyes say something else. Dave stares at me from beside the cooker. Jason sits at the kitchen table and slowly turns his coffee cup as if it is something to be examined. His long fingers are stained with paint.

'Where are the kids?'

'With my mum, being spoilt rotten.' Kaz says, still looking at me. Her eyes seem like Jason's when he looks at me. What is that, pity? Stop it, normal conversation is required.

'How's your mum? I miss her.'

'She's good. Really well. She loves being a nana, says it's given her a new lease of life. She sends her love.'

'That's nice, is it OK if I sit down?' My legs still don't work properly.

Kaz says, 'Of course, you don't have to ask.' Then a look passes between her and Jason.

He says, 'Coffee?' His mouth is still a line.

'Yes please.'

I hate that I've taken his smile. He stands up and pours from the pot he has on his cooker, then adds milk from a jug on the table. Harold Lloyd is wandering amongst all the feet, trying to find someone to stroke him.

Dave sits next to me and takes my hand, 'Matt was asking after you, he's back from Abu Dhabi. He wanted to come but had to work.'

My hand disappears inside Dave's, I'd never noticed he had huge hands. Or maybe mine are tiny? Everything is quiet, what were they saying? Matt, they were talking about Matt, 'Oh, OK. Is he happy to be back?'

'Yeah, we think so. His wife and kids are having to adjust to living in Britain, must be a big change for them.' Kaz says as she sits down as well.

I conjure an image of Matt in my mind, he was kind. Maybe I should have stayed in the village with him. If I'd never come to London. If I'd stayed in the tiny village and pumped out babies like Kaz...what? What would I have done there, except lose my mind? Too much stuff there, too much to forget. Probably would have got into this state sooner. But then I would never have met Charlie. Beautiful Charlie, I jerk my hand out of Dave's and wrap both around my mug of coffee, then take a sip. Mustn't cry, got to get better. Got to get out of here. They need to think I'm fine.

Kaz says, 'Mm.'

Then she and Dave exchange a look.

'What? Whatever it is I can handle it.' Kaz looks at Jason who nods slightly.

'What... stop treating me with kid gloves. Tell me what you have to tell me.'

Jason looks at me, 'Just tell her.'

Kaz says, 'Right, OK, I don't know if you've spoken to your mum and dad lately...'

'Is one of them sick, are they OK?'

'Yes, it's just Tigger died and Kevin... well..'

'Oh. Tigger, the cat.'

Kaz nods.

'And Kevin?'

'He continues to be a twat, got done for drinking and driving.'

My face twists into a grimace, 'Yup. Usual twatage. No surprises there. God, I thought it was something really bad. Thank fuck.'

Kaz starts to laugh, 'Jesus, we were terrified it was going to really upset you.'

Dave is smiling. Jason watches me. I snort a laugh, then look down at my mug.

Kaz continues, 'I mean, Tigger was really old and your mum said he died peacefully in his sleep. Cats don't usually live to over twenty, do they? So, he must have had a great life, for a cat.'

Kaz is nervous around me, why is she nervous? I say, 'Yeah, for a cat.'

Jason's brown eyes look black again, he's tired. Why's he staring at me? I look away first.

'Anyway, we thought it would be nice to go out for a meal tonight if you were up for it?' Kaz says.

'Sure, why not.' I stand up, 'Let's pretend my husband isn't dead, that my cat isn't dead, my cousin isn't a twat and that I'm not a drug addict. Let's do that. Fun.'

Picking up my coffee, I leave the room. There are hisses

of whispers behind me. In Jason's bedroom, I put the mug on the bedside table and flop, face down onto the bed. The muffled sound of another person in the room. Jason.

'What the fuck, Em. They've travelled all this way to see you, left their kids. All so they can support you and talk to you and you do that. Stop being such a fucking bitch.'

Rolling onto my back, I glare at him for a moment, there are no words. He sighs, then leaves.

A little later, he comes in and starts to get changed. As he's undressing, he says, 'You have half an hour to change into some clean clothes then we're going out.'

'No.'

'Yes.'

'Fuck off.'

'Fuck you.' He goes to the wardrobe and grabs something, 'Here.' He throws a dress at me. I pick it up and throw it back.

'Prick.' I return to my lying down position with my back to him.

His hands are on me. What's he doing?

'Stand up.'

'No.' He's lifting me and making me stand up, I haven't the strength to fight him.

'Arms up.'

'No.' He lifts my t-shirt and heaves it up so my arms are forced over my head. He puts the dress on, putting my arms in one at a time as if he were dressing a reluctant doll. He takes off my leggings and sits me on the bed to take them off my feet. I glower at him. I've given up fighting. He puts my feet one by one into tights and then gets an old pair of brogues and laces them up. He stands me up again and hikes up the tights. When he's finished, he lets go of me and I slump back down. He stands back and looks at me, frowns and disappears. He comes back with my hairbrush, tugging out the bobble I have holding my hair in a ponytail and starts brushing.

'Ow.'

'You could do it yourself.' I ignore him. It feels nice having my hair brushed, but I'm not going to give him the satisfaction of telling him.

When he's done, he looks at me again, 'You look almost like you.' He still isn't smiling.

'I'm sorry I took your smile.' Tears again. Damn it.

He looks at me and kneels by the bed, wrapping his arms around me and holding me tight.

'I don't think I'm me anymore Jas. I think I've gone. I don't know who I am or how I'm expected to be. What do I do now?'

Leaning back so he can look at me, 'Ah Em, you'll always be you. Whatever you do, you'll do it in your own good time, when you're ready. OK.'

'OK.'

'Thanks Jas. I still hate you.'

'I know.'

———

We're in a restaurant. I can't remember when I was last in one. Was it our one-year anniversary and we went back to the Italian place, or was it after that? I don't think it was after unless you count the hospital one. I won't count that. Kaz, Dave and Jason are talking. I'm watching their mouths move but I'm not listening to them. Instead, I'm eavesdropping on the couple at the next table. They're in love. Kaz and Dave are laughing, Jason is smiling but it's not his proper one, he's lost that. I think the real me might have it somewhere, maybe it's inside me screaming to get out. But the real me would let it out. This me won't. This me is horrible. This me is cruel. This me deserves everything that's happening. The man behind us is telling the woman that he loves her to the moon and back. A bit of a cliché but he sounds like he means it. I wonder if she's smiling, no...they're kissing. I miss kissing Charlie. He had the best lips for kissing. Our starters have arrived, what did I order? It's orange. Soup. I ordered soup. Soup is OK. Hang on did someone say my name?

'Em. Emma. Em...'

Voices, saying my name? They look familiar, I'm confused.

'It's John and Ken, remember, from Charlie's Uni photo-shoot. How's Charlie, is he here?'

I stand up, Jason next to me, Kaz has taken John and Ken away, trying to hide their shock and sadness.

'Em. It's OK, do you want to sit down?' I nod, Jason is holding me up. Dave is looking from me to Kaz to Jason. He doesn't know what to do.

Jason says, 'We can stay or we can go, it's up to you.'

Ken is crying. John is hugging him while Kaz rubs his back as she looks at me. Charlie had said they owed him a favour, I never found out why, I should ask them. I stand up.

'What're you doing?' Jason, black sad eyes.

'I need to ask them something.'

I walk over, 'It's OK Kaz.'

Moving to their table, I dodge people, chairs. Is everyone watching?

Ken is still crying.

John says, 'I'm so very sorry, we didn't know.'

'It's OK, but there's something...' Their faces are different. Sadder. What am I doing? I have a question. That was it.

'On the day you modelled, you remember, Charlie said you two owed him a favour. I never asked what he had done for you to get the favour.'

John smiles, then looks at Ken, who is slowly getting himself together, 'He modelled for us, for our final pieces. Didn't he tell you?'

'No. What kind of modelling.'

Ken looks down as he says, 'I was on the same course as Charlie. I took his photographs, he was beautiful.' His eyes meet mine.

John adds, 'And I did art and he did some life modelling for me.'

Ken's face is wet, 'He was such a gorgeous darling boy; I can't imagine what you're...'

'Please don't. I cry all the time, I can't... not here. I would love to see your work, I have so few photos or anything of him really, he was always behind the lens.'

'Oh my God, yes, we would love to.' Ken takes my hands in his.

'Jason will probably come too; he won't let me out of his sight. I've, er...struggled with...well everything, lately.'

Ken is rummaging in his bag, 'Here, this is our address, come this Sunday, I'll make lunch. About midday?'

I take the card and hold it in my hand rubbing the sharp corners with my thumb, 'Yes and thank you. It's lovely to see you.'

1990

We've been living in the flat in Barnes for about a month. After a day at the library in Kensington, working on my thesis, I walk in through the front door and something smells wonderful. Charlie's cooking has vastly improved since we were students living together. Saliva forms in my mouth.

'Hey you.' Charlie grins at me.

'Hello, what're you cooking? It smells amazing.'

'Oh, just a veggie bolognese. I have a surprise for you.' I can't work out what is going on, it reminds me of Charlie at Christmas, overflowing with joy at everything.

'What have you done?' I squint at him.

'Come with me.' More grinning as he grabs my hand.

In the living room, I find out what Charlie is so excited about.

'Oh! Hello... Who's this?' I'm having a staring contest with a tiny black and white kitten who's standing on the top of our sofa looking extremely cute. He has two black circles around his eyes and black and white splodges everywhere else. Picking him up, I'm greeted with loud purrs. 'Oh Charlie, he... she... is gorgeous.'

'He's your housewarming present.'

'What shall we call him? What shall we call you?' I'm holding him in one hand, tickling his tummy as he plays with my fingers.

'Well, I was thinking, seeing as how he looks like he has a thick pair of glasses on, and because I'm Charlie, because of Charlie Chaplin, that we could call him Harold Lloyd.'

'Oh, that's perfect. Hello, Harold Lloyd. And you, come here.' I grab the front of Charlie's shirt and tug him towards me so I can kiss him, 'Thank you. I love him and I love you.'

'I love you too. Now I must get back to the dinner. You've about five minutes of playtime with Harold Lloyd before we eat.'

'OK. I will say thank you properly later.'

'You may end up with dozens of kittens if you're not careful.' There's desire in Charlie's gaze.

'Maybe dinner can wait?' I say, leaning in for another kiss.

'No. I've worked hard on it. How many dinners have we wasted? I'm standing firm.'

'OK, but only if you're sure...'

Dinner is burnt by the time we're finished and we end up ordering a curry. As we eat it on the sofa, Harold Lloyd attacks our toes. His tiny claws are like needles and we both struggle not to spill our food.

'The bedroom is off limits, that's my only stipulation. I don't want him putting us off.' Charlie is looking at the kitten.

'Fair enough.'

That idea lasts until we hear him crying outside the bedroom door later as we're trying to get to sleep.

'Fuck.' Charlie climbs out of bed and lets him in. We hear the purring as he clambers up the bed towards us.

I whisper, 'Hello, Harold Lloyd.'

He circles between us until he's a tiny ball.

'OK, but when we're having sex, he's not coming in.'

Charlie is whispering as well.

'OK, seems fair. Do you hear that Harold Lloyd, no watching us have sex.'

I buy Harold Lloyd toys and when he's big enough, we fit a cat flap in the door. The first time he goes out we're terrified he'll never come back. Charlie and I wait anxiously, unable to settle, like parents on their child's first day at school.

When we finally hear the click of the cat flap, I'm overjoyed to see his bespectacled face. Much purring and cat treats follow. Charlie tells me not to spoil him, which is easier said than done.

Charlie has whole conversations with Harold Lloyd, about his plans for the day, about what he does when he's at work. Seeing Charlie with Harold Lloyd makes me start to think about children. Charlie would be an incredible dad. He's patient, loving, kind. I bring it up one evening as we're flicking between channels on the TV.

'Have you ever thought about having kids?' I have my feet on Charlie's lap and Harold Lloyd is on top of my feet.

Charlie mutes the TV and looks at me, 'I already have you two. Why?'

'Just wondering. I don't mean now, this minute... but sometime in the future.'

'Yeah, I suppose, I always assumed I would. When I had Hodgkin's, they said I may have trouble because of the chemo, so they asked me if I wanted to store some sperm. I did.' Charlie is stroking Harold Lloyd's head.

'Oh. I didn't know that.'

'I suspect everything will work fine, but better safe than sorry.'

'Yeah, better safe than sorry.'

'What about you?'

'I don't know, I never thought about kids until you.'

'Ah, so I'm dad material.' He smiles.

'Maybe.'

'You want my babies.' Now he's laughing.

'Not if you carry on like that!' I try to move my feet off his lap, dislodging Harold Lloyd who looks at me with disdain and jumps off the sofa onto one of the comfy chairs to lie down. Charlie leans over so he's on top of me.

'I could put a baby in you right now if you wanted.'

'I think that would be tricky as I'm on the pill.'

'But we could practise.'

'We could...'

1993

Kaz and Dave leave the following day. Before they go there are more whispered conversations with Jason. I know I should have been nicer, particularly to Kaz. She's my oldest friend, I'm Godmother to her kids and I was a shit. I know all of that and yet my head is unable to make sense of anything. Everything feels broken; the world, my friendships. I stare out of the car window as Jason drives us to Ken and John's. Houses, streets and shops flash past me moving quickly. Everything is moving too quickly.

I'm trying to breathe more slowly so Jason doesn't notice, my heart feels like it could escape my chest and fly away. Maybe that's what will happen, maybe I'll die right here in the car. I could be with Charlie. I close my eyes and a tear drops out. Fuck, he's going to notice. Stop it. Stop. IT. NOW! I'm pinching the skin on my arms, which are wrapped around me. There'll be a bruise. Doesn't matter this is all my fault. It's OK, it's OK, I'm OK. Pinch. Pinch. Pinch.

We're standing outside a pretty terrace house in Brixton.

'Are you sure about this?'

Jason is observing me like I'm an experiment. Instead, I

focus on their front door. Number nine is my lucky number. Their door is blue. Charlie's favourite colour.

'No, but I need to see.'

'OK then.' Jason walks in front of me and rings the bell.

Ken opens the door wearing jeans and a white T-shirt, 'Hello, come in, come in.'

I step onto the original Victorian tiled hallway floor as we go towards the back of the house that opens out into a modern open-plan kitchen. There's the smell of roasting food and something else, sweet and warm. A candle is burning on a huge modern sideboard as we walk in, vanilla. John is at the cooker, he's dressed almost identically to Ken, except his T-shirt is black. He leaves what he's doing and hugs me. Ken hugs Jason, then they swap. I see it, over Ken's shoulder. It's huge, maybe six feet by six feet, Charlie is looking right at me.

'Oh.' I walk towards it. It's incredibly beautiful, painted in muted tones. Jason is in the painting as well, the two of them are naked and curled up together, I can't... I turn my back on it and say to Jason, 'You never said.'

'We did it as a favour for John.'

I turn to the picture again, Charlie is looking straight out of the picture, his eyes follow me as I get closer. He's curled around Jason who is looking down. Both of their bodies look lean and muscular, it reminds me of sketches I've seen by Leonardo De Vinci.

'It's beautiful,' I say to John, 'have you got any smaller sketches or anything else?'

'Yes, I have them ready to show you.'

'And I have the photographs. I've made some prints for you to take with you.'

John goes back to the cooker and turns whatever is cooking down, then tells us to follow him. We go into a room at the front of the house that he's using as a studio. There's a sofa. I half sit, half fall heavily on to it. I'm exhausted. In the room, there are sketches everywhere, hands, lips, noses. Some I recognise as Charlie's. Jason sits down next to me, into my ear, quietly, he says, 'I'm here.' Black eyes, line for a mouth. His face makes me want to cry. I touch it with my hands, feeling the warmth from his skin. I'm causing him so much pain, 'Hey, hey, you're OK. It's OK.'

Jason holds me, rocking me like a child. I calm down a little.

'I'm OK. I'll be OK.' I take a deep breath. John looks concerned as he sits in front of his desk. Ken hovers in the doorway.

'Please show me the rest.'

John glances at Jason.

'Please.'

'OK.'

John hands me a large folder. It's too big for my knees so I slide onto the floor and cross my legs. Opening the folder, it's Charlie, all Charlie. His hands, his face, his lips, his body. It's my Charlie. His hands are on Jason's body, gently holding one of his hands and the other resting on his hip. They're relaxed. So many sketches. I find one and it's Charlie looking straight at me, his mouth relaxed, the grin behind his eyes.

'Can I have this one? Would that be OK?'

'You can take whatever you want, my sweet girl.' John hands me the folder.

'No, just this. The rest would be too much. You're very good, very talented. Why didn't you sell the picture in the kitchen?'

'I couldn't bear to give it away. I was offered something ridiculous for it, but it felt special.'

'It's incredibly special.'

'Would you like to see the photos now, or after lunch?' Ken asks softly.

Jason says, 'Shall we wait until after lunch?'

I nod. I'm holding the picture of Charlie in front of me.

John says, 'Well, I better get back to the kitchen. Ken, can you give me a hand?'

They disappear leaving me on the floor with all the pictures of Charlie surrounding me, Jason still sits on the sofa. I know he's watching me.

I try to stand up but struggle to move from the floor, his hands are under my arms before I need to ask. I'm next to him, his arms around me.

'No wonder he didn't mind me kissing you. Why did you keep it secret?'

'I don't know, two heterosexual guys have their painting done in a homoerotic way. I suppose I... we were a little embarrassed.'

'You shouldn't be.'

'Yeah, seems stupid now.'

Where's Jason? He looks like he might cry. I've broken this man, we, Charlie and I, have broken him. He's looking at the pictures spread out on the floor. I stand up slowly and lean down to get the one where Charlie's hands are on Jason's body. I flop back down on the sofa holding the sketch.

'Is it stupid that I'm jealous of this.' I turn to look at Jason, a tear has escaped and is falling down his cheek. He shakes his head.

'No.'

'I'm sorry that I forgot you missed him too.'

Jason brings me into a hug,

'It's OK Em. We're OK.'

We stay like that for a while. When we're both a little more together, we go back into the kitchen. The table is covered in food; there's a roast chicken, dauphinoise potatoes and loads of vegetables.

'Woah, that's a lot of food.' I say as Ken ushers us to the table to sit down.

John says, 'Sorry, I'm a bit of a feeder.'

Looking down, I say, 'I'm so sorry for all of this.'

'Oh no, Em it's fine, I just feel terrible that we lost touch and didn't know. We're dreadful friends.'

'Shut up, it is easily done. Charlie and I didn't keep in touch either. Life is busy. I'm just glad we bumped into you. It's so lovely to see you.'

We eat and chat about uni, Jason seems to brighten up. Watching him talk to Ken and John, he is laughing at something. That's nice, I like Jason's laugh. When was the last time I heard him laugh? I can't remember when I laughed. When did we last really laugh? I watch his hands; they move as he talks. He has paint under his nails. Have I ever seen his nails completely free of paint? When did we meet, 1982 or was it 83? Have I known Jason for ten years?

'Em... Em?' Jason is saying my name.

'Sorry, what was that?'

'We lost you there for a moment, don't forget to eat your food.'

Everything is still on my plate; I haven't touched it.

'Right, OK. Sorry.' I pick up my knife and fork and cut into a sprout. They're all looking at me. It's suddenly very quiet.

Ken breaks the silence, and says, 'I told you about the exhibition we did in Chelsea, didn't I?'

'Yeah, I would love to have some of your work in our studio.' They continue talking, I chew half a sprout. It takes ages, I swallow it and look at the plate again, I put the other half of the sprout in my mouth. Jason is cross when I don't eat. It tastes like iron. Do I like sprouts? Charlie loved them, they reminded him of Christmas. He liked them with bacon. Maybe if I ate meat, I could have sprouts with bacon. I should eat meat. Why don't I eat meat, why did I stop? My head's a jumble? Jason is talking about a commission he is working on for the British Museum. I went there once. Not with Charlie, who did I go with? Can't remember, some shitty date. We went to the restaurant and he ate a toastie. Ha.

Toasties at the British Museum, that would be a good name for a book. I was writing a book, before Charlie... What was I writing about? It was about a girl. It was probably crap. I didn't know about anything then. I know even less now. I better eat some potato, before they look at me again. It tastes really rich; my stomach won't like that. I'll stick to the other vegetables, a carrot. Ken and John are handsome. I wonder if they draw or photograph each other, I bet that would be beautiful. Someone is saying my name, 'Em.'

'I'm eating.'

'Yes, that's good. Em I was just explaining about Harold Lloyd, you tell it better.'

'Harold Lloyd's mine and Charlie's cat.'

'Yes, but... come on Em explain why he's called Harold Lloyd.' Jason is looking at me, he looks like he's smiling but it's not real, inside he's black like his eyes, bottomless sadness. I should try to make Jason happy. He's been looking after me. I think I was horrible. Yeah, definitely horrible.

'Harold Lloyd, yes. It's because he wears glasses and Charlie is Charlie because he was named after Charlie Chaplin.'

All three of them are looking at me. I didn't explain properly. I'll eat another carrot, maybe they'll talk about something else. Why are they all looking at me. I'll just put these down quietly onto the plate and then I'll go.

'Em. What are you...' Jason's voice follows me down the tiled hallway. Need to lie down for a minute on the sofa. Very tired.

'Em, wake up.' Jason is rubbing my arm, I put my hand over his. I don't want to come back to reality. Charlie was having his portrait painted by John, he was smiling at me. I was going to kiss him.

'Em. Come on.'

'Mm.'

'We should go, we can look at the photos another day.'

'Today. Please let me look today.' I start to sit up. There he his, black eyes, a line for a mouth. I touch my fingers to his lips. He takes my hand away.

'You're exhausted.'

'I'll be alright, I just need to wake up a little. Can you help me up, please?'

Jason lifts me into a sitting position. I cross my legs in front of me, then wrap my arms around my knees. He's looking at me but I don't know what he's thinking, his eyes are just blackholes drawing me in, I could disappear in those blackholes.

'I'll go and get Ken and we can take a quick look, then I'm taking you home. Harold Lloyd will be wondering where we are.'

'OK.'

As Jason walks down the hall, his trainers squeak on the tiles, male voices, more steps. The three of them. Jason's hand is out, I take it, and it curls around mine, his thumb strokes my thumb. His fingers are rough from painting, I like the feeling on my skin. We are across the hall in Ken's office. It's full of photos. There's the one Charlie took of me, with John and Ken at my feet wearing nothing but leads. I didn't know they had it. I don't recognise the me that's standing there looking powerful in skin-tight latex and a corset. Jason glances across at the image. Is that a smile?

He says, 'I wondered where that one went.'

'Hey, he got us into Skin Two. We're very proud of that.' John is beaming at me. I look down, I don't know how to respond.

'Right well here they are. There were larger versions that we sold but this folder is for you. I have put all of them in, even the ones we didn't use, I think you'll like them.' Ken is holding it out like a tray. I take it off him, it's heavy, but bring my arms around it so it is close to my chest.

'Where can I, shall I just sit...er...'

'Here,' Ken stands up from his seat at his desk, 'sit here.'

'Thank you.'

Ken and John disappear again. Jason moves some things off a chair in the corner and sits down. The folder seems huge on the table.

When I open the first page, Charlie is right in front of me, half of the photograph is in shadow the other half is brightly lit, he isn't smiling. Instead, he is staring down the lens of the camera like he hates it. It's not my Charlie, where's my Charlie, I turn the page, a photo from behind with his hands on his head, he's naked, his body looks great. Another, lying on a chaise longue, nude. He isn't smiling, another and another they don't look like my Charlie. Then I find him, towards the back, the photos between the staged ones, he's laughing, his head back and his mouth wide open. There's my beautiful boy. There he is. I close the folder and pat it gently.

'Enough now.' I don't need to turn my head. Jason waits for me to speak.

Quietly, 'OK.' He comes behind me and helps me up, I hold the folder to my chest and keep it there. I walk to the other room and find the drawing, I put it between the plastic sheets holding the photos in the folder. My Charlie is safe inside.

'Thank you, for this. Em and I really appreciate it.' Jason shakes John's hand, but John isn't having it, pulling him into a hug. Ken does the same. Then they come to me. If I speak it will all just be too many words. I nod at them keeping my eyes fixed firmly on the ground.

'Please come again, or we'll come to you. OK.'

Jason says, 'OK.'

Outside. Rain is falling heavily hitting my head. Jason is in the driving seat of my car. I get in on the passenger side and put the folder on my knee. I pat it with the flat of my hands pushing the rain off it. It's safe. I put my seatbelt on. My fingers lie still on the top of the folder. Out of the window, houses, trees, cars but they don't matter. I place a snapshot of Charlie in my mind, there he is, there he is.

'Em. Emma, we're home.' Jason has unclicked my seatbelt.

He lifts me out of the car and takes me up the stairs to his studio. The folder is safe in my arms. He puts me on top of the bed.

'You need to eat; you hardly touched your food.'

'OK.'

'I'll bring you some soup.' Jason knows soup is all I can cope with.

Later, in bed. The folder's on the floor. When Jason comes to bed, he climbs in next to me.

'Oh, I thought you were asleep.'

I look at him, how long can he stand this?

'Why are you doing this?'

'Doing what?'

'Looking after me.'

'I promised Charlie.'

'And?'

'And I love you.'

'Still? How could you?'

'I don't know, I just do. I don't know how not to love you.'

'I'm not the same.'

'Neither am I.'

'I don't understand.'

'Em.' His hand is on my cheek.

'Jas.'

'I have loved you since the first day I sat in a van going to a fair with you, since you fell asleep on my shoulder since you fell in love with everyone but me.'

'I've loved you too.'

'Not in the same way.'

'No. Probably not.'

'No.' His hand falls away, but the shape of it, the warmth of it, the sense of his sandpaper fingers gentle on my cheek remain for a moment. I lean forward and kiss him. His lips are not new to me. He's pushing me away.

'Stop. I don't wan... I need you to... please stop.'

'I'm sorry. You've been so...'

'I made a promise. Turnover, let me hug you and we can go to sleep.'

'OK.' I turn over, he moves closer to me wrapping himself around me so I'm enclosed in him, I'm small and safe. His erection is against me, I try not to move, he doesn't want me to. We fall asleep.

1985

It's nice to be on the bike again, I grin as I start to enjoy the familiar feeling of my legs pumping up the incline towards the dip where I freewheel down to the parade of small local shops. I get there first and lean my bike up against the wall in front of the chippy, sitting next to it, letting my legs swing. When Kaz approaches, I wave and jump down to hug her.

'Do you want a can of pop; I could do with a Coke?' she says, as we go back towards the chippy and my bike.

'Nah, I'm ok but you get one.'

I follow her into the chippy as she buys the drink.

'So, how's Dave? Things in general?'

'It's OK I suppose. To be honest, work is boring. All I do is wash people's hair and sweep up the cuttings. When I'm at Tech for training, they've started to let us cut these big dolls head's hair...it's a bit like a horror film when you think about it, but I'm enjoying that part, so hopefully one day I might get to cut some real human hair.'

She puts the ends of my hair between her fingers, it reaches below my shoulders.

'You could be my first customer; you could do with a trim.'

Kaz picks up a clump of my hair and puts it in front of my eyes, 'Have you seen these split ends!'

'You know what, I've no money and you're right, it needs a trim, when can you fit me in?'

My guilt at not seeing her because of all the pressures of Sixth Form, makes me want to do anything to make her happy.

'Really?'

'Yep! Someone has to be first, so why not your old bestie?'

'Yay.'

She throws her arms around me and gives me a bear hug.

'Oops.'

'Oops?'

'Sorry, I may have spilt a bit of Coke down your back. Hang on, I have a hankie somewhere.'

After Kaz has cleaned me up, we wander up to Top Field chatting about nothing. When we get to the gate at the top, we climb up it and perch on the top. She takes out a packet of cigarettes from her back pocket and produces a pre-rolled joint, lights it and passes it to me. As she exhales, she says, 'Yeah, yeah, so you've told me all the boring stuff, tell me the juice. How're the clever fellas you're meeting? Are they all swots with glasses or are there some hunky swotty ones?'

'Nah, no one to write home about, some of the geography students are quite hunky though.'

'God, I miss that.'

'What? You and Dave are OK, aren't you?'

'Yeah, but I miss the thrill of the chase, you know.'

'But you still have fun, right?'

'Yeah, I s'pose, sometimes.' Kaz takes the joint off me and exhales, 'Oh, speak of the devil.'

I squint to see what she's talking about, it's nearly dark. Dave and Matt are walking up the path towards us. I give them a wave and they wave back.

'Hello stranger. Bored of your fancy college friends then?' Matt says as he approaches us.

Kaz hands the joint back to me and mutters, 'You better take a big pull on that; he's been in a foul mood with you lately.'

I do as she says whilst raising an eyebrow at her. As I exhale, I pass Matt the joint.

'Nope, just slumming it with you low lives for an evening.'

Dave pipes up with, 'Ah, you mean back where you belong, then.'

'Fuck off.' Kaz and I say in unison.

Laughing, I start to climb down the gate, my head's gone and I'm feeling a bit spinny up high; my foot slips as I step down.

Matt is behind me, his hands on my waist, 'Here let me help.'

He tightens his grip as I make it to the ground, his breath on my neck.

'Thanks, I'm fine. It's been a while. I've been off the joints; I must be out of

practice.' He lets me go but stays close. When I turn around he's facing me.

'Yeah, that must be it.'

In the dark, he looks angry.

'You always were a lightweight,' says Dave, breaking the tension. He lifts Kaz down from the gate easily, she leans into him and says thanks, it's brief but intimate. They're really relaxed with one another, even with other people around.

Matt has got on my bike and is pedalling up the path, he shouts, 'I can't believe you're still riding this old thing.'

'Hey, I love her, she's faithful and true.' I shout back, he's turned around and is pedalling back. He's filled out, he's been working as a labourer, and his arms and legs look broader. He does a brief wheelie and then skids to a stop beside me; my jeans get splattered with mud.

'Fucking hell Matt, look at this. These were clean on!'

'I'm sorry, shit, it was an accident.'

He's off the bike and rubbing the mud off my jeans with his hands. Dave and Kaz have walked on ahead, they're laughing about something else. His fingers are on my legs, I imagine them on my body, touching me. I realise he's stopped moving, one hand is on my thigh and the other on my knee as he kneels in front of me. Our eyes meet. Shit. Can he see what's going on in my mind? What's wrong with me, why am I thinking about Matt like that, he's my friend. Fuck, shit. I take a couple of steps back as Matt stands up, his hands loose at his sides. I try to gather my thoughts, 'It's fine, now look, you're all dirty too.'

He's covered in mud, along with the knees of his jeans.

'I'm OK, it'll come out in the wash.'

'Are you OK, you looked a bit out of it there for a moment. Maybe less of this.'

He makes the toking on a joint gesture at me.

'Yeah, maybe. Shit, where've they gone, it's pitch black down here.'

It's a cloudy night and the moon is out of sight, with that and the tree cover the path to Top Field has suddenly got very dark. I hear Matt pick up my bike, then feel his hand on my arm, 'Come on, let's get back onto the street where there are some lights. Those two will be canoodling somewhere nearby.'

I make a snorting sound. 'Canoodling, who says that?'

'Me, apparently.'

We laugh as we go towards the light.

I realise I've missed my friends.

1993

Jason has gone out and left Harold Lloyd and me to fend for ourselves. Mooching, I end up downstairs where Jason paints. He's painting me. There are about thirty sketches and paintings. But they don't look like me. I'm too thin; there are no curves. I stare at the paintings, why are there so many? Then I find some others in the corner. Looking through them, I find one of Charlie and me. I take it out to get a better look. I'm laughing and Charlie's kissing my neck. Jason's paintings have always reminded me of the pre-Raphaelites, this one is like that. We're on a riverbank, water lilies in the river next to us; it looks like there was a picnic. Wait, I remember this day. Jason had been there, he had brought...what was her name? Shelley...Stella... something like that. It had been a perfect summer day. We'd drunk something bubbly. I touch the painting. It's not the same. I traipse upstairs again; Harold Lloyd follows me.

I prowl from room to room, like an old tiger in too small a cage. I begin rummaging in the kitchen cupboards, I know he must have something somewhere tucked away. My search takes me to the bathroom cabinet, empty. Jason's clothes drawers. I rifle through them; they smell of him. I try not to disturb his clothes. Nothing, still nothing. High up, he will have put it high up, where I can't find it. I push a kitchen chair in front of the kitchen cabinets and climb up, carefully, my legs still aren't my own. Up, up. There at the back, there they are. Come to Mama. Hello, old friend.

I put the bottle of vodka on the kitchen surface and open Jason's tin. I know Jason's tin, we all had one. It's where we kept our stash. Jason's is an Old Virginia tin. It still smells of tobacco. I poke my finger around in it, what do we have here? Hello, a little bit of weed and three pills. I fill a small glass with vodka, put two pills in my mouth and neck the vodka and pills together. The vodka hits the back of my throat hard. I cough and shake my head as it goes down until the warmth of it hits my chest. The last pill, I put under my glass and crush it. I tilt my head back and lick the bottom of the glass, don't want to waste any. Then snort the crushed pill on the table. Finally, I wet the end of my finger to get any crumbs I left behind, ugh, tastes disgusting. Glug of vodka, swill it around my mouth, swallow. Cigarettes, rip one open and start the process of making a joint. The feeling of hazy softness has already started from the snorted pill, I need to be quick. Harold Lloyd jumps on the table. To get rid of him I give him some food. He's purring when I return to the job at hand. As I light the joint and take a drag, I get a head rush. Leaning back in the kitchen chair I refill my glass with vodka. Music, I need music. Holding the joint, I head to the living room and put a tape into the stereo. Rockafeller Skank starts playing. Shit, there's ash on the carpet, back to the kitchen to get the ashtray, vodka and my glass. Finally, I collapse onto the sofa. I'm exhausted again, all the searching and climbing has worn me out. My eyes close as the weed and pills do their job. Half an hour later I'm throwing up, rushing my tits off. When it's eased off, I clean my teeth. Minty good. Back in the living room, there's half a joint left. The music has stopped, I turn the tape over. Born Slippy. Back to the sofa, my foot taps to the rhythm. I'm taking the last drag from the joint as Jason comes in, I didn't hear him arrive. Shit.

'What the fuck...?' He's taken the joint out of my hand and put it out in the ashtray.

'Hey. It's OK.' I attempt to stand, nope not happening. Angry face. Jason is taking away the vodka, he's shouting.

'What did you take? Em. What did you take?'

'I dunno. Your stuff.'

'Shit. Em. Fuck.'

Jason is pacing in front of me. I pat the sofa, 'Come and sit down with me. It's all good. I'm fine.'

He's shouting, 'It's not fine, you're a fucking addict. It is not fucking fine. Fuck.'

I try to get up, legs are resisting. I fall onto the floor. Jason turns off the music. I roll onto my back and grin at him.

'Funny, let me touch...' I have my arms in the air, ah, the air feels good. I remember now. Dancing, clubbing, kissing. I beckon Jason to me with my hand, he looks like a giant standing over me looking down. This makes me giggle. Jason is lifting me up. Whirly head. Settling, settling, ah there he is, his jaw is very tight. A muscle is twitching. No smiling. I touch his bristles, they feel nice on my fingertips.

'Stop that Em, I need to straighten you out.'

'Been sick, nothing else you can do.' I'm grinning at him.

'Fuck. Right, coffee then. Lots of coffee.'

'I like coffee, but I love you.' I touch his ear, mmm soft, 'Let me just...' I try and kiss him.

'No Em.'

'Old time's sake. Please.'

He's still carrying me, but he's stopped moving and closed his eyes. He takes a breath, opens them and leans towards me. I put one hand on his face the other in his hair. Nice kiss, Jason always did nice kisses on E's. His lips are gently moving, the warmth of his tongue in my mouth, he's helping me stand and drawing me to him. His body against mine. This isn't how we used to kiss. Something's changed. I open my eyes and see him looking straight at me. Black eyes. His hand is on my back. His other on my arse. It's nice. He's kissing me hard and long. Warm body, lifting me, my legs around him, a hand moving under my shirt. A thumb on my nipple.

'Charlie.'

'Fuck.'

Jason, it's Jason.

'Jas... shit. I'm sorry.' He's putting me down.

'I'll go and make some coffee, come on. Kitchen.'

He's walking away. The E's are buzzing around my body, I want to hug, I want to fuck, I want to dance. I've more energy than I've had for months. Following Jason into the kitchen, I realise how twisted I am. I use the walls for support. He's at the counter making coffee. I put my arms around him.

'Stop it Em. Enough.' He's holding my wrists and pushing me away.

'Jas, please, I just want to..,'

'You just want what? To fuck me and call me Charlie. To walk all over me until I'm nothing, to do what you want without a thought for anyone else. I fucking hate this and right at this moment I hate you.'

He leaves the kitchen, just as the kettle turns off. Moving to the cups, there's instant coffee in the bottom of one. The bedroom door slams. I follow him, opening the door gently.

He's lying on the bed looking at the ceiling.

'Fuck off Em.'

'No.' I lie down next to him.

'Please, leave me alone.'

'No.' I place my hand on top of his chest and push myself up to face him. He won't look at me. So, I climb on top of him and take my top off.

'Em, please. This isn't fair.'

'Please, I love you.'

'No, you don't, not like you should. You're off your head. You don't know what you're doing.'

'I do, you know what Es are like. I do, Jas.'

'You just want closeness with someone. Get off.' He lifts me off him. I push my whole body next to him and touch his cheek.

'Please, just kiss me. Just kisses.'

A sigh as he turns to kiss me again, his hand on my back, bringing me closer, the rhythm of his hips rocking me. I wonder why I never fancied Jason. I stop kissing him to look at him, 'You still haven't got your smile back.'

'No. You have it. When you smile, I'll smile.' His fingers gently caress down my arm.

'I'm smiling now.'

'This doesn't count Em. You are going to feel worse tomorrow.'

'I don't care about tomorrow.'

'That's what worries me.'

'You need to stop worrying about me.'

'I can't.'

I kiss him again. I taste salt. Why do I taste salt? Those big black eyes are crying. I try to kiss the tears away. I mumble, 'Please stop.'

'I can't Em. I fucked up, I should've got rid of my stash and the vodka, I shouldn't have left you on your own. I thought you were getting better.'

'I am getting better.'

'No. No, you're not. You're not eating and the first opportunity you had, you went off the rails again, fuck?' He has sat up and is sobbing, big body shaking sobs.

I hold onto him but I'm not big enough to contain them.

'Please, please stop. Please.'

Eventually, he does, but then he turns his back on me, so I just hold onto him from behind.

When I wake up the bed is empty. My head aches and legs

feel like they've run a thousand miles, I hobble into the kitchen. Jason isn't there. Tentatively, I walk downstairs to his studio; it takes me ages.

'Hello.'

'Hm.' He's painting, he doesn't talk when he's painting. Maybe back upstairs is a better idea. I make some coffee and bring a cup down for him, leaving it on the table he uses that holds all the paint. He looks at me then turns away.

I have no energy left. I trudge with my coffee into the living room and turn the TV on, I can't be arsed to change the channel. I flop onto the sofa and let whatever is on telly wash over me.

Later, Jason comes into the living room, he looks tired. I look at him but don't say anything.

'You need to pack.'

I don't understand.

'Come on, I'll help.'

'Why?'

'I can't do this anymore, I'm not qualified. I nearly fucking had sex with you while you were off your head. That's not OK.'

He can't look at me.

Standing up, I put my arms around him. He leans down and kisses the top of my head.

'It's time to go, I've found a place to take you.' I don't understand what he's saying. I'll just hold on to him.

'They specialise in drug addiction.'

'I'm not a drug addict.'

'Yes, you are.'

'No, I'm just struggling a bit, after Charlie...'

'You need professional help.'

'Please don't make me go.'

'I have to.'

I lean back to look at him. Black eyes, line for a mouth, 'No. you can't make me.'

'If I have to I can, but I'd prefer not to get you sectioned if we can avoid it.'

He's stroking my hair; the residual part of the E makes me want to kiss him.

'Please let me stay,' I put my hand on his arm. Why am I so short? Can't. Get. To. His. Lips. I'm on tiptoe, if I could just...

'Stop it, I know what you're doing. I'm not going to kiss you.'

He gets up and walks to the bedroom. I follow him, he's packing my things.

'What about Harold Lloyd?'

'He can stay here until you're well enough to go home.'

'I can't afford this.'

'I can.'

'How?'

'I have a number of well-paid commissions, people like my art.'

'Where do I have to go?'

'Wimbledon.'

'Will you visit me?'

'Yes, but you're not allowed any visitors for the first six weeks.'

'Oh.'

I don't like this; I don't want to go. Harold Lloyd walks in; I pick him up and sit down on the bed. Harold Lloyd isn't in the mood to be held and wiggles free. I burst into tears. Jason keeps packing, his jaw muscle is twitching. I've seen that before. When was it? Last night, just before... Oh... I tried to make him... Flashes, like snapshots. I called him Charlie. Shit. I'm sniffling.

Jason zips up my suitcase. 'Do you want to take this with you?' He's holding the folder of photographs of Charlie. I nod at him.

'OK. Put your shoes and coat on. Come on.'

We're in the car. I don't want to go. I fucked up last night, I know I fucked up last night. I'm staring straight ahead, we aren't talking. While Jason is parking, I gaze out of the window of the car. It looks new, all red brick. We walk into reception, it smells like a hospital, I don't like the smell, I try to turn around, but Jason is ready for me and puts his arm tightly around me.

'This is Emma Richards, I signed her up for your programme this morning, I'm Jason McGinty.

'Ah, yes, Mr Mc Ginty. I spoke to you. Hello Emma, if you could just wait there, I will get someone to take you to your room. I turn around and look at Jason. He's looking everywhere but me.

'I'm sorry Jas. I'm sorry about last night, I'm sorry for what I did. I do love you. I do. Please look at me. Please don't make me come here.'

Jason looks down at me, his jaw tight. Tears and snot are free falling out of me.

'I love you Em, which is why I have to. I'm sorry.' He turns away and walks out of the automatic doors. They close with a blast of cold air and a swoosh sound. I fall to the floor, screaming and crying. Someone picks me up and half carries and half walks me to a room, they close the door and lock it.

1986

I start lectures after Freshers Week. The reading list is huge. If I hadn't swotted up over the summer reading some of the course material, I would be in serious trouble. Still, I'm out of my depth, I'm expected to read at least two books a week, plus reference material, write essays and go to lectures. The other students I meet seem more than equipped to deal with the workload, why am I struggling? After two weeks, I'm doubting my thinking. I hate the halls of residence; everything costs too much and I miss home.

Contacting Jason seems my best option, the last thing I should do is worry my mum and dad. He can be my home from home. He's always been there for me. Ever since we started working for the Turner Boys and going all over the country working on their burger vans at the fairs.

We agree to meet at the Trocadero in Leicester Square and be tourists for the day. As I sit on a bench waiting for Jason to arrive, people traipse back and forth across the famous square in front of me. I can't help wondering, where they going, what are they doing? Some are people who look like they work in the city on their lunch breaks, wearing power suits with massive shoulder pads, whereas others are tourists with their bum bags and cameras. When Jason appears through the crowd, I'm so happy to see a familiar face, I run over to him and throw my arms around him, nearly knocking him off his feet.

'And hello to you too,' Jason says, wrapping me in a bear hug.

'I've missed you sooooo much!' I wasn't going to let go anytime soon, his smell reminded me of all our journeys for work, to and from fairs with him sitting next to me, joking with me, letting me sleep on his shoulder. He's like a hot chocolate on a winter's day.

'I've missed you too. Now come on if we're going to be proper tourists you've gotta let me go.'

I slowly detangle myself from him and then hold his arms so I can look at him.

'Now what are you doing?' Jason says, raising an eyebrow at me.

'Seeing if you're still you, or a pretentious Royal College of Art student with aspirations of being the next Warhol.'

'How do I fare?' Jason grins at me and puts his hands on his hips to pose.

'I'm not sure yet. There's a twinkling of pretentious, but I got here just in time to bring you back to earth. At least the guyliner has gone!'

'Hey, that was a great look. Come on. I have a plan. Time is of the essence.'

Jason strides off towards The Trocadero, I quickly trot after him. He really does have a plan. We start by having old-timey photos taken inside The Trocadero, he's dressed as a cowboy and I'm a saloon gal. Then we walk to Chinatown and have an amazing lunch. Jason tries to show me how to use chopsticks but all I succeed in doing is getting noodles down my top. He tries to help me remove them, but I slap his hands away. I make him go into a cheap clothes shop so I can buy a new top as I stink of Chinese food. He tells me we haven't got time for shopping. I ignore him and try on several tops as he stands around looking slightly uncomfortable holding my handbag. When I've found something, he mutters that I've 'wasted enough time shopping and we need to pick up the pace.'

We walk quickly along The Thames crossing over the bridge to the South Bank to visit The Hayward Gallery. I'm full of energy, dancing around him, 'Have you been clubbing?'

'Yes.'

'What was it like? Where did you go?'

'I don't know, loads of places.'

'Rubbish. What about Harrods? Or Liberty's?'

'Neither; why would I want to go shopping in those posh crap holes? I'm a

student and have very little money.'

'Have you got a job?'

'Yes, two.'

'What are they?'

'I work in a pub and as a night shift cleaner at a big office.'

'Oh.'

'Enough questions.'

'Fine. For now.'

When we get to The South Bank Centre and enter The Hayward Gallery, Jason is taking the viewing seriously explaining stuff about each piece. In the end, I ask him to be quiet, so I can absorb all the images for myself.

We finish the day in Soho, mooching from bar to bar until we find one we like enough to stay in for a few drinks, bar snacks and a natter.

'So, truly, how is it here? Are you enjoying it?' I'm desperate to know if a year down the line, I'll feel better.

'Honestly?'

I nod, I need to know I haven't made a mistake.

Jason says, 'I found it hard at first. It's very different to home. It feels so big and there are SO many people, but then you find your tiny space in it. You start to make friends. I love my course; I'm learning so much and I may be able to make a career from something I enjoy.'

'So, you, it, everything is good?'

'Yes, me, it and everything is good.'

'Any ladies to tell me about?

'No one serious, I've been having a lovely...erm...open time.'

'Right. Oh! I hooked up with Matt before I moved here.'

'Wha...! That's massive. I've been with you all day and you're telling me this now?'

'Yeah, well. It isn't a thing. It was nice but we knew it wasn't going to last.'

For some reason, I play it down to Jason.

'Em. You know he used to have the biggest crush on you. He's probably crying into his big muscly arms right now.'

'Yeah, he told me. And yes, they were muscly weren't they,' I say, grinning at the thought of Matt's arms.

I lean forward and neck the last third of my pint, just as the bell for last orders goes, 'Go on then, it's your round. I need to be quick if I'm gonna catch the last bus home.' I say, pushing my empty glass towards him.

Jason is watching me, his brown eyes look black in the dim lighting, 'Maybe you've had enough. I could catch the bus with you, make sure you get back safely.'

'I'm fine, I can handle myself and they gave me a rape whistle, which is obviously right to hand...' I rummage in my bag.

'I know you are. Just keeping an eye on my little weirdo.'

'Aha!' I hold it up like it's a trophy.

He takes my glass and goes to the bar.

When I go to catch the bus, he walks me to the stop. We

continue to chat about this and that as we walk, until we both see the bus coming.

'I'll call you. I've got your number now. No escaping.' Jason says as he gathers me into one of his big hugs. I breathe in his familiar smell and notice he feels bigger than I remember. I squeeze him back, tightly.

DAY ONE

The snot and tears are drying by the time I finally look at my room. It's a square box. There's a picture of some roses. The frame is screwed into the wall. The bed is up against the wall with a duvet that has a geometric pink and blue design which reminds me of the duvet cover I had in the flat with Jason and Charlie. No. Stop. Not that. Stay with the now, there's only one pillow, I pick it up and shake it, I don't know why. There's no TV, radio or mirror, just a bedside table and a tiny window above the bed. The window, when I try to open it, is locked. Checking the bedside table drawer there's a King James Bible, I jiggle it to see if any money drops out. Nothing.

Through the only open door, is a very small shower room, with a toilet and a wash basin, the whole room is hospital green and there's no window.

Looking around this box of a room, I can't help but think how bland and depressing it all is, what's the point? What's the point without Charlie? Is this my life now? I clamber onto the bed and curl up. I don't know what else I'm supposed to do.

I'm woken up by a woman dragging a chair towards the bed, the legs of the chair are screeching against the floor. She looks a bit older than me and even sitting down, seems tall. Her hair is light brown and tied back into a ponytail; she's holding a clipboard.

'Hello Emma, I'm Rosie.' She frowns, 'I've some questions I need to ask you.'

I move on the bed into a sitting position. Need to sound sober and sane, need to get out of here.

'OK.'

'Can you confirm your name, please.'

'Emma Joyce Richards.' I hate my middle name, it's my mum's name.

'Date of birth?'

'Twenty-second of September nineteen sixty-seven.'

'Good. Now can you tell me why you're here?'

Fuck, no. I don't know. Didn't Jason tell them?

'Er... Because my husband died.' I hold her gaze, her attention returns to the clipboard. Her mouth looks like Jason's, gripped tight. She looks like she may be clenching the muscles in her jaw.

'And?'

'And I may have overdone it a little with some drugs and stuff.'

'Which drugs, specifically.'

'All of them.'

'Uh huh.' I can hear her pen scratching the paper as she writes, 'Can you list them please.'

Fuck.

'Oh, OK. Weed, dope, speed, coke, acid, ecstasy and H.'

'When you say H, do you mean heroine?'

'Yes.'

'What about alcohol?'

'I drink alcohol.'

'Yes, but would you say you prefer spirits over, say a glass of wine.'

A flash of me necking the vodka at Jason's.

'Yeah, I s'pose.' I've brought my knees to my chest and wrap my arms around them, I don't like this. She continues to scribble stuff.

'How's your eating?' She looks at me, observing my pointy elbows and knees.

'I eat. I like soup and coffee. Is there coffee here?'

'Yes, we let you have coffee.' Half a smile. Rosie isn't a robot.

'Would you say you eat three meals a day?'

'Er... no. Probably not. Can I smoke here?'

'Yes. But you have to earn your cigarettes.'

'Oh...'

'When can I see Jason?'

'In six weeks.' I remember, he said that. I put my forehead on my knees, my head is really achy.

'When did you last take heroine?'

'About... I don't know. Maybe a couple of months.'

'Good, so you've been through withdrawal?'

'Yes.'

'When did you last take any drugs?'

'Last night.'

'Hm. And what did you take.'

My finger poked the baggie in the Old Virginia Tin.

'Three E's, some weed and some vodka. Hah!' I congratulate myself on the accuracy of my memory, tapping my arm. Rosie glances at me briefly, more scribbling.

'Emma, we keep you in here for twenty-four hours, then you'll be paired up with someone to share a room. I'll bring you some food, coffee and cigarettes to keep you going.'

'OK.'

Rosie picks up the chair and drags it to the door, which she unlocks before dragging it out of the room and closing the door. There are clicks and clanks and the sound of a massive key locking the door. I briefly imagine Rosie as Mrs Danvers with keys dangling from her belt.

This must be what prison is like, except without a picture of a rose on the wall. I lie down again.

When I wake up, Rosie is there with a tray. She leaves it on the bedside table. Coffee, a packet of cigarettes, matches and a plate of food which is divided into three, grey mush, green mush and whitish mush. I put one of those little plastic cartons of milk into the coffee, it barely changes colour, I put the other one. It stays a very dark brown. I light a cigarette and look for an ashtray. There isn't one. I decide grey mush can be the ashtray. Grey mush is probably some kind of meat. I still don't eat meat, I don't think.

I touch the side of the cup, still boiling. My mouth is dry, I take a sip. Burning. The roof of my mouth is burnt and it tastes shit. I glance at my bag, there doesn't seem any point in unpacking. On top is the folder of photos. I climb out of bed and get it. I'll just hold it. I don't need to look at it, I know Charlie's inside.

Later Rosie is back with the clipboard, a tape measure and some scales. She tells me to strip to my bra and knickers. I struggle to get my leggings off but she makes no attempt to help me, just watches with her arms folded around the clipboard. She weighs me first, then measures my height, chest, waist and hips. She writes it all down. Then disappears again only to return minus the scales to take the tray of food, after making a note of, I assume, what I did or didn't eat. I didn't eat.

Through the little window, I notice it's getting dark. I stay on the bed and let the darkness wrap around me until Rosie comes in and turns the light on. It's very bright and fluorescent, I cover my head with a pillow. She has brought more food and coffee. I ask her about an ashtray, but she doesn't come back that night, so I stub my dogends out in the food. I wonder if she sleeps here too or goes home to a cosy semi, with kids, husband and dog. She looks like a dog person, outdoorsy, she probably hikes. She has the long legs for it. When I eventually fall asleep, I dream of nothing but eternal night.

1983

Ugh. Two-thirty in the morning is too early. I turn the bedside light on, get out of bed and dress quickly. I chuck a couple of bits of makeup and a purse into my bag, then go to the bathroom and wash. As I come out, my mum is standing on the landing looking like a spectre in her white nightdress.

'Jesus! You scared the life out of me.' I whisper.

'I was checking you got off OK.'

'Yeah, I'll be back about the same time tomorrow. I've got a key. Don't worry.'

'Be good.'

'Go back to bed, Mum.'

I tiptoe downstairs and out the back door after grabbing my house key off the hook. It's brisk outside, a crescent moon is high in the sky. My eyes adjust as I walk off our drive onto the pavement and towards the main road. The road divides the village in half, the old half where I live and the new half with all the new houses where my friends live. I walk half a mile down the main road. A single car passes me, going towards the next town. As I reach The Wheatsheaf Inn, I cross the road and go down Handway Lane. I notice the lights as I turn the corner and hear the low rumble of male voices at work.

The Turners have owned this bit of land and the three terraced houses next to it for as long as I can remember and probably longer. Rumour has it they were gipsies that settled here, but this small arse place is great at creating imaginatively crafted backstories when there's no story to tell.

I spot a lad who was the year above me at school huddled, watching the men work. He's holding his tracksuit top around himself to keep warm.

'Alright.' I stand close so we can share our heat.

'Yeah. You?'

'These early starts are shit.'

'Yeah.'

'Oi, you two, you coming to work or not.' Bobby Turner is shouting across to us. The Turners don't care that the rest of the village is asleep around them, they'll make as much noise as they like.

We shuffle forward, 'You two are on burgers with me today.' My stomach sinks.

'Here, start loading these into the back of the van.' Bobby indicates the burger bun boxes. We start to load, it's light work.

By three-thirty, we're on the road. I sit in the middle of the cab; Bobby is driving and I've found out my fellow passage is called Jason. He's by the window. It's not ideal for a comfy sleep, I was hoping for the window seat.

Bobby has put his country music tape on low and turned the heat up in the cab. Johnny Cash is singing about his Ring of Fire.

'Hey, hey...'

Someone is nudging me. I wake up and find myself curled into Jason's shoulder and chest.

'Shit, sorry.' I'm blurry with sleep.

'It's OK, I was asleep too. Bobby's stopped for a quick break; do you need the loo or anything?'

I realise there are loads of floodlights. We're at a truck stop somewhere.

'Yeah, that would be good. Any idea how long we've been driving?'

I'd forgotten to put my watch on when I got up. I try and stretch out my knees and arms.

'A couple of hours, I think. Only a couple more to go. Bobby says we'll be there by seven.'

'Fair enough, let us out then.'

Jason opens the door; the cold air comes pouring in. He jumps down and I follow him.

'Alright, see you in a minute.'

I wander towards the lights, enjoying getting my circulation going, but as I head through the doors, the bulk of Bobby is coming towards me.

'Don't take too long girlie, we're on the clock.'

'Two minutes.' I speed up my walk. I wouldn't put it past him leaving me in the middle of nowhere. Everyone knows he has a mean streak.

When I get back, Jason jumps down again to let me into the middle. I wonder if this is what Bobby has asked for. As I get in, the light from the cab makes Bobby's face even more ghoulish than it already is, casting shadows where he got glassed, giving him a permanent lopsided grimace. He looks at me, longer than I would like, as I climb in next to him. I avoid looking back. Then we're on the road again.

We're going to a big fair, somewhere on the coast just before Cornwall in Devon. I don't pay attention to where; I never get to see the places we go. I work in the van, do the job, then come back again. I've been doing this for a year off and on. The winter is less busy with only the odd job, but in the summers, they want us to work most weekends. We drive, set up, serve, clean up and then drive back again. Twenty-four hours for twenty quid, cash in hand. It's good money, but hard work.

There are six Turner boys. Although, they aren't boys anymore. John, the eldest, is about thirty. He rarely works the vans anymore, he is mostly back on The Terrace, accounting, organising permits and paperwork. Then there's Bobby, the second oldest. He got himself into trouble when he was younger. He had a massive fight that left his face in tatters. Now he drinks and gets handsy. The other boys are all about two years apart. I can't tell one from the other. Usually, when we go to the fairs, or flower shows or whatever, there are three vans, two burgers, and one ice cream. Ice creams are cushty. On the burgers, you come home stinking of meat fat, with greasy hair, but I don't mind it. As long as it's busy, the time goes quickly. We have to arrive early to get a decent spot.

As Bobby drives, Jason and I have a quiet chat about the work. We agree he'll do the morning cooking and I'll take over in the afternoon. When one is cooking, the other is serving the customers. He's been doing the job longer than me. I'm jealous that he's a year ahead of me, he'll escape first. I'm about to ask him how his O Levels are going when Bobby says, 'What are you two gossipin' about?'

'Just deciding who's doing what, when we get there, is all,' Jason says, leaning forward to look at Bobby as he speaks.

'Right yer are.'

That stops the chat. Dolly Parton is singing Jolene for the umpteenth time. I try to go back to sleep.

It's after seven when we arrive on site. Bobby chats with the fair management and agrees on the spots for the three vans. We're near the entrance. It's a good place, we should be busy if the rain holds off. We all know what we need to do to get ready. By eight we're done. Bobby has disappeared and Jason and I sit in the cab waiting for the fair to open at nine. There's no point cooking anything until then.

I say to Jason, 'Hopefully, that's him off for the rest of the day.'

'Yeah. Fingers-crossed. Look out for him, yeah.'

'I know, I will.'

'He watches you.'

'I know. He's mostly harmless. He can't do anything with everyone about.' I don't believe this. Bobby gives me the creeps.

The fair opens and we get to work. Around midday, Bobby puts his head around the door, 'Tom will drive you back. Alright.'

'OK.' We reply in unison, not paying much attention as we're busy with customers.

By three, it's a bit quieter. The rain has gone from a drizzle to a downpour.

Jason says, 'Is it OK if I take a bit of a break, I could do with stretching my legs?'

'Yeah, I'm fine. Don't get drenched!'

I busy myself cleaning the surfaces as I hum along to Prince on the radio. Suddenly, there are arms around me. One hand is on my breast, the other on my leg with a thumb pushing its way between the top of my thighs. I smell the stink of alcohol and cigarette breath on my neck.

'Hello, gorgeous.'

It's Bobby. His head is over my shoulder, we are cheek to cheek. He must've been in the drinks tent most of the day. His hips are pushing up behind me and I can feel the shape of his dick growing through my jeans.

'Fuck off, Bobby!'

My hands are on his, as I try to get him off me, but he's clamped on like a limpet. I kick his shins with the heel of my shoe as I try to wiggle free.

'Ah, come on you know you want to; you were giving me the eye all the way here.'

He's so drunk he doesn't seem to notice the pain I must

be inflicting on his shin. His hand has moved from my breast and is trying to get under my crop top.

I hiss at him, 'I don't think so.'

My eyes flit around, everywhere is deserted. Shit. Bobby licks my neck and tries to turn me around. I manage to wiggle free. Face to face, he staggers and holds on to the tiny sink as he tries to get to me. I consider the stuff my dad taught me, but then think maybe I'll be able to talk my way out of this.

'Come on, Bobby, you don't want to do this. I'm just a kid.'

He licks his lips and does a fake step towards me and laughs when I jump back. Talking isn't going to work. I notice the knife we used to cut the lettuce and tomatoes. Grabbing it, I hold it out in front of me. Bobby seems to find this hysterical, but then his expression changes and he stops laughing almost as quickly as he started.

'Hey, Bobby, what's happening here.' It's Jason.

'Piss off Jason, you can take another ten... no, fifteen minutes.' Bobby doesn't look away for a moment as he says this. I can't get past him; the burger galley is only about half a metre wide.

'Jason, go. I've got this.'

I'm hoping Jason will get the message and run and get one of Bobby's brothers.

'Yeah, she's got this, haven't you baby.'

Bobby licks his already wet lips and I shudder inside as Jason disappears from behind him.

As soon as he hears Jason step away, he's back on me; he grabs my wrist and forces the knife out of my hand. My five-foot-two petite frame is nothing to his towering drunk six foot. He isn't in great shape, but his weight is on his side. I try to punch him with my free hand but it's like I'm punching a marshmallow. He's oblivious.

He has an arm around my waist and his other hand behind

my neck; he's forcing me forward to kiss him as his hips continue to grind against mine. All the time, he's talking, 'Come on baby, come on, a kiss for Bobby, come on baby. You want it bad; I know you want it, little slut.'

I'm almost in a backbend as he leans over me. I'm trying to push him away. He bites my neck as I turn and twist, I scream. His feet move, using one to push my leg. I lose balance and we tumble to the floor. We're out of sight. I'm scared now, I've felt like this before. I couldn't escape then. I feel bile rise in the back of my throat as I start to panic. He starts to dry hump me as I continue to fight him; I realise he still has the knife in his hand and is using it to open my top. When he sees my bra, dribble falls from his mouth onto my cheek. He pants like a dog when he pushes the knife under the middle of my bra and jerks it up sharply. The material rips and something hurts. He uses his teeth and tongue to move the rest of it. My breasts are exposed. All the time, I fight, scream, push and hit him, but he seems to feel nothing.

'Look at them titties. Good enough to eat.' He bites my nipple and yanks up. I shout at him to stop. I realise I'm hoarse from screaming.

Then he's off me, suddenly. I scrabble back into a sitting position and try to cover myself with the shreds of my clothes.

Jason, his hoodie already off, is wrapping it around me. In the distance two of the Turner brothers are lugging Bobby away; he's cursing and fighting with them.

Jason helps me into the hoodie, he can't look me in the eye.

'I got them as quickly as I could. They thought I was messing about at first.'

He's talking but I'm not hearing it.

'I'm OK. It's alright, could have been worse. I'm OK.'

I'm standing up. The rain has eased off and someone is waiting for a burger.

'We're closed, sorry mate.' Jason says, pushing me out the back of the van and sitting me down on the step.

'I'll get you a coffee or something. Tea?'

'Coffee, two sugars and milk, please. Thanks.' Jason half walks, half trots away. The smell of wet grass and diesel leaks into my consciousness. I clutch my knees and put my head down. The hoodie smells of Jason. It's nice. Better than the smell of Bobby. I shudder. People are milling about as the sun pokes through the clouds. They're laughing, enjoying the fun of the fair. I try not to think. Behind the vans, one of the brothers punches Bobby whilst the other one holds him. He sneers and shouts at them. I can't hear what they're saying. There's a lot of shouting and pushing back and forth between them. I'm glad they punched him, I'm glad he's in trouble with his family. When Jason returns, he hands me the coffee which I take in both of mine, I'm shaking. I flinch as his thumb comes towards me.

'What're you doing?'

'You're crying. I'm sorry. Let me get a napkin.'

He goes past me back into the van and comes back with a wodge of the tissue-thin napkins we give to the customers. I let him wipe away my tears.

'Well, that happened.' I say, staring at my coffee.

'Yeah. Men are shit.'

'Ha! You're not kidding.'

'Will you be OK?'

'Yeah, nothing happened, it could've been worse.'

'It looked pretty bad.'

'Yeah.'

———

We drive back in silence. I don't sleep. Jason holds my hand all the way home. Tom, one of the middle brothers is driving. He's quiet for most of the journey. As we arrive at the village he says, 'Can you stay for a minute? We need to have a word.'

I'm nervous. It must show because Tom says, 'Jason can stay with you if you'd feel better about it.'

I ask Jason, 'Is that OK?'

'Yeah, no problem.' He squeezes my hand.

When we park up, Tom tells us to wait in the cab.

'What do you think they want? Do you think I've lost my job?'

'I bloody hope not,' Jason says.

The van's headlights are on. Tom walks towards the other brother that grabbed Bobby, they say something to each other, then go towards one of the terrace houses. Bobby follows behind. He doesn't look at me.

About five minutes later Tom comes out of the house with, I think John, the eldest brother.

'Shit, this look's serious.' Jason says.

Tom indicates for us to come out of the cab to him and John, who's standing in the beam of lights. Jason keeps his hand in mine, when we get closer, John speaks, 'I hear there's been some trouble today.'

'Yeah. I s'pose.' I stare at my feet stepping from foot to foot. I want to go home and reset.

'Look, I'm sorry. Bobby's a dickhead. You're a good little worker and we appreciate what you do. I'm going to give you fifty quid for today. Call it compensation or whatever, yeah.'

When I look up, he looks like Bobby but softer, kinder.

'OK. Do I still have a job? I need the money.'

'If you still want to work for us, we're happy for you to stay with us. You won't have to work with Bobby again. He'll be staying here with me for a bit.'

'Yeah, that would be good. Thanks.'

'We'd like it if you didn't say anything about this. Bobby... well, he's not been right since the fight, his face... I'm goin' t' get him some help. Right.'

'Right, OK. Yeah. No problem. Can I leave now?'

'Yeah, you can pick up your wages in the week, as normal, and check your shifts then. OK?'

'OK.'

Jason and I walk out of the yard and go towards the main road.

'I'll walk you back to yours.' Jason says.

I realise Jason is just in his T-shirt, his arms are wrapped around himself.

'I'm OK, you must be freezing; I'll get this back to you next shift.'

'It's no problem and I could do with the walk after being in the van.'

We start walking towards my parent's house.

'It's not your fault... you know... what happened, ' he says, frowning.

'Yeah, I know. But...'

'No buts. That was all him. Not you. Are you OK with what John said?'

Neither of us is looking at the other.

'Yeah, why not? One of those things. It's not like he raped me, or anything is it.'

'He came pretty damn close. He hurt you.'

'Yeah, but I'd rather move on. My mum would stop me working there if she knew.'

'I don't think fifty quid covers it. What he did was wrong. You should go to the police.'

'And what're they going to do? I don't want them in my business. They'll make out I'm a slag and deserved it. I could do without that.'

'OK. But I'd back you up if you needed a witness.'

'Thanks, Jason, I'll be alright.'

When we get to the house, Jason watches me go in, and then he wraps his arms around himself and walks away. I like him, clever, arty and all skin and bone, hardly bouncer material, but I'm safer with him than without.

I shake my head, exhausted. I need a shower and to get the smell of Bobby off me. After the shower, I assess my injuries. I have bruises on my elbows and across my back from where I fell. There are bite marks on my neck and breast and he's managed to nick me with the knife on my chest when he ripped my bra off. I'm crying again. I need to sleep.

DAY TWO

I've been taken to another part of the building. I'm in another square box; this one has two beds in it. There is a female shape lying on one of the beds. I put my bag on the other one. This room has a picture of irises screwed to the wall. The door is left open. Rosie has shown me the canteen, the TV room, a room for group therapy and the way to the garden. She has explained that there isn't work but I will have occupational therapy. I get tokens for turning up, which can be exchanged for cigarettes or snacks at the small shop. The shop is open Mondays, Wednesdays and Fridays. I don't know what day it is.

Everywhere is bright and very noisy. Women are milling about, some are talking, others are crying. There is a background noise of screaming. Someone is always screaming, but I don't know where they are. I lie down and put my hands over my ears.

Someone plucks at my jumper sleeve.

'We have to go and eat, come on.'

A large pair of hazel eyes that are mostly hidden behind a dirty blonde fringe that needs cutting are staring at me.

'OK.'

I get out of bed and follow dirty blonde fringe until we are queuing in the canteen. She turns around to look at me, we're about the same height. She's skinny.

'I'm Cat. It looks like we're sharing a room.' She is blank, no expression.

'Em.'

'Why're you here?'

'Drugs and stuff, you?'

'Same.' I nod and look down, we shuffle forward.

I gently tap her arm, she is looking towards the front of the queue, 'Is it just women?'

'No, there's another building with men in, you see them in the garden. We're not s'pose to mix. Except for group therapy. They think there are,' She holds her hands up and does air quotes, 'benefits to hearing both genders' points of view.'

'Oh. OK.'

'Have you met your therapist yet?'

'Is Rosie a therapist? She's the only person I've met other than you.'

'No, she's a nurse. Interesting, I wonder who you'll get?' She grins at me for the first time, she has three teeth missing, two on the bottom and one to the left at the top.

We're at the food. It's mushy stuff, is there soup? I ask. They say yes and hand me a bowl, with a roll and butter.

I find a huge urn of coffee and pour a cup. At least here they have a jug of proper milk.

Cat tells me to follow her. We go to a table with two other women, Cat nods at them.

'This is Em.'

I move my lips a little bit upwards while placing the tray on the table.

'Hi Em, I'm Tiff and this is Kerry.'

'Hi.'

So many voices, so much noise. What sort of soup is it? Green coloured. I lean down and sniff it, maybe pea?

Tiff says, 'When did you arrive.'

'Yesterday.'

'Ah, newbie. Withdrawal?'

'No, did it before I came.'

'Impressed, why're you here, then?' Flashes of Jason's lips and the sound of him sobbing.

'I fucked up.'

'Welcome to the fucked-up club. We all have, that's why we're here.'

'Got your therapist yet?'

Cat answers this for me, 'No, she's still waiting.'

'Well, good luck with that.'

The three of them exchange a look. I don't know what it means.

We're back in our room. Cat has returned to lying on her bed with her back to me, I have curled up with the folder.

Outside the screaming, crying and laughing seems to go on and on. I try to zone it out.

A man walks into a room, he has on grey slacks, a blue V-necked jumper, and a polo shirt under his jumper. He looks about my dad's age and holds a clipboard. He glances at me and then the clipboard, 'Emma Richards?'

I half nod.

'Can you follow me please.'

Getting off the bed slowly, I manage to stand up. My legs remain old lady legs.

He's gone. Trying to pick up the pace I follow him, but he's rounding a corner. As I get to the corner, he disappears around another one. Is this a test? Fuck. I'm almost jogging; I've nearly caught up as he goes into a room. I'm out of breath.

Somehow, he's already sitting behind a large desk that seems to be covered in folders of various pastel shades, they are overflowing with sheets of paper. He puts on a pair of wire-rimmed glasses and scrutinizes me over the top of them.

'Hello Emma, I'm Dr Joseph, your therapist. Please take a seat. Have you ever had counselling before?'

I sit down on the plastic chair in front of his desk.

'Yes.'

'And may I ask what that was for?' No, fuck off.

'Just stuff, you know.'

'And why are you here now?'

Why does everybody keep asking that? Rosie wrote it down, Jason told them. Why do I have to keep telling people stuff?

'I... er... My husband died, I didn't...I haven't been coping very well...'

My jumper has a loose thread at the end of the sleeve I roll the thread between my fingers.

'Have you ever been to a facility like this before?'

'No.'

'OK then,' Dr Joseph makes a bridge with the tips of his fingers as his elbows rest on the desk, 'We use a mixture of techniques here to help you. Most importantly, we offer a routine in a safe, drug-free environment. We have one-on-one therapy and group therapy and encourage exercise and time outside in nature. Nature has been proven to aid recovery. I understand you had your withdrawal before joining us, how was that?'

'I...don't...' I was cold, then hot and my skin crawled with the itches. I started remembering, the smell of pine sap. And Charlie, beautiful Charlie... Jason held me for a long time. I got sick, I tried to ... oh no.

'Emma, please finish what you were going to say.'

'I don't remember.'

'OK. When you took drugs did you do anything that, when you were sober, you regretted?'

'Yes.'

'What did you do Emma?'

He's looking at me. I don't like how he's looking at me.

'No, nothing, I can't remember. I blacked out mostly.'

'OK, we'll return to that. Tell me about your husband, what was his name.'

Don't look at him.

'Charlie.'

'Tell me about him.'

'He was a photographer.'

'Interesting, did he photograph you?' Dr Joseph is looking at me over his glasses again.

'Sometimes.'

'Anything I would've seen?' I think about the picture in Ken and John's studio.

'I doubt it.'

'Hm, shame.'

I have twisted the piece of wool so tight the tiny strands start to snap; I keep twisting.

He's stopped talking. He's writing something down in a large notebook in front of him. He has a fountain pen. I had a fountain pen. Where is it now? Mum gave it to me when I went to Uni, where did I leave it? I'm imagining our flat in Barnes, where's my pen?

'Emma. Emma. Ah, there you are. You weren't with me for a minute.'

'Sorry.'

'Nothing to apologise for, this is a safe space.'

I don't feel safe here, I check the door is still open behind me. I want to go home. I want Charlie. Don't think about Charlie. His cheekbones looked as sharp as razors in the end. He wasn't him anymore. The door, is it? Yes... I need...

'Why are you crying? Can you tell me what you're thinking about?'

'Hm... Charlie. Just Charlie, that's all.'

'OK, you don't need to diminish his death.'

I raise my head and look at the man sitting in front of me, blink once then stand up. I don't want to be here anymore. I feel trapped. I leave the room and walk away. I don't know where here is. I don't know how to find my room. All the corridors look the same, all sour green, lots of doors, keep walking. I want to lie down. Then there's chilly air on my skin. Outside. There's a door to outside. I'm outside. I rummage up my sleeve, cigarettes and matches. I light one, take a drag and look around. There's grass and some trees spotted about with a few Hebe bushes in varying shades of purple. Charlie and I had a Hebe in the garden. People are walking around. Men and women. It's cold, I don't have a coat. Did I even bring a coat? I can't remember. I'm losing the sensation in my fingers; I stamp my feet as I walk to try and stay warm. That hurts my legs. I stop stamping. Nobody looks at anyone, we all keep our eyes down. I bump into someone. I'm on the floor.

'Shit, sorry.' He's helping me up, 'Are you OK?' I glance up at him, he's thin with long straight brown hair.

'Yeah, fine, wasn't looking. My fault.'

'Fuck, you're bleeding.'

My left hand has a gash across its palm, I still can't feel it.

'Oh.' It's bleeding quite a lot, the blood feels warm.

'Hold it up.' He's grabbing my wrist, holding it in the air. The blood is dripping down from my hand over my wrist, to my elbow and dripping on the floor.

'Shit. Shit. Shit, come with me.' He's tugging at my elbow, I'm lightheaded. Knees and legs still not great, down again. Floor. He's lifting me up. It feels like an effort for him. His arms are thin.

Warm air, warm body, nice, sleepy.

'Stay awake, please, shit. Please stay awake.'

Men's voices, lots of them. A different wall of noise, wailing and crying, men wailing.

'Dr David, I bumped into her and she's bleeding and now I think she's passed out.'

'It's OK, Seth, you did the right thing, put her here.' Soft male voice sounds grown up and sensible. Safe hands on me, feels safe here. I need to sleep.

'Hello, what's your name? Miss, can you open your eyes for me? OPEN YOUR EYES!'

Why are they shouting? My eyelids are heavy but I do my best. Two men, Long Hair and Nice Voice.

'Miss, what's your name?'

'Em. Emma.'

'And your surname?'

'Richards.' I want to sleep now.

'Seth, can you write that down for me please, Emma Richards? We need to get her back to The Women's as soon as I have patched her up. Emma, Em. You'll feel a little pinch.' I open my eyes long enough to see him put a needle into my hand. It stings then, numbness.

Someone is holding my free hand. Who's holding my hand, is Jason here?

'Jas?'

'No, I'm Seth. I'm so sorry.'

'Hello Seth, s'alright. I'm tired now.' He squeezes my hand as I fall asleep.

I'm in a wheelchair, someone is pushing me. There's a blanket over me, swoosh. Warm air, reception. I remember reception. Is Jason here? No.

'Hello Dr David, who have you got there?'

'One of ours bumped into her in the garden, she fell and cut her hand. I've patched her up, the stitches need to come out in ten days. She'll need the dressing changed every other day and she mustn't get it wet. Also, you will need to check her medical notes to see if she has had her tetanus jab recently.'

'I'll pass all of that on. We'll take her from here, thank you.'

Someone else is pushing me. I'm back in the room I share with Cat. Cat is sitting up in bed looking at me.

'What happened to you?'

'Bumped...fell into... er, fell down.'

'Come on Emma, time to get up.'

I stand up out of the wheelchair. Rosie was pushing me.

'Don't get it wet, I'll change the dressing the day after tomorrow.'

'OK.' I'm climbing onto the bed, why is it so high? When I finally make it, I lie down looking up at the ceiling. Dirty off-white Artex. Charlie and I had an Artex ceiling, we painted it together, swirly. I close my eyes, there he is, green eyes smiling,

Rosie has left and Cat sits on the end of my bed.

'Tell me what really happened.' I just want to sleep, but I drag myself into a sitting position.

'I was in therapy with...what's his name? Dr Joseph. I didn't like him, so I left.'

'Shit, you just walked out of a session.'

'Yeah. He was asking stupid questions.'

'You're not s'pose to do that. They can be really funny about it. Although, Dr Joseph is a total creep, just wants to hear about the dirty sex we've all been having when we're off our heads. Anyway, tell me what happened then.'

I mumble a short version of what I remember.

'Oh, my, God. You were in The Men's?'

'Yeah, I suppose.'

'Who'd you see, any hotties, celebrities? Anyone worth fucking?'

'I ... I passed out.'

'Fuck. Well, that's a real shame, how does it feel.'

'Sore.'

Later Cat is getting ready for bed, I glance over as she takes her top off. She has a huge tattoo running from her shoulders to the base of her spine, it's a snake. It looks like it's in the Garden of Eden. It reminds me of one of Jason's paintings.

'That's beautiful.'

'What... Oh, the tattoo, I forget it's there, had it years. You got any?'

'No, never had the nerve.'

'You should, I know someone who'd give you a great deal.'

'Maybe.'

DAY THREE

I wake up with a start. Cat isn't in the room. What time is it? Nine o'clock. Shit. Shit. I just lay down for a second after breakfast. I should be in occupational therapy.

I half walk, half trot to the room I'm supposed to be in, quietly congratulating myself that I've managed to get there without getting lost although I'm wheezing and have to bend over to catch my breath. When I stand up still wheezing, all the women in the room are staring at me. They're all holding knitting needles. Fuck.

'Come and take a pew. You must be Emma. I was just beginning to worry.'

A woman with blonde, neatly curled hair is talking to me. I realise I'm just standing there looking nervous and still trying to catch my breath.

'Hi, er... yes, that's me.'

The woman is patting an empty plastic chair, which I assume means I should sit on it.

'I'm Sally and I'm going to teach you how to crochet or knit. Have you ever done anything like this before?'

I mumble, 'Yes, years ago, my mum taught me to knit.'

She's smiling at me and being unnecessarily cheerful, 'Bril-

liant, knitting it is then. We're knitting baby hats for the
neonatal unit this week. You know, for the little babies that
are born too early.'

'Right, OK.'

Sally hands me some knitting instructions, needles and
yarn. I glimpse around the room as I start to cast on, my
hand is bandaged and sore so it's slow progress. The women
have started to chat again. There is a general mumble of
voices and click-clack of knitting needles filling the room.
Then tea and biscuits are on the table in the centre of the
room. It reminds me of visiting my mum at the WI. I've
dropped a stitch, shit, I'll just keep my head down and knit.
I'm not here to make friends. When we finish, the needles
are counted as we hand our knitting back to Sally.

After OT, I lie on the bed, I'm just dozing off when Dr
Joseph reappears. Fuck.

We're back in his room.

'We've certain conditions you have to adhere to, Emma.'
Dr Joseph is looking at me over his glasses again, his fingers
joined in a bridge. I'm finding my hands in my lap very
interesting.

'Emma, can you look at me, please.'

I raise my head and stare at a certificate just behind his
head, I don't want to make eye contact. There's something...
I turn towards the door, it's still open.

'Emma, as I was saying. There are certain conditions of
your stay. These daily therapy sessions are mandatory. Do you
know what mandatory means?'

'Yes.' Patronising dick. Look at the certificate. Face
neutral, hide it, Em. Come on.

'Good. So, let's talk about regrets, shall we?' No, let's not.

'What do you want to know?'

'When you were taking drugs, did you do anything that
you regret?'

Jason, I broke Jason.

'No. I told you; I blacked out a lot. I don't remember.'

'Let me help you. Close your eyes for a second.'

I don't want to do this.

'OK.' I drop my head down and hope it looks like I've done what he said.

'Can you think about the last time you took drugs, can you do that for me.'

A cigarette would be good right now. I feel up the sleeve of my jumper. There they are.

'Now take a deep breath and tell me about that.'

I sigh.

'I found some drugs in a tin, I took them, I listened to some music, I drank some vodka, I passed out.'

'Nothing else?'

'No.'

'Why are you here Emma?'

'To get over Charlie.'

'And?'

What is with this "And" business, for fuck's sake.

'To acknowledge I'm a drug addict and get better.'

'Yes, but is there anything else?

Isn't that enough?

Dr Joesph says, 'Now, tell me have you ever felt suicidal.'

'Oh, fuck off.' Shit, that came out, shit.

'Emma, we don't do bad language here, nice young ...'

'Is this fucking Victorian England. Normal women swear, whether they take drugs or not. It's none of your twatting business whether I've had fucking "Suicidal thoughts"!'

I cross my arms, suddenly I want to make eye contact. I stare at him until he looks away.

'I apologise, Emma, of course, you should have freedom of expression, in whatever form it may take. Let's try this again. Please remember we're all here to help you.'

I continue to stare at him. He's just a little man, in a little job. I'm better than this. I just need to make him believe I'm well enough to get out of daily sessions. I soften my expression.

'I'm sorry Dr Joseph; it's been a difficult year.' Look contrite.

'That's OK Emma now let's try again. Have you got any regrets?'

Play the game, give him something. Something that doesn't matter.

'I had sex in an alley with a man I'd just met for some speed.'

'Good, good... Can you tell me how that felt?'

I spend the rest of the session telling him I'm a dirty slut, giving him as many sordid details as I can think of. I won't talk to him about Charlie or Jason. He's a creep.

As I leave, he says, 'Great work today, Emma. I think you're going to progress well.'

I turn back towards him and make my mouth do something it hasn't done whilst sober, for nearly a year. I smile.

'Thank you, Dr Joseph, you've been a real help.'

Dickhead.

I get back to our room, after several wrong turns. This place is a fucking rabbit warren.

'You lasted a whole session and had no further incidents of falling down. Wow, progress.'

'That's what Dr Joseph said.'

'Really?'

I'm trying to climb back onto my massive frigging bed again.

'Yeah, I gave him a juicy titbit and he was thrilled.'

'Ah, I like it, playing the game. Do you want to get lunch?'

'Not really, but I need to eat if I'm going to get out of here.'

'A girl with a plan. What changed?'

'I think, I got angry.'

1987

We're on the tube. Before our final stop Jason says, 'Look, I've got something that might loosen us up a bit. I bought them from someone I trust who's had some from the same batch. He says we'll have a great night clubbing.'

He looks surreptitiously around; everyone is focused on their own thing. He pulls out a small clear plastic bag with some tiny off-white pills inside.

'What're they?'

I'm looking at Jason and thinking when did he start doing drugs?

'Ecstasy. E's.'

'What do they do?'

'I've never done them but from what my friend said, lower your inhibitions and make you want to dance. He says drink plenty of water.'

I'm relieved this isn't a normal thing for Jason.

'You had me at lower inhibitions, pass one over. Are you doing one?'

Jason says, 'Yeah, definitely? What about you Charlie?'

'Nah, not my sort of thing. You go ahead though.'

'Fair enough, I'll keep one back in case you change your mind. One other thing, my friend says, about forty-five minutes in, you get a 'rush', he says you feel sick and a bit shit for about five minutes then you feel amazing, so be prepared.'

I nod and say, 'OK.'

Jason says, 'open wide,' and leans forward placing the tiny pill onto my tongue.

'Down in one.' He swallows his shaking his head, 'Ick, tastes disgusting.'

He's right it's foul, but I manage to get it down.

We arrive at the club. As the door opens, the music is loud. It's warm inside but I'm not ready to take my coat off yet. I had decided to wear a clingy mesh dress with a black bra and G-string underneath which left little to the imagination, as soon as we left the house, I started to have doubts. Charlie and Jason give their coats in the cloakroom. As we're walking in, I hang back a bit with Charlie, as Jason goes ahead, 'Watch out for us, I haven't done anything like this.'

'I've got you. Enjoy yourself.'

I'm glad Charlie has loosened up a bit. After that first meeting, he slowly started to warm up to Jason and me, joining us for chats around the table and eating with us. There's still a part of me that believes that was more self-preservation than actually liking us because Charlie can't cook. Jason thinks it's because he's taken a shine to me. I don't know what I think about that.

We walk through a long corridor as the music becomes louder and louder until we reach the end, one way leads to a massive dance floor, the other to a bar. The dance floor is quite dark except for an impressive light show above the people. Everyone seems to be really going for it – men have their shirts off and the women are wearing either similar things to me but are braless with just black tape in a cross to cover their nipples or in crop tops and cargo pants. All of them are glowing with a sheen of sweat. It looks frenetic, tribal and wild. And yet they're all perfectly in sync, at one with the music as the DJ transports them, I have never seen anything like it. We go to the bar where Charlie buys Jason and me bottles of water and he has a lager. The music is still quite loud, it's crowded and people are shouting to hear each other. Jason somehow manages to find a table with three seats.

I've just sat down when, suddenly the room is spinning. What's happening? Pinpricks of sweat form on my forehead.

'Em. Emma. Are you alright?' Charlie's next to me.

'I need to close my eyes for a moment.'

The nausea washes over me, I lean against Charlie's arm. It feels like I'm going to throw up. I hear Charlie say to Jason, 'Mate, what's going on you're as white as a sheet?' There's panic in his voice.

Jason says, 'I'm riding the wave, need to breathe. In through the nose, out through the mouth... Em... breathe...'

I do as Jason says, it helps. Within a couple of minutes, my foot is tapping to the music. It's like someone has switched from black and white to colour, everything is brighter, shinier, nicer. I've a warm feeling spreading through my whole body. I shrug off my coat so it's on the back of the chair. The air on my skin feels amazing. Jason is grinning at me.

'Oh my God. Jason, can you feel it.'

'Yeah. I feel it.' His body is moving, 'We need to dance.'

Jason is already on his feet stepping from foot to foot. There's a hand on my arm. Charlie. I turn to look at him. His eyes look incredibly green. I touch his chin, with my fingers, feeling stubble, my thumb runs over his lips.

'You look really good.'

'Do you want me to take your coat, I'll meet you on the dance floor?'

'Hm, OK.' The beat of the music is inside me; I want to dance but Charlie's lips are so... I put my lips to his and they feel soft, warm, like home.

Charlie gently leans back from me, he's smiling, 'Go and dance.'

I want to focus on his lips, his smiling eyes, but Jason is tugging at my arm, 'OK. But come back. I'm not done.'

'OK, Em.'

Jason grabs me and holding hands we walk to the dance floor. There are light trails as we move.

I notice a woman in a red rubber dress leaning against a wall, she looks incredible. I say to her, 'You're very pretty.'

'So are you.'

She leans forward and kisses me. Her lips are different even softer, her lipstick tastes nice. Is this what it's like for men? Jason is still holding my hand. He's dancing on the spot, watching us kiss.

'What's your name?'

'Lucy.'

'Lucy, this is my friend Jason. He's lovely.'

'Hello Jason.'

They kiss, but the music is tweaking my insides, I need to dance. I say, 'Come on let's go.'

Jason says to her, 'I'll see you later,' as I drag him away. We're on the dance floor. The bass is deep inside me, I'm dancing. Jason gives me a hug and shouts, 'This is amazing Em.' We're jumping, hugging each other, hugging strangers and dancing. I notice Charlie in the crowd and go to him.

'He says, 'Shall we look around?'

'OK. Jas, are you coming?' He shakes his head and nods in the direction of Lucy who's coming towards us, I nod as he continues to dance, 'We'll be back soon.'

Charlie follows me, 'Who was that?'

'That's Lucy, she's lovely.'

'OK.'

As I wander through the club it seems to go on forever. I briefly think of Alice Through the Looking Glass.

We're in a different room. Hello Charlie, 'It's really bright in here. Have you got any water?' He takes a bottle out of his pocket and gives it to me.

'Are you alright, Em?'

'Yeah, the lights kinda take the soft edges away. I feel the drug but it's like I'm really together as well.'

'You and Jason look really happy. Maybe I should've had one?'

'You still can, come on. Let's go find Jason and get you sorted. Honestly, you will feel unbelievable. I promise.'

Grabbing his hand, I tug him back to the dance floor. As soon as I'm back in the darkened corridors, I'm warm, soft and beautiful, but it's not as strong. We find Jason who's dancing still. He has taken his T-Shirt off and is wiping his face with it. His skin is a light pink without a pinch of fat. There's enough muscle to make him not skinny.

'Look at you.' I touch his chest.

'Look at you.' The E makes you want to have skin-to-skin contact with people, 'Do you wanna dance.'

'Uh huh.'

Jason's hand is on my arse and mine on his back. I grin at Charlie. He is leaning against a wall smiling as he watches us.

Jason leans in and says into my ear, 'My god, you're beautiful.'

'So are you. So was Lucy, where'd she go?'

'She had to leave; she had an early morning. I have her number.'

'Nice one.'

He grins, then leans in for a kiss.

Jason stops for a second and says, 'Mm... cushions for lips.'

Kissing feels incredible, I press my body against Jason and feel his grip on my arse tighten.

A hand on my arm, 'OK you two enough, come and sit down and drink some water.' Charlie.

He has a pill off Jason and we take another. While we wait Jason and I talk. It's like we can't stop.

'You know I love you.'

'I love you too, but you know I think of you as a friend.'

'I wish you didn't. I really fancy you.'

'I wish I wanted more; you would make a perfect boyfriend.'

'I would make a perfect boyfriend. Why aren't I your perfect boyfriend.'

'I don't know. But you're my bestest friend, apart from Kaz. Oh, and Matt.'

'Hmm. Friend zone, story of my life.'

'I will find you someone. Better than me, you deserve someone better than me.'

'I love you.'

'I love you.'

'Can I kiss you again.'

'Yes.'

Jason puts his hand gently in my hair as I lean in to kiss him. It's soft and gentle. 'Hey. You two remember I'm here.' Charlie. He has hold of Jason's arm and is moving him away from me.

'Mate, she said it was OK.' Jason is looking at me for help.

'It was OK, I said it was OK. Because Jason is my friend and I love him and he's going to call the lovely Lucy tomorrow.'

'OK.' Charlie is looking serious. He's gone pale. I hold his hand.

He says, 'Shit.'

Jason is looking at me and grinning, I can feel it too. I close my eyes and let the rush come. There's something about not fighting it and accepting it, knowing what it leads too. It makes this rush better, yes, I feel sick, but I will feel amazing soon. I breathe my way through it. Charlie's hand is in mine, it's clammy. I look at him. He's still going through it whereas Jason and I are already up. Maybe, as we had already had one pill, our bodies were quicker to deal with it. We wait, both of us have jiggly legs that want to move, our feet are dancing. Jason has found the beat and is tapping his legs with his hands. When Charlie opens his eyes, he looks at me. There they are – the pools of liquid green. He's smiling. He touches my face with the tips of his fingers and kisses me. Fireworks: I thought it was a myth. The kiss feels like it goes all over my body.

'Come on, let's go.' Jason is grabbing my arm. I'm reluctant to stop kissing Charlie, but my body wants to dance. We grab our water bottles off the table and head for the dance floor.

We dance for what feels like half an hour but it must have been more, the club is closing and it's time to leave. We queue for our coats and go out into the night. The cold hits us as we leave the club, there's a frost and London is sparkling, it looks incredible. We'd decided before we came out that we would catch a taxi as trying to get a night bus would be a nightmare. As we walk towards the main road we notice the moon, bright and beautiful in the cloudless sky, even with all the light pollution that London throws up in the air, it stops us in our tracks for a moment. In the taxi, it's warm again, I sit between Jason and Charlie, holding their hands. We're quiet as we watch the world whizz by. It's after two am when we get in, nonetheless Jason holds up the baggy of pills and says let's do another one each. We all nod, take them with water and sit at the kitchen table.

I say, 'Hang on a sec.'

I disappear into my room and grab my stash of dope in my tobacco tin. When I return to the table I open the tin and start to roll joint. Charlie looks at me and says, 'How long have you had that?'

'Oh ages, been doing it off and on since I was about four-teen. It's nice from time to time.'

'You're a woman of many surprises.'

I grin and get on with the serious business of making three joints. Jason has put some music on in the background. We're conscious we don't want to wake the people down-stairs. We start smoking the first joint straight away as we chat. Passing it between us. We chat about how happy we all are living together. How it's worked out. Charlie tells Jason and I that he had Hodgkins's disease and that was why he had a year out of Uni and says that's why he was a bit weird when he first met me, he says his head was a mess. We all hug. Then the rush comes and we all go quiet for a moment as we wait for it to pass. As we come up, we're beaming.

'Jason this was a great idea.' I give him a peck on the mouth. He touches his lips after.

'Yeah, mate. Awesome night.'

I lift my bottle, 'To clubbing.' They tap my bottle with theirs, 'These chairs are really uncomfortable, let's go to Jason's huge room.'

I disappear and climb onto Jason's bed, taking off my shoes as I do. I'm on all fours moving pillows making myself comfortable when I turn around and see Charlie and Jason staring at me.

'She's doing it again.' Charlie's talking to Jason.

'Yep. Do you think she does it to torture us?'

'I don't think she realises.'

'What? I was getting comfortable.' I sit down in the middle of the bed.

'Em,' Charlie sits down on one side of me and Jason on the other.

'Yep.'

'Well, right now, you are practically naked, you were on all fours, you're super relaxed and very touchy feelie. You're going to get yourself in trouble.'

Jason says, 'It is only because myself and my wonderful friend Charlie here are gentlemen, that your honour remains intact.'

I stand up, 'Shall I get changed, seeing as this is bothering you so much?'

'No. Definitely not, no.' This is from both of them who're still sitting on the bed, looking at me.

I take my hair out of the ponytail. I get that wonderful untightening feeling in my scalp except its times ten, I run my fingers through my hair to loosen up the hairspray and feel the hair on my skin.

'That feels good.'

I'm gently swinging my long hair back and forth so that it rubs against me. New Order's Blue Monday is playing on Jason's tape deck and I'm dancing with my eyes closed. An arm comes around me. It's Charlie, his hand is on my stomach as we dance slowly in unison to the beat. Jason has lit one of the joints and passes it to me as I dance. I do a blowback with Charlie and then with Jason. I'm incredibly blissed out.

Later Jason says, 'You two need to be alone. I'm going to have this last joint and try and sleep. Have a good night.'

Charlie follows me into my room. There's no room to dance. Charlie climbs onto my bed as I find some music to put on quietly.

We lie down next to each other side by side.

I say to him, 'Can I touch you?'

I yank off the mesh dress, as Charlie takes off his T-shirt. His fingers run slowly down the length of my arm, as I touch his chest.

'What's this?' I've found a scar.

'I had my spleen removed.'

'Oh. Does it hurt?' I let the end of my finger gently caress the scar.

'No.' He's smiling, I smile back then lean in to kiss him.

He unclips my bra one-handed. His mouth is on my neck, then his tongue is circling my nipple.

Mm... my fingers are in his dark curly hair holding his head in place. It feels like my tits are directly linked to my clitoris. He continues for a minute, if he continues, I might come right now, my hips are grinding into him with drug-induced internal rhythm. When he takes his mouth away, I'm bereft.

'Why did you stop?'

'Other one.'

I'm not the only one in this state, his eyes say it all. My top leg wraps around the back of him clamping his hips to mine. He stops kissing me and returns to my breast, holding, licking, sucking, warm. I arch my back and feel him caress my nipple between his forefinger and thumb. His mouth is back on mine and his hand has moved down to between my legs he moves the G-string, his fingers are inside me. He's kissing my neck, my tits. I find the fly for his jeans and unbutton, as he pushes against the material. I find him and wrap my hand around him. Pulling him towards me.

I'm manoeuvring myself so I'm on top of him.

'I... Stop... Em, stop.'

He puts his arms around my waist and lifts me off him.

'But... I thought?'

'Em, I want you. God, I really want you. I've wanted you since the first moment I saw you, but I need us to be one hundred percent sober and straight and knowing exactly what we are doing.'

I lean into him and kiss him again then say, 'But imagine how this would feel.'

'I'm sure it would feel amazing and if after, we want to do it like this, we can. OK.'

'OK.'

'But I can help you out, right now, if you want.' Charlie says, his fingers already moving down my body.

'No, that wouldn't be right,'

'I don't mind. I'd like to watch you.' There is a petulant part of me that's going no, even though my body is going yes.

'No. I'll wait. We can do this together. Do you want a joint, it might help us sleep?' I lean over and take the last pre-rolled one out of the tin. We smoke it and chat some more; it's getting light.

WEEK TWO

By the end of week one, I have a routine. Knit at occupational therapy, go to group therapy, then every other day, therapy with Doctor Joesph. Plus, sleep, eat, smoke, knit some more and sleep. I mull over the word therapy. I remember learning it comes from the Greek for healing. This doesn't change the fact, that if you say the word often enough, it sounds weird. I spend about fifty nine minutes of every hour day craving drugs, trying not to think about drugs, or Charlie, or the other thing. The boredom makes it worse.

Occasionally, I go outside, I find a coat Jason must've packed for me. Outside seems vast, pathways, lawns, trees, bushes. People walking, no one looking at each other. Some of them seem to be fully in withdrawal, scratching at themselves, their hands shaking, they look like death has her mighty foot on their chests and is pressing down so they can't breathe, can't think, can't eat. My habit was short-lived, but some of the people here have been addicts for years. Sometimes, I try to imagine what they looked like as children, with some it is impossible, they are wraiths.

Group therapy is weird. A person talks, the rest of us listen. It feels like oversharing. But I'm not the only person to lose someone I love. There's a woman whose child died. On a scale of terrible that feels worse, little people who have never had a chance of life, it's just wrong. Some people have had one thing after another happen to them, a parent died, an accident, a sibling disappears. People have been raped, abused, tortured. My stuff is nothing. Not nothing. I know it's something, but these people; how are they still getting through each day? I avoid sharing. I'm a fraud.

One day after lunch, Cat, Tiff, Kerry and I saunter outside to smoke and continue our conversation. Kerry is telling us about jumping out of a first-floor window to avoid a beating from her husband. She broke one of her ankles after the fall and discovered the joys of prescription morphine as she recovered. She says she didn't shit for a month. I wonder, is that even possible? I say nothing as I don't want to ruin her story. Kerry continues to talk; I'm daydreaming, thinking about Charlie, about drugs, half listening when I notice a long-haired skinny bloke looking at me. I tell the others I'll be back in a minute and go towards him. He can't keep eye contact, looking at his feet as I approach.

'Seth?'

'Yeah.'

'Thanks for helping me the other day.'

'How is it.'

'Better, itchy. They're going to take the stitches out in a couple of days.'

'Hm. Good.'

'Do you want one?' I push my cigarette pack towards him.

'OK.'

I strike a match and I hold my hands around the flame, he leans forward to light the cigarette. He looks at the match rather than me.

I take a drag and ask, 'Have you been here long?'

'Mm. About a month, I think.'

He's nudging a loose pebble with his shoe.

'How's it going?'

'I would kill people to get high.'

'Me too.'

We both smirk and continue smoking. We've started walking slowly but I don't think either of us knows where we're going.

He inhales, then exhales and says, 'Drug of choice?'

'Used to be E, but I got into smack before...before... er... I was here.'

'Me too. Although to begin with it was Charlie, you know...'

I have never been able to call coke, Charlie. It feels odd hearing his name used that way.

'My husband was called Charlie.' I say it without really thinking.

'Overdose?'

'Cancer.'

'Oh... Is that why?'

'Yeah, I'spose.'

'Makes sense. You're young to be married.'

'Hm.'

'Young to be a widow.'

I stub out my cigarette, crushing it under the sole of my shoe. I don't want to talk about this anymore. He's looking at me with his sunken eyes. He's too thin. I can't. I walk away. As I leave, I hear him say, 'I'm sorry, Emma.'

When I get back to the others, Cat gives me a look and I just say I'm going back in. I lie down in my room and stare at the Artex swirls on the ceiling until they blend and merge and I'm back to the beautiful oblivion of sleep.

When I'm in sessions with Dr Joseph, I tell him stuff that never happened to keep him off my back, the more disgusting the more he likes it. I swear I caught him licking his lips. I bet he has an erection behind his desk. It makes me want to puke but I need to get out of this place. I plan the stories I'm going to tell him before my sessions. Using some of my tokens, I buy a pad and pen from the shop to scribble some of these ideas down and end up writing other stuff as well, poems, thoughts, descriptions of people, things I've seen. My pad is kept under my mattress, away from prying eyes.

My legs are starting to work a little better and I'm less exhausted each day. I try eating some mush instead of just soup. Some of the mush is less bad than others. I still avoid the grey.

Rosie comes on Wednesday and takes my stitches out. The gash ran from one side of my hand to the other. I count the stitches as she removes them. Twelve. In the tiny shower room, the plastic mirror distorts everything. My right eyebrow still has a gap in it where I was punched at school. And below my bottom lip, you can still see a small scar from where I burst my lip, when I fell off my bike. My hair has got long, it hangs between my shoulder blades. There are four or five white hairs among the strands of dark brown. I pluck one out and look at it. I'm twenty-six. How did this happen?

WEEK THREE

I'm desperate to leave the walls closing in tiny-box- trapped-so trapped-can't be here-boredom-boredom-help-me-vomit green-disappearing-in a box-boxed up-packed away- disappearing.

I'm spending more of my time outside. There's a weeping willow where I go through the thickly hanging branches to lean against the trunk and smoke, invisible to the world outside. I'm invisible. In the spring I won't be able to see out once the leaves return, if I'm still here in spring, that's too far away to think about. The tree is up a small bank, which gives me a great spot to observe most of the building. The tall 1970s windows in the glass-fronted canteen at the end of the structure look like giant eye sockets with people milling about inside them. The main building is red brick with all the small windows for all our vomit green rooms. It's pointless, we all wander aimlessly from one place to the next. We have no purpose. In the canteen, they've put up a Christmas tree. I don't want to be here for Christmas.

Charlie loved Christmas, I remember last year, we spent Christmas Day with his parents, Boxing Day with mine. We played board games, pulled crackers, wore Christmas jumpers. I remember the creases around his eyes as he laughed in the candlelight, as he sang carols in church with my mum, giving Silent Night everything he had, with his deep tenor voice. I can't be in here for Christmas. It's December the first. I have twenty-four days to get out. Jason is due to visit me after six weeks of being here. That takes me to the twenty-third of December. He could take me home then. I could be home for Christmas. I could go to my mum and dad's house. No. I would see my arse of a cousin, Kevin, I don't want to go there, not on my own. No, can't see Kevin. Maybe Jason will stay with me? Although, he'll want to see his family. What if he doesn't come for me? What if he hates me? Has he told my mum and dad I'm here? What if no one else knows I'm here and Jason just leaves me here? I could ask Kaz and Dave to take me, would they take me with Arthur and Gracie there as well. Would I want a recovering drug addict around my children? No, of course not. Matt maybe, Matt's married to someone else now. No, no, no. Breathe. Breathe. Breathe like I'm rushing, in through the mouth out through the nose. Breathe.

What's Seth doing? He's looking behind him, then looking forward. He doesn't look aimless. He looks like he's up to something. Moving from my tree hideout, I stay high on the bank in parallel to him. He keeps checking behind him. He's going to the back of the canteen, he's out of sight. I move down the bank to the path that goes all around the outside of the building and wait. It's a dead end, it just leads to the back door where the canteen takes deliveries, so he has to come back this way.

Lighting a cigarette, I lean against the wall until he comes around the corner, he looks shifty. I block his way and ask him if he wants a smoke.

'No, I'm fine. Got to go. Got to go.'

One of his hands is behind his back and he keeps looking everywhere but at me.

'Come with me.' I say tugging the sleeve of his jacket. He doesn't want to but I'm an unknown quantity. Whatever he's up to he doesn't want any fuss.

'Fine.'

We go underneath my willow tree.

'What have you got?'

I'm looking at him, waiting for him to stop glancing around. Eventually, they settle on my face, there's resignation, anticipation and something else... excitement.

'I've got some weed. Just a bit. One of the delivery drivers gets it for me.'

'Weed?'

'Uh Huh.'

'Can I have some with you?'

I know he doesn't want to share, I wouldn't, but he's fucked because if he doesn't share, I could tell someone.

'OK.'

I nod.

'Here?'

'Where else?'

'Fine.'

His skinny fingers take out some Rizlas, his fingernails are dirty. He pulls out five and licks them, his hands are shaking,

'Here, I'll do it.'

Taking the Rizlas from him, I break one of my cigarettes into it. He gives me the small baggie of weed, there is enough in it for maybe two joints. I put half on top of the tobacco and roll it together, pinching the end to stop the contents from falling out and make a filter from rizla cardboard. I put it in my mouth and light it. Deep breath in.

Fuck, yes.

It's good weed. FUCKING YES!

I pass it to him; his fingers are still trembling when he takes it from me.

'How much did this cost?'

Seth looks down. Ah, not money then. Of course, not money, none of us have money.

Muttering, he says, 'A hand job.'

'Mm. What else can he get?'

'I don't know, that's all I would do?'

'Is he gay?'

'I don't know.'

'What if I offered him... something?'

Seth looks up at me. He blows out some smoke and passes me the joint, his hands are steadier now.

I inhale and say, 'I need something to take the edge off, this place.'

'I know.'

This is the best I've felt since I got here. I pass Seth the joint. He's watching me.

'You're really beautiful.'

I consider him, his blue eyes, his hair tied back in a pony-tail. He has angular cheekbones. I briefly wonder what he looks like when he isn't strung out.

'Thanks.'

'I don't think you should do anything...He's not... kind.' He exhales.

'I'd be OK.'

'No.'

I take the joint from him.

'The way I see it, you don't have a choice. Either you let me meet him, or I tell someone about this.'

I know I'm ruining his buzz. He shakes his head slightly.

'Fine. But I'm coming with you.'

'Whatever. When?'

'Next Monday, three o'clock, meet me here.'

'OK.'

Five days, five more days to wait. I hope he has E's. I would do pretty much anything for an E.

We finish the joint in silence. When we are done, we stay by the trunk of the tree a while longer.

Eventually, I say, 'So, you. How'd you end up here?'

Seth starts picking at the skin around his fingers, 'Addictive personality. Parents got divorced when I was a teenager, been off the rails ever since. Mum got remarried recently and decided she should finally take responsibility for me, that's how I'm here. Parent guilt.'

'You ever been clean before?'

'Nah, not really. I spent a year inside for petty theft, but even in there, you can get most things. Compared to that, this is nothing.'

'A year for petty theft?'

'A lot of petty theft.'

'Ah.'

'Who put you here? Your parents?' Seth says.

'No. God no. They haven't got a clue. I don't think they even know I'm here. My friend, Jason. He put up with a load of shit from me and I... I tried to...' There's something in his eyes I recognise, 'I tried to make him fuck me whilst I was off my head.'

'And did he?'

'Nearly, that's why I'm here.'

'He must really love you.'

'How'd you mean.'

'I imagine you're hard to resist.'

'Charlie used to say... Charlie used to say I had a thing, a thing men found...'

'Your husband's right. Even like you are, all fucked up and skinny and everything, it's there, the thing.'

Tears prickle. Too many thoughts of Charlie, flooding in. Christmas Charlie, crinkly twinkling eyes.

'Shit, what did I say.'

'Sorry, not you... just my stupid brain.'

Seth takes my hand and squeezes it. I lean against the

trunk of the tree and try to draw the tears back in. I wipe the snot off the end of my nose with the back of my hand as I sniffle.

'Yeah, now you're really sexy.'

This catches me out and makes me laugh.

'Tell you what, seeing as how you're willing to blackmail me anyway. Do you want to meet me back here the day after tomorrow for the other half of my weed?'

Seth is doing the half-smirk thing.

'Yeah. That would be great.' He lets go of my hand.

When I'm back in my room, Cat is lying as normal with her back to the wall. I get my notebook out to write something. I've had an idea for a story, about a small-time thief with a ponytail.

WEEK FOUR

Under the weeping willow, Seth and I chat more about family as we smoke the rest of his weed. He has a younger brother that he feels he should have been a better big brother to when his family broke apart.

Seth is easy to talk to. I ask him, what did he want to be? He tells me he was good at technical drawing at school, he thought about becoming an architect. When he relaxes, he's naturally funny, making me laugh more than I can remember laughing for ages.

He stops talking and looks at me, 'You smell good.'

I lean in so he can kiss me.

Eventually, we stop kissing and talk more. I tell him a little more about Charlie and he tells me about the girl he loved and lost because he was an addict.

He kisses me again as his hand wanders under my shirt. I climb onto his lap so he has easier access. I'm cursing my stupidity at wearing leggings. More kissing, our hips are moving together. Then hands on my shoulders that don't feel like Seth's.

Rosie's scowling at me. Seth takes his hands away from my breasts. There's a man with Rosie. He's talking.

'Seth, I knew you were up to something. Come here. Time for a drug test, and garden privileges are on hold. Say goodbye to your new little friend.'

I stand up, Rosie's hand is on my elbow, it's warm. Seth comes towards me to try and kiss me. He has me for a second, then we're pulled apart.

It's dark except for the light from the canteen lighting up the bank. Rosie and I walk down it. Seth is taken back to the Men's.

In the doctor's office, it's very bright, I cover my face with one arm as they take blood from the other. They want me to pee in a cup, but that just makes me giggle. Rosie takes me to another room, it's like the one I was in to begin with. I hear her lock the door. I wrap myself in the blanket. Turn off the main light and put on the bedside lamp. I imagine I'm back in a club with Charlie and Jason, tapping my feet to the music. I'm kissing Charlie; I'm kissing Jason. Jason's brown eyes laugh as he grins at me. There's my Jason. Charlie is smiling as he watches us kiss.

When I wake up the next morning my head is killing me. I run to the toilet and throw up. It's mostly bile, I haven't eaten for twenty-four hours.

Rosie comes in with a clipboard. Clipboard Rosie doesn't smile. I'm curled up on the bed under the scratchy blanket, that I could have sworn was as soft as velvet last night.

Rosie drags a chair to by the bed, the shriek as it is dragged along the floor slides into my bones. I shudder.

'Sit up Emma.'

My pathetic attempt to move myself into a sitting position leaves me half sitting, with my head on the pillow as it doesn't want to stay upright on its own.

'Where did you get the drugs?'

'Don't know, what drugs?'

'The weed that you took yesterday, according to our test results.'

Fuck.

'Don't know.'

'Did Seth Moore give you the drugs.'

'Who's Seth Moore?'

'Seth is the man you were kissing last night.'

'Oh.'

'Hm.'

'The drugs Emma, tell me where you got them, otherwise we will have to leave you in here for longer.'

I shake my head and don't look at her.

'We've had to let Jason McGinty know about last night.'

'Why? Fuck.'

'He was quite upset.'

'Can I speak to him, phone him? I need to explain.'

'No. That's not how this works. You have just reset the clock, Emma.'

'What do you mean?'

'Your six weeks start again from now.'

'No, please. Let me talk to Jason. I can't stay here for Christmas, I can't.'

Tears are falling, 'I'll tell you everything, just please, don't make me stay.'

'If you tell me where you got the drugs, I may be able to sort out a phone call with Mr McGinty for you, but I would need to speak to my superiors first.'

My head is in my hands, I don't want to lose my only source of drugs but I really need to speak to Jason. Shit. I won't tell her anything until she has the authority to get me that call.

'OK.' She's standing up, 'I'll be back shortly. If I get the call for you, you must tell me everything, do you understand.'

I need to talk to Jason. I nod and wrap the blanket tighter around me. She slots the pen into the gap at the top of the clipboard and goes out of the door, locking it.

After she's gone, I sob, until I'm hiccupping and gasping

for air. I wonder what's happening to Seth. He'll be in worse trouble. I fall asleep until the sound of the door unlocking wakes me up. I'm heaving myself back into reality as Rosie brings the chair and sits down again by the bed.

'OK, you have yourself a deal. You can have a five-minute call with Mr McGinty if you tell us everything about the drugs.'

Five minutes doesn't seem very long. I tell her anyway, I need to talk to Jason, I need to get out of here. I tell her about the delivery man, about everything Seth told me. She isn't happy. I'm sure they probably vet everyone who comes in and out of the building and somehow this fella got by them. Dr Joseph is going to have a field day with this.

When I finish telling her, I ask her, 'When do I get to talk to Jason?'

'Tomorrow. Come to reception after you've finished your occy health session, I will meet you there at ten.'

'OK. Will I be going back to my room today?'

'Yes. You can go now. I do have to do an internal exam before you go to check you for drugs.'

'Really?'

'Yes, you can't be trusted.'

'No, fair enough.'

Rosie produces some latex gloves from somewhere and snaps them on. She asks me to lie down, put my feet together and relax my knees. Her fingers go inside me; she isn't very gentle as she pushes down on my stomach and probes around. Then she tells me to stand up, so I can squat on the floor as she checks my arse. I'm something less, somewhere below human.

Back in my room. Cat is waiting.

'Is it true, you got drugs and shagged one of the men?'

How did this get out, so much for confidentiality?

'I got some weed, but I didn't have sex with anyone.'

'But you were with a man?'

'Yeah, there may have been a little bit of kissing.'

'You fucking fucker. Lucky fucking git. Where'd you get the drugs?'

'Some fella bringing food in.'

'What did you have to do to get the drugs.'

'That's for me to know. He won't be coming anymore. I had to give him up so I could speak to Jason.' I've told Cat about Jason before.

'Shame, I would have fucked a donkey to get anything.'

'I was pretty much planning to until Rosie put a stop to it.'

'Bitch.'

'Yeah.'

Later, in bed with my notebook, I'm trying to think about what to say to Jason, but my mind is all over the place. I pad out of my room and think about going outside, then remember I'm not allowed.

Shuffling through the corridors, you can't help but absorb all the noise - the laughing, crying and screaming. I long for silence, or music, or my bed. The panic attack arrives quickly and makes me feel as if my heart will pump out of my chest as the corridors close in on me, it's like a waking nightmare. I am utterly trapped. Stumbling, I manage to get back to my room and into the bed. Eventually, sleep takes me back into black nothingness.

After breakfast, I'm doing my knitting but keep dropping stitches. The hat I'm making isn't going to be any good at all. Cheerful Sally doesn't get cross but does take the knitting from me. She pats my hand then takes the thing apart, rerolling the wool into a ball.

'I think you best start this again when you can concentrate a little better – we don't want the little babies' hat to be full of holes, do we?'

I mutter, 'No,' as I take the wool and needles back.

I run to reception to get there on time. Rosie is waiting,

she takes me into a small office to one side. She tells me she'll be listening to the call from another room and once the five minutes are up, she'll hang up the call. I nod as she disappears. The only things in the room are a desk, a chair and a dark green phone. I'm pressing the numbers for Jason, listening to the clicks until it rings. An image of him in his studio slips into my head. His phone is covered in brightly coloured paint fingerprints.

'Hello, Em?'

When I hear his voice, there's an ache of tears, I breathe in.

'Yeah, it's me.'

'How are you?'

'Please let me come home.'

'I can't. You had a blip, you were doing so well, they tell me. I talk to Dr Joseph often.'

'Hm. Dr Joseph is a creep.'

'He's just trying to help you.'

'Help me to tell him every dirty sexual thing I've done.'

'I'm sure that's not the case.'

'Look, Jas, I miss you. I promise I won't do anything.'

'Em, you managed to get drugs in a place that does everything they can to stop them. You can't be trusted.'

'I need to be home for Christmas. Charlie loved Christmas. I don't want to be here.'

'I'll visit you on Christmas Eve.'

'Really?'

'Yes.'

'Oh Jas, that would be brilliant, will they let you? I've missed you so much.'

'Yeah, they'll let me. I've missed you.'

We're silent for a moment as I stare at more dirty green walls. I've wrapped the curly phone wire around my fingers.

'Jas, you know I love you.'

'I love you too.' His voice is cracking.

'I'm so sorry for everything, for what I did.'

'I know you are, but you're ill, I need you to get better.'

'I wish I could be with you. I need you Jas.'

'I need you to be better, we can't go on as we are, it isn't healthy.'

'I know. I'm sorry.'

'You don't need to apologise Em. Just work on your recovery, can you do that?'

'Yeah. I'm trying to.'

More silence, I'm wasting valuable time.

'Jas.'

'Em?'

'When I finish here, can I stay at yours again for a bit? I don't know when I'll be ready to go back to mine and Charlie's place.'

'Of course you can.'

'How's Harold Lloyd.'

'He's good, he misses you. He sleeps on your side of the bed.'

'I miss him too, give him a chin rub for me.'

Quiet again, just his breathing.

'Are you painting?'

'Yeah.'

'What're you painting?'

'You.'

Click – we've been cut off. No. NO. I slam the receiver down over and over again until the plastic crunches, then wrench the wire out of the wall, throwing the phone so it breaks into pieces as it hits the floor. Rosie comes in and tells me to calm down. I'm screaming at her, shouting, punching walls. Rosie goes away and comes back with someone bigger. I've run out of steam. I curl up in a ball in the corner of the room. I hate being here. I'm lifted and carried back to an isolation room for twenty-four hours.

When I get out of isolation, Rosie seems to be everywhere I am. The only time I don't see her is when I'm knitting, at group therapy or in Dr Joseph's office. He's very keen to talk to me about what I've been up to.

'How did you pay for the drugs, Em?'

Fingers in the bridge, he's squinting at me above his glasses, elbows on desk. Assume the position, Dr Joseph. I tell him everything, every sordid detail of what I nearly did with Seth. He's almost vibrating; I know I'm giving him masturbatory material for later. I touch my breasts as I talk, it's a brilliant performance, maybe I should have been an actor. When I finish, he's leaning back in his chair. His glasses pushed up onto the bridge of his nose. I fear for what's happening below his waist. Thank goodness for the large desk.

'Hm. Emma, that's very descriptive. And how did it make you feel?'

How did it make you feel Dr Joseph?

'Er... dirty. I had to go and have a long foamy soapy shower after.'

'Good, good.'

'When they found us, he was sucking my nipples. It was nice to have human contact with someone. Do you know what I mean Dr Joseph?'

'I do Emma. I understand your need for that, but do you think it was appropriate in this context.'

'I defy you not to find pretty much everything appropriate when you're like me.'

'Hm, but rationally, do you think it was appropriate, considering your feelings for Jason McGinty.'

'Jason's my friend.'

'But you have other feelings for him as well.'

'Jason's my friend and I'm not sure what you're implying.'

'But you did try to have sex with Mr McGinty before you came here.'

I don't like where this is going.

'Yes. But that was just because he was being... And I missed Char... he reminds me of a time... I did, but not because... I don't know, what are you asking.' Damn it, tears are coming. How did I let Dr Joseph get in my head?

'I understand on the phone call you told Jason you loved him.'

'I do love him, but not...'

'And you asked if you could go back to live with him after you left here.'

'Yes, but...'

'And he paints you.'

I'm staring at the doctor as warm fresh tears stream, dripping onto my shirt. I refuse to lift my hands to wipe them away.

'Would you like a tissue?' The doctor is handing me a box of tissues, I take one and blow my nose noisily.

'Why do you think Jason, paints you, Emma?'

I have squished the tissue into a ball in my hand, I squeeze it tightly, my knuckles are white.

'I don't know. Because we've known each other a long time?'

'Or could it be that he's in love with you.'

The tears continue to roll. The doctor puts the box of tissues in front of me on the desk and leaves them there.

'Who's paying for your stay here?'

I take another tissue and wipe my eyes before I answer whilst still looking at the balled-up tissues in my hands.

'Jas.'

'Emma, before I meet with you again, can you think about what we've talked about today and about Jason and what he means to you? Can you do that?'

I nod, but my interest remains on my clenched fists.

'OK, we're done for today, I'll see you tomorrow.'

'OK.' I get up and leave.

1989

The city changes to the countryside as we get closer to Worcestershire, my stomach is churning. I'm nervous about Charlie meeting my parents for the first time.

Charlie interrupts my thoughts as he squeezes my hand and says, 'Your relationship with Jason is the strangest thing. I feel sorry for Lucy.'

'Why?'

'Because he loves you, has done ever since I've known him, but he knows you will never love him like he wants. So, instead of disappearing and getting on with his life, he stays near you, like a permanently loyal guard dog.'

'It's not like that. And he has Lucy now and I've never led him on.'

'I know, apart from the odd kiss and him copping a feel when you're both off your heads.'

'Pish, that's nothing.'

'I know and I'm glad I knew you both. Otherwise, I could be very jealous.'

'Do you remember when you said I had a thing? Is that the problem?'

'I was being a dick. You were right, it's not your problem,

it's men. You're the sexiest person I know. You don't do it on purpose, you don't flirt, you're you. Men find that irresistible. They look at you, they want you. But they don't know you like me. I love you and want you.' He looks so serious as he speaks.

'Wow, you really have given this some thought.'

Charlie leans forward, 'Yep, you're my specialist subject. So, tell me more about your mum, dad, and Kevin.'

'I've told you, my mum doesn't work, my dad's an Insurance Inspector, we live in a big house because Mum inherited it, so people think we're posh and most importantly, Kevin is a twat and will say vile things. Be prepared.'

'OK. Got it. Posh, big house, Insurance Inspector, twat.'

'Yup. That's it. Do you think your mum and dad will like me?'

'What's not to like? I'm glad you're finally meeting them.'

'Yeah, me too. Can I sit there now?' Charlie indicates the seat next to me.

'Yes. Come here.' We spend the rest of the journey, kissing and talking as I point out landmarks on the way. As the journey is coming to an end, he puts his hand up my shirt.

'Goodbye my friends, I will see you in a week.' I giggle at this. Then kiss him until he tells me to stop it, adjusting his trousers.

'I don't want to be that pleased to meet your parents.'

I laugh

as we get our bags.

WEEK FIVE

When I get into our room, Cat isn't there. I climb into my bed and heave the covers over my head. It is several hours later that Cat wakes me, so many dreams. I'm exhausted, too many emotions, too much crying. She tries to get me to go for food. I'm not hungry. I stay in bed. Rosie appears five minutes later and pulls the covers off me. She tells me to get up and go to the canteen for dinner, then frog marches me out of my room with a hand on my elbow. We queue for food. I try to get soup but she makes me have green, orange and cream coloured mush. She holds my arm and sits me at a table putting the tray in front of me loudly. The usual clatter of plastic cutlery and plates has stopped, the room is quiet and everyone's eyes are on me. Rosie sits opposite me and hands me a spoon.

'Eat.'

This isn't a request. I take the spoon and put orange mush in my mouth as I keep my eyes on the food. I continue spooning and swallowing. Turns out the orange one is the worst of the three, it's fibrous as well as mushy. The white one is like eating paste, I think it may be potato and the green tastes like cabbage and salty water. Just keep swallowing.

When I finish, I put the spoon on my tray. Rosie gets up, picks me up by the elbow and marches me back to my room.

'Tomorrow, if you don't eat. I'll put you in isolation and I'll tell Jason he can't visit.'

Fuck.

I'm completely under their control. What's the point? What's the point of anything without Charlie? It was perfect before and now it's not, it will never be perfect again.

I'm in the little bathroom snapping my toothbrush in half to get a sharp edge. I turn the shower on and sit in it as I stab the inside of my arm near the elbow and drag the broken toothbrush down through skin, through sinew, it hurts but I don't care. I repeat it on the other arm. Warm now, warm heat, gushing blood-Charlie-Charlie- Charlie-Charlie. I need Charlie-can't do this anymore-too hard-Charlie-blood pumping-wrists bleeding-water pounding-Charlie-water falling in a veil all around me, mixing my blood-water and blood-down the plug hole-down the plug hole. Tired now-warm-tired-Charlie-Charlie-Charlies not smiling-Charlie-Charlie-angry with me? Why's he shouting? So much shouting. Charlie-blackness coming-Charlie, it's OK.

I wake up in a bright room. I don't want to be awake.

'Ah, there you are. Hello, Emma, Em. Do you remember me, we met before? I'm Dr David.'

'Mm.' Nice Voice. Sensible, kind, safe. I remember.

'Emma, you need to wake up, I'm going to sit you up. OK.'

Warm hands are on my waist, my arms. Pillows are moved, I'm sitting, leaning back. A pillow is cushioning my head.

'Come on Emma, eyes open for me.'

A torch is shining in them. I don't like it but feel fingers holding them open.

'No, please don't.'

'I just need to check for pupil reaction. One second, good. Good.'

'Em. Tell me your full name.'

'Emma Joyce Richards.'

'Good.'

'Can you tell me your date of birth.'

'I've told you before.'

I'm still blinking as white spots pulse around me, but can make out the kind-faced doctor smiling.

'Humour me.'

'Twenty-second of September nineteen sixty-seven.'

'Good. I think your noggin is still functioning as it should.'

'Noggin...Ha.'

I want to sleep, white spots pulsing there as well.

'You needed stitches in your wrists and lost quite a bit of blood. I'm going to keep you here for a day or two, OK.'

'Mm.' I just want to go back to sleep.

'OK, go back to sleep and I'll see you again in a few hours.'

He lifts me and puts the pillows flat again. As he walks away, he says to someone, 'Twenty-four-hour observation, do not let her out of your sight.'

'Yes doctor.'

I smirk, as I start to doze, 'yes doctor...'

The next time I wake up my wrists are killing me. Is someone prodding them with knives? What happened to me? Where am I?

'Emma, it's OK. It's Dr David, you're in the ward at the rehab centre. Do you remember why you're here?'

My bandaged arms are on top of the bed covers. What's happened? The doctor looks concerned. My wrists, the shower, I was in the shower.

'I was going to see Charlie.' I'm crying, I'm not with Charlie. I'm here. Still here.

'Who's Charlie, Emma?'

'My husband.'

'Where's Charlie, why did you think cutting your wrists open would get you to Charlie?'

'He died in March.'

'Ah. Now I understand. OK. You're OK. Nurse. Nurse.' He beckons a nurse over who puts her arms around me and hugs me. He is blurry over the shoulder of the nurse.

'I'm not allowed to hug the female residents.'

'I bet you hug good.' I say as I drip snot down the nurse's uniform. He smiles calmly and looks away.

I start to hiccup cry as my tears ease off. The nurse lets go of me and hands me a box of tissues. Dr David is still sitting by my bed.

'Which therapist are you seeing?'

'Dr Joseph.'

'Good and how's that going.'

I cast my mind back to the last session.

'He wanted me to think about Jason.'

'And who's Jason?'

'He's my friend, he was looking after me, then I messed up and he put me here.'

'OK.'

'Dr Joseph says Jason's in love with me, but I already knew that. I manipulated Jason, I've always... Charlie said Jason was my loyal dog.'

Oh God, I'm going again. When will I stop crying? All year, this is all I've done.

'Is that why you tried to kill yourself.'

My wrists. There are tiny bits of pink where blood has seeped through the dressing. Suddenly, I don't want to cry or talk or anything, just switch off.

'Yes... No... I don't know.'

'Can I get Dr Joseph to come and talk to you here? I'm a

medical doctor. I think you need more care than I can give you.'

'Yeah, I s'pose.'

'Good. Now you rest.'

'K.'

I fall asleep almost instantly. When I wake up a nurse is re-doing my dressings. The jagged cuts and black stitches go from my wrists to nearly my elbow. I did a proper number to myself. She's very gentle; her small efficient hands neatly clean my wounds then reapply more dressing.

When she's finished, Dr Joseph is watching me from a chair by my bed.

'Hello Emma.'

'Hello Dr Joseph, I'm sorry.' I don't know why I'm apologising but it feels like I should.

'It's OK Emma, I should apologise. I should have realised you were at the end of your tether.'

'That's one way of putting it.'

'Hm. I've chatted to Dr David and we're both quite concerned about you. Physically, you will heal, apart from a couple of nasty scars.'

He's looking at my bandaged wrists and I end up looking there as well.

'But mentally I need to do more to help you. Have you heard of Prozac?'

'Housewife's choice.'

'Hm. As far as anti-depressants go, it is quite effective and doesn't have the nastier side effects that we used to get with Lithium and the like. Obviously, we would continue with the talking therapy but you would have a little more help at controlling your emotions with the Prozac, especially after you leave. I would recommend you stay on it for at least a year.'

'Will I be like a zombie?'

Dr Joseph says, 'No, it just takes the edge off, you'll feel things slightly less. I'm going to put you on 20mg of Fluoxe-tine and see how you get on.'

'Fluoxetine?'

'It's just the posh name for Prozac.'

'OK.'

'You probably won't feel any different for the first few weeks, you need to give it time. I will see you daily until you feel a little better, OK?'

'OK, thank you.'

'I've also brought you this.'

It's my notebook that I stash under the mattress.

'I thought you might want to do some writing. Jason says that's what you are, a writer.'

'Have you spoken to Jason?' Oh God, here are the tears, I'm always crying.

'Yes, he's the one who has authority for you here, you signed a waiver for him to make decisions for you.'

'Did I? Why don't I remember?'

'It's not uncommon to have gaps, considering what you've been through.'

'It makes sense, I wouldn't want my parents to... Does Jason know about this.' I hold up my arms.

'Yes.'

'Oh.' Shit.

'He said he thought you'd tried this before, but you claimed it was an accidental drug overdose.'

'It was.'

'Was it?'

'I don't know. I don't know anything anymore.' I don't look at him. I'm tucking in the sheets around me.

'Emma, Em. You know what – and I know you don't think this right now – but today you're making huge progress. Jason said to remind you that he would see you on Christmas Eve.'

'What day is it, how long is that?'

'It's the sixteenth today, not long. Eight days.'

'Eight days. OK.'

'Well, you must be exhausted. Dr David wants to keep you in for another day, so I will see you here tomorrow, then in my office after that.'

'OK. Thanks, Dr Joseph.' He stands up and leaves, was I mistaken about him? Do I think all men just want sex from me? What the fuck is going on in my head. I pick up the notebook on the bedside table. So much for it being a secret. I bet Rosie dug it up.

Dr David comes around later and I take my first Prozac, one a day he says. I have to have them individually here. I can't be trusted.

WEEK SIX

When I am released from the ward, Cat greets me like I'm a long-lost sister. Her scrawny arms embrace me as our ribs bang together like two bags of bones.

We sit facing one another on my bed, cross-legged, she tells me it was her who found me.

'I'm so sorry, that must have been awful.'

'It wasn't great, I thought you were dead, to be honest, I've never seen a human look that white and there was SO much blood. A proper Carrie moment. It's a fucking miracle I'm talking to you.'

'Well, thank you for saving my life. I think I want to be alive. It's just hard.'

'Hey, I took a bottle full of paracetamol and had to have my stomach pumped a couple of years ago, half of us in here have been where you are and we didn't even have a dead husband to blame.'

'I don't blame Charlie, it's not his fault.'

'Not what I meant. But you know what I mean.'

'I do.'

'How much longer have you got here Cat? Do you get out before Christmas?'

'I do, I'm going back to my parents' house in two days, so you'll probably have a room to yourself for a while. So don't do anything stupid without me to look out for you.'

'Ah, that's great news.' Inside I'm terrified, Tiff and Kerry left a couple of weeks ago. I'll be here on my own.

'You know Christmas Day is mixed.'

'What do you mean?'

'I mean, I've heard they let the men come and eat with us. You could reconnect with your friend.'

An image of Seth under the willow tree comes to mind. My cheeks colour slightly.

'Hm. Maybe. I'm looking forward to seeing Jason on Christmas Eve. How long do you think they will let him visit for?'

'I don't know, they might give you a couple of hours because it's Christmas.'

Only a couple of hours. It's not enough time.

Two days later, Cat's bed is empty and my room suddenly seems very quiet. I don't want to make friends with anyone else, I just want to have my sessions with Dr Joseph, write in my notebook and sleep. Only five more days until Jason.

Dr Joseph asks me what I write in my notebook. I tell him it's like a journal, jotting down what's going on in my head. He says that's good and asks if I will share one thought each session. I tell him the one that comes up the most is my feeling of being trapped. I ask him if my outside privileges could be reinstated. He looks at me over his glasses and says, 'And what will you do if you see Seth Moore.'

'I'll say hello, probably.'

'Is that it?'

'Yes. I think so. I don't know.'

'I'm going to ask you something and I want you to think about it before you answer, so if you want to wait a couple of days to come back to me, that's fine.'

'OK.'

'Do you think men only like you because you might have sex with them?'

'Oh. Hm... I'll think about it.' Yes, yes, I think that, of course I do. Duh!!!

'So can I, can I go outside?'

'Can I trust you?'

'Yes. I will do my best not to do anything stupid.'

'OK. I will authorise it, from tomorrow.'

'Thank you.'

The next day I'm outside and breathing crisp cold frosty air making clouds with every breath. I walk up to the bank and look down. Rosie is watching me like a hawk so I don't go into the weeping willow. Instead, I walk along the top of the bank, trying to pick up the pace. My legs starting to ache with the effort but I keep going. I'm looking for Seth but I don't see him. He mustn't have got his privileges back. After about thirty minutes, I get cold, so go back in and have a cigarette in the canteen with a coffee. I feel better than I have for ages just from being outside. Maybe I'll go out later as well.

WEEK SEVEN

I should have gone home today. I try not to think about it. I'm still crying a lot. It doesn't feel like the Prozac is working, but Dr Joseph says it takes a while. I walk outside twice a day, I can manage a whole circuit from the top of the bank to the entrance, down the bank and back again a couple of times over, but usually need to sit down in the canteen for a bit before going back to my room. I still haven't seen Seth.

One day to Jason. Dr Joseph wants me to talk about that.

'What are you looking forward to?'

'Seeing him, hugging him. His smell. Talking to him, catching up.'

'How do you think he will be with you.' Dark eyes, line for a mouth. I shake my head.

'I don't know.'

'Have you thought about my question from last week, you still haven't answered it.'

Drawing my attention away from the scabby skin around my fingers, I glance up at Dr Joseph, he's leaning back today, hands on the arms of his chair. He isn't going to let this go.

'Yes.'

'Yes, what Em?'

'Yes, I think men only like me if they think they might have sex with me.'

'Why?'

'Because that's what they've said.'

'Have they? Or have you heard something else?'

'They, men. Um... The men I've slept with... The men liked me more after I slept with them.'

'What about Jason?'

'What about Jason?

'You haven't slept with him.'

'No, but it's like there's a promise of it somewhere tucked into the back pocket of our friendship.'

'Why did Jason stay friends with you after you married Charlie? He knew how much you loved Charlie. Maybe he just liked you as a friend.'

'Maybe. I don't know. I didn't fancy him then, I told him.'

'And now?' Soft lips, laughing, hard body.

'I don't know, I miss him, who we were before everything went to shit. I knew him before I knew Charlie.'

'To be fair to Jason, you need to decide if you only want to be with him because he reminds you of your time with Charlie, or if you actually like him.'

'Harsh, Dr Joseph, very harsh.'

'But true, isn't it?'

'You're much better at what you do than I gave you credit for.'

'And I'm ashamed to say, I should have realised there was more to you than a pretty face.'

'Truce?'

'Truce.'

I smile at Dr Joseph, 'Can I tell you about my first proper boyfriend, Matt.'

'Please, go ahead.'

———

It's Christmas Eve. It's before six in the morning when I wake up, excitement is bubbling in my stomach. I have a shower, then mooch about my room tidying before breakfast. Porridge with honey. Coffee, cigarette. Knitting, dropping stitches again. Sally doesn't seem to notice so I just keep my head down. I'm killing time. There's less screaming today. There's a feeling of anticipation permeating the place, that has made it quieter. We're told we can show them around, including our rooms, but no closed doors. After knitting I'm looking at my clothes in my room. There's nothing nice. Just leggings and tops that still hang off me. I find the newest-looking pair of leggings and a T-shirt with Guns and Roses on and put a dark grey cardigan over the top, I think the cardigan is Jason's. By ten twenty-five I'm in reception, he's due at ten thirty. Where is he? Standing up, I walk from one side of reception to the other. I contemplate the notice board with all the activities we could do, I've never seen it before. Apparently, there's a swimming pool. I had no idea. Swoosh. The automatic doors go, I turn around. Not Jason. Somebody else, hugging. People hugging. Ten thirty-two, what if he doesn't come? What if he's realised, I'm a complete waste of space? There's a chess club. Really? Swoosh. Jason. I run to him, jumping, throwing my arms around his neck and my legs around his back.

'Em. Hey you.' He says it quietly, just for me. I lean back, I need to see him. He looks tired. I put my hands on the sides of his face and kiss him. He pulls away and sets me down.

'Sorry. Excited to see you. Come on.' I hold my hand out so he can take it and follow me. He takes it, it's warm and big and familiar. Hello, Jason's hand.

He's half smiling as I bounce down the hall towards my room.

'This is my box. Do you like the irises? Cat used to sleep there but she got better enough to leave. Come and sit on my bed, here, let me take your coat.

'Breathe Em.'

Jason puts his hands on my shoulders. I've missed him so very much. Losing Charlie was one thing but losing both of them felt unbearable. Jason takes his hands off my shoulders and takes off his coat, puts it on Cat's bed and sits down on mine.

'Don't they have chairs here?'

'We're not allowed, too many hard, dangerous parts.'

'Oh, OK... And how are you?' He is looking at my wrists, I tug my cardy over my hands.

'Fine, getting better. Dr Joseph has me on Prozac now and I'm talking to him properly. I think it's helping.'

'That's what they thought before, Em.'

'I know, but this time it really is.'

'Em, you're a clever woman, so I know how you do this. You can sound so sincere...' He is looking at my hands again.

I move towards him, trying to curl my body into his.

'Don't do that, you don't need to do that to get my attention.' He gently pushes me off him.

'I know, but... I need ... I need you.' I put my hand over his, 'Please look at me Jas, please see who I am now.'

He lifts his eyes; his long dark eyelashes making shadows, he lifts my hand and kisses my palm.

'I want to trust you Em but what you nearly made me do. What I nearly did. I've been in counselling too.'

'Have you?'

'Yeah, it's all so fucked up, all our feelings about Charlie, both of us loved him.'

'I know.'

'And then he made me promise to look after you and you nearly died on my watch. Fuck.' He looks away and I see the beginning of tears, 'Then you nearly did again here, which made me question if I should have tried to keep going on my own with you. I don't know what's best for you. I just want you to be happy, for both of us to be happy.'

'Me too.' I wipe a tear off his mouth with my thumb.

'And you're so thin.'

'I'm eating again and walking. I'm trying to get better.' Then I say something I didn't know I was going to, 'I think you did the right thing and if it is OK with you, I will stay here a bit longer. Dr Joseph is really helping.'

'Really, you want to stay?'

'Yeah, not forever or anything, but I know I have a problem and I need to be better so I can come back to you and we can be friends again.'

'Yeah. Friends again.'

'Maybe more.'

'We'll see, Em.'

'OK.'

'OK.'

'Let me show you around, you'll need your coat on because I need to show you my circuit.'

He puts his coat on, his long messy wavy blonde hair is longer, his hands are covered in paint.

'How's your painting going?'

'Slowly, I finished the thing for the museum, now I'm working on a mural for Brixton Council.'

'Oh, that sounds amazing. Have you seen anyone?'

We are walking down the corridor towards the canteen.

'No, I spoke to Kaz on the phone, oh, I did go out for a drink with John and Ken. That was a good night.'

'Say hello from me if you see them again. This is the canteen; They serve various colours of mush for our delicate palettes.'

I sweep my arm around in a majestic gesture so he can take in the magnitude of what is basically a school canteen.

'I've also discovered that out of all the mushes we are offered at lunchtime, the yellowish one is my favourite. I have no idea what's in it but it tastes better than orange and green.'

'Hm good, remind me to take you out for dinner when you get out of here.'

'I'll hold you to that.'

'It looks, er...very nice?'

'Come on. Circuit time.'

I walk the circuit with Jason. It is only at the end of the circuit I notice Seth. He's right in front of us with his head down.

I say, 'Oh, hello,'

Seth isn't looking at me, 'Hi. You must be Jason.'

'Yeah?'

'I'm Seth.'

Jason's expression changes, shit.

'Oh, so you're the one who got her drugs in here. Dickhead.'

'Hey, she took the drugs herself.'

They're starting to square off, I can't have trouble, they won't let Jason visit again.

'OK, enough macho bullshit, come on. Nice to see you, Seth.' I nod, then drag Jason away.

'What was that?' I've never seen Jason behave like that.

'I have no idea. I don't know. Fuck.' He pushes his hands through his hair.

'Come on, we haven't got much longer.' As we go to the canteen, I glance at the clock. Eleven forty-five.

Back in my room, Jason and I take our coats off. I get him to sit on the bed again as I climb up and sit cross-legged in front of him. He's gone quiet again.

'Jas?'

'What, Em?'

'It wasn't Seth's fault, he's right, I did it. Me.'

'They told me what you were doing with Seth.'

'Oh.' Fucking hell.

'It makes me wonder what else you've done.'

I don't want to spend the next forty minutes telling Jason

the worst things I've done just to get off my head. The tears are aching again, they're always so close.

'Jas, if you really want to know I'll tell you every horrible detail. But can we not do it now, we only have a little time. Please look at me. Jas. Please.'

Damn it, they've escaped. I promised myself I wouldn't cry. Shit. Jas looks up and draws me to him.

Oh God, it feels better in his arms than any drug I've ever taken. If I could just stay here forever. Home.

As he strokes my hair I'm still, his other hand rubs my back. I'm frightened if I move, I'll ruin it. I'm just going to be here. Still.

'Em.'

'Mm.' Don't move.

'Look at me, Em.'

Damn it, I lean away from him slightly, as his arms fall away from me. Must. Not. Cry. His face is in shadow as he looks down at me.

'You asked me if you can stay with me after you get out of here.'

'Yes.'

'You can, for a bit. But you need to go home. You need to learn how to live without Charlie. You need to become independent. You need to find out who you are without Charlie. Without me.'

'Without you?' Tears dripping like a tap.

'I will be there for you always, but I think I'm not helping you, I'm enabling you. That's not healthy. When you're you, we can decide what we are. Are we friends? Or is there something more? But not until you know who you are.'

'Jas, I don't know if ...'

'You're a warrior. You've just forgotten how to fight.'

'I don't know if I've any fight left.'

'I think you do. I know you do. You have hidden reserves. You can do this Em. I know you can.'

'How can you have such faith in me after I've treated you so badly? I'm a terrible friend, I've taken advantage of you, manipulated you...'

'Yeah, I should kick you to the kerb.'

There's the hint of a smile, he's still there, he's still mine.

'Yeah, you should, but you won't because you love me.'

'I do.'

'I love you too, Jas.' He pulls me back into the hug. I'm glad of it, I don't want him to see me cry again.

'Before I leave, I've something for you, a Christmas present.'

He jumps off the bed and rummages in one of the pockets of his coat, taking out a small square present.

'I haven't got you anything.'

'That's alright, I wasn't expecting anything, this is from me and Harold Lloyd. Open it tomorrow, yeah?'

'Yeah. Thank you.'

I hold the present in my hand as I hug him again, as I stop hugging him I push my lips onto his, feeling him resist for just a second, then his hand moves from my cardy and my shirt onto my back, the heat of his warm fingers touching my skin.

'I can't.'

He's gone again, black eyes, line for a mouth.

'Jas.'

'I better go.'

He's standing up, straightening his clothes putting on his coat. I take his hand. His fingers close over mine. I leave the present on the bed as we walk back to reception in silence. One more hug, I need to remember every last bit of him.

He kisses me on my lips quickly, then turns and walks out. Swoosh. I stand in reception until he's gone. I'm heavy, like someone has put lead in my stomach, my legs. I drag myself back to my room.

Under the covers. I want sleep. I wrap my arms around

me, and imagine his mouth, his smell, his everything, as I curl into a ball.

———

Christmas Day comes. I wake up in a terrible mood. Dr Joseph isn't in until the day after Boxing Day. I'd like to talk to him. Instead, I try to scribble my thoughts into something coherent in my notebook. I'll share them with him when he's back in. I keep eyeing the present on the bedside cabinet. The urge to open it is huge but I don't want the anticipation to be over. Just before lunch, I give up and rip it open. It's a tiny painting of Harold Lloyd sitting on Jason's kitchen table looking very smug indeed. I'm grinning. On the back, Jason has written, 'Merry Christmas Em, Loads of Love, Jas & Harold Lloyd xxx' Underneath Harold Lloyd's name there's a tiny painted paw print. I lean the picture on the wall on the bedside cabinet so it's visible when I'm in bed.

At lunch, they have set out the tables differently, so they're all joined together. The men are already in the canteen when we get there. Where's Seth? I would rather sit with someone I vaguely know than someone I don't. When I spot him, he has a spare seat next to him. I push through people until I'm there.

The low mumble of noise is louder and deeper than usual.

'Hey.' I say as I sit down.

'Ah, you found me.'

The kitchen staff are bringing plates already made up to us today. There's no choice, you get what you get. There's no mush. Instead, we have whole baby carrots, sprouts and roast potatoes.

'Do you want my meat, I'm vegetarian.'

'Sure, I didn't know that.'

'Yeah, strangely not part of the conversation whilst smoking weed under a weeping willow.'

'Ha.'

Seth smirks. 'Yeah, probably not our best move.'

'No. How're you doing?'

'I just got my garden privileges back and my appetite, so this is nice.' He says chopping up some of the meat I've put on his plate and putting it in his mouth. He does look less gaunt, less grey.

'Yeah, me too.'

'How was your visit yesterday? Jason seemed...er... bubbling with testosterone.'

'He isn't normally like that. They'd told him, in detail, about the weed and you.'

'Oh. Wow. OK. Fair enough. I'd probably be pissed off with my girlfriend's new friend if she did that as well.'

'He's not my boyfriend.'

'He thinks he is.'

'No. He doesn't.' I think about the conversation yesterday, about moving back to mine and Charlies, 'Can we talk about something else?'

'OK.' Seth looks at me, his mouth full.

'Did you get any visitors?'

'My mum came. It was the usual, lots of tears, lots of why have you done this? Is it my fault because of the divorce? It was hard.'

'Have you got a release date yet?'

'Nope, you?'

'Nope.'

'Yeah, we really fucked ourselves over.'

'Yeah.'

We eat for a while in silence as we mull on our stupidity, but I can't help but be cheered up a little. I'm sitting next to Seth, not eating mush and they've put Christmas music on over the speakers which are usually only used for announcements to bring us to reception or therapy. I haven't heard music for so long. I start to sway as Last Christmas plays.

Seth says, 'What're you doing?'

'What?'

'Your legs.'

I realise I'm dancing; my feet are moving under the table.

'Do you think they'll let us?'

'I'm not dancing.'

'Ah, come on.'

'I've never danced sober in my life. Not going to happen.'

'OK.'

I leave it as they take our empty plates away and bring us bowls of Christmas pudding and custard.

As I take my first spoonful, I say, 'I wonder if there's alcohol in this.'

'Doubt it. They would never...'

'I think I can taste it.' I'm grinning at him, my cheeks full of food. My feet are still dancing.

'How much do you like Christmas on a scale of one to ten.'

'Eleven.'

'Oh, so you're one of those.'

'One of what?'

'You're like a fucking Christmas Elf, irritatingly happy whilst everyone else is getting drunk and crying.'

'What's not to love, the music, the dancing, the food, the presents. It's brilliant.' Momentarily Charlie's in my head, laughing in the candlelight at one of my novelty presents for him. No. Not going to cry, we were happy. It was wonderful.

'But we're here.'

'Not forever, next Christmas we'll be somewhere better.'

'I'm not so sure.'

'I am. Believe the elf.'

Some of the other residents have left their bowls of food and are swaying in the middle of the canteen to Mistletoe and Wine. I'm on my feet, 'Come on.' I'm standing next to Seth grabbing his hand and jigging from foot to foot.

'This is not happening.' He stands up, 'If you ever meet any of my friends this absolutely did not happen. What happens in rehab stays in rehab.'

'Yeah, yeah. Whatever, come on.'

I grab both of his hands and make him dance with me; we dance to all the classics until White Christmas comes on. I wrap my arms around Seth's neck and he puts his hands on my hips.

'Slow dance, surely you've done this.'

'I have. Maybe a couple of times.'

He leans into me until our hips and bodies are together. My head is on his chest.

'I forgot how short you were.'

'Fuck off, you are unnaturally lanky.'

'Hm, so romantic. You know how to charm a gentleman.'

I'm smiling, as we dance.

I've moved my hands to his back. One of his hands is at the base of my spine. His fingers are edging under the belt of my shirt.

'When are they taking you back?' I say into his chest.

'In about half an hour.'

I turn to see who's around. Rosie and all her friends are everywhere.

'Do you wanna see my room?' Bad idea Em, what are you doing.

'That would be nice, but tricky. The thought police are abundant today.'

'They are, but if you go down there,' I point to the corridor leading to my room, 'and say you are going to the loo or something, wait a few minutes and I'll catch up with you.'

'No harm in trying.'

It's like I'm back at a school disco trying to get off with someone without the teachers noticing.

I mither about for a minute or two then follow Seth down the corridor. He's leaning against a wall halfway down. Grabbing his hand, I'm giggling like a kid as I lead the way. When we're inside, I don't close the door completely but close it enough for some privacy.

'Ah, I have an identical box where I am, who's your roomie?'

'I haven't got one at the moment.' I jump onto the bed. Lately, it doesn't feel as tall. I pat the space next to me.

'Lucky. Mine is fat and farty.'

'Shush.'

I kiss him, why am doing this? I need someone to touch me, I need to feel something. Seth is easy on the eye and makes me laugh. Jason sees me as a friend. This is OK. I'll just do this now, here. What's the worst that can happen?

It isn't long before both our hands are wandering. I'm touching him, because I want to touch him, not because of drugs. It feels nice. He feels nice. There's stubble on his chin, it feels nice against my skin. I move to get astride him. He's pushing my top up, leaning in to get to my nipples. He has filled out a little since I last touched him, but he's still lean.

'Can I see you naked?' he says.

I take my top off and get off him, to climb under the covers and remove my leggings and pants.

'Get in and get you're kit off.'

He quickly strips. Nice. He's under the covers with me, on top of me, in me. When did I last have sex? Man in the alleyway, can't remember that much. It was Charlie. Beautiful Charlie. This feels different. We haven't time to waste.

He has his hand under my arse as he pushes deeper into me. His mouth is on my neck. There is sweat and heat and urgency, his mouth moves to my nipple. I think I might...

'Emma.' Shit, fuck. Rosie.

'Emma and whoever is with her, stop what you're doing immediately.' I peer at Seth who is still inside me.

He whispers, 'This is not over.' As he slowly comes out of me, leaning down to kiss my nipple as he does.

'Do you mind?' Seth says to Rosie.

She turns her back, as Seth leans back in to kiss me, long and slow.

'Quicker. I need to get you back to the canteen immediately.'

We get dressed then move past Rosie who scowls at me, 'Ah, you. I might have known.' She gives Seth the once up and down.

'Yeah me. Is this not allowed?' I'm trying to look innocent, big eyes.

'You know perfectly well it isn't, no fraternising between residents.'

This makes me giggle again, 'Fraternising...'

'Come on.'

We follow her down the corridor, stopping to snog quickly. It's definitely just like school.

When we get to the canteen, Rosie goes off to speak to her equivalent person from the Men's as we both stand there grinning like idiots.

'If I get to keep my privileges for outside, I'll see you outside, 2pm under the tree, yeah. We've unfinished business.' Seth has turned to me.

'Same. I'll turn up as soon as I can, at 2pm. OK.'

'OK.' A man has taken Seth's arm.

'Come here.' He doesn't look happy.

I grimace at Seth who grins back.

Rosie takes me to her office.

'I thought you were making progress.'

I sit down opposite her.

'I am.'

'Another flagrant breaking of rules.'

'Ah, come on it's Christmas.'

'It doesn't make any difference, what you were up to isn't allowed. I will be talking to Dr Joseph when he is back in but from the off, no outside privileges for a week. That may be extended depending on what Dr Joseph decides. Do you understand?'

'Perfectly.'

Rosie softens her expression and says, 'You know there are many types of addiction.'

'What are you saying Rosie?' I frown and fold my arms as I continue to stare at her.

'Nothing. It isn't for me to say. Talk to Dr Joseph. I'll be letting Mr McGinty know about your latest activity.'

'No, oh, come on now. No. There's no need for that, please can you wait and talk to Dr Joseph first, please.'

'Hm.' She briefly looks down then back at me, 'I'll wait, I don't see the need in ruining Mr McGinty's Christmas.'

'Thank you.'

Fuck, fuck, fuck. Why do I do this?

WEEK EIGHT

Dr Joseph says a week is enough of no outside privileges. I also persuade him not to tell Jason about me and Seth.

I'm relieved but feel guilty like I've been unfaithful to Jason, even though he made it clear he doesn't want me as a girlfriend. I say all of this to Dr Joseph because I don't see the point in lying. I also ask him about what Rosie said, about all sorts of addiction.

'Ah. I see.' Bridge of fingers today.

'What do you see?'

'Let me ask you a question. Do you think you associate sex with love?'

'I hate that, by the way, when I ask you a question and you throw a question straight back.'

'I'm not here to give you answers, I'm here to help you find them.'

'Alright Yoda, fine. No, I think you can have love without sex. I loved my gran, my mum and dad, there was no sex there.'

'Hm. You didn't mention...' Dr Joseph, looks at his notes, 'Kevin. Your cousin that grew up with you.'

'No, no need, definitely no love there.'

'And why is that?'

'Just because,' Dr Joseph is looking at me over his glasses.

'He was a dick to me.'

'Can you expand.'

'No.'

Silence, I'm not falling for the ‐ if I stay quiet for long enough, she'll speak thing.

After a moment, 'OK, let's talk about Seth.'

'OK.' Safe ground, I can do this, 'What do you want to know?'

'Why did you take him to your room, did you plan to have sex with him?'

'I didn't plan it, but then I saw him and we had a slow dance. It was nice, he made me laugh. I haven't had sex with anyone I like since Charlie.'

'Ah. Interesting, how did it make you feel.'

'Bloody brilliant. It would have been even better if we'd had five minutes more.' Dr Joseph looks down. Are his shoulders shaking slightly? He seems to take a

breath then leans back in his chair.

'What about contraception?'

'What about it?'

'I know you stopped taking the pill after Charlie. What if it had continued and you'd got pregnant.'

'Oh, come on. The chances of that... Have you seen the state of me?'

'Are you having periods?'

'No, not at the moment. Too thin.'

'What about sexually transmitted diseases?'

'Maybe we should be given condoms. I'd have got him to use one if we had them.'

'Emma.'

'Fine. Fair point. Seriously, I could really use some condoms.'

'So, you still plan to have sex with Seth, even though you know it's breaking the rules.'

'It's not like we're doing drugs, is it? It's natural. When a man likes a woman…'

'Have you considered that you might be using sex like a drug?'

'No. It's just nice. I've always enjoyed sex.'

'I'm not saying it isn't something you should enjoy. It gets endorphins going and oxytocin which both attach to the pleasure centres in the brain. Remind me again what was your drug of choice.'

'Fine, I get where you're going with this. Maybe, but fucking hell, is being here just about being miserable. Surely recovery can have some joy in it.'

'Joy isn't the point. The point of rehab is to stop you from taking drugs and understand the root causes of why you did them in the first place. For you Emma, sex and drugs are intrinsically linked.'

'Well, that's shit.' I slump in my chair like a teenager, crossing my arms, 'so, definitely no condoms.'

'I wouldn't be doing my job if I gave you condoms. Can you think about what I've said?'

'Yes. I understand what you're saying but no sex. Really. That's fucked up.'

Dr Joesph reigns me back in, 'Tomorrow, we should talk about your first sexual experience.'

Kevin flashes front and centre, holding my arms, the smell of pine. Nope, no. Not that.

'Hm. OK.'

'Go on, I'll see you tomorrow.'

As I leave, I walk to the canteen to get coffee before going back to my room. I know that he's right, I know I use sex to make men like me. But I don't see the point in digging about in my past. Why wake up old ghosts?

When I get back to my room, I realise I've been missing

doing my circuits and wonder about the mythical swimming pool. I drink my coffee, then go to reception.

'I'm interested in using the swimming pool. Can you tell me where it is and how to access it, please?'

The receptionist looks at me like I've asked the stupidest question in the whole world.

'Have you got a blue card?'

'No, what's a blue card?'

'Your therapist will give you one to give you access to the swimming pool. No blue card, no swimming.'

'Right. And just for reference, should I ever get a blue card, where might a person find the swimming pool?'

'It's at the back of the canteen, follow the corridor past the canteen then you can't miss it.'

'Right. OK then, thanks.' I decide I'll go and check it out blue card or not. I move along the hallways, past the familiar smell of boiled cabbage from the canteen and down a gloomy corridor I've never been to before, which has more screwed-in flower pictures along the wall. They must have got a job lot. The smell of chlorine starts to permeate around me. Suddenly, I'm in a bright room with a wall of windows on one side and sofas on the other. I sit on one of the sofas and light a cigarette. In front of me, behind the window, is the swimming pool. It's not huge, maybe fifteen metres by ten but it's busy. People are swimming lengths. All of them look too thin, but some of them are smiling. That's new. And it's mixed, there are men and women in the pool. I take a drag and stand up. I keep watching, someone is running an exercise class. I hear loud music, dance music. Oh, my fucking god, I could get to hear music, often. I need a blue card.

———

'Before we start, can I ask you something.'

'Yes, ask away.' Dr Joseph is wearing a green tank top

today with a brown checked shirt underneath, I briefly wonder if he's a farmer in another part of his life.

'How'd I get a blue card?'

'How did you hear about the blue cards?'

'Can you just not, this isn't a learning thing, just tell me. I want to go swimming. I think it would be good for both my mental and physical health.'

I've planned what to say.

'I agree, swimming would be good for you. I'll give you a blue card when I believe you won't have sex with every man you meet in the pool.'

'Oh. You think I'm some kind of nymphomaniac. I wouldn't have sex with *every* man. And that isn't why I want to go.'

'Why do you really want to go? Be honest.' He gives me his stern over the top of his glasses look. He means business.

'They play music.'

'Ah, yes. They do.'

'I miss music.'

'I'll think about it.'

I nod and look down at my hands, I know what's coming next.

'Can you tell me about Kevin.'

The bandages and stitches have been removed from my wrists now, I have a raw red jagged line going from wrist to nearly my elbow on both arms, they're still scabby. I start to focus my attention on them, picking at them with my fingers.

'Em. Emma, come on talk to me. Tell me your first memory of Kevin.'

I don't look up. 'I was scared. I used to get nightmares. I would go and sleep in his bed when I was small.'

'So, he looked after you.'

'Yeah, until the summer before I went to secondary school.'

'Then what happened?'

'Stuff. He changed; he was being bullied. He offered me up to them. Like meat.'

I find and tug harder at a scab, as I peel it off, pinpricks of blood start to rise through my cut.

'How old was he then?'

'I... thirteen or fourteen.'

'When you say, 'like meat' what do you mean?'

'We were under the trees, in the garden. The smell of pine sap... it makes me... They were there, four or five of them, he let them touch me. Put their dicks in my mouth. Stuff. Fuck. I was on my knees and the pine needles dug into me, hurt me. They hurt me... He made me...'

'So, the person you went to for comfort suddenly wasn't offering that anymore.'

'No. He definitely wasn't.'

'Did Kevin make you have sex with him?'

'Nearly...When I realised, I managed to push him out of my room. I locked my bedroom door. Can we stop, I don't wanna... Look, I made my peace with this, he was a scared kid.'

'Have you ever talked to him about it?'

'No. He hates me. We don't talk.'

'Have you told anyone else about this?'

'Only Charlie.'

'That's good, it's good that you trusted him enough to share this with him. And it's good that you're sharing it with me.'

'You won't tell Jason, please don't tell Jason.'

'I can't, what we talk about in this room, unless you're at risk, is confidential.'

'OK. OK.'

'Do you want a tissue?'

I touch my cheek, I hadn't noticed I was crying, I take one from the box on his desk.

'Emma, your first sexual experience was forced on you.

That changes a person's perspective. It's made you view sex in a way that others don't. Most people who've been through what you have really struggle to maintain relationships of any kind. It's a miracle that you had what you had with Charlie and with Jason. The fact you still maintain a consistent family life with your parents shows strength of character. I'm not surprised you ended up here and I'm surprised you weren't in a worse state.'

'I was pretty bad.'

I'm struggling to speak, crying noisily, snot running from my nose. Leaning across Dr Joseph's table I take the box of tissues and hug it to my lap, 'Please stop being nice. I'm better when you're mean to me.'

'And there it is. Your normal is when people are horrible to you, when they aren't, you don't know why, so you give yourself to them body and soul.'

'Is it stupid that it upsets me that I don't remember my first kiss? I know there are far worse things I should be worrying about, but it was one of those boys and I don't remember which or know their names or anything.'

I'm sobbing, it's hard to breathe and talk.

'Not at all, a person's first kiss is a rite of passage, you've grown up hearing other peoples' versions of their story. I bet you have a made-up version you tell people.'

I nod.

'Em, you've done very well today. In the next week, I think you may be ready for the blue card.'

I sniff, 'Really?'

'Yes. This is good.'

'Doesn't feel like it.'

'It will.'

'Promise?'

'Promise. Now go on, you need to rest, get some sleep, oh and happy new year.'

I had completely forgotten it was New Year's Eve.

WEEK NINE

I wake up the next day feeling better than I expected. Is the Prozac working? It's also the first day I'm allowed back outside. After breakfast, group therapy and knitting, I walk my circuit, watching for Seth but don't see him, which doesn't bother me as much as I thought it would. The walk makes me feel good.

My first thought this morning wasn't, I need drugs, sex or something to take the edge off, instead it was a desire to get outside. It's like a huge weight has been lifted. Saying that a part of me is still thinking about what I would like to do with Seth.

I spend an hour on the bed scribbling notes until lunch, then go and eat before my session with Dr Joseph. After, in my room I undress, my stomach's still concave and my breasts look like deflated balloons. When I touch my face, it feels bony. There are no mirrors in my room as I'm still considered at risk, even the plastic one has been removed. I put on my uniform of leggings, t-shirt, cardy and coat and go outside. It's five to two. Glancing around for Rosie, I realise, she's nowhere to be seen, maybe she's finally taken some holiday. I disappear into the weeping willow and wait.

After about thirty minutes I give up. He mustn't have his privileges back. I'll come back tomorrow.

This goes on all week. My days are on repeat.

Friday is my last session with Dr Joseph. My feelings about him have completely changed, mostly to gratitude. Over the last week or so, we spend a lot of time talking about Cousin Kevin. More than I ever thought I would want to. He believes Kevin, must always have felt abandoned by my Aunt Tilly, Mum's sister. Kevin was just looking for love and support and didn't know how to stand up to bullies, leaving him emotionally withdrawn. So, he took it out on me. I don't hate him anymore for stealing my childhood, I just feel sad. Sad for Kevin, sad for Aunt Tilly who eventually committed suicide because of untreated mental health issues and sad for my parents who have no idea why Kevin and I hated each other so much. I also feel a huge amount of empathy for my Mum who lost a sister and took on her angry child. I hope Kevin finds some peace, somehow. Dr Joesph has been crystal clear that I need to work on my grief counselling when I get out but I feel like the invisible dark cloud that has always hovered above my head has disappeared.

To say thank you to Dr Joesph, I write him a short story about a therapist who secretly wants to be a farmer.

He thanks me and says, 'When you're a famous author, I will sell it and retire to the country.'

'As you should Dr Joesph, the country would suit you.'

I ask him to read it after I've gone, it feels a little embarrassing, the last person I showed anything to was Charlie. I can't seem to stop writing and had to buy a new pad this week from the little shop. It feels good, like the walking. It's like I'm getting closer to the old me, the me before Charlie died.

Dr Joseph gives me a blue card.

'Any idea how to get a swimming costume in this place, I doubt they stock them in the "shop"?'

'You could phone Jason.'

'Could I?'

'Yes. Here, he hands me a yellow card.'

'What's this?'

'Take it to reception, you can use it once a week, you get five minutes on the phone.'

'Really?'

'Yes.'

Unbelievable! How do I not know this?

'OK, Dr Joseph, truthfully, are there any more secret cards that give me special privileges?'

'No, that's it, just the yellow and the blue. You've earned them.'

'And how much longer will I need to be here?'

'Ah well, that's up to you. A couple of weeks of group, while we make sure you have a counsellor you can visit on the outside every week, then I would say, you'll be ready to go. You're planning to stay at Jason's first, aren't you?'

'Yeah, then when I'm ready I'll move back to my place. Thank God Charlie put life insurance in place, otherwise, I'd have been fucked, the flat's paid for.'

'Jason has told me that he has been popping in just to check it's OK, paying bills and stuff.'

'Fuck. I owe him big time.'

'Yeah. I think you do, but as a friend.'

'Yes, Dr Joseph, note to self – will not throw myself at Jason in fit of gratitude.'

'That's right. Good work.'

'I suppose I'm not allowed to hug you either.'

'Officially no, but unofficially, if you are OK with it, I am too.'

I stand up and walk to the other side of his desk. We hug. On the front of his drawers that sit under his desk, there are loads of children's drawings and stickers.

'You have kids?'

'Two. A girl and a boy.'

'How old?'

'Five and seven.'

'My godchildren are five and three.'

'Someone let you be Godmother to their kids? Interesting.'

'OK, rude. I don't think we're there yet. Thanks again, Dr Joseph.' I'm grinning as I release him, 'You hug well, maybe you should introduce it into the therapy sessions.'

'Probably won't, these things can be... misconstrued.'

'Fair enough, and with the greatest respect, I hope I don't see you soon.'

'Me too.'

WEEK TEN

Producing my yellow card with a flourish that is wasted on the sour-faced receptionist, I make an appointment to use the phone. My appointment is scheduled for today after therapy. What if he's not in? They tell me they call him first to arrange it, so there are no surprises. I'm in the small room where I smashed the phone last time. More stern looks from the receptionist. I'm not trusted.

Listening to the rings, I think about Jason. I miss him. More than anyone else in the world. It's different to how I miss Charlie. Charlie's never coming back. When Jason answers my stomach flips.

'Hey.'

'Hey, how're you doing?'

'Better.'

'I heard; Dr Joseph is pleased with your progress and you have started to open up in group therapy.'

'Yeah, it's good. The Prozac's working. I'm in a better place. He thinks I'll be out in a couple of weeks.'

'He said. Are you OK with that?'

'Yeah, if it's OK to stay at yours first. I still don't know how I feel about going home.'

'Of course, it's OK. I'm just happy you're feeling better.'

'Can I ask you a favour? I need a swimming costume.'

'There's a pool?'

'Yeah, I know, it's the best-kept secret ever. I've a blue card now, which means I can go swimming, but I've nothing to swim in.'

'Sure, I'll drop one in, I think I'm allowed to visit. Would you like that?'

'Yes. Very much.'

'Tomorrow, OK?'

I'm going to cry. I try and hold it in.

'Yes, I think I can fit you into my busy schedule.'

'Hah, funny. What time is good?'

'You'll have to check with reception, but I finish group therapy by eleven.'

'I could do eleven.'

'Yeah.'

'Yeah.'

My face feels weird, I'm grinning.

'OK, well I'll see you then and I'll bring your costume.'

'Great. See you then. And Jason...'

'Yeah.'

'Thanks.'

'It's not a problem.'

'No, I mean for everything.'

'I know.'

When we hang up, I practically skip to my room. Tomorrow is a Jason day. After lunch, I wander up to the tree. I've almost given up on seeing Seth but want to keep my promise. I'm surprised to see him leaning against the tree smiling.

'Hello.'

'I've been coming for over a week, hang on what's going on there?' He has bruising around his eye. I lift my hand and touch it, it feels swollen, he flinches.

'Ah. Yes, that will be why I got a week added on.'

'What happened?'

'Oh, just me and another resident had a disagreement about something.' He's not looking at me.

'What, what did you disagree about?'

'It was nothing. Don't worry about it. I'm out and about again now.'

'And how're you doing, are you still in one-to-one therapy?'

'Yeah, my issues don't seem to be getting less no matter how much I talk. You?'

'I had my last one on Friday. Did you know they have a pool here?'

'I'd heard a rumour, but you need a blue card.'

I grin at him.

'Oh my god, how did you get a blue card?'

'I delved deep into my saddest darkest secrets and surprisingly that did the trick.'

'Hm, interesting.'

He's watching me; his eyes move to my lips.

'Apparently, I confuse sex with lots of things.'

'Really.'

His hands are on my waist.

'Yep, very confused. And of course, when you have sex there are the hormones that hit your pleasure centre in your brain, a bit like taking drugs, apparently.'

'So, if we had sex, it would be like taking drugs.'

'Hm, maybe we should sit down. There's a lot to think about.'

'There is.'

The grass under the tree is brown from lack of light and fairly dry. He starts to undo my coat buttons, 'I've thought about you a lot since... last time I saw you.'

'Me too. I was told specifically not to do this.'

'Me too.'

I unzip his coat. Then he leans forward and kisses me. I don't want to hang around, I need to get my shoes and my stupid leggings off. Whoever invented leggings didn't want people to have any fun. I'm wiggling underneath him as I attempt to undress.

He stops kissing me, 'That's not helping.'

He sits up and takes my leggings and pants off in one smooth move. Then his hand is between my legs, at the same time as his mouth attaches to mine. My hands have moved to his trousers, I'm unbuttoning his fly.

He's inside me, his one hand has gone under my T-shirt to find my breast, the other he uses to hold himself up. We move together, slowly at first then quicker. It's been so long, I stop kissing him for a second and moan, his hand goes over my mouth. We need to be quiet. I don't want him to stop. It feels amazing, I don't care if it's bad for me or if I'm doing it for all the wrong reasons. I like Seth and it makes me feel alive.

When we finish, we are both breathless, neither of us are at the peak of physical fitness.

He rolls off me and does his trousers back up as I put my clothes back on. Then he holds me close.

'That felt great. You're great. I've been thinking about doing that since after Christmas dinner.'

'Me too. How can they say this is bad for us? I don't get it.'

'Me either. I tell you what I would like. I'd like to do that in a bed.'

'We both have to get out of here, do you have a place, outside of here?'

I don't want to bring him to mine and Charlie's flat and I can see Jason being very happy if I brought him over.

He says, 'I had a flat I rented, but I think I've lost it. My mum wants me to go into a halfway house. She doesn't want me home and I don't want to be there. I think it's my only option. I need to try and get a job, then get a cheap flat.'

'Have you thought about going to Uni as a mature student? You could get the qualifications you need to be an architect. You'd get a grant and live in student accommodation.'

'I hadn't thought of that. I've been drifting these last few years, working as a waiter, cleaner, that sort of thing, just enough to make ends meet. I never thought about the future.'

'Maybe you should.'

He looks at me and leans in to kiss me again, this time it's soft and tender, his fingers are in my hair.

When he pulls away from me, he says, 'You make me want to think about the future.'

'Mm.' I lean back towards him to kiss him. I move to sit on his lap.

We continue like that for a while, eventually, I say, 'We need to stop, I'm supposed to be at occy health. I'll be missed and they'll come looking. Tomorrow?'

'Mm. Yeah, tomorrow.'

It's like he can see inside me. When I stand up, I'm stiff from the cold and sitting in one position I stretch my arms above my head and stand on my toes to try and loosen up.

'You were a dancer.' It's not a question.

'I was, a little, never professional.'

'You went en pointe, yeah.'

'Yeah.'

'Sexy, always had a thing for ballet dancers.'

'When we're out of here, remind me to show you some pictures.'

As soon as I say it, I feel guilty. Those were pictures Charlie took, they were for him for his final project at Uni not for titillating future fuck buddies. SHIT, shit.

'OK.'

He tries to put his arms around me, but I move away, 'I better go.'

I leave quickly, without looking at him, then remember to slow my pace to avoid further trouble. I wipe the tear with the sleeve of my cardigan.

I sleep poorly, tossing and turning, slipping into half-dreams about Charlie, Seth, and Jason. These men merge in my subconscious. All their eyes, blue, green, brown then black when they're angry. He'd be angry.

When I wake up it's with a start and I catch my breath. I get dressed slowly, I'm excited to see Jason again, but have started to feel guilty about that as well. At occy health, I try to knit my thoughts away. It doesn't work.

With fifteen minutes to spare. I run back to my room, tidy up the dirty clothes from the floor and have a quick wash, before arriving in reception at ten fifty-five. Rosie is already there, so's Jason. They seem to be having a serious discussion. I don't care. All my thoughts of guilt disappear at the sight of him, I bounce up to them like Tigger and grin at Jason, taking his hand.

'Hi.'

'Hello.' I can't stop smiling.

Rosie says, 'Right, I'll leave you to it. Two hours.'

'OK, thanks,' says Jason, as I drag him towards my room.

When we get there, I hug him but try to keep in mind what Dr Joseph and I talked about, especially in light of yesterday with Seth.

'Here.' Jason hands me a carrier bag. My old swimming costume is inside. It looks huge, but I don't have any choice, it will have to do.

'Thank you. I'm really looking forward to swimming, they have exercise classes and there's music, real music.'

'That sounds good. How's everything else?'

'Like I said yesterday, I'm improving. The Prozac has helped, but mostly it's the talking to Dr Joseph and the

Group Therapy. I think I get it now, all this talking about our dark stuff. What about you? You said you were seeing someone.'

'Yeah, she's made me realise I need to just be your friend and get on with the rest of my life.'

'Weird, that's what Dr Joseph said too. Do you think they're all in cahoots and gather information?'

Jason smiles and says, 'Maybe, but I think they're right. Don't you.'

'Yeah. I do.'

'No more kissing.'

'OK.'

'Or cuddles that are more than cuddles.'

'OK.'

'Promise.'

'Yeah.'

We hug again. Like friends. Less guilt.

'What did eagle-eyed Rosie want?'

'Oh, she was just saying you were doing well, but needed to be careful to avoid that Seth bloke.'

'Oh yes, why's that?'

'I don't know, she said he was a bad influence.'

'Oh. I haven't seen much of him.' That's basically true, I haven't seen him naked, well not recently.

'Yeah, so just steer clear.'

Let's move this away from Seth, 'OK. How's Harold Lloyd? And thank you for the painting, it's gorgeous, I love it.'

'Good, I'm glad you like it. He's good, he brought me a live mouse which has taken up residence somewhere in my studio. It's probably chewing through my art as I speak.'

'Oh, God. Sorry, you need to get a humane trap from the hardware shop near you. He was always doing that. He's bored of them after he's brought them in, it never occurs to him to kill them.'

'So, I've come to realise, this is the third one. The last two I managed to rescue and take back outside, but this one is proving more elusive.'

'You'll miss him when I take him home.'

'Maybe. Although I've been thinking about getting one of my own, I've enjoyed the company.'

'Better than me?'

'He's much better company than you and far less trouble.'

'Rude. But true. Come on, let's go and get a cuppa in the canteen, the coffee is pig swill but it'll put hairs on your chest.'

'Hey, I have hairs on my chest.'

'If you say so.' I'm laughing, this feels like us. He's smiling. This feels good.

When we've got our coffees and sit down, I push the sleeves of my cardigan up without thinking. Jason is sipping his coffee, but when he sees my arms, he puts it down. He takes my hands and turns them upwards so he can see the full effect of the damage I did to myself. He doesn't let go.

'Oh Em.'

'They look better than they did.'

'And what's this?' His thumb is running along the scar on my hand from when I fell and cut it. When I met Seth.

'I tripped over just after I arrived. I was outside, I accidentally cut it on a rock.'

'Accidentally?'

'Yes. Absolutely accidentally.'

He lets go of my left hand and runs his forefinger down the scar on my right arm.'

It is still quite red and raw-looking,

'Does it hurt?' His mouth is back to a line.

'No. It's getting better, honestly.'

'Did you really think this was your only option?'

'It felt like it, I felt... trapped, alone, frightened. I felt like you and Charlie had both left me. It felt unbearable, I couldn't imagine my life without you in it, as well as losing him.'

'I never left you Em, I was trying to help.'

'I know that now, but my brain wasn't working right, there was no logical thinking, I just reacted.'

'I'm so sorry Em, I'm still not sure I did the right thing putting you in here.'

'You definitely did the right thing. I feel better, like before Charlie... Before Charlie died. I'm still sad, but I know now, Charlie wouldn't want me to be like this. You did the right thing. I was awful, uncontrollable. I would've probably had more success at killing myself out there. I probably wouldn't be here if it hadn't been for you.'

Tears are rolling down his cheeks. I move to hold him tight as he stays seated in his chair. I dig around in my pocket and find a tissue that looks cleanish and hand it to him.

'Thanks.'

Sitting back down opposite him, I notice Seth looking through the windows. He doesn't look happy. When he sees I've seen him, he walks away.

'Do you want another cup of coffee?' I'm trying to distract myself from thoughts of Seth's angry expression.

'No thanks, you're right it's disgusting. Shall we go for a walk outside?'

No, we definitely shouldn't go for a walk outside.

'Nah, it's a bit cold for that, let me show you the swimming pool.'

'OK.'

I take him to the pool. We sit there on the sofas for a while people watching as they flay about in the pool. The thump of dance music plays in the background.

'I'm hoping to go for a dip today and I then find out when the exercise classes are to build up my strength.'

'That's good Em.'

'Yeah.'

Jason still seems sad. I'd like to cheer him up. Old Emma would kiss him, touch him. I don't know what to do. In the end, I say exactly that to him. As Dr Joseph used to say, 'Use your words, Em.'

'It's OK. It was just seeing your arms. I think I've let Charlie down. I had one job. Look after you and I don't think I did it.'

'I think you did. I think you did the best you could with me. I was not easy to look after.'

Jason leans forward pushing his hands into his hair that falls down over his face. God, this is impossible! I put my hand on the back of his neck and squeeze it slightly. He moves his hand to cover mine and leans back.

'That feels nice.'

I lean back, keeping my hand where it is. The warmth of his neck is under my fingers, the thickness of it. It feels wider.

'Have you been exercising?'

'A bit, why?'

'Your neck...'

'Ha. Yeah, just some jogging and I brought some weights. The counsellor said it might help. I'm thinking about joining a gym.'

'It feels nice.'

'Em.' His voice is stern, he turns his head towards me but lets my hand stay where it is.

'I know, I'm just saying. Although, it feels weird. I've always... We've always had, I don't know.'

'We've always felt comfortable with each other.'

'Yeah.'

'So, now it feels weird not to touch anymore.'

'Yeah.'

'But somewhere, after Charlie, things changed. Do you remember? How much do you remember?'

Inwardly, I cringe at this.

'More than I care to admit.'

'Right, and that's why we aren't supposed to, you know. Touching, kissing. It's not good, not healthy. Not normal.'

'Hm. I agree, but I don't like it. I like touching you, with your new big neck. Are there more new muscles in other places?'

I use my other hand to squeeze a bicep. Jason lifts my hand off his arm. I let it drop to the sofa.

'Emma. Stop it. You know what you're doing.'

'Emma? Since when have you ever called me Emma.'

'Since you started misbehaving.'

'I like misbehaving, that's part of my problem.'

'Oh, I know. It's part of my problem too.'

We stare at each other for a moment, God, if I could just kiss him. I really don't remember when I started fancying Jason, it wasn't when Charlie was still alive, but after he became more...

'Can you stop looking at me like I'm food. You, literally, just licked your lips.'

'Shit, sorry. My mind was, er... elsewhere.'

'Yeah, you've never been able to hide what you're feeling.'

'Fuck, this is harder than I thought.'

'Yep, but we're going to be strong, be good friends. I'm going on a date; did I tell you?'

I don't like this, what's happening?

'A date, who with?'

'Do you remember Lucy?'

Lucy, red PVC dress, banging body. Gorgeous blonde. Yep, kissed her as well.

'Yeah, from the club we first went to, when we did Es for the first time.'

'Mm, bumped into her in Clapham. Weird right.'

'Hm. When's your date?'

I hate her.

'Tomorrow.'

'That's great Jas. I'm thrilled for you. Lucy was lovely.'

Too fucking lovely. Shit. He went out with her for ages, they've loads of shared history. Bollocks. Arse. Fuck. And I'm stuck in here. I can't do anything about it except Seth, I can do Seth. Why am I jealous, Seth's lovely. What's happening?

'Em. Stop it.'

'Stop what.'

'Your mind is whirling.'

'I hate that you know me so well. I'm jealous. I know, we're 'Friends' we're not good for each other. Not healthy. Yep, fine, I just need a moment to process it. You definitely should see Lucy. You and she were a great match, I never really understood why you split up. Why did you split up?'

'Same as the rest, you know why.'

He's looking at me like he used to. God.

'I'm sorry. I'm sorry I ruined your love life.'

But can you kiss me now?

'You didn't ruin it. It wasn't your fault how I felt.'

Felt? Past tense. Not surprisingly, I'm a bag of bones, my boobs are like puppy's ears and I can't walk more than half a mile without needing a rest.

I turn away from him and put my hands around my knees, staring at the pool. It's OK Em, you're OK. Jason still loves you but as a friend. It's fine, it's how it's always been.

'Em, come on. We're fine.'

'Yeah, OK. I know.'

I've had enough for today.

'You better go, time will be up soon.'

'Em, come on.'

'No, I think it's better if you go. We can talk when I get out, when I'm at yours before I move back to mine and Charlie's.'

'OK.'

'We're fine. It's all good.'

God, he looks sad. He looks at me with those pools of

blackness. I lean in and kiss him gently on the lips. Warm, soft, familiar. His hand goes around my back and draws me closer. Warmer, more familiar.

'Shit.'

'Sorry.'

I'm not sorry. I know I should be sorry, but I'm not.

'Come on, I'll walk you to reception.' I take his hand and he squeezes it as we walk. Nothing more is said. When we get to reception we hug.

'I'll see you soon.'

'Yeah, soon.'

———

I'm pacing, I could go and see Seth, I said I would go and see Seth, but Jason. Jason. I can't walk, because I may bump into Seth. Shit. Swimming, I need to clear my head. I could switch it all off when I danced. What's wrong with me? Why did I sleep with Seth, why did I kiss Jason? Both things, both have completely fucked my head. I've probably ruined Jason's chance of happiness with Lucy. I slap myself in the head. Ouch. Well, that didn't help. What would Charlie think? He'd be laughing at me for being such an idiot. Swimming. I strip and put my swimming costume on, it hangs off me but should cover enough to keep me decent in the pool. I throw the clothes I have taken off into the carrier bag the costume was in and wrap myself in a towel.

When I get to the pool, I hand the person on reception the blue card.

'Name?'

'Emma Richards.' He's looking at a clipboard. He finds my name and adds a tick next to it.

'You get an hour then we'll call you out. OK?'

'OK, how do I join one of the exercise classes?'

'Just turn up, either eleven or two o'clock.'

'OK, thanks. Is there somewhere to leave my stuff?'

'Lockers are in the changing rooms.'

'Thanks.'

I find my way to the changing rooms; the smell reminds me of swimming lessons at school. I haven't been to a pool since. Charlie and I didn't go swimming. The changing rooms are exactly as you would expect. Beige ceiling-to-floor lockers split the room into sections with wooden benches. There are no cubicles. It looks like the men and women just all get changed in the same place.

At the pool, I tentatively step down the ladder into the water, holding tight to the handrails. It's cold, why isn't it warmer? My body is instantly covered in goosebumps. I continue down the steps until I am submerged up to my chest. People are swimming up and down the pool or standing at the end talking. I drop down so I'm crouching underwater. It's freezing. When I come up for air, I push my hair back and start swimming. The first lap seems easy and it's warmer, but by the second I'm struggling. I'm arguing with myself. My body is knackered and wants to rest but my mind is saying stop being such a wuss and keep moving. On the third lap, I need to rest when I reach the edge of the pool at the deep end. My teeth start chattering almost immediately, so I start swimming again. Fourth lap finished; I'm standing in the shallow end with my arms around me. One more lap come on, Emma. My body is shivering. I keep going, my arms feel like jelly, I try turning onto my back and do backstroke - that feels easier for a moment, pushing my head back into the water so I'm as flat as a plank. The water's supporting me. My arm hits the end of the pool as I get to the deep end. Now, I just have to get back to the other end, then I'm done. Backstroke again, I narrowly miss someone on the way. The water feels like treacle. I just about make it to the end.

As I climb out of the pool, I realise the crutch of my

swimming costume is between the middle of my thighs and my nipples are poking out. Hiking the wet costume up takes all the energy I have left.

In the changing room, I wrap my towel around me. The teeth-chattering thing is getting old. I try rubbing my hands up and down on my arms. No good. I need to get dressed to get warm, but it's all a little too much. I sit down on the hard wooden bench and tuck my feet up under me. I'll just rest for a second.

'Hey, hey. Wake up.'

It's the man I talked to earlier. There's a small crowd of dripping-wet people standing behind him looking at me.

'Is she dead?'

'No, she's not dead, just cold. What's your name love?' The man says as he wraps something that looks like tinfoil over me.

'Emma.'

'OK Emma, he says gently then he's shouting, 'Go on piss off you lot, mind your own business.' Then more quietly again, 'Can you stand up?'

'I think so.'

'Which locker are your clothes in?'

'Number nine, no nineteen. Yes, nineteen.'

He pushes people out of the way like they're sheep, then goes to the locker where he grabs my bag of clothes.

'Come on, I'm just going to take you to the office to warm up.'

'OK.'

He puts his arm around my back and puts a hand on my elbow. Every time someone does this to me, it makes me feel like an old woman, I remember my dad doing it to my gran.

We only have to walk for a moment and then we're in a tiny office, with a desk, chair and filing cabinet. There are some papers on the desk but it's tidy. The man puts me into the chair and plugs in a little fan heater that's on the floor. The heat hits my toes almost immediately.

'I'll give you five minutes to get dressed. You need to get some dry clothes on.'

I nod, as he backs out of the door. The warmth feels good. I drop the towel and the costume to the floor and rummage for my knickers. I get them and my top on easily enough but the leggings with damp legs are a nightmare. It's like I'm in a wrestling match. I eventually manage to haul them up and put my cardigan on, depositing the wet things into the bag. I sit back down in the seat enjoying the dry heat. I'm just dozing off again when there's a knock on the door.

'Hello?'

'Are you decent?'

'Yeah.'

The man comes back in and crouches down in front of me.

'Emma, I've seen this dozens of times, you pushed yourself too hard on your first day in the pool. You need to take it slowly. Come back tomorrow and try again but do less to begin with.'

'OK, sorry to be a problem.'

'It's not a problem. I just don't want you to do yourself an injury.'

'OK.'

'Back tomorrow?'

I nod. I enjoyed swimming until it got too hard. My brain switched off, which was nice. I'll be back tomorrow.

———

I sleep fitfully, Charlie, Jason and Seth slip into my dreams again. When I dream of Charlie, it feels so real, we were in the flat playing with Harold Lloyd. Then we were in bed, he was kissing me and fireworks were going off in my head, his beautiful body, naked next to mine, laughing. Doing things to me that only he knew I liked, a smile at the edge of his lips as he watched me, wanting me. Those green storms gazing down at me. Telling me he loved me. Then he was sick and thin and I was screaming after he stopped breathing.

Rosie is in my room. Why's Rosie here?

'Are you OK?'

'Yeah, I just woke up.'

'You were screaming Emma.'

'I'm sorry.'

Rosie is sitting on the end of my bed; she hasn't got her clipboard. I must've caught her unawares.

'Nothing to be sorry for, did you have a nightmare?'

'Sort of, I was dreaming about Charlie... my husband.' I'm twisting the slim white gold band on my ring finger.

'That's good.'

'It didn't feel good.'

'When someone has taken a lot of drugs or been through a trauma, dreams kind of disappear, you pass out rather than sleep. It takes a while in recovery for people to get their dreams back. You're getting better, Em.'

'Oh. It doesn't feel like it right now.'

'No one said it would be easy. You haven't allowed yourself to process your grief. This is your mind telling you it's time.'

'Oh.' I study the ring on my finger, I think I'd forgotten it was there. If I didn't see it, then Charlie didn't die, didn't marry me. None of it happened. Suddenly, I feel the weight of it. I visit the picture in my mind where he's grinning and crying as he puts it on my finger.

Rosie stands up and fetches a tissue from the box on my bedside table and hands it to me. I blow my nose as Rosie rubs my arm, 'You're doing well, I'm proud of you.'

'Thanks.'

———

I'm back at the swimming pool the next day after group therapy, to join in the class. Moving to the music in the shallow end feels brilliant. The exercise is gentle and reminds me of the warmups I used to do before ballet class. Slowly, slowly, I keep telling myself.

I avoid going to the willow tree. My body wants to but my mind is so full of other thoughts, I don't know if I have room to squeeze Seth into them. I feel bad for Seth, worried about Jason and guilty about Charlie. I write everything down but it doesn't help. I need to explain to Seth what he saw through the window of the canteen, so I have one less thing on my mind.

On the third day, I decide to see Seth. When I get there, he's already there leaning against the tree smoking, he isn't smiling.

'Three days? Three fucking days Em?'

'Sorry. My head was all over the shop, but what you saw wasn't...'

'What I saw wasn't what?'

'Jason's my friend.'

'Looked like more than that to me.'

He's stopped leaning and is standing over me his shoulders curved so he can look down at me, the smoke blows into my eyes as he speaks.

He's raising his voice, 'Look at me!'

Suddenly, an image of Bobby Turner dribbling on me is in my head, where the fuck did that come from, I flinch and take a step back.

'Let me explain.'

He turns away from me, there isn't much room for movement. He throws his cigarette on the floor and stubs it out with his shoe, grinding it into the grass. Is that what he wants to do to me? His face is a mask; I don't recognise him.

'Go on then, explain this one away Em.'

'Jason was sad about this.' I roll up the sleeves of my coat and show him the scars, 'He feels responsible.'

'When did that happen? You didn't mention it.' His expression softens.

'After we were caught with the drugs, one of the days after, I'm not sure. I felt...trapped.'

'Hm.'

He rifles in his pocket for the box of cigarettes, takes one out and offers me one. I put it between my lips. Seth comes closer to light it. He's back, normal Seth.

'Sorry. This place. Too much time to think. It does my head in.'

'I know, me too.'

He hasn't stepped back after lighting the cigarette.

'I imagined all sorts. I got jealous.'

'Jealous?'

'Yeah. Shouldn't I?'

'No.' I think of Jason. Yes, you should be jealous. No, Jason went on a date with Lucy, we're just friends. That's how it is.

He puts his hand behind my head and pulls me to him so we can kiss. I think of the kiss with Jason in front of the pool. That was nice. My hands move inside Seth's coat, under his clothes.

We've both thrown our cigarettes away. He takes my coat off and turns me so I have my back to him, he's kissing my neck, pulling my leggings down, using his feet to push my legs apart, pushing me forward so my palms are against the rough bark of the tree. His hands bring my hips to him. I bite my lip trying to be quiet, arching my back to help him push in deeper. He leans over me when he's done, feeling for my breast, drawing me up. I pull my leggings up before I turn around. It's Seth, of course, it's Seth. I wasn't thinking of Seth.

He kisses me, then rummages again in his pocket for cigarettes. He lights one and we both sit down leaning against the tree to share it.

We're both still breathless. I miss feeling fit. More swimming tomorrow.

'Any idea of the time.'

'None.'

'I need to go and do knitting soon before they miss me.'

'I know, will you come tomorrow?' He's looking at me, we're shadowed in the dim light under the branches of the tree.

'Yeah.'

'I'm sorry for shouting earlier.'

'I know.'

'I'm angry so much of the time and I don't want to feel angry with you.'

'I don't want you to feel angry with me either.'

I kiss him softly. He looks like he may cry.

'You know, when I had this...' He points at his eye, there's still a little yellow bruising around it, 'someone said something about you, they somehow got wind of what happened at Christmas. They asked me about...fuck. They said...' Tears are falling now, slipping down onto his coat.

'They said I was a slag.'

'Yeah, more or less.'

'Yeah. Men are dicks.'

'Ha! Yeah.'

We sit there quietly for a moment.

'Right time to knit hats for babies. I'll see you tomorrow.'

'Yeah.'

We both stand up. I'm just about to walk away before he tugs me back to kiss him again.

'I need to go.'

'I know, I really want you to stay though.'

'No, we'll get in more trouble. I'm going.'

'Tomorrow.'

I walk away.

WEEK ELEVEN

I'm in Dr Joseph's office; I've been summoned. I fear they have found out about Seth and I'll be in trouble again.

When I walk in, I remain cheery.

'Hi. How's things.'

'Good, nice to see you looking so well. You're filling out.'

'Are you calling me fat, Dr Joseph?'

'I wouldn't dare.'

Dr Joesph is looking at his notes on his desk. He looks up over the top of his glasses.

'I have some good news.'

'Good news?' I'm in unfamiliar territory; I don't get good news.

'Yes. You can go home. On...' Another look at his notes, 'Wednesday.'

'I can leave, the day after tomorrow?'

'Yes.'

'Fuck. Sorry. Shit, that is good news.'

He's smiling when he says, 'I have issued you a three-month prescription for your Prozac, you can pick it up from reception when you leave. I will pass on all the relevant information to your doctor, you should be able to get a repeat prescription fairly simply. I've also sorted out weekly visits with a counsellor, here are her details. She's very good, I think you'll like her. Your first appointment is the Friday after you leave here. I've recommended grief counselling as a priority. I think you already know; you really need to process your feelings about Charlie so you can move on with your life.'

I'm looking down; the ring feels heavier on my finger.

'Em. Emma. Are you still with me?'

Focus Em.

'Yes, yes, I am. Thank you. I really appreciate everything you've done for me. Patience of a saint.'

'Part of the job description.'

'Yeah, s'pose it is.'

I pick up the details for the counsellor off the table. As I leave, I say, 'Thanks again, Dr Joseph.'

Walking back to my room, I'm trying to persuade myself this is good, but I know I'm scared. Scared of all the temptations outside. Scared of facing moving back into mine and Charlie's flat. First though, a little respite at Jason's. Jason, I need to call Jason, so I make a detour to reception and ask for a telephone appointment with him. They tell me they'll try and arrange it for six o'clock this evening.

Back in my room, I mull over how to tell Seth. I don't think he'll take the news well, although he must have seen it coming. I've been exercising in the pool every day, doing my circuits, building up muscle. I half-jogged around this morning; it was exhilarating. When I get out of here, I'd like to book into an adult ballet class. I miss dancing. I have plans, all my scribbles in my notebook might be something. I need to get my electric typewriter from home and start putting it all together. I think I've about enough money from Charlie to last me a couple of years. If I could get a contract for a couple of novels... It's a dream that has started to bubble in the last few weeks, I have finally started to think about my future and Charlie had such faith in my writing. I could honour his memory and write something beautiful. It'll be for him. But before that, I should tell Seth I'm leaving. It's midday. Lunch first, I won't miss the mush.

———

I'm under the tree before him, pacing. I light a cigarette. They're on my list of things to give up. One day at a time. As I inhale, he appears.

'Hey.'

'Hey.'

He comes forward and kisses me. His hands circling my waist. I twitch away, I need to tell him before I get distracted.

'I have to tell you something.'

'Hm.' He has moved to my neck, his hands are moving up my back, undoing my bra.

'Seth, stop. Look at me, it's important.'

He stops but keeps his hands on my waist.

'What's so important?'

'I'm leaving on Wednesday.'

His hands drop from my waist.

'Wednesday?'

'Yeah.'

'Oh. I mean, I knew you were doing well. That's good.'

He's looking at the floor, he's feeling in his jacket pocket for his cigarettes. I watch as he lights up, then looks at me. The flame from the match makes his eyes look like there's a fire in a pool of dark water.

'Yeah, it's good. I'll be staying at Jason's for a bit before I return to my flat.'

'The friend.'

'Yeah, the friend.'

'Hm.'

'When you get out, will you look me up? Tomorrow, I'll give you my numbers, Jason's and my flat.'

'Yeah, I'll look you up.'

'We have plans to do things in a bed?'

I need to lighten the mood. Seeing Seth disappear into his head is worrying.

'Yes. We do. Speaking of which.'

He moves back towards me.

'Please don't be sad.'

'It's in my nature.'

I kiss him.

We have sex lying on the ground, but it's like I've lost a piece of him. Almost as though he's hardly there.

Back in the Women's Unit, I'm despondent. After occy health it's dinner time. I eat my food after a fair bit of pushing it around the plate.

Just before six, I turn up to reception for my call with Jason. I need to shake off this fug. Before I make the call in the tiny room, I spend a couple of minutes jumping and stretching to try and get my endorphins going. What it does is make me feel breathless so when Jason picks up the phone and I say hello, he says, 'Have you been running?'

'No, I was just stretching. Getting my brain into a better place.'

Instantly, I hear the concern in Jason's voice.

'Are you OK?'

'Yes, it's good. I have good news.'

'Oh.'

'Yeah. Can you come and get me on Wednesday morning?'

'They're letting you out?'

'Yeah.'

'That's great news.'

The happiness and relief in his voice is palpable.

'And you're sure it's still OK for me to stay at yours for a bit, just as I reacclimatise.'

'Yeah, absolutely. You're always welcome. Harold Lloyd will be thrilled; we'll probably have multiple mice presents.'

'Oh, did you catch that one that was lost?'

'Eventually, it had set up home in one of my paint cupboards, it was building a nest.'

'Wow.'

'What time shall I come and get you?'

'They said nine-thirty. Is that OK?'

'It's perfect. I'm so happy for you Em.'

'Me too.'

I'm smiling. I should be happy. Sod Seth, I've worked hard to get better. I'm going to keep getting better. I want to live.

———

My last full day. I eat, knit, go to group, go to swim class, eat again and then wait under the willow tree.

I wait and wait. I'm out there over an hour becoming angrier with each passing minute. Fuck him. Fucking tosser. How dare he not be happy for me. How dare he. He was bad for me anyway. Bad influence. When I'm back in my room I kick the door to the bathroom which makes my toe throb. This just infuriates me more. Last shower in the tiny shower. Last sleep under the scratchy blanket, last everything in this place. Another night of weird dreams. These are every night now. I tell myself, I'm healing, or at least that's what Rosie said.

My few belongings take no time to pack. They can all go to the charity shop when I leave. I never want to wear these clothes again. Picking up my folder of Charlie's photos I pat the folder gently, I haven't looked at them. The three notebooks filled with the things I scribbled whilst I was here are in my bag.

Jason is there when I get there, smiling. There he is. My Jason. I drop the bag and let him hug me as I hold the folder.

I ask reception if they have my prescription. They give it to me. It feels odd to just walk through the automatic doors. I can leave. Jason picks up my bag and takes my hand. He leads me out of rehab. I never want to come back. Swoosh.

OUT

Being in a car, seeing the outside world, is odd. A few Christmas decorations dangle morosely in shop windows, but most have been taken down. It's one of those typical British end-of-January days in London. Bitingly cold, with light clouds covering the sun so everything is just varying shades of grey.

Within forty minutes we're in Jason's studio flat again. I've spent so much time here that it feels as much like home as my place with Charlie.

I dump the bag of clothes in the bedroom, then place the notebooks and folder under a chair out of the way. Back in the kitchen, Harold Lloyd is on the table and Jason is making me coffee, which smells incredible.

Harold Lloyd bumps his head against my chin as I scratch behind his ear. I have a brief conversation with him about bringing in mice. How very kind it was to show his appreciation to Jason for letting him stay, but now it's time to stop. Harold Lloyd purrs, I say to Jason, 'He says thank you, but he may still have to keep giving you presents.'

'Does he now? When did you learn to speak cat?'

'Oh, come on now, that's been on my CV for years.'

'Hm. Here.' He puts a mug of coffee in front of me. I lift Harold Lloyd off the table, I don't want him knocking it over or getting fur in it. Leaning closer, I put my nose as close to the liquid as possible without touching it. It smells glorious. Jason is watching me; I grin.

'Don't drink it until it's cooled down a bit.'

'OK, Dad.'

He comes and sits next to me and takes my hand.

'So, what's the plan?'

'The plan. Straight to the point. OK. Step one, get my prescription filled. Step two go to my counsellor appointment on Friday. Step three get my typewriter from the flat. Step ...'

'Wait, have you been writing?'

'Maybe, a little.' It's stupid, I'm shy when I mention it.

'Em. That's brilliant. I'm so incredibly proud of you. Come here.'

He lifts me off the chair into a bear hug. I have to tap his shoulder when I stop being able to breathe.

When we sit down again, he says, 'I promised to take you for dinner. I've booked us in at the Italian place. Lucy is going to come too. She says she would love to catch up.'

'Oh, OK. That'll be nice.' I put my hands back around the coffee and inhale, 'How's the mural going?' I don't want to talk about Lucy.

'Good, nearly finished. And I'm doing an exhibition at my gallery with John and Ken in March.'

'Really? That's amazing. Can I see what you've been working on?'

'Er... No, not yet.' He looks away, nervous. This is strange, 'Do you want anything to eat now? Like brunch or something?'

'No, I'm OK, just an ashtray. Which is point four, give up these. But not today.'

He stands up and fetches an ashtray, while Harold Lloyd replaces Jason in the chair. I stroke the cat, while I watch Jason move from sink to cooker to fridge and back again, Something's up. I can't tell what it is.

'How's Lucy about our sleeping arrangements.'

'Ah, yeah, that. I'll sleep on the sofa in the studio, I think. I don't think I should... You know.'

He has come back and put the ashtray down, I fumble in my large pocket to get my cigarettes. I put one in my mouth.

'Hm,' I take it out as I say, 'Have you got my Zippo?'

'Yeah, let me go and get it. I put it away. Hang on.'

When he's gone, I pick Harold Lloyd up from the chair and put him in my lap scrapping the chair back so the table isn't in his way. When he's settled slightly, I pick up my coffee and take a sip. It's still hot but the flavours ping around my mouth. I have my eyes closed when Jason comes back into the kitchen.

'What are you doing?'

I jump, spilling coffee on me and Harold Lloyd, who jumps down as I stand up. 'Shit, sorry. I'll get a cloth.'

'I was enjoying the flavour until you made me jump. You're like a frigging ninja.'

He's wiping at the top of my chest with a tea towel. I've put the coffee down. I take the cloth off him and our fingers touch, butterflies. As I peek up at him, he's looking down, we both look away as we sit down again. There are definitely weird vibes going on.

'Here.'

Jason slides the Zippo across the table. I put it in my hand enjoying the weight of it, rubbing my thumb over the inscription, 'Always.' A gift from Charlie.

Reliable as ever, it sparks up as soon as my thumb quickly rotates the wheel. I put the cigarette in my mouth, light it and inhale, then lean forward and take another sip of coffee.

There's nothing better than this, good coffee and a cigarette. Bliss.

'The coffee's great, thank you.'

'When you're done shall we go and get your prescription and we could go to your flat and get the typewriter?'

The thought of going to the flat feels too big. I need to get some clothes as well. Shit. I'm pushing my wedding ring around with my thumb as I smoke. Jason is watching me.

'Or that might be too much, I could go in and get the typewriter. Would that be OK?'

'Yes. That would be OK.' Relief washes over me. I'm not ready. 'Could you get me some other clothes, all I have is leggings and T-shirts and big cardigans, which I think maybe yours.'

'Yeah, the cardigans are mine, you totally nicked them.'

'Well, those I like, so I'm keeping them, but everything else I've been wearing can go to the charity shop. I need to smarten up. It'll make me feel a bit better. Could you get my make-up bag as well?'

'Sure.'

'Can I just stay here today, until tonight? I just want to mooch if that's OK?'

'You can do whatever you like. I'll go and get your prescription and everything else now. I'll be an hour or so.'

He grabs the car keys from by the kettle and disappears. Silence.

I haven't been completely alone for months; I pad towards the living room and lie on the sofa. Harold Lloyd jumps up and starts kneading my stomach with his paws. I pet him until he's a ball of black and white on my tummy, then relax. A little traffic noise makes it through the windows. A rev of an engine. Somebody walking past talking to someone else, too quiet to make out the words. Harold Lloyds purrs vibrating through me.

'Hey, are you OK?' Jason's hand is around my arm, he's leaning over me looking concerned.

'Yes... wha...'

'I think you fell asleep.'

'It was nice, quiet.'

I try to sit up, Harold Lloyd, is still there, but my movement disturbs him so he jumps down onto the floor and stalks off with his tail in the air. I swivel slowly around into a sitting position; Jason sits down by me.

'You looked pale, I thought...for a moment.'

'I'm not going to do anything like that. Please stop worrying. They wouldn't have let me out if I was at risk.'

'I know. I know.'

He brushes his forehead with his hand and pushes his hair out of the way.

'I was just tired. That's all.' I touch his arm, with the end of my fingers, then think better of it and let my hand drop in my lap.

'OK. I got everything; I think. Although you have a lot of clothes, I picked them randomly. I hope they're OK. I left them in the bedroom and put the typewriter on the desk in there.'

'Speaking of bedrooms. It should be me on the sofa. As I've just proven, I sleep perfectly well on the sofa.'

'No, it's fine. The sofa in the studio is a sofa bed.'

'Hm. OK.'

The rest of the day is spent reacquainting myself with Jason's flat. I take a long bubbly bath which is something I didn't even realise I'd been missing. Then go and sort out the clothes Jason has picked up for me. There's a mixture of skirts, tops, trousers and underwear. It looks like he just emptied my underwear drawer into a bag, probably not wanting to root around in there. I hang up what needs hanging in the space Jason has left for me in his wardrobe and put everything into the drawers he has left empty since last time.

The typewriter is on the desk. My Mum and Dad got it for me for my twenty-first birthday, it's electric and was top of the range then. Now people are using computers and sooner or later I'll have to bite the bullet and get one. But not yet. That's just one step too far. Jason has picked up a ream of paper as well and put it by the side of the typewriter. I put a piece in and type - The quick brown fox jumped over the lazy dog. My fingers feel stiff on the keyboard from lack of practice. I clench and unclench my fists wiggling my fingers, then bring my notebooks from under the chair and put them on the desk on top of the paper. There's a pot on the desk with pencils and biros.

Looking out of the window in front of me, there's a small square of garden that Jason has access to. It's been block-paved and there are a couple of large plant pots whose plants have withered and died. Across from there is another identical terraced Victorian house. All around here the houses have been split into flats. Jason has two floors, the basement is his studio, it's open plan except for a small kitchen and toilet. Some steps lead up from his studio to the second floor of his flat. This is more traditional, kitchen, bathroom, living room and bedroom, all coming off a small, tiled hallway. Another person has separate access from the side of the house and lives above us in another flat. I don't think I've ever seen them; they must have a traditional nine-to-five job. You only occasionally hear them in the evening as they move from room to room.

I follow the smell of food into the kitchen.

'Ah, there you are. I made something to tide us over until dinner.'

Jason puts two plates of beans on toast on the table. I grin at him.

'One of my favourites from Putney.'

'Yeah. Back to student days.'

'Nice.' I tuck in, I'm hungrier than I thought. Between mouthfuls, 'Thanks for getting everything.'

'No problem although it felt a bit pervy when I got to your underwear drawer.'

'Did you just put everything in?' I'm smiling as I eat.

'No, I rifled through it, individually.'

I nearly choke on my food.

'Yes, of course I did. I took the whole drawer out and threw all of it

into a bag.'

'Fair enough,' I'm smiling. This is nice. It's good, it feels like us.

The rest of the day I potter around, watch a bit of TV, read a book, look at my notes until it's time to get ready to go out. Jason's in the shower as I decide what to wear, finally settling on a short red dress. It's straight up and down, hiding my body's sharp angles. I put on a pair of thick black tights and some ankle boots and find a long black cardigan to wear over the short sleeves. I don't want people looking at my arms, their thinness paired with the raw redness on the inside of my forearms is not a good look.

My makeup is a struggle; I can't remember the last time I wore it. It was probably when Charlie was still alive. I take a deep breath and try not to think about that. No tears. I'd like to look nice and feel like myself again. Eventually, I manage a smoky eye with black eyeliner and nude lipstick. The reflection in the mirror makes me think it's a passable effort.

Jason is wearing black jeans with an open black shirt and a black T-shirt underneath. He's bulked out. The shirt is tight around his biceps, and his arse seems more compact in the jeans. He doesn't notice me taking in his new body shape. He's busy feeding Harold Lloyd, bending to put the cat food in the bowl. It's like watching a well-oiled machine, I lick my lips. As he stands up, he looks around and sees me. I rearrange my expression and grin. Grinning is safe.

'You look good. I haven't seen you wear makeup for ages.'

'No, it was a bit of an effort, this is about my third attempt. When do we need to be there?'

'Seven, Lucy is meeting us there. Her place is in Clapham.'

'OK. Are you driving or are we catching a taxi?'

'I'll drive.'

In the car, the smell of Jason's musky aftershave mixed with the smell of soap from his shower seems to seep into me. He seems more relaxed than I've seen him for ages.

When we get to the place, Jason shakes hands with the maître d', who leads us to the table. Lucy is already there. She looks gorgeous. Her blonde hair is long and very straight, her make-up perfect. She stands up to greet us. She's wearing a skin-tight knee-length dress with heels. I instantly feel frumpy. Jason wraps his fingers around her waist and kisses her on the mouth, when they stop, she rubs the lipstick off his lips with her thumb. There's a familiarity there. They're definitely sleeping together. She sees me watching and smiles, perfect teeth. Embraces me, rubbing my back. Which is weird. Like I need pity. After the initial, How are you, we sit down. There's an awkward silence as we look at the menus. A waiter comes over and asks us what we would like to drink. Jason asks for sparkling water, Lucy a glass of white wine. I order a large glass of Merlot. Jason looks at me and frowns, 'Are you allowed to...'

'No one told me not to.' That's a blatant lie. Alcohol weakens the resolve and makes you more likely to want drugs.

'Really?'

'Really.' I scowl at him. The waiter has gone anyway. I return to the menu. Proper food. Not mush. This is exciting. Ignore Lucy patting Jason's hand and giving him a concerned look. Hold it together Em.

After we order, I ask Lucy what she's up to these days. For the life of me, I can't remember what course she did at uni.

'I've just started my own consulting firm.' She leers at me again; did she always look a bit snaky? Jason is squeezing her hand. They make me want to puke. Poker face Em. Come on.

'Oh yes, but what does that actually mean?'

'Well, I offer advice to businesses about how to improve their performance, profitability and infrastructure. That kind of thing.'

'Right, so you encourage businesses to fire people.'

'Em.' Jason is giving me daggers.

'No, however, sometimes a restructure is required to maximise efficiency.'

'Wow. Good. That's very, er... helpful.' I smile sweetly at Jason.

'Yes, I enjoy it and so far, my little business is going from strength to strength.'

Another squeeze of her hand.

The waiter comes over with the drinks, I take a large gulp and offer a cigarette to Lucy, who declines with a little shake of her perfect head. I light up, as we wait for our starters.

Lucy looks at me, 'And you, what are your plans now? You did literature at uni didn't you?'

Great, her memory is better than mine.

'Yes, I'm just trying to get straight at the moment, you know.' I give her a stern look. I don't want to share my plans with her. Jason has different ideas.

'But you've been writing, whilst you were...'

'In rehab. Yes. I wrote some stuff in rehab.'

Another large mouthful of wine. Its warmth runs smoothly down my throat. My cardy is too warm. Can't take my cardy off because of my stupid arms. Damn it. Lucy is looking at me again.

'What was that like, rehab? You hear stories.'

'Oh, yes, what sort of stories?' I'm not going to make this easy for her.

'Oh, I don't know. It's supposed to be awful.'

Memories of the constant noise, the screaming. I shake my head.

'Yeah, it can be, um, challenging.'

Jason is watching me like a hawk. I stare at him as I lift my wine glass and take another sip. He looks down at his hands. Good.

When the starters arrive, I ask the waiter for another glass of merlot.

I have a caprese salad. It looks amazing. God, she's still talking.

'But you're better now?'

I put some tomato and basil in my mouth and enjoy the flavours as they hit my taste buds. It's glorious. I refocus.

'I'm an addict Lucy, it's not something I'll ever be better from. I have to live with it every day. It's a bit shit to be honest.'

'Oh, I'm sorry.'

No, I don't want your pity. I ignore her and focus on the gorgeous food. The mozzarella is beautifully creamy and there's a basil vinaigrette over the tomatoes which is making my tongue sing.

'How's everyone's starters? These tastes incredible, thanks for bringing me here Jason.'

His shoulders relax slightly.

'It's alright Em. Mine's good, what about you Luce?'

Luce? Ugh.

'Lovely. Thank you.'

She's eating an undressed green salad. She'd said some bollocks about watching her calorie intake when she'd ordered. It looks green, probably tastes like the green mush, I'm oh so used to. No thanks.

My next glass of wine arrives as they take our starter plates away. Lucy is talking about our clubbing days.

'Do you remember when we were trying to get you zipped back into that rubber skirt, just as we started rushing. That was a brilliant night, you looked incredible in that outfit.'

'Thanks.'

I don't want to think about that. It was a great night. Charlie and I had just got together. No don't think about that. A shiver, as the tingle of tears pulse to be released. No.

'Maybe we should talk about something else,' Jason says, always watching me. I take another sip of wine. The restaurant feels too warm.

'Shit, sorry. My mistake.' Lucy is apologising.

'It's OK. It was a good night.'

Our main courses arrive.

Mushroom tagliatelle. Yum. I get my fork and start winding it. Taking a huge mouthful. Jason cuts through his steak, it's still pink in the middle. Another salad for Lucy. It looks boring. I feel a bit sorry for her. I taste the parmesan in the sauce of my pasta dish. I had forgotten how much I missed good food. I rip a piece of garlic bread off the plate in front of me and run it around the empty bowl licking the creamy sauce off my lips. Jason is staring at me. That's different. His hands are holding his knife and fork, but they're not moving. I suck the garlicky butter off my fingers.

'Well, that was lovely,' says Lucy, oblivious to breaking the spell.

Hm. Another sip of wine, it tastes better and better.

'Yeah, it was good. I love Italian food. So, tell me how'd you two managed to bump into each other again.' The wine must be making me more affable. Maybe?

'Oh, it's such a funny story. Isn't Jason,' She kind of leans against him and they bump shoulders as she smirks at me, 'I was literally walking down Clapham High Street, when I dropped my cahier and papers were flying everywhere, when who should come to the rescue? So lovely.'

'Hm, so lovely.' Jason glances at me. I ignore him and beam at Lucy, 'Then what happened? Do tell.'

'Well, we got talking and went for a coffee. Then a date and well, the rest is history.'

'That's nice, you two reconnecting. You have so much in common.'

'Oh, not really, but that doesn't matter when there's a connection, you know.'

'Yeah. I know.'

'Well, I just need to visit the little girl's room. Won't be a tick.'

She unwinds her long lean body. I wonder how someone so slender has such great-looking tits. Are they real?

As soon as she is out of earshot, 'What the fuck are you doing Em.' Jason is glaring at me.

'I'm not doing anything,' I say, making my eyes bigger as I stare back at him.

'You are. Bloody leading questions, stop being a little bitch and play nicely.'

'I am. She's just...A consultant? Really, seriously, what do you talk about? You have nothing in common.'

'She has an interest in art.'

'Yeah, and capitalism and voting conservative.'

'You don't know that.'

'Do you?'

Jason looks down as I take another large glug of wine. I'm coming to the end of my glass. There's the waiter, I point at my glass, he nods.

'You are very annoying when you want to be.'

'I'm just saying I can't see it. Lucy is lovely, beautiful. Amazing tits. But I don't know, she doesn't seem right. Why did you split up last time?'

'I told you why.'

Shit.

'Oh, yeah. Sorry. I haven't touched you once tonight.' I'm grinning at him.

'No. Good. That's how it is, just remember. Friends.'

'Friends.' I use my finger to cross my heart and wink at him. He shakes his head at me but his lips are twitching.

Our desserts arrive at the same time as Lucy arrives back from the loos. She has a black coffee whereas me and Jason have both chosen a tiramisu. Just as I take my first bite my glass of wine appears; Jason squints at me. I don't care, I'm savouring the coffee, chocolate and liquor unctuousness currently living in my mouth. Nothing can ruin it.

'Jesus, I would fuck this tiramisu if I could.'

'Oh.' Lucy is looking at me, as I realise, I said that aloud.

'Sorry. But I would.' Jason's shoulders are shaking as he keeps eating, 'How's your coffee?'

'Yes. Nice.'

She has reapplied her perfect pink lipstick, it leaves imprints on the rim of the cup.

'You didn't fancy a pudding then, or something stronger in your coffee.'

'Oh, no. These days, one glass of wine and I'm drunk. I'm such a lightweight.'

'Right. OK.'

When everyone's finished. I light up again, savouring my wine, knowing it will probably be my last, ever. The restaurant feels boiling. Fuck it, the cardigan needs to come off. Lucy gasps. I don't know whether it's at my sticks for arms or the scars. I don't care. I'm full of food, warm and a little bit tipsy. Nothing could ruin this.

Jason and Lucy are making quiet conversation as I smoke. I'm watching them, she touches his shirt, his arm. He just stands there. Yeah, he doesn't fancy her. She's gorgeous, but there's something off.

I stub out my cigarette and make my excuses to nip to the

loo. People are looking at me as I make my way there. Ignore them Em, they're all just dickheads. Nothing to see here. When I'm washing my hands, I scan my face in the mirror. My loose up-do, is coming down slightly and falling around my cheeks which are a little flushed and there's no lipstick left on my lips. I don't care, we'll be going home in a minute. I smile into the mirror and see my teeth have that slightly purple stain you get from red wine. Oh well. I briefly wonder if Jason has more wine in the house. I doubt it. He probably got rid of everything before I got home. Shame. I'm enjoying the buzz and want it to continue. Naughty wine.

By the time I get back, Jason has paid the bill and he's helping Lucy into her coat. We walk out together. Jason gives me the keys to his car so I can get in while he says goodbye.

I plonk myself down into the passenger seat and watch them kiss. His hands are still on her back as they do. Again, the rub of his lips with her thumb afterwards. I sniff and look away, suddenly finding the dashboard really interesting. Jason climbs into the driver's seat. A blast of cold air hits me, followed by his musky scent. I continue to stare ahead, inhaling his smell.

He doesn't say anything as he starts the car and we drive back to his place.

When we get to the flat, I disappear into the bedroom to put on something comfier. I choose a pair of tracksuit bottoms, a cropped top and one of Jason's cardigans. In the kitchen, he's boiling the kettle.

'Coffee?'

'Yes please. Although I would love another glass of wine.'

'I bet you would.' Hm, grumpy Jason.

'So, that's a no then.'

'You're not supposed to drink, are you?'

He's turned around to look at me as the kettle boils. I've taken my usual seat at the kitchen table.

'Probably not, nope.'

'Fucking hell, you've been out for less than twenty-four hours Em. Don't you want to get better?'

Lighting a cigarette, I glare at him through my exhaled smoke. Then suddenly find the cuff of my cardy fascinating and start picking at it, I say, 'It wasn't drugs, Jas. It was just a couple of glasses of wine.'

'Yeah, and you became a complete bitch. You were horrible to Lucy.'

'Wasn't.'

'You were. There was no need for it.'

I mumble a reply to the table, 'Sorry.'

He turns around with a sigh and makes the coffee, bringing it to the table for us to drink together.

The wine is still buzzing around my system. It's nice, but Jason's grumpiness is making it hard for me to enjoy it. He takes a cigarette out of my packet and lights up.

'When did you start smoking?'

'When you came to live here.'

'Did you? I don't remember. Then again, a lot of that time is a bit of a blur. Is it my fault?'

He looks at me for a second too long before saying,

'Nah.'

I watch his lips as he inhales, that mouth. Nice mouth. Mustn't touch. He says, 'You looked nice tonight, it's good to see you getting dressed up again.'

'Thanks. You looked good too.'

'Hm. Right, well I'm going to finish this and go to bed.'

'OK.'

He stands up, stubs his cigarette out and takes his mug to the sink, then disappears downstairs to his studio.

When I'm in bed, I have to move Harold Lloyd off my side of the bed to get in. I must have fallen asleep straight away, as that's the last thing I remember.

'Em, wake up. Wake Up!' Jason is holding my arms, shaking me. The bedside light is on.

'Wha...?'

'You were screaming, I thought someone... I thought you were in trouble.'

I remember, the nightmare, Jason with Charlie, both of them dancing with Lucy in her green dress. Their hands on her, everywhere. Then she's stamping on them, on their heads.

I lean closer to Jason, he's OK, his face is OK.

'Sorry, I've been having these nightmares. Should've warned you.'

'Hey, hey, it's OK.' His arms around me. His big arms. Wow, his arms have got big. I feel tiny within them. I put my hands around his back, I can't reach around him.

'Em.' His chin is on my head. I'm not letting go.

'Yeah.'

'You're naked.'

'Yeah. I didn't bother putting anything on as you weren't going to be in bed. I normally sleep naked.'

'Oh. I didn't know. I should probably go.' He's letting go.

'One more minute. Please.'

'One more minute.'

My hands move across his back. There are muscles he didn't have before. I let my fingers slip down to his boxers, pushing past the elastic.

'Em.'

'Jas.'

'Stop it.'

Leaning back, I know full well that nothing is stopping him from seeing everything.

'Em. Please stop.'

Letting go I push my fingers into his hair, bringing his head down to me.

He leans towards me and our lips brush then he moves to my neck, my shoulder and back up again, then the other side, I arch my back to come closer to him. His lips are on my nipple. His tongue circles it. I moan, as he moves back up, now his mouth is on mine. Kissing me, like I've wanted him to since after Charlie when it changed between us. Even in my drug-addled state I knew it had changed. Jesus Christ he can kiss. I have nothing going on in my mind but his lips on mine, his tongue pressing against mine. He's lying us down. The length of him solid beside me, his hands roaming my body, my nipples, he is opening my legs, gently feeling me, finding his way. I'm writhing. I tug at his boxers, taking them off. My hand finds him.

'Em?'

'Don't talk. There's been too much talking.'

My body and soul wants him. He's gentle, filling me up, his body over mine, enveloping me absorbing me, as I hold onto him with my arms, my legs. We're in a perfect rhythm, like when I dance. I'm completely at peace as we orgasm, our bodies shuddering as he holds me tight.

When he loosens his grip, he's crying, I try to wipe the tears away.

'Why are you crying, didn't you enjoy...?'

'I've wanted to...for so long, I've wanted you. I never imagined...'

I lean back and hug him; he hasn't come out of me.

I say, 'It's OK. We're OK. Maybe we're more than friends?'

I hear the warmth in his voice.

'You think?'

'Yeah. Do you think our counsellors will be cross?'

He says, 'Yep, definitely. I just hope I haven't taken advantage of you.'

'Yeah, cos I'm an innocent Victorian lady. I don't think so, I was completely sober, well nearly. I knew what I was doing. You have never, would never take advantage of me.'

'You sure?'

'Yeah.'

'OK, in which case.'

Jason leans in to kiss me. We're both getting our smiles back. We don't get much sleep after that. Mid-morning, Harold Lloyd, walks across us, meowing.

'I'll feed him.' He clambers out of bed, his body is incredible, tall and lean, but powerful looking, 'You're staring, you'll make me shy.'

'I just like watching you go.' I shout as he leaves the room. I stretch and grin. Today is a good day. I'm tired but happy. When he comes back, he climbs back into bed and hugs me. I climb on top of him as his hands cover my breasts.

'Hm. I'm not going to get much work done with you here. You always were a distraction.'

'That's me.' I say as we grind hips.

Eventually, we stop long enough to have coffee and eat breakfast. Jason makes me fried eggs on toast.

'I need to build you up. I love you, but...

'You love me?'

'Oh, this is a surprise?'

'S'pose not. And yeah, you're right, I miss my tits and my hips. I was thinking of jogging and finding a ballet class.'

'I'll jog with you, but the ballet you can keep for yourself.'

'Wuss, it's brilliant and builds strength. I feel weak.'

'You're anything but weak, and I don't doubt the ballet, just not my thing.'

'Fair enough.'

We sit down to eat. I wolf my food down. I'm running my finger around the plate, when Jason says, 'I love watching you eat.'

'I noticed, last night.'

'Shit. I thought I was doing such a good job of hiding it.'

'Nope.' I put my finger in my mouth and suck the butter and egg yolk off it.

'Jesus Christ woman. Come on.' He is lifting me onto the

table, pushing the plates off, I hear a smash but don't care as he opens my dressing gown.

A little later we hear the phone ring.

'I'd better get that.' Jason disappears out of the room. When he comes back he looks serious.

'What? What's happened?'

'That was Lucy.'

'Oh.'

'Yeah. She didn't take the news very well.'

'Don't worry about it, she'll optimise her efficiency or something and restructure herself.'

'You really were a bitch last night.'

'I was jealous.'

'No shit.'

NIGHTMARES

I'm in our flat, Charlie is shouting, throwing things.

Harold Lloyd is cowering under a chair.

Suddenly, he's holding my arms, raging, awful words tumbling from his mouth, but I don't understand, what's he saying?

He's shaking me again. My hands are on his chest, pushing him away.

'Em... Wake up, you need to wake up.'

Jason. Fuck. My palms are spread across his chest, I was pushing Jason.

'Sorry.' Charlie's angry face is still in my mind as the wetness of tears drip onto the pillow.

'Nightmares again?'

'Yeah, shit, I'm sorry.'

'Hey, it's OK. It's OK.'

'Charlie was so cross, Jason. Do you think he'd mind, us? This, you know.'

'No, he knew how I felt, I made no secret of it. I think he knew what would happen, which is why he told me to look after you.'

'Do you?'

'Yes, definitely. Talk to the counsellor tell her what is going on in that noggin of yours.' Jason lightly taps my head with his finger, then pushes some hair behind my ear.

'Noggin. You're so weird. I will, promise.'

Holding onto Jason, dozing in and out of sleep, Charlie keeps pushing through. I'm forced awake when Jason jumps out of bed and says, 'Come on then, jogging time.'

He sounds positively perky.

'Can't we just stay a bit longer... ?'

'Nope.'

Jason jumps out of bed and jerks the duvet off me.

'Ah. No!'

'Yes.'

He disappears into the bathroom, as I scrabble to wrap the duvet back around me.

We attempt to go for a jog around the local park. Jason is fit as a butcher's dog, whereas I nearly throw up after half a mile. He jogs slowly, next to me, backwards and forwards. I walk the rest of the way, scowling.

'You'll get there, Em. It's going to take time.'

'I know. It's just frustrating.'

In the afternoon I have my counselling appointment. It's the first time I've been behind the wheel of a car for over a year. I refamiliarise myself with everything before driving slowly to where the counsellor lives. As I arrive in one piece, I quietly congratulate myself on another tiny milestone being reached.

I ring the bell of a nicely presented nineteen-fifties semi. A lady of about forty in bright red-rimmed glasses and wildly curly mid-length hair opens the door beaming.

'Hello, you must be Emma, come in, come in. I've been looking forward to meeting you. Dr Joseph has told me so much.'

'All good I hope.' I know it's not.

As she leads me through her home there are children's

wellies and shoes strewn about the floor and small coats hung precariously off low-level hooks in the hall. We pass a framed finger painting in what looks like a living room; it feels chaotic but cosy. We go out the back through a small garden to a large, converted shed. Inside, a sofa and comfy chair are sitting on an expensive-looking Persian rug. Huge glass doors give a view of the garden. The lady sits in the chair and indicates I should sit on the sofa. It is squishier than I expect, so have to adjust to avoid my feet dangling off the edge. I end up perching, with my hands on either side of me to keep steady.

'So, as you know, I'm Dr Akhtar. I've looked over your case notes and spoken to Dr Joseph. You have been through the mill, my dear, haven't you?'

She's looking at me, waiting for me to answer, I stare back for a second too long, 'Yes, I suppose. But there are lots of people worse off than me.'

'No, no. We don't do that here. No trivialising your issues or comparing yourself to others. You've had a tough time and it is a miracle you're sitting in front of me today. So, well done.'

'Er...Thank you.'

'Right, can you talk to me about Charlie? Tell me all about him.'

'OK, well when I first met him, I thought he was a bit of a creep, but then I got to know him.'

We talk about all the good stuff. What a great talent he was, how he was going to be a famous photographer and how he was just making a name for himself.

I'm avoiding the bit where it's about him getting sick. So, instead, I mention the nightmares and Jason instead. Dr Akhter says the nightmares are normal, especially in light of the relationship with Jason. She says we're programmed to feel guilty, even when we think we don't feel guilty it may come out in our subconscious, in our dreams. She does say that she thinks getting into a relationship with Jason straight after rehab is a mistake.

I'm just building myself up to talk about when Charlie got sick when a ting sound goes.

'Well, that's our time up for today. You've done brilliantly. Next time, we need to talk a little bit about your feelings when Charlie got sick and more about you and Jason. So, have a think about that. We'll meet every Friday at the same time until you don't need me anymore. How does that sound?'

'Good and thanks.' I can't remember the last time I didn't cry when I talked about Charlie. It feels good. Although I know the next few sessions are going to be more challenging. Somewhere during the session, I've manoeuvred myself to a more comfortable sitting position with my legs beside me on the sofa, I uncurl and put my shoes back on.

'You're welcome, dear.'

And she is up and leading me back through her home. Until I'm saying goodbye at the door and driving back to Jason's, smiling.

When I open the door, he's in the hall to greet me. His gaze is steady as he looks for signs of upset, 'How was it, are you OK?'

'It was… good. Really good, I just talked about Charlie, before he was sick. It felt nice.'

'That's great.' His arms go around me, a kiss into my hair. This is nice too.

Harold Lloyd winds around our legs.

'Do you fancy meeting up with Ken and John on Saturday for some food?' The massive painting of Charlie and Jason in their kitchen pops into my head. That was a difficult day.

'They suggested lunch at a bistro near them.'

'Oh, yes. That sounds good.' Relief. I'm not quite ready for their house again.

We go jogging again on Saturday morning. Once again, my

legs turn to jelly and I nearly get Jason to carry me home. It seems worse rather than better. But I decide not to let the momentum of exercise stop and get the Yellow Pages out to look up dance classes near us. I phone about ten places before I find a place for experienced adult ballet. They're in the middle of the term but say I can start in a month as someone is leaving the class. I put a cheque in the post to secure my place. I'm hoping a month is long enough to get my fitness levels somewhere close to good enough for a ballet class. I suspect not. But fuck it.

———

I'm trying to get ready to meet Ken and John, I've found an old pair of jeans that Jason bought back from the flat. They are ridiculously baggy, so I rummage around for a belt. The belt is too loose. Jason makes another hole in it for me to tighten it enough to hold the jeans up. He puts his hands around my waist and his fingers not only touch but overlap. He's looking at me with those big sad brown eyes and holds his hands in front of me in a circle with the fingers not touching.

'Like this, this is how I remember your waist.'

'I know. Soon.' I kiss him and smooth his frown with my fingers.

Ken and John are sitting in the bistro window, at a table for four. Ken is picking lint off John's top as John smiles at him. They're such a gorgeous couple. I squeeze Jason's hand as we walk in. There are lots of hugs before we sit down.

'So, baby girl, tell me you're doing OK.' Ken leans across the table and holds my hands.

'I'm doing a lot better. I think it will take me time but, yes. I'm on the mend.'

'You look better. Although, you're way too thin, darling.' This is John.

'I know, I'm working on that. He's cooking me huge meals.'

'He always was a great cook.'

'Still is, we'll have to have you come around.'

'We?'

I grin at them.

'About time. I'm so happy for you.' Ken is up and around the table hugging me again. He whispers into my ear, 'Be good to him, he's been worried sick about you.'

'I will.'

John is hugging Jason; they swap places for more hugs. We all sit down again and I say, 'Right let's order, what's good here?'

We have a relaxed, long lunch, conversation flows easily. I don't have any alcohol. Although it's tempting when both John and Ken have glasses of wine.

'Jason says you're putting on an exhibition together in March. What's the theme? Jason won't tell me anything about it.'

Both John and Ken look at Jason, who shakes his head.

'Sorry, lovely. Not our place to say, you'll have to get your information from him.'

'Damn it, this is very annoying.' I turn to Jason, 'I will find out, you know I will.'

'No, never going to happen. You'll have to wait for March, just like everyone else.'

'Ahh.'

I punch Jason gently on the arm, who just grins at me.

When we get home, I disappear into the bedroom and get changed into something more alluring, I have a cunning plan. Jason has made a couple of coffees and gone into the lounge and is lying on the couch. I stand in the doorway with my arms high holding the door frame.

'Hello. You look...nice.'

'Nice?'

'Sexy. Definitely sexy.' He has sat up.

Coming towards him, I kiss him and lean into him, so he can feel my body.

'So, what's brought this on?'

'I just thought I should show you another side of me.'

'Hu huh.'

He's nudging the strap of the black lace bra that is still too big for me but it seems to be having the desired effect.

I slowly push the strap back up.

'Nope.'

'Nope?'

'Nope.'

'Why nope?' Jason looks genuinely upset.

'No more of this, until I get the theme from you or you show me what you're working on.'

'Ah,' He quickly switches position. I'm suddenly, lying underneath him. The bulk of him above me as he takes his weight on his arms. He lies on his side and runs a finger down my body and leans in for a kiss. His hand moves over my thigh, slowly. Then it's covering my breast, his thumb on my nipple through the lace of the bra. I try to resist him, but it's so good.

He pushes me onto my side and now his hand is going down my back over my arse bringing me closer to him, I wrap my leg around him. Fuck... His mouth around my nipple, teasing, nipping. I'm arching, he is ripping my knickers off me as I am undoing his jeans.

He puts his hand over mine and stops me.

'What, no. Now. Jas. Come on...'

'But I thought I wasn't allowed until I told you the theme...'

'Don't care, just let me...'

I'm trying to move his hand to get to the fly on his jeans. His fingers of his other hand are still inside me.

'Are you sure...' He's kissing my neck.

'Yep, definitely sure.' Nibbling my ear lobe.

'OK then.'

He undoes his jeans.

As I lay next to him afterwards, I curse my lack of resolve.

'And you're sure you won't let me see what you're working on.'

'Em, it's not finished and I'm not happy with all the pieces yet.'

His hand is running down the length of my spine. He is looking down at my body, absorbing details, taking everything in. He seems sad.

'You know, I'm OK. You know this is OK, don't you?'

He says, 'I worry that I let my desire for you win over actually looking after you and making sure you were better. I don't think I put up much of a fight.'

'Jas, I didn't give you a choice. This was inevitable, after Charlie something changed between us, I couldn't tell you when or how but it did. I was just too wasted to deal with it. Although, I tried, unsuccessfully, because you were doing right by me. It's time for us now.'

'Hm, maybe. But the day after you came out of rehab. It feels too soon.'

I kiss him.

'Does that feel too soon?'

'No.'

I kiss him again.

'Or this?'

'No.'

'Sometimes it's better to stop thinking and just do.'

'Hm.' Jason leans forward and kisses me.

RECOVERY

Weeks pass, Jason and I fall into a pattern. We jog every morning. I'm getting stronger, now managing a couple of miles without collapsing in a heap. I've started to fill out. Jason keeps feeding me large meals, which is what I put the nausea down to. I'm just not used to all this food.

After the morning jog we shower, then work until lunch. I've been collating everything I wrote into an order that makes sense. Jason won't let me in his studio and is increasingly secretive about the work he's completing. But I don't let him read my stuff either as it's not ready. So, I get it.

After lunch, we go back to work. Our evenings are spent reading, watching TV or just enjoying one another's company. It feels idyllic. The Friday sessions with Dr Akhtar are proving to be a good deal harder than the first one but I'm working through a lot of my feelings about Charlie's death. She's suggested I spend at least one night at our flat as a test, without Jason. She thinks Jason and I are enabling one another. I don't bother telling Jason that, although I suspect his counsellor has told him the same thing.

I also have my first ballet class. I need my pointe shoes and a leotard. I decide to drive to the flat to get them. Jason offers to come with me, but I say no. This is another step that I need to do alone.

Entering the flat, it smells different. Sort of musty from the lack of people and activity. It's cold, colder than outside. I wander from room to room. It doesn't feel like mine and Charlie's place anymore, although all our things are dotted around. Ornaments we bought together at antique markets, books we both read, his photographs. I'm detached from it. In our bedroom, I search through drawers for my pointe shoes and leotard. I don't want to stay any longer. It's like Charlie will walk around a corner. In the car, I breathe through a panic attack. Too much. Too soon. I feel guilty for not feeling enough. Jason and I talk about it when I get back, he holds me tightly and says I must have felt more than I thought, why else would I have had a panic attack? He's probably right. I'll talk to Dr Akhtar on Friday.

The ballet class is in a gym about a mile from Jason's flat. I'm nervous. I haven't danced since I did Charlie's final photos and that was hardly dancing. I've been building up my flexibility at the flat stretching my inactive muscles into splits and pliés. My body is not happy with me. I keep pulling muscles that leave me sore and cross. I'm sick of feeling weak and small. Bathing in Epsom salts help soothe some of the aches and pains away and Jason massages my legs and back, but more often than not that leads to other things.

When I walk into the ballet class, the other students turn around to look at me, they all look incredibly fit. As I'm putting my bag down, I check out what everyone has on their feet, just soft shoes. Relief. I went en pointe at Jason's and it nearly killed me.

The teacher is an older woman with a tight bun and a pronounced slightly hooked nose, she reminds me of an eagle that sees everything.

She asks us to go to the barre and starts a warmup. I'm wearing a cross-over cardigan over my leotard as I don't want anyone to see my arms. It is exhilarating to be back in class but I'm struggling. At one point she comes over pushing her hand into the base of my spine to get me to straighten my back. Muscle memory kicks in and puts me back into the correct position. She appraises my posture, 'Good. Good.'

I'm ridiculously proud of this small piece of praise, I suspect she doesn't offer it often.

By the end of the lesson, I'm sweaty and exhausted, but endorphins are coursing through me, I almost run back to Jason's flat. I shout his name as I come through the door. There are voices in the kitchen.

Kaz is standing with Gracie and Arthur by her side. Gracie comes running towards me.

'Em. Em. I've missed you.'

I crouch down on my sore legs to embrace her.

'Ooh you're all sweaty.'

'I'm sorry, I've just finished a ballet class. I need a shower.'

'How was it?' Jason is making drinks by the kettle; he looks at me over Kaz's head.

'Oh, good. Great. Exhausting and brilliant.'

Kaz is grinning at me.

'You look great. Go and have a shower, we're not going anywhere.'

'OK.'

I quickly run over to Kaz and give her a peck on the cheek, before going for a shower.

When I come back the kids are square-eyed watching a video of Aladdin. Kaz and Jason are sitting at the table drinking coffee.

'What a nice surprise, I didn't know you were coming.'

'Oh, it was a bit of a spur-of-the-moment thing. Jason says you're a lot better.'

'I am.'

'And you two are a thing?'

'Yeah.' I grin at her.

'About time.'

'That's what everyone says. Are you here to stay over, we can go in the sofa bed and you and the kids can have our room. Or you could stay in mine and Charlie's place, it's just sitting there empty.'

'If it's alright with you, could we stay here?'

'Of course.'

Jason stands up from the table, 'I'll just go and put some clean sheets on the beds. You're welcome to stay as long as you need. He takes Kaz's hand and gives her a look.

'What's going on?'

'I've left Dave.'

'Oh.'

'Yeah. It's not been right for a while. He was always at work and I was trying to work too and rear the kids. We lost each other somewhere in the mix.'

'There's not anyone...'

'No, God no, not for me anyway and I don't think for him. We just stopped making each other happy.'

'Oh Kaz. I'm so sorry I haven't been around more.'

I stand up and go and hug her as she stays sitting in the chair.

'It's not your fault, there's nothing you could have done and life happens, it happens to all of us.'

'Yeah, it does that. Have you got a plan?'

'I think so and Dave and I are still friendly, we don't want to upset the kids. They're the priority. I'll stay in the house. Dave is moving his stuff out this weekend, which is why I came here, I don't want to be there for that.'

'No, I understand. Where's he going to live?'

'He's putting his stuff in storage and has been staying in Matt's spare room but he plans to get a flat with enough room for the kids to stay.'

'That's good Kaz. I'm glad you're all still friends. It could be so much worse.'

'It could, it's just a massive chunk of my life, I've been with Dave since I was fifteen, that's nearly twelve years.'

'I know. But just think of the adventures you're going to have now. And the men you can date. That's exciting.'

Kaz grins at me, 'Trust you to go straight to sex.'

'I didn't say that, exactly. Well, how about we take the kids to the zoo tomorrow and then maybe Hamleys afterwards.'

'Yeah, that does sound good.'

'And then you need to come back down without the kids in March for Jason's exhibition.'

'He's putting on an exhibition?'

'It's some kind of top-secret project, a couple of our other friends are joining him and showing their work too.'

'Well, that's a date. It sounds intriguing.'

'If you can get him to spill the beans, will you let me know?'

'Of course. Girl code.'

'Look, I'm sorry about last time. I was awful.'

'Pfff! It was nothing, we've had worse fallings out. Friends forever remember.'

Kaz holds her hand out and we do our not-so-secret hand-shake. It's like I'm back in the village giggling about boys again.

'Hello, what are you two scheming?'

We both say nothing but start to giggle. Jason ignores us and says, 'I've put you in our room, we'll sleep in the studio, although I need to tidy up down there a bit.'

'Ooh, I get to go into your studio, finally?' I'm grinning at Jason.

'You won't find anything I'm going to put everything away under lock and key.'

'Damn it.'

Kaz and the kids stay until Sunday evening. It's lovely

having them stay, but the kids are a lot of work. When they leave, Jason and I flop onto the sofa.

'Bloody hell, that was knackering. How she has brought those two up, practically on her own these last few years, I'll never know.'

Jason puts his arm around me, 'Shame about her and Dave, though.'

'Yeah, but if they're not making each other happy. I always thought they had kids too young.'

'Really? You never said, when do you think people should have kids?'

I turn and look at Jason, this conversation has taken an odd turn.

'I don't know? When they're ready, I suppose. When it feels right.'

'Hm. Yeah.'

I climb onto Jason's lap.

'Enough talking, we've not had nearly enough alone time.'

'No, we haven't.'

SURPRISE

I'm throwing up again. Jason is rubbing my back.

'I've made an appointment for you at the doctor. There's something wrong.'

I spit into the sink and nod. I haven't any fight left in me to argue with him.

It's the third week in March. Jason's exhibition opens the following Saturday on the twenty-sixth. Overall, I've been feeling good, fitter and stronger. But the nausea and vomiting has become more frequent. I'm starting to think there may be something very wrong with me.

I sit down and explain my symptoms to the doctor, an older gentleman behind a huge desk. He has a tweed jacket on. A shiver passes over me, the room feels cold.

'Could you be pregnant?'

'Wha...No, I haven't been having any periods for nearly a year...I can't be.'

'Just because you weren't having periods doesn't mean you can't get pregnant; it's less likely but not impossible. Here, if you could urinate in this for me, we should be able to clear this up nice and quickly.'

Shit. Shit. Shit. I take the small plastic container from the doctor and disappear to the loo, returning to him a couple of minutes later.

'OK, let's see shall we.' He puts a cardboard strip into my urine and nods, 'Yes, as I suspected. You're pregnant Mrs Richards, congratulations. It is congratulations, isn't it?'

The doctor clearly hasn't read my notes.

'How pregnant? How can I tell how pregnant?'

'We'll send you for a scan. You'll get an appointment in the post.'

'Right, OK. Good. Yes, thank you.'

I walk out of the surgery in a daze. What am I going to say to Jason? Do I tell him about Seth? I had sex with them both within a week of each other. It could be either of theirs unless I'm only a bit pregnant, if I'm just five or six weeks then it's Jason's but anywhere in the eight to ten weeks region... Fuck. I'll wait for the scan. I won't say anything, I've got to say something or he'll worry. Do I just tell him the truth? I should tell him the truth. I could speak to Dr Akhtar. She would tell me to tell him, straight away regardless of the scan and everything.

I sit down on a bench outside the doctor's surgery and light a cigarette. I take a drag and feel sick. I need to knock this on the head as well now. Arse. I throw the cigarette on the floor and stub it out with my foot. Do I even want a baby? I love Gracie and Arthur but I get to give them back. I'm a mess, I'm a drug addict who's still processing the death of her husband whilst sleeping with my best friend. And now I could break his heart. Fuck. I'm an idiot. Fuck. Fuck.

When I get back to Jason's flat, he comes and meets me in the hall as I come in, 'How was it? Are you alright, you look pale? Come on in, let me take your coat. You need to sit down.'

Fuck, stop being nice.

When I sat down at the kitchen table, Jason sits next to me and holds my hand.

'What did the doctor say.'

'I'm pregnant.'

He becomes suddenly very still, like the air has left the room and we are both holding our breath.

'How pregnant?'

'I don't know until I have a scan, they're sending me an appointment.'

'Right.'

We are silent for a second, I can't look at him.

'Ask the question, Jas.'

'Is it mine?'

'I don't know.'

He lets go of my hand and stands up, turning away from me and putting his hands on the kitchen surface. His head goes down.

Fuck.

The tears are coming, I can't do this without him. I'll have to get a termination; I should still be OK. Yes. That's what I'll do.

'I'll get rid of it. I'm not ready, it wouldn't be right, the not knowing.'

Jason turns around looking at something on the wall, anywhere but at me. His fists are clenched, his knuckles white, and my stomach lurches, I need to escape, but he beats me to it, 'I need to go.'

'Jas?' I stand up and go towards him. He brushes past me; I hear him grab his coat and then the sound of the front door opening and closing after him.

I crumple onto the floor. I want him to come back and for my life to be less fucked up. If Charlie hadn't died, this would never have happened. Jason and I would still be friends, I wouldn't be hurting him like this. Fuck Charlie. Fuck Jason. Fuck me. I stand up, grab a dirty cup from out of the sink and smash it on the floor. It feels good, I get another and do the same, again and again. God, I want drugs, to get wasted or drunk or something. I could go out and buy alcohol. I'm getting rid of the baby anyway. It wouldn't matter. I light a cigarette. Ugh, it makes me nauseous again. Fuck you, baby! Damn it. I head to our bedroom, taking my shoes and clothes off as I go leaving a trail behind me, then climb under the duvet and shout, scream and cry until I can't anymore, until I'm asleep.

I wake up when the front door bangs, it's dark outside. I turn on the bedside lamp as Jason staggers into the bedroom.

'There she is.'

He's swaying, glaring at me. He takes his jacket off and drops it to the floor. Then he's tugging at his T-shirt, it comes off and I'm reminded of how big he is, how strong. I wrap the duvet around me and hold my knees.

'You. The one I wanted, soooo long. Sooo long. Knew you opened yer legs a lot, fer anyone. Jusss not me. Till nows. Nows yous pregnant. Baby inside. Maybe mine, maybes not. Buts you kill it anyways. Don't care.'

He takes a step closer to the bed and bends down, putting his hands on the end of the mattress. The muscles in his shoulders, his arms hard and solid looking as he moves closer, crawling up the bed to me, my heart is beating hard in my chest. He flops his head down on the pillow next to me, his eyes are pulling me apart. He puts his hand around my wrist.

'I loved you sooo much...put up with sooo much. Come here to me now.' He tugs at my arm to try and get me to go closer. I don't want to. I use my body weight to hold my position. He pushes himself up on his elbow. He lets go of my wrist and puts his hand around my back and brings me closer.

'Please don't Jason. Please.'

'Pleeeese don't. Beggin' you, your lips lied. Made me believe.' His arm is clamped around me so my chest is pressed against his, 'Who's else. Who could be the baby daddy, part from me. Tells me. Truth now.' He has brought his hands to my face, holding it tightly. His breath stinks of spirits.

'Seth.'

'Ponytail boy. Addict, great genes for baby, s'pose you weren't thinking of that.'

'Please. Jas. I'm so sorry. You told me we could only be friends.'

'Friends! Hah.'

His eyelids are drooping. I bring my hand to his cheek, he pushes it away but it's half-hearted, his limbs are getting heavier. I wiggle free of him. I grab the spare blanket and go into the living room. I'll sleep on the sofa tonight. I need to think about moving back into mine and Charlie's place. I can't do this, I can't do any of it, not without Jason.

In the morning the sound of the shower wakes me up. Everything comes flooding back, I feel sick. I run to the kitchen and throw up in the sink. I've forgotten all the broken cups on the floor. My bare feet have bits of crockery stuck into them. Warm blood gathers under my soles as I continue to retch. Jason walks into the kitchen with a towel around his waist.

'Shit, Em. You're bleeding.'

'I know, just need to...' More retching, my stomach is empty. Jason has disappeared by the time I stop. I run the tap in the sink but don't want to move my feet. I'm standing in a small pool of blood. My body relaxes a little when Jason comes back, he has some tracksuit bottoms on and trainers. Lifting me away from the broken crockery, he deposits me on a chair as he kneels in front of my feet.

'I'll get the first aid kit.'

'OK.'

I'm struggling to hold back the tears; he shouldn't be kind to me. He returns with the first aid kit in hand and kneels in front of me. As he tugs out the bits of crockery one piece at a time a frown creases his brow. I wish I could smooth out the frown. I can't. I just watch as he places a piece of gauze over each new wound once he has cleaned it. They really hurt but that's not why I'm crying.

'I think you need stitches; your feet are in tatters.' He picks me up and takes me to the bedroom and puts me on the bed.

'What do you want to wear?'

'I don't know. Jas, can we talk.'

He looks at me, I still can't read his expression.

'Not now, I have a hangover from hell and you're bleeding on the carpet. Later.'

'OK. I'll wear a dress, can you pass me the black one and a cardy, please.' I put the dress over my head. I know he's watching me.

'Can I have some knickers please?'

He goes to the drawer and finds some, he puts my feet gently through the leg holes one by one and then lifts me to pull them up. He smells of the musky aftershave he wears and soap. My hand touches the back of his head feeling his warmth, my fingers move through his hair.

He steps away from me, then puts a T-shirt and a jacket on and throws one of his cardigans at me.

He carries me to the car. We drive in silence. The hospital reminds me of rehab, the screaming, crying, the smell, the vomit-coloured walls. I stare straight ahead and try to think about nothing, but my brain is whirring. I'm spiralling, this place is full to the brim with drugs, I could just... but I can't walk. FUCK. FUCK. I could just scream and cry and vomit and just give up. Jason is sitting with his arms crossed. We don't talk. It takes two hours before we manage to see a doctor.

'So, tell me, how did this happen?' The doctor is young, about my age, although he looks tired.

'I felt sick and forgot I had broken some cups the night before and not cleaned them up.'

'Hm. Do you have any medical conditions I should know about?'

'She's pregnant.'

The heat of his body tells me he's next to me but he feels a hundred miles away.

'Ah, congratulations. How far along are you?'

'I don't know, I'm just waiting for my scan.'

'Is this your first?' He's looking at both of us.

I say, 'Yes.'

'You're going to need some stitches. I'll just give you a local anaesthetic. You'll need to stay off your feet for about a week or two until these have healed, will that be a problem?'

Jason says, 'No, no problem.'

We drive home. The silence between us feels like a wall being slowly made brick by brick. I'm trapped for at least a week, totally reliant on someone who is extremely pissed off with me.

When we get back, Jason carries me back to the bedroom and puts me on the bed. He says nothing as he walks out of the room. I punch the pillows. Harold Lloyd comes and pads onto the bed, briefly sniffs my feet and then jumps into my lap. I'm raining tears on his head when Jason comes in with two cups of coffee.

'I'm sorry about the mugs, I'll replace them.' I sniffle and grab a tissue from the box beside the bed.

'Hm.' He has put the mugs on the bedside cabinet and sits on the bed next to me.

'I'm sorry for reacting so badly.'

'I think your reaction was more than warranted. I deserved it.'

'This baby, are you seriously thinking about a termination.'

'Yes, no. I don't know. If the scan says I am eight to ten weeks pregnant then it could be yours or Seth's. I could do a paternity test. I think I should if I keep it.'

'Rosie had told me you were having sex with Seth.'

'Really. I'm surprised she knew and didn't stop us. You never said.'

'It didn't seem important and then you never mentioned him when you came out.'

'No, he was. I don't know, a way to feel better. A way to remember I was a human being. I don't want to make excuses but it was really hard in there. No physical contact with people... I struggled.'

'I can't say I understand because I don't know what you went through. But I know you. You've always been...'

'A slapper?'

'I was going to say, touchy-feely.'

'Oh.'

'I'm sorry for the stuff I said when I came back home. I didn't mean it.'

'I'm surprised you remember it. I haven't seen you that drunk for years.'

'I haven't been drunk like that for years. If it hadn't been for your feet, I was planning to spend the day with my head in a bowl of ice-cold water.'

'I'm sorry. I'm sorry I'm always apologising. I do nothing but hurt you.'

He finally looks at me, his whole countenance softens, 'I would like a family, Em. I've thought about it before. I saw what you were like with Gracie and Arthur. You'll be a good mum.'

'Will I? I'm a recovering drug addict. What if I go off the rails? All I've wanted to do since I found out is get off my head.'

'But you didn't. I did.'

He smiles at me, it's a half smile, but I'll take it.

'We'll do the paternity test, but I'm with you, regardless of the outcome. I love you. I shouldn't, you're not good for me, but I can't help it.'

I draw him closer to me, to kiss him. He holds on to me tightly. I never want him to let me go.

ANNIVERSARIES

It's a year since Charlie died. Dr Akhtar said this day would be difficult and she's right. It's made more difficult by everything else that's going on. I need to be able to walk before the exhibition, it's only a couple of days away and Jason has been so busy finishing off his paintings that I've hardly seen him. I mostly stay in bed writing or crawl from room to room when he isn't there to carry me. I've decided today's the day I try to stand on my own two feet, the irony isn't lost on me but I don't mention it to Jason. I slide my legs over the edge of the bed and lower my feet gingerly onto the floor. Ouch. Just stand still. OK, one step at a time. Ouch. Ouch. Ouch. Moving slowly towards the living room, keeping my hands on the walls for support I finally make it to the couch. This is good, I'm doing it, it hurts but it's not impossible. One thing's for sure, I won't be wearing heels on Saturday night.

The appointment for the scan turned up, it's tomorrow before my appointment with Dr Akhtar. Jason has said he'll come with me.

When we arrive in the waiting room, there are several other couples holding hands, smiling. I don't know what to feel, we're both adjusting to the news. Sometimes I'm excited but at other times I'm devastated. Jason takes my hand and squeezes it, just before we're called in. He carries me into the scan room, he's still trying to stop me from walking as much as possible.

'Well, that's a first, I don't normally have my ladies carried in.' The nurse is smiling at us.

'I cut my feet, I'm just waiting for them to heal, he's being overprotective.'

'Ah, many new fathers can be like that. Lie her down here' I don't look at Jason, this is all too new, too weird and too much to think about. He gently lowers me onto the examination bed.

My belly is exposed as the nurse doing the scan squeezes out some clear goo onto my tummy, 'A little cold.'

I realise I haven't got a concave stomach anymore. It's back to being flat.

She presses down firmly as the TV screen next to us lights up.

'Good. There's the heartbeat, do you want to hear?'

She doesn't wait for us to say yes but just flips a switch and there's this swooshing sound like the sound of the automatic door at the rehab centre, but as if it was underwater and opening and closing really quickly, Jason says, 'Should it be beating that fast?'

'Yes, it's perfectly normal. It's a good strong heartbeat.'

I look at Jason before I ask, 'Can you tell how many weeks I am?'

'Based on the length of the spine and general development, I would estimate you are about...yes, nine weeks along.' My heart sinks.

I take a breath, 'And do you know how I could get a paternity test?'

The nurse stops pressing on my tummy for a second and looks at us both.

'Yes, I can sort that out for you today if you'd like.'

'Yes please.'

'I will need to take some blood from you both. Then it's sent to the lab, it could be a few weeks before you get the results.'

'OK.'

Jason looks at the nurse,

'How accurate is it?'

'About ninety-nine per cent accurate, or so I understand. You're lucky, ten years ago we wouldn't be able to tell you.'

I don't feel very lucky. The nurse asks me if I'm taking folic acid. I say no and she tells me it's a good idea to take it daily.

'We'll get some on the way home.' Jason is gathering me up in his arms again. We have both had a vial of blood taken.

Jason drops me off at Dr Akhtar's house.

'I'll be back in an hour.' I put my hand up to wave, I can't turn that would involve more footwork. I know he's watching me as I walk slowly towards the front door.

Back in Dr Akhtar's fancy shed, I explain what's happened this week.

'Well, you can't say your life isn't exciting.'

'I think I would prefer boring.'

'There's a lot to unpack. Let's talk about the pregnancy.'

———

That evening I try and pad about the place. I feel slightly better about everything after today's session with Dr Akhtar but the enormous feelings of guilt weigh heavily. The constant craving for drugs is like a low background hum these days, but it's still there. We have to wait for the results of the paternity test, hopefully, the baby's Jason's. I know he's said he's OK either way, but would he be? There's the nurture over nature argument and I have no doubt he would make a good dad. But would he resent me or worse, the baby? Would it tear us apart in the end?

Jason is in his studio putting the finishing touches to his pieces. Kaz is due here tomorrow morning. I'm excited to see her and although I know I'm not supposed to tell people I'm pregnant until you hit the three-month mark. I have every intention of telling her. Tonight though, I'm doing something for Jason, so he realises how much I appreciate him.

I've been cooking for a couple of hours when he comes up, covered in paint.

'Did the paint pots explode?'

He looks down at himself and grins.

'Nah, I was just in the zone. I think I'm done. I'm happy with them.'

'Good. Now will you go and clean up so I can feed you.'

'How long have you been on your feet?'

'No time, I've sat by the cooker and chopped at the kitchen table.'

Jason squints at me, 'You know I've got better at knowing when you're lying to me.'

He comes over to me and draws me to him, he smells of turps.

'Nope, I'm not going to let you put me off, I've been cooking for hours.'

'Hm, you sure?' His hands are on my arse bringing me closer.

'No.' He lifts me, so I wrap my legs around him.

'Better.' He kisses me. There's paint in his hair and on his face.

'I have to cook.'

'No.' He switches all the knobs off on the cooker and takes me to the bedroom. He is tugging my clothes off as he moves.

'I've been thinking about you all day.'

'While you were painting?'

'Yep.' He places me on the bed, then grabs the front of my shirt and tugs, the buttons ping in all directions exposing my chest.

'You look so good.'

I've filled out lately, my breasts look more like they used to and my nipples have gone slightly darker which must be a pregnancy thing. He's taking his T-shirt off, then his jeans. He's naked in seconds.

He watches me lose myself in the moment until we are both done.

'Holy fuck, where did that come from.' We're lying on the bed, sweaty and breathless.

'Like I said, I've been thinking about it all day, about you. What I want to do with you. I think about you a lot. You'll see.'

'What will I see, Jas.'

He's smiling at me again.

'Not long to wait.'

'This is so annoying. I don't understand why I can't look now.'

'Because you can't.'

'Fine. Are you hungry, I have a lovely meal you've ruined ready for you in the kitchen.'

'Yeah, starving, we should eat, I have other things planned for you tonight.'

'Really.'

'Yeah...'

He is looking at me like he's ready to go again. I'm determined that we eat the meal I've made.

We make it through the first course before I'm lying on the table.

EXHIBITION

Kaz arrives at lunchtime. Jason lets her in and brings her to me in the kitchen, he's still trying to stop me from walking too much, although my feet feel a lot better.

Kaz looks amazing. Her long auburn hair falls down her back in big waves, as she folds her willowy figure around me.

'Hello, you. How are your feet, you idiot?'

I glance at Jason, how has he managed to impart so much information from the front door to here? He shrugs and quirks a smile.

'They're nearly better, he's just worrying. Cuppa?'

'Yeah, tea please.'

'Ugh, devils' water, fine. I'll get it.'

'No, you won't. I'll get it, how do you like it?' Jason has moved to the sink and is filling the kettle.

'Just with milk, but let it stand I like my "devil's water" extra strong.'

After Jason has made us all a drink, he mutters something about bits to finish downstairs and leaves us to chat. When he's gone, Kaz looks at me with a different expression.

'Something's changed, what's going on?'

I hate that she knows me so well, 'Ah, your powers are strong today.'

I've always said that in another life I thought she was a witch. She punches me gently on the arm.

'Seriously, how did you hurt your feet?'

I sigh and tell her everything.

'You're pregnant?'

'Yeah.'

'That's amazing Em.'

'Hm, yeah, if it's Jason's.'

'Shit.'

'Yeah, shit.'

'Does he know it may not be his.'

'Yes.'

'Ah, hence the weird atmosphere.'

'He says he's OK with it and will support me, but there's a part of him that's still really pissed off. Understandably.'

'Definitely understandably. You don't make your life easy Em. What're you going to do?'

'We've done a paternity test. We get the results in a few weeks, until then we just have to wait.'

'Well, it sounds to me like you've done as much as you can. You've been honest, you're talking to your counsellor, you're taking your medicine. My baby is growing up.'

'Shut up.'

'It's true.'

'It's lovely to have you here, now tell me about you. How are things with Dave and have you been on any dates?'

We spend the rest of the afternoon, laughing and gossiping. Mid-afternoon, John and Ken turn up and whisk Jason and his work away in a van so they can set up. He tells me he'll see me there.

'Look after her, she's wilful.' Jason says to Kaz as a parting shot.

'Oh, I know.'

'Rude.'

A little later we start to get ready. Kaz is wearing a dark red dress cut on the bias that hangs beautifully over her long body.

I put on a tight short black dress, tights and over-the-knee flat boots. My makeup application has improved and my lipstick matches Kaz's dress. I order a taxi.

'Will there be wine at this thing?' Kaz is looking at me oddly.

'Yeah, I think so, and nibbles, apparently.'

'You won't be having any though, will you?'

'I haven't touched a drop, except a few glasses the first time I went out for a meal with Jason and Lucy.'

'Who's Lucy?'

I'm telling her all about Lucy when the taxi arrives, we laugh all the way from Jason's to his gallery where the exhibition is.

I've only been there a couple of times. It is a place Jason opened with two other people he met at Uni, to show their work but also to support emerging artists. It's been a profitable business for him and his friends, they have excellent taste, showing and selling other artists' work for premium prices. Jason doesn't normally show his personal work but instead does commissions for councils or schools. He's built a reputation as a reliable commercial artist. I know tonight is important to him as he will be showing what he really wants to paint.

As we pull up outside Kaz is pointing at the window.

'Oh, my God. Is that you?'

There's a massive painting facing the street. It's definitely me. It's different to the paintings I've seen Jason paint before. This is more like Lucian Freud's hyper reality with the colours of Gauguin. We walk from the car to get a closer look. In it, I'm wearing a black dress that's almost iridescent like birds' feathers but the dress looks like it is made from ribbons and they are becoming unwound by the wind, part of my breast is exposed, a length of thigh, it's sensual. My hands are trying to stop the unwinding. As I look more closely, I notice tears in my eyes and my lips are parted. I appear incredibly sad. It's beautiful. There is a small white card underneath the painting which says, The Weeping Widow.

Kaz leads me to the door where there is a poster with the name of the exhibition – Muse. Kaz squeezes my hand as we go inside.

People double-take when I walk in. A drink would be very nice right now. Jason is at the centre of a small crowd of arty types talking with his hands. He's surrounded by large six-foot by six-foot paintings. I glance at them; they all look like me. It's overwhelming, my heart is beating hard in my chest and it feels too warm. I notice, there are photographs in another section, Ken's work. I walk towards that, Kaz is by my side. Ken's photographs are macro photos of parts of John. They are poster size; it is hard to know which part is what. They're in shades of sepia. I kiss Ken on the cheek and tell him they're stunning. He asks me if I've seen Jason's paintings yet. I say no.

'You should look. They're outstanding, his finest work.'

'Hm, I will. Where's John?'

'Over there.' He points around another corner. John is talking to yet more people, Kaz has grabbed a glass of wine and a nibble and is following me.

'These nibbles are yum.' Her mouth is full, for someone so elegant-looking, she eats like a pig, it makes me laugh.

'What?'

'Nothing, let's look at this.'

John's work reminds me of the painting of Charlie and Jason in their kitchen, super realistic but drawn like Leonardo da Vinci's drawings. They're all of Ken. Ken laughing, Ken sleeping. Ken eating, they're fantastic. I compliment John who kisses me on the forehead and asks me the same question Ken did.

'I'll go now. I just...'

'Come on, since when did you shy away from anything?' Kaz has my hand again and is taking me towards Jason's section of the gallery. He's schmoozing and smiling, he looks relaxed. When he sees Kaz and I approaching, he says something and comes towards me.

'Hey.' A kiss on the lips.

'Hey.' Kaz lets go of my hand and wanders away casually to look at the paintings.

'Shall I show you?'

'Hm.' His hand is in mine.

The first painting shows me when we were younger. I recognise my Dr Marten's and my hair is in a bob. The colours, everything about it look clean and fresh, I'm full of life, happiness and something else. I'm wearing jeans and a loose-fitting top but my nipples are hard and you can still see my curves. I'm leaning against a burger van, grinning, it's almost like a snapshot. The title is - Small Town Girl.

We move to the next one, I'm in a club. People are all around me like shadows I am wearing latex, my eyes are wild and my lips look full and wet. My tongue is just visible. This is how Charlie saw me. There's a hand around my waist and another one on my breast, different hands, in the shadows you can make out two male figures - Cushions for Lips – That's what Jason said to me before he kissed me in the club. That's what this one is called.

It's another from the same time, I'm in the kitchen in Putney with a silky dressing gown, I used to wear at the time. It's open, nothing is left to the imagination as I eat toast with buttery fingers, one is in my mouth. A shadow of a male figure crosses the table behind me. It's all so exposing. The crowd in the gallery are staring at me as I consider the paintings. My cheeks feel warm as I start to sweat. I shrug my cardigan off as Jason brings me to the next picture.

I'm curled around a thin man, on a hospital bed. You can't see his face, but you can see the ridges of my spine through the dress I'm wearing. My knuckles are white holding his arm, my hair is greasy and my feet are bare. One leg is wrapped around the body I'm holding. Machines surround the bed and IVs are hanging all around us. The man's arm has needles and tubes coming out of it, Charlie. It's Charlie. Through the hospital window, a seagull is on the ledge looking in. I don't remember a seagull. Flying Away is written in stark black letters on the card.

Tears are falling. Jason should have warned me. I tug my hand out of his and stumble away, the panic rising. My feet hurt. I push through warm bodies to get away, I need fresh air.

Outside, shambling forwards, the pain is unbearable. Pain in my feet, my heart, everywhere. Moving from the front of the building to down the side, leaning against the brick wall and lowering myself into a crouch as I try to sort out my breathing.

'Em.'

I'm still breathing hard.

'Em, are you OK?' A hand outstretched, I take it. He pulls me up.

'In through your nose, out through your mouth, like they showed us. Breathe Em.'

I do as he says, looking at him. He looks the same, except he's cut his hair.

Eventually, I manage to speak.

'Seth, what are you doing here?'

'I got out. I've been trying to find you. You're impossible to trace. Then I remembered your friend was an artist, I found out about the exhibition in Brixton and hoped. Then I saw the picture in the window, I knew I was at the right place.'

'Why? I thought you didn't want to know me; you didn't show up on the last day.'

'I know. I was behaving like a complete dick. I'm sorry.'

I hear running, Jason comes around the corner.

'Hey, get away from her.'

He's between us, pushing me behind him.

'Jason, it's OK.'

'It's not OK. Fuck off.'

He's squaring up to him, I can't believe this is happening, again.

'No. Jason, stop it.' I move from behind him, to between them. Jason isn't looking at me, he is looking over my head at Seth. Seth has his hands up.

'I just wanted to talk to her, that's all.'

'No. You're an addict, you need to stay away.'

'Yeah, and so's she.'

Jason is moving me out of the way, he shoves Seth with the flat of his hands, pushing him so he stumbles back.

I stand in front of Jason, 'What the fuck are you doing.'

'I don't want you hanging around with this twat.'

This riles me, he has no right and Seth should know about our situation.

'He wasn't hanging around, he was helping me through a panic attack, which I had because you didn't tell me what was in your paintings. Charlie dying, for fuck's sake Jason. You didn't think that would upset me!'

I shove Jason in the chest. He doesn't move.

'Look, you two obviously have something going on. Em, this is my number, call me, yeah.' He hands me a scrap of paper which I scrunch up in my hand.

'She's not going to call you, mate.'

Seth walks away. I'm left seething as I stand opposite Jason who is watching Seth leave. When he's out of sight

Jason focuses back on me, his anger gone. There's a moment of silence between us as we contemplate one another.

Jason says softly, 'You haven't seen all the paintings. Please come back in. I think you'll like the rest more.'

'You should've told me.'

'Yeah. I should've told you. I just... I think painting was my way of expressing how I felt and talking about them with you, I don't know...They're about me as much as they are about you.'

He takes my hand, then leans in to kiss me, I turn my head and start to walk away, yanking my hand out of his. I understand, but can't help but feel angry.

Behind me, he says quietly, 'How are your feet?'

'Sore.'

I've stopped walking. He lifts me, cradling me like a child. I lean my head against his chest, his heartbeat steady in my ear.

'I'm sorry Em. I never want to upset you.'

I know he means it.

'There're two other pictures I think you might ... I don't know. Then a couple I hope you'll like. It's supposed to be positive.'

'OK.'

We go back in; the gallery is warm and condensation I forming on the large window at the front of the building. Kaz is talking to John. Jason puts me down as we go inside but holds my hand to take me back to his paintings. I push Seth's phone number into my bra as I have no pockets. I need to speak to him, but I'll worry about that tomorrow. One thing at a time. Jason leads me to the next picture.

This one has me leaning forward; my eyes are glassy. A couple of the buttons on my blouse are undone, exposing black underwear underneath. There's a cigarette in my mouth which I'm holding between my teeth as I smirk, the rest of my face looks miserable. My skirt is short, there's a ladder running up the length of my tights. One of the stilettoes I'd been wearing is in my hand so I'm sort of lopsided. I'm off my head, my relaxed posture, my dilated pupils, the clench in my jaw. Again, it feels like a snapshot which has been enlarged and brightened into something almost other-earthly.

The next one is the day Jason found me in the flat, there's all my paraphernalia around me, my Zippo open on the floor, a dirty spoon on the table. My thin arm in a ligature, my hand holding an empty needle. Eyelids half closed. I'm lying on the sofa with a leg dangling over the side. I'm in knickers but nothing else. My hip bones are jutting out and my stomach is concave. There are bruises on my arms from the needles. My chest looks like it has been carved open, inside there is an anatomically correct heart that looks as if it's been cleaved in two. Blood slips down the edges of the opening in cascades, pooling under my body which is various shades of grey, going from pale to a bluey white. I look dead, I'm whispering when I speak, 'Jas. Why?'

'I wanted you to see what I saw.'

The card says Being Nothing.

Fuck.

'Why did you call it that?'

'That's what you said. You said, you were being nothing.'

'Oh. I don't remember that.'

'I know.'

He moves me to the next. I'm in a long grey cardigan, it covers one of my arms and most of my body, I'm sitting holding my knees. One sleeve is rolled up. In one hand I'm holding a burning cigarette and my lips look like I have just exhaled smoke which puts a veil of grey across my face. It's the rehab canteen, all white plastic and glass. The sun is coming in and Jason has found refracted colours in the whiteness. There's some colour in my cheeks, but my cheekbones jut through my hair at sharp angles. My eyes are black in shadows. Along my exposed wrist to my elbow, you see the scar, it's bright pink with small flames flickering as they cast more smoke into the area around me. A smile is sitting at the very edge of my lips. The card says – Healing.

In the next, I'm sat on the kitchen table in jeans and a crop top. My body is filling out. My eyes tell you everything you need to know. I don't know how he paints that, how it's so obvious. I'm an animal choosing what to eat next, except it's not food I'm after. Again, there's a large shadow of a man cast across the table. The card says, Beginnings.

In the last painting, I'm laughing on the sofa, my mouth wide. My hands are in front of me, it looks like I'm explaining something using my hands to help me express it. There's a hand on the top of my thigh, squeezing the soft flesh, the arm it belongs to disappears out of the painting. Harold Lloyd is on the back of the sofa watching me. It's a beautiful version of me I don't recognise. It's called Home. I turn to Jason, I'm crying again, but this time for a different reason, I understand now. No, I didn't like all the paintings, but he's trying to show all the versions of me, including the times I've been ugly and harsh. The paintings are incredibly honest and as much a part of him and his view of me as they are of me. I understand now.

'I'm so proud of you. These are incredible.'

'I'm sorry I didn't show you before. That was a mistake. I was so caught up in them, I forgot these are about you.'

'I think they're about us. But yeah, you should have shown me.'

He leans down and kisses me long and slow. I don't care that people are looking.

The rest of the evening is spent talking to people, a few well-known art critics have come to see the work, and the feedback they give seems positive. I hope they're kind to Jason, John and Ken. People slowly disappear until it's just the five of us. I leave the rest of them in reception on the sofas as they drink wine and eat the remaining nibbles. I move around the exhibition again, without people and noise. It's a completely different experience, I notice things I didn't the first time, little touches. Harold Lloyd is in more of them but less noticeable, he's licking up the blood on the floor in Being Nothing. The only one I still struggle to look at is the one in the hospital bed. The memory seems so raw and yet Charlie died over a year ago.

When I think about Charlie it still hurts. I miss his lips, his hands, everything. I know I'm in love with Jason, but I still love Charlie. I don't know whether I will ever stop loving him, or if I need to. Arms come around me from behind.

'Are you OK, you should get off your feet.'

His mouth is on my neck, the smell of wine on his breath.

'I'm fine, these get better and better each time I look at them, how long has it taken you to paint them?'

'I don't know, I started them a couple of years ago.'

'Is that how you see things, like snapshots, moments in a life?'

He lifts me up again, cradling me, I put my arm around his neck.

'I suppose, sometimes. I'm just a visual person, I interpret shapes and patterns in everything.'

I push my fingers gently up the back of his neck into his hairline, he leans down to kiss me.

'We better go back, I shouldn't leave Kaz.'

'She's fine, John and Ken love her, they want to take her clubbing.'

'Really?'

'Yeah.'

When we go back into reception, they all have their coats on.

Kaz says, 'Is it OK if I go out with John and Ken, they've said I can stay at theirs tonight.'

'Go for it. It's not like I'm up for dancing. You deserve to have fun.'

'Thanks, I'll be back in the morning.'

'We'll bring her back in the afternoon, there's no way she'll be up in the morning.' Ken winks at me.

'Be good and don't do anything I wouldn't do.'

Kaz comes over to kiss me on the cheek, Jason has put me down.

'Well, that leaves my options very open.'

'Rude.'

'Congratulations on tonight Jason your paintings are fab.'

'Thanks.'

After they're gone. Jason locks up and we hail a cab for the short journey home.

Harold Lloyd greets us at the door. I manage to hobble into the kitchen and sit down.

'Let me check your feet.'

'My feet are fine.'

'No, come on.'

Jason kneels on the floor in front of me pulling off my over knee boots. I stand up and take off my tights, then sit back down. He frowns. You've been bleeding again. I'll clean you up. He disappears to get the first aid kit.

When he comes back, he takes off the old dressings and redresses my wounds.

'No walking tomorrow, these feet need rest.'

'Fine. I really want to go back to jogging and ballet, I'm going to get fat.'

'Yep, you are definitely going to get fat,' he says, smiling.

'I didn't mean like that.' I prod him with my toe.

Jason moves forward, opening my legs with his hands. He puts his hand to the back of my head, gently bowing my head down to meet his lips. His hand is on my neck as he uses the other to push my dress up to my waist. His fingers are on my breast squeezing and teasing through the material. I push Jason back slightly and lift the dress over my head so I'm left in my bra and knickers, he takes his shirt off. I put my fingers on his chest, feeling the warmth of his skin.

He's undoing my bra, taking it off. The scrap of paper flutters to the floor, shit, I'd forgotten.

'What's this, Em?'

'It's Seth's number.'

'What the fuck. Why do you want that loser's number?'

'Because...' I'm struggling, I don't want to say it.

'What?'

He's standing up, moving away from me.

'Jas. Please.'

'No, what? You kept is number in case the baby's not mine?'

I don't say anything, I know whatever I say won't sound right to him.

'He's a drug addict and a tosser. I've told you; I'll support you either way. You don't need him, he'll only let you down.'

I respond quietly, I don't want to have this discussion, not now, not while he's so cross.

'I'm a drug addict and a tosser, I've let you down. Yet you believe in me.'

'I know you.'

'I know him.'

'Yeah. Don't I know it.'

He can hardly look at me.

I stand up, my feet are killing me, I do up my bra as I walk towards him, he turns away from me.

'Please. Jas.'

'This is killing me, Em.'

'I know.'

'I'm really trying to be the better man, but the idea of his hands on you...'

'Jas, I only want your hands on me. Since Charlie, it's always been you.'

I hold his arm, trying to get him to look at me.

'Then why did you sleep with him?'

'I've told you why.'

Silence again, just the sound of us breathing and the kitchen clock ticking.

'I'm going to bed.'

I'm an awful human, tonight should have been all about his success, his paintings and yet again I've ruined it.

Walking carefully into our bedroom, I shoo Harold Lloyd off the bed. Then wait for him to finish, when he comes in, I brush past him to go to the bathroom. It's awkward and uncomfortable.

When I come back, he's pretending to be asleep. I get in bed and curl around him, which reminds me of the picture of Charlie. Then I'm angry, so turnover. We fall asleep back-to-back. I sleep fitfully until the early hours, then finally fall into a deeper sleep.

In the morning, I wake up alone. In the kitchen, Jason is sitting eating a bowl of cereal. I sit down opposite him.

'I think, I should move back to my flat for a bit.'

He stops eating for a second, then looks at me, spoon half raised.

'OK.'

'Right. I'll let you know when I get the twelve-week scan appointment through.'

'Hm.'

I get up again and go back to the bedroom, grabbing my bag from under the bed, I throw clothes in.

I take the bag to the car. I'm not sure how my feet will cope with driving, but I don't care, I'll manage. Back inside, I put the typewriter in its case and put it in the boot. Finally, I grab the papers, notepads and the folder with the pictures of Charlie and throw them in the back seat of the car. I'm crying.

Jason is still in the kitchen, his bowl of cereal empty. He's staring into space.

I ask him, 'Where's Harold Lloyd's basket?'

'I'll get it.'

Wiping my nose with the back of my hand, I fetch Harold Lloyd from the bedroom, where he is sleeping on the bed. I carry him into the kitchen, he starts to purr until he sees Jason return with the cat basket, he is less than happy but I get him in.

'Hang on.'

Jason gets a carrier bag and puts Harold Lloyd's food into it.

'Thanks. I'll see you then.' The tears are still streaming. Jason isn't looking at me but his jaw is clenching.

I take the keys to his flat off my keyring and leave them on the table. Harold Lloyd is mewling unhappily as I grab him and his bag of food. Closing the front door quietly after us, I place Harold Lloyd's basket in the passenger seat next to me and strap it in. It feels very final.

Weeping, I lay head on the steering wheel until I run out of tears. What have I done?

BACK HOME

Harold Lloyd and I arrive at the flat. Quickly, I let him out. He has been meowed all the way to Barnes. He immediately starts to reacquaint himself with the place as I gather everything from the car.

I close the door and sit down on the sofa surrounded by my things. It's cold. I push myself back up and shuffle to the cupboard in the hall. I press a few buttons and hear a woosh of the boiler firing up. I'm relieved it works. The last thing I need is to have to call a plumber.

Back on the sofa, I wrap a blanket around me. I'd like a cup of coffee but there's no milk in the house. I consider going out to get milk and food and decide against it, who needs milk? It'll do black. The radiators are ticking as they warm up. The enormity of what I have done hits me. Dr Akhtar is going to have a field day with this, I was supposed to stay one night, not move back permanently. Shit.

With the blanket still around me I shamble to the kitchen, opening the cupboard to find coffee. There it is, next to the tea Charlie liked. Trying not to think about it, I boil the kettle, then bring the mug back to the lounge and put it on the coffee table. Switching the TV on, I rewrap myself in the blanket and curl up on the sofa.

I'm woken by the doorbell buzzing. Still fuzzy with sleep. Why am I here? Then it all floods back, get up, sore feet, keep walking. Go to the door. Kaz.

I'd forgotten about Kaz. I'm a shit friend. Fact.

'What the fuck is going on? Jason's in a right state.'

'I... we... Shit.'

'Come here.' I fall into her, as she wraps her arms tight around me.

When I calm down a little, she sits me down and offers to make some tea. I tell her the milk situation. She looks at me like I'm an idiot.

'Jesus Em. Where's the nearest shop?'

'On the corner, there's a little Spar.'

'Fine. Give me ten minutes and your keys, you need to rest those feet, there's blood coming through your bandages. She's right, I've left bloody footsteps all over the flat and there are stains on the sofa. Damn it.

When she comes back, she unpacks the shopping in the kitchen.

'OK, I've got bread, butter, cheese, some vegetables, milk and fruit. It should be enough to keep you going for a bit. I'm gonna make some tea, do you want a coffee.'

I nod, my face wet with tears, thank goodness she's here. I've undone my bandages, one of the cuts stitches have burst, it doesn't look too bad but it needs to be redressed.

When Kaz comes back in and sees my feet she asks where my medicine cabinet is. I tell her. She sorts out both my feet. Then finds some salt and sprinkles it on the blood stains on the sofa.

'Give it an hour, then I'll sponge the stain away.'

'Thank you.'

'Now tell me, what happened?'

'I don't know. We argued about Seth. He showed up last

night and gave me his number. I would like to tell him about the pregnancy, you know, in case... Jason said he was a drug addict loser. I reminded him I was a drug addict loser which didn't go down very well. Then I was angry about the painting of me and Charlie, he could have warned me.'

'So, all the emotions then, from both of you.'

'Yeah.'

'The way I see it, you've probably done the right thing. Since Charlie died you've been living in each other's pocket and you haven't exactly been easy to be around.'

'Er...thanks?'

'Em, come on. When was the last time you talked to your mum and dad, or came home or did anything that wasn't about Charlie or Jason or you?'

'Wow, don't hold back.'

'I'm just saying it as it is, my love. You disappeared and lost the plot completely. We were all devastated when Charlie died, that's a massive thing to happen to anyone, but you just went into self-destruct mode and imploded.'

Kaz leans over, rolls up my sleeves and says gently, 'Jason told us about this. Your mum was in pieces, she wanted to come but Jason asked them not to. He struggled with putting you in rehab.'

'I know.'

'I thought it was getting better but this whole pregnancy thing has thrown up so many things. Of course, Jason's upset. He loves you. But he knows you, warts and all. Yes, he should have warned you about the painting but is it comparable to what you've put him through? No. Should you be sad about Charlie still? Yes. Should you feel guilty about being with Jason? No. Should Jason be pissed off that you could be pregnant with someone else's kid? Shit yeah.'

'Oh.' I'm looking at my oldest friend feeling the tears come again, 'How can I fix it?'

'I don't know. Time. See what the paternity test says.

Jason said you were going to contact him when the appointment for the twelve-week scan comes through?'

'Yeah.'

'Wait till then, that's a couple of weeks. See where you stand then and personally, I wouldn't contact this Seth fella unless he turns out to be the dad.'

'OK.'

Kaz smooths my hair.

'I just need to make a call, then how about I make you some macaroni cheese?'

'Yes please.'

Kaz goes into the hall, as Harold Lloyd jumps up next to me on the sofa in Kaz's spot.

When she comes back in, she says, 'Well, that's all sorted, Dave has the kids tonight and then my mum will take them tomorrow. I don't have to be in work until Wednesday. So, I can stay here until Tuesday evening, just to help you settle back in.'

She comes over and hugs me, I feel better knowing she'll be with me for a while. I'm not sure how I'm going to be sleeping in mine and Charlie's bed for the first time in a year.

Kaz makes dinner and we eat it on the sofa sharing the blanket while watching a video of Pretty Woman. Charlie hated it, calling it ridiculous and unrealistic, but I always loved it. I know it's a stretch but the romantic in me wants it to be real.

Eventually, bedtime looms. Kaz pushes the situation, saying, 'I'm knackered, I didn't get in until the early hours this morning, we went to Heaven and then onto somewhere else. It was a fabulous night. John and Ken know how to have fun.'

I grin at her.

'Now, I could sleep in the spare bedroom or in with you, which would you rather.'

'Can you sleep in with me, just for tonight.'

'Not a problem. Go on, you go first, I'll catch you up.'

In our bathroom, Jason has tidied away things. There's no sign of Charlie's toothbrush, flannel or shaving stuff. I wash and look in the bathroom mirror, an image of Charlie, his mouth full of toothpaste foam grinning behind me before kissing minty foam onto my neck. No. No, I shake my head and go to the bedroom. The bed has been remade with fresh linen, Jason again. I get in, it doesn't smell of Charlie. It smells like Jason's bed, his washing powder. I peer at the large wardrobe in the corner and wonder if Jason has left Charlie's clothes for me to sort out or done it for me. I suspect he's left them out of respect. I don't get up and look. I don't need to think about that right now. Or what Charlie and I did in this bed, this room, every room of this flat. Stop it, stop it, I don't want to think, I could go out and get drugs. I could just... Kaz bounds into the room. Jumps on the bed and climbs under the duvet. She turns the bedside lamp off and says, 'Do you want a cuddle?'

'Yes please.'

Kaz curls around me, there are advantages to being a short person in a tall person's world. I fall asleep quickly, but my nightmares are full of Charlie and Jason.

Nausea. Ugh, where am I? Home, Charlie, Shit. Bathroom, I need to get to the bathroom. I'm throwing up as Kaz sleepily follows me in, holds back my hair and rubs my back. I finally stop retching.

'How long does this go on for?'

'Hopefully, you'll start to feel better after the first three months, some people have morning sickness all the way through, day and night. Be grateful yours is only in the mornings. Upside, they say it's a sign the baby is super healthy.' Kaz stretches and yawns.

'Whoop.' I say, unenthusiastically as I push myself up from the toilet seat, splash water on my face and clean my teeth.

'I'll go and put toast and coffee on.'

'Mm, thank you.'

Realisation, no Jason. He's really upset with me. Is this the final straw? Fuck. Don't think, so many things bubbling in my head. I hear the doorbell and the sound of Kaz going to the door. There's talking and then the sound of the door shutting.

In the kitchen I find the toast, I'm always starving after throwing up. Kaz comes back frowning.

'Seth is outside.'

'Oh.'

'Do you want to see him?'

I don't know. I stare at Kaz like a rabbit in the headlights.

'That's a no then, I'll tell him.'

'No. Hang on, will you stay while I talk to him.'

'Yeah. Are you going to tell him?'

'I don't know.'

'On your head be it. Much as I'm a believer in honesty... Can't say I blame you, for a drug addict he's good-looking.' Kaz grins at me as she disappears back into the hall. I hear Seth come in, as Kaz talks quietly to him. When he comes into the kitchen he's smiling, I smile back, 'Hey.'

'Hey, you OK, you look sick?'

'Thanks?'

'Sorry, I mean, you look great.'

'It's too late now, the moment's gone.'

Kaz goes to the kettle, 'Coffee?'

'Yeah, that would be good.'

'How did you find me this time?'

'I tried here first when I got out, you're in the phone book, I didn't think you were living here, which is why I came to the gallery, but it turns out you are.'

'Hm, yeah, kind of.'

Seth looks around, 'Nice place, nice area. You've done alright.'

'Yeah. Dead husbands' life insurance makes life so much better.'

'Shit, yeah, forgot.'

Kaz puts the coffee on the table in front of Seth and sits down next to me and opposite him.

'Well, you two seem to have skirted around British politeness and headed straight into really honest shit.'

'Rehab does that to you.' Seth says grinning at Kaz.

'Sorry, where are my manners, this is Kaz my oldest and most long-suffering friend, mother of my godchildren and drinker of the devil's juice.'

'Wow, that's some title, I thought Jason of the big muscles was your best friend.'

Kaz looks from me and back to Seth in horror, I snort a laugh through my nose, 'Attractive. And, oh my God, when did I get demoted? It was the kids wasn't it, they ruin everything!'

'Yeah, that's what it was.' I'm laughing, it's nice.

'So how long have you known each other?'

Kaz says, 'Since we were about three, maybe younger, we were in playgroup together.'

'That's a long time. So, you know all her secrets.'

'Yeah, most, I think.' Kaz looks at me more seriously.

'Yeah, she does.' I say nodding at Seth.

'So how did you find rehab?'

'Hard.' He's stopped smiling, 'Although, this one made it a little easier.' He looks at me, his expression serious, 'I missed you when you were gone.'

I didn't miss Seth. I hardly thought about him until the pregnancy thing. Not good. Suddenly, my coffee cup is fascinating. I need to tell him. Fuck. When I peek up both he and Kaz are looking at me.

He says, 'Spit it out. You want to tell me something.'

How does he know, he can't know? No, it's just my stupid face, showing every single thing I'm thinking.

'Yeah, there's something, you should know. I was going to ring you once I knew one way or the other.'

'Shit, it's Gonorrhoea isn't it.'

'No! It isn't. For fuck's sake!'

'What then?'

'I'm pregnant.'

'Ah.' He looks surprised, then concerned to... he's withdrawing, yep, what did I expect?

'It's not just that. It's not necessarily yours, it could be Jason's, we've done a paternity test. I should have the results in a few weeks.'

'Hm. OK.'

We're all quiet for a moment, I take a sip of my coffee and watch him from behind my mug.

Seth says, 'Well, that's a lot.'

'Yeah.'

'What did Jason say?'

'It's complicated.' I don't want to discuss Jason with Seth; it would be disloyal.

Silence again. Harold Lloyd jumps onto the kitchen table, purring, he clearly hasn't read the room.

'Hello, this must be Harold Lloyd.'

'Yeah.'

'If it's mine, I'll do right by you and the child. Do you want to get married?'

'Romantic.'

'Ha, funny, I'm serious.'

He's sincere, but I don't know him. I liked him enough to sleep with him but forgot him as soon as we were apart.

'No, I'm in love with Jason.'

'Ah. So, what do you want?'

'I don't know. It depends on the paternity test, but if it is you, I think you have a right to know and decide if you want to be part of the child's life.'

'Fair enough. If you love Jason, why are you here.'

'More complicated.'

'Is it because of all this baby stuff?'

'OK, maybe not that complicated.'

I hear Kaz snigger, I cast some daggers her way, 'Why did you come looking for me?'

'I like you, I thought we had something, but it's OK, I understand. It was a rehab thing.'

'Yeah.'

Seth says, 'That's going to be an interesting conversation if it is ours. Where was I conceived, Mummy?'

'Haha, funny.'

Kaz is smirking, she says, 'He does have a point.'

'Shut up.'

'Do you want some breakfast?' Kaz has stood up.

'Yes please, what about you?'

Seth hasn't filled out completely.

'Yeah, the halfway house has cereal and that's about it.'

'Scrambled eggs.'

We both say yes. I ask him how it is there.

'It's alright. Although, I thought about what you said, about the mature student thing. I've applied for a course in September. In the meantime, I'll work and try and get enough together for a deposit to rent a flat.'

'That's good. You should. Having something to occupy your mind really helps.'

'Have you been writing?'

'Yeah, a little. I might have something.'

'That's great, Em.'

He leans across and takes my hand. I look at his solemn blue eyes. My baby might have his eyes.

'So, Jason. He's a bit full-on. He doesn't like me much.'

'Can you blame him?'

'He told you he could only be your friend at the time, we were...er...together. It's not like you were in a relationship with him.'

'I know, but...there was something, after Charlie. Our relationship changed. Jason has always...'

'He's always fancied her.' Kaz puts three plates of scrambled eggs on toast with grilled tomatoes on the table. I gently slide my hand from Seth's and pick up the knife and fork Kaz has put by the plates.

'Looks good, thanks' Seth is grinning again, 'So he's always fancied you, and yet you never...'

'Not until after Charlie.'

'Right. When emotions were high.'

'That's what I said,' Kaz is nodding at Seth.

'And how close were Jason and Charlie?'

I turn my attention to the food and mutter, 'Best friends, I suppose. He was the best man at our wedding.'

'Oh, lordy girl. That poor fella. He lost his mate, has been in love with his mate's girl, starts shagging said girl, finally, then gets her pregnant maybe, just after girl has fallen apart and been in rehab. He's in a spiral of guilt. What have you done to him? No wonder he doesn't like me.'

'We're so on the same page.' Kaz holds her hand up and she and Seth high five.

'This is not how I remember group therapy working. I feel very ganged up on.'

Kaz says, 'Do you fancy staying, we're planning a movie marathon. This one has knackered her feet and can hardly walk so needs looking after for a bit. I'm only here until Tuesday.'

'I can help out after that; I haven't got a lot on. Surprisingly, people don't want to employ a recovering drug addict.'

I don't want Jason finding out Seth is here, 'Jason won't like it.'

'Jason's not here and to be honest, we'd be doing him a favour, the poor man needs a break.' Kaz says, taking our empty plates and putting them in the sink.

'So, what films have you got and tell me about your feet?' Seth says, as he goes and grabs a drying-up cloth.

It seems I have no choice; he's staying.

Briefly, I explain how I hurt my feet. As I move from the kitchen to the living room, Seth sees me wincing.

'I'm not Mr Muscles, but should be able to get you from A to B, come here.'

He lifts me easily. It feels odd to be so close to him again. I relax and put an arm around his shoulders, he smells... cleaner. He places me gently on the sofa, holding me for just a moment too long.

We spend the day watching romantic comedies. At one point Seth finds Charlie's video of A Midnight Clear a WWII film but is immediately outvoted. It's a relaxed and easy day; we order pizza for dinner. Around eight o'clock, Seth says, 'OK, well I have outstayed my welcome. I'm going to leave you two ladies to it. Shall I pop around tomorrow?'

'Yes, that would be great, I could do with doing a supermarket shop before I go and this one needs watching.'

'Oi.'

'Sure, about ten.'

'Great.'

Seth leans in and kisses Kaz on the cheek, 'Thanks for today, it's been good. You. I'll see tomorrow.'

He leans down and kisses the top of my head. I hear Kaz and Seth talking as he leaves. When she comes back, she seems too bright.

'What are you up to?'

'Nothing.'

'What were you and Seth talking about?'

'You. Jason. Stuff.'

'What are you planning. I know that face. You're interfering.'

'Would I? I like Seth, by the way. For a drug addict loser friend, he's OK.'

'Can we stop with the drug addict loser thing? It's not funny.'

'It's a little bit funny.'

Kaz is grinning and curling up next to me on the sofa.

'Shove over, for a teeny tiny person you take a lot of space. Speaking of which do I get a bed alone tonight and a duvet I don't have to fight to keep over me?'

'A, I am not that teeny tiny and B, I do not steal the duvet and C, you can sleep in the spare room. I need to get used to being on my own.'

'OK, but if you need me just shout, I'll be down the hall. Now, one last film then bed.'

———

The next morning, Seth turns up just after ten. Again, I hear serious voices as he and Kaz slowly walk towards the living room. I'm lying on the sofa with Harold Lloyd on my lap. Seth sits down next to me then lifts my feet and scoots under them so they can go on his legs.

'Probably good to keep them up a bit.'

'OK.'

'How do they feel?'

'A bit better today.'

Kaz comes into the lounge with her coat on, 'Right, I'm off to the supermarket. Be good. And if you can't be good, be careful.'

She grins, knowing this is something my mum used to say to me.

'So, how have you been really, since getting out?' Seth is looking at my massive socked feet, his hand on my ankle.

'Alright, it's been a bit of a whirlwind. I was exercising, going to ballet classes, jogging and stuff until I hurt my feet.'

'Hm, you've filled out. You look good, Em.'

'Thanks. What about you?'

'Not gonna lie. It's been tough. I've struggled not to slip. To be honest, looking after you will help me have a bit of a project, I need to keep busy until September.'

'I just don't want you getting the wrong idea. I'm going to get back with Jason, we're just straightening out our heads.'

'I know, it's a lot to process, the idea of being a dad is huge. I meant what I said yesterday, if Jason lets you down, I'll step up.'

'I appreciate it, but I don't think we'd be very good for each other.'

'Yeah, you're probably right. Your friend Kaz is nice, is she single?'

I grin at him.

'Maybe, but you need to complete that course and show some potential then I may let that happen.'

'Blimey, you two are tight.'

'Yeah.'

We read the papers and listen to the radio in companionable silence. In the Sunday arts section of the Times, I find a massive article about Jason's paintings, the critic reviewing his work loves it. They say he will be the next big thing. I show the article to Seth. There are pictures of some of the paintings in the paper as well. I'm grateful that the one of me curled around Charlie on the hospital bed isn't one of them.

'Wow. He's good at what he does. He totally sees you, the whole you, doesn't he?' Seth is looking at the paper as he speaks, he doesn't see my tears forming until they are falling.

'Shit, fuck. I'm sorry. Insensitive. Let me get some tissues.'

He dashes out of the room and comes back with kitchen roll.

'Sorry, all I could find.'

He shoves a wadge of them into my hand. I separate a few

sheets and blow my nose. Eventually, I say, 'He knew me before Charlie, I met him when I was fourteen, maybe fifteen. A man attacked me where we worked together and he looked after me. He's always looked after me.'

Seth shakes his head, 'So, Jason has known you and probably loved you since you were a teenager. He has watched you have relationships, fall in love, get married. Befriended the man you fell in love with. All to be your friend first. Wow. He's a better man than me.'

'Yeah.' The burn of tears again.

'Hey, you could have at least pretended to think about it.'

'Sorry.' I sniffle, 'I've treated him like shit and I don't know how to make it better. This whole pregnancy thing. It's so big. I suggested a termination and he was devastated, even when he knew the kid might not be his. What do I do?'

'You know this is weird, right? Asking advice off the man who is one of the potential fathers of your baby on how to get back together with the other potential father. I tried to find you because I really, really like you.'

'Oh, now I'm being insensitive, I didn't think...'

'Yeah, sorry. When I fall for someone, I fall hard.'

'So, not just a rehab thing for you.'

'No.' His blue eyes look inky today.

'Maybe, you shouldn't come around once Kaz goes, I'll be OK. We keep it more formal. I'll call you with the results from the test and we go from there. I don't want to lead you on.'

'Hm. That would be the sensible thing to do, but I'm a glutton for punishment. I need to keep busy. You're in safe hands; you've made your feelings clear. I promise, cross my heart, not to make any moves on you.'

'Cos' us drug addicts promises are so reliable.'

'Yeah, they are.' He grins at me as I hear the key in the door. Kaz is back. Seth stands up and goes and helps her with the bags. More serious sounding mumbling. This is doing my head in. I know they're up to something.

We're sitting around the kitchen table, Kaz has made a roast dinner. She needs to leave in a couple of hours to get the train home. The mood is sombre as we eat. Eventually, I can't stand it anymore.

'OK, enough. What are you two up to?'

Seth freezes, his fork with roast potato doesn't make his mouth. Kaz looks down at the food.

'Nothing.'

'Karen Beatrice Cherry-Warner. I have known you long enough to know when you are lying to me. Tell me what all the whispering is about in the hallway or I swear...' I have picked up my knife and I'm pointing it at her.

'Fine.' She puts her cutlery down and looks at me, 'So, I've been going to see Jason. He's not doing great. His head's a mess. His counsellor has told him you both need space and I agree. I have told him that Seth is in the loop. Which pissed him off, I didn't realise he had such a temper. Anyway, I've suggested that he and Seth should talk, which he thinks is stupid. I have asked him to speak to his counsellor about it. He calmed down a bit and said he would. He's promised to call you after he speaks to his counsellor next week. I'm hoping then you two can have a conversation without Jason killing you.' This last part is directed at Seth.

'Oh. OK.'

'His biggest issue is that he feels he is constantly sharing you with other men. The memory of Charlie, now Seth could be in the picture for years because of the baby. He said, and these are his words, not mine, "I just want her to myself for a little while." It's fair enough after all this time.'

More tears, for fucks sake, will they never end?

'Yes. It's fair enough.'

Seth nods, 'Even I feel for him and every time we've met, he's been a complete dick.'

I put my head in my hands, I've lost my appetite. I stand up, Seth gets up to lift me but I can't have his arms around me right now. I push him gently, shaking my head. Kaz takes Seth's arm, as I shuffle slowly to my bedroom. I need to hide, rest, stop being me for a bit, God, I would kill for an E right now, for anything, just to take it all away. I climb into bed and look at my wrists, remembering why I'd broken the toothbrush and scrapped it down my arms. It made sense. It makes sense. I just make people miserable, Jason, Kaz, Seth, my parents. But... I've got to be responsible. There's another person inside me. I curl up and cover my head under the duvet. It would be so easy to lose myself in drugs right now. I pull the duvet over my head and hope for the oblivion of sleep. It's a long time coming.

I wake up with Kaz lifting the duvet off me, the light's on, I squint at her. She's talking quietly.

'I have to go.'

'Oh, yes, let me...' I start to try and get out of bed.

'No, you stay here. Seth has gone, he'll be back tomorrow, between ten and eleven. I gave him your spare key so he could let himself in. I'll call tomorrow evening. Everything will be OK. I promise.'

She leans down and hugs me.

'Thank you, give kisses to the kids. I'll try and come up. I should come up. Once my feet...'

'Yeah. Come up when you feel a little better. It might help clear your head a bit.'

'OK. I love you.'

'Love you too.'

The front door closes after her and I get another sense of loss. I'm alone again and feel very awake.

In the kitchen, Kaz has tidied up, everything is clean and put away. In the lounge, she has plumped the cushions and Harold Lloyd has taken up residence in one corner of the sofa with a cushion supporting his back. I move around, looking at the books, the records, then go back into the bedroom and open the door to Charlie's side of the wardrobe. All his clothes are there. I lean forward. There he is - the smell of him. It's like he's in the room with me. I run my fingers down one of his favourite shirts. I take it off the hanger and put it on the bed so I can take off my T-shirt, I want the smell of him on my skin. When it's on I close the wardrobe door and wrap my arms around myself; I don't want the smell to escape and disappear. The folder with the pictures is in our little office. I climb back into bed with it, then quickly go past the more posed photographs and find the ones at the end where he's smiling and laughing. Everything would have been so much simpler if Charlie hadn't died. We'd talked about having a family. I'd said, the kids would have dark hair as my mousy curls were boring. He had told me I was beautiful. I fall back to sleep eventually, surrounded by the photos of Charlie.

I wake up to a worried face too close to mine, 'Fuck, thank God. I thought you were dead. I couldn't tell if you were breathing or not.'

'Sorry.'

'Is this Charlie? Now, he's a handsome dude.' He's picked up one of the more posed pictures, 'I thought you said he was a photographer, not a model.'

I'm trying to wake up and take in all the information tumbling about my brain, Seth is here, asking me about Charlie. Seth puts the photo down and opens the curtains.

'You should try halfway house living, they get us up at seven every day for their shitty supermarket brand cereal breakfast. You know it's nearly eleven 'o' clock.'

I start to get out of bed, as I sit up, nausea. I move swiftly, for someone with sore feet, to the bathroom.

Seth isn't far behind me. He finds a bobble and ties back my hair as I continue to throw up everything I ate yesterday. At this rate, I will be very thin very soon.

When I've finished and cleaned myself up, Seth carries me to the kitchen.

'Right, what has the beautiful Kaz left us for breakfast, well you breakfast. Me, brunch. Ah, melon and oranges. Maybe, with some toast and coffee, obviously. Is all this caffeine good for my possible child?'

'Jesus, you're a morning person. We definitely aren't compatible. Yes, to all the food, the alien inside me is hungry all the time. Yes, to coffee. I'm only having three cups a day AND it's my last vice, I can't give everything up.'

'Grumpy.'

I glare at him.

'Right, I'll get on with it.' He turns on Radio One and starts moving about the kitchen, dancing a little as he does. I ignore him and have a look at the newspaper he has left on the table. Harold Lloyd jumps up and meows, he hasn't been fed. I start to move off the chair.

'Oh, no you don't. I've been given strict instructions from Kaz. Minimal use of feet for another two days at least. I will feed the cat, where's the food?'

I point at the cupboard under the sink, Harold Lloyd jumps off the table immediately to wind appreciatively around Seth's feet. I mutter, 'Traitor.'

After breakfast, Seth says, 'Do you want to get dressed?'

I'm still wearing Charlie's shirt, some of the buttons have come undone at the front. Seth is looking at my body.

'Yes. I'll get dressed.'

He comes over and lifts me slowly off the chair, his hand circles my waist as his other arm goes under my knees. Is he spreading his fingers, moving them slightly as he takes me towards the bedroom? He lowers me onto the bed, not letting go. I put my hand onto his chest, 'Seth. You promised.'

'Hm.'

He's looking down, the side of my breast is exposed.

'Seth. Let me go.'

His gaze moves to my lips, for a second, then he's back.

'Right, yeah. Sexy in the shirt thing. Sorry. Got a bit lost there, with the carrying woman, felt macho. Fuck, this is not going to be easy.'

'Sorry. Like I said, maybe we shouldn't.'

'Nope, just a lapse. I'll be good.'

'OK then.'

I look at him and then the bedroom door. He's still staring.

'God, shit. Sorry. Right, give me a shout when you're done.'

He turns away and closes the door after him.

I breathe again. That would be too easy and very wrong. It was sleeping with Seth that got me in this mess in the first place. It would only complicate the issue, but my stupid head doesn't always have any power over what my body wants. I get changed quickly into joggers and a t-shirt; I need to be as unsexy as possible. I walk slowly out of the bedroom and down the hall.

'What are you doing, you're not supposed to be walking.'

I'm scooped up and put on the sofa. Seth goes and sits on a comfy chair. This is good. Not too close.

'Seth, can you drive?'

'Yeah.'

'On Friday, I have my appointment with the counsellor for an hour, any chance you could drive me? I've got a car.'

'Sure. What sort of car is it?'

'Just an old Jetta. But she's reliable. Are you seeing a counsellor?'

'Yeah, I do Mondays on the other side of Battersea. Where's yours?'

'Back in Brixton, close to Jason's.'

'Makes sense. What do you want to do today? Do you know how to play poker, Texas Hold 'em?'

'I do.'

'You are a woman of many talents. Kitchen table?'

'Kitchen table.'

'What can we use for chips?'

'There's a bag of peanuts somewhere. We can literally play for peanuts.'

'God you're weird. But fine. Is it alright if I put some music on?'

'Yeah, help yourself.'

He kneels by Charlie's and my record collection. He pulls out my album of Cats the musical and laughs, 'You, presumably?'

'Yep.'

Then he takes out another album, The Mission, 'Charlie?'

'Me.'

'Colour me impressed.'

He settles on Siouxsie and the Banshees. He asks if this is me or Charlie.

'Me again. I was a bit of a Goth before I started clubbing and got into Dance music.'

'Yeah, you being all gothy in black sounds about right.'

'What do you like?'

'Dance, acid house, a bit of metal stuff from before, like you, there's the music from before drugs and after drugs.'

'Do you ever listen to dance music straight and still find you can conjure up some of the feelings you used to have.'

'Yeah, it's like an echo of it. I wish we'd met clubbing; we would have had a lot of fun.'

'Mm, I was with Charlie then. I never went clubbing with anyone but him and Jason.'

'So, Jason did drugs with you. I didn't expect that.'

'He was the one who got us our first E's, he even put it in my mouth.' The memory of that night makes me happy; we were so naïve and up for it.

'Oh, he is going to be going over that in his mind. Bet he feels responsible.'

'Maybe. Most of my memories of clubbing are positive. It's only after Charlie died that I started using them differently.'

As we start to play poker, we talk about clubs we both went to, realising we would have probably bumped into each other at some point.

'So, you were into all that latex and stuff.'

'I wasn't and then Charlie did this thing on subculture for his final project, I modelled for him, that's part of how we ended up together.'

'Where are the photos now?'

'Most of the big ones were sold, but I have the originals, do you wanna see?' I grin. They remind me of a much happier time.

'Yeah. Oh, and you're bluffing.'

I put my cards face down on the table and squint at him.

'So where are these photos?'

'In the office.'

'Your chariot awaits.' He lifts me and carries me into the office, dropping me onto the desk chair. I swivel and find the folder from Charlie's finals.

'And up again, come on.'

He carries me back to the kitchen. I pass the folder over to him. I haven't looked at them for years.

He opens them, the first picture is one of me with Ken and John, I'm wearing a latex skirt and bra and thigh-high leather boots. John and Ken are at my feet on leads with nothing but black latex G-strings on, their hands on my legs. It's a powerful image.

'Holy shit, Em.'

He turns the pages slowly. Looking at each picture carefully, as they delve into the hidden depths of sadomasochism. The pictures are beautifully crafted stark black and bright whites, the only colour one is a close-up of my lips with iced water dripping off them. I'm wearing bright red lipstick.

Some of the pictures are more explicit than others, but I figure I've slept with Seth, it's not like he hasn't seen my body.

His thumb is rubbing his lips as he turns each page. When he finds the ones when I'm en pointe. He looks at the photo, then at me. He closes the folder without looking at the rest.

'Em, I told you I had a thing for ballet dancers, do you remember.'

'I'd forgotten.'

'These are not helping...fuck, I think I'd better go, before I do stuff to you, we both regret.'

He is looking at me seriously.

'Shit, sorry.'

'Yeah, I need a cold shower. Will you be alright?'

'Yes, I'm sorry.'

He picks up his coat and he's gone before anything else is said. I grab the folder from the other side of the table and look at the pictures. They're beautiful, but I'm full of lust for Charlie. To anyone else, it just appears as lust for whoever is looking at the photo.

My body was so strong. I built up my strength back then and I can do it again, even with stupid cut feet and a baby inside me. I shift to the floor in the living room and do some stretches. I feel better moving and using my body. As I move and start to sweat, I listen to my body and remember why I like to dance. It's somewhere to lose myself. I need to dance, the sooner the better.

Just as I'm finishing up and thinking I should go and have a shower, the phone rings. I lift myself and go to it. It still takes me four or five rings,

'Oh hello, I thought you weren't going to answer.' It's Kaz.

'Sorry, I was stretching, trying to do some exercise.'

'Is Seth not there with you?'

'Ah. Er... he had to go.'

'What happened.'

'I showed him Charlie's photos from his finals.'

'Jesus, Em. Do you want to sleep with him? Because any red-blooded male who sees them will want to sleep with you.'

'I haven't looked at them in years I forgot they were so...'

'Explicit. They're fucking explicit...' I hear a small voice, 'Sorry Gracie, Mummy is talking to Em. I know, I know, it was a bad word... No not right now, you can talk to her when I finish. Now go back to painting... Sorry, I thought they were engrossed in what they were doing, Gracie doesn't miss a trick.'

'Reminds me of her mother.'

'Hah. So, is Seth coming back or have you broken another man?'

'He said he'd be back tomorrow.'

'Good. Just don't do anything stupid.'

I promise I won't and ask her about her journey home, then I talk to Gracie for a bit and have an odd conversation with Arthur about a monkey he's seen recently. When they finally give the phone back to Kaz, I ask her more about Dave and how it is all going. She says they are still behaving like adults and trying to think about the kids. I'm pleased it isn't acrimonious. It would be weird. Just before we say goodbye she says to me, 'So, what aren't you going to do?'

'Anything stupid.'

'Specifically?'

'Sleep with Seth.'

'Good. Now try and rest those feet and hopefully, I will see you soon, up here.'

'Yeah, hopefully.'

I'm in bed, trying to get to sleep when I hear the phone ring again. I pad cautiously to the hall and pick up the receiver, 'Hello?'

'It's me.' Jason.

I sit down on the floor with the receiver to my ear. Softly, I say, 'Hey. How are you?'

'Is he there?'

'No.'

I hear him sigh. I wait for him to say something. I miss him, it hurts like a physical twist in my gut. It's easy to imagine his dark hooded eyes, his soft mouth, I need to make him smile.

'Em. I miss you.'

'I miss you too.'

Another silence. In the end, I say, 'I'm sorry. You've done so much for me and... what do I give you? Nothing but misery and trouble.'

Another sigh, then, 'I think you're right; we need to just press pause for a moment. But this is just a pause, I want you back, Em. We may not be together, but we're together.'

I know what he's getting at.

'I won't sleep with Seth.'

I hear him exhale.

'But you're seeing him, he's coming to the flat?'

'Yeah, but just to help out as I can't walk much still.'

'Right.'

I stare at the wall in front of me. It's midnight blue, I remember choosing the colour with Charlie.

'How is it, being there?'

'Hard.'

'But you're coping?'

'Yeah. In some ways having this baby inside me is a good thing, it stops me doing ... what I really want to do right now.'

'Are you going to see Dr Akhtar on Friday?'

'Yes.'

'Promise.'

'Yes.'

Exhale.

'Good.'

Silence.

I unbend my knees and stretch out my legs. My feet look ridiculously large, I have a pair of Charlie's woolly socks covering up the bandages underneath. Eventually, Jason says, 'I love you and miss you. This is horrible, Em.'

I rest the back of my head against the wall. It would be so much easier to go back to Jason's flat.

'I love you too. But we've got to work through all this by ourselves, you have to let me be by myself for a little while I get my head straight.'

'What if, when your head is straight you don't want...'

'I will. You're the only thing I'm sure of. But it isn't fair on you to be my counsellor, nurse, friend and lover. You should just be my friend and lover.'

'Mm.'

I change the subject.

'I saw the review in the paper. They loved your paintings.'

'Yeah. They want to interview you. I told them, you were unavailable to comment, which made them want to talk to you more.'

'Ah, I'm a woman of mystery.'

'Yeah.'

'You're right, I don't know if I'd want to talk to them about some of the pictures just yet.'

'I'm sorry about...'

'Shut up, the paintings were beautiful, I'm just overly sensitive and need...'

'Yeah.'

'Yeah.'

'Right, you should rest. I just needed to hear your voice.'

'I'm glad you phoned. We can still talk, like this until... we're ready to...'

'Yeah.'

'OK. I love you, night night.'

'Night.'

I hear the click. More tears, I crawl to the bedroom, crying as I go. I get into the bed and fall asleep weeping.

———

'Fuck, you sleep like the dead. Seriously, tiny little breaths.'

Seth is standing next to the bed.

'I would like to think you're eyes are all puffy because you're weeping over me. But I suspect not?'

Wearily, I push myself into a sitting position as Seth perches beside me.

'Jason and I spoke last night.'

'Ah. Was he OK?'

'No.'

'Are you OK?'

'No.'

'Coffee?'

'Yes.'

'Come on then.'

Seth throws the duvet off me and carries me to the kitchen. I'm tired, even though I slept heavily. As soon as Seth puts me on the chair, the wave of nausea hits me. I'm pushing myself up.

'Oh, no you don't, bathroom?'

I nod, he has me again and takes me quickly to the bathroom. I am left kneeling in front of the toilet. As I vomit, I hear him put the kettle on and move about in the kitchen.

I'm cleaning my teeth when he comes back in for me. When I finish I'm carried to the kitchen again.

Seth seems too comfortable in mine and Charlie's kitchen as he makes a boiled egg with toast fingers. It feels wrong having him here.

We sit eating not talking until I finally say, 'Sorry about yesterday.'

'S'alright.' He has toast in his mouth.

'I didn't mean to...'

He swallows and then looks at me.

'It's my problem. Not yours. I'll keep my promise.'

'OK.'

We slip back into silence, but something has changed. We spend the day quietly, reading and watching TV until he leaves.

The next day he drives me to Dr Akhtar. He tells me he'll wait for me in the car after he deposits me at her door.

'I've got a book, it'll be fine.'

He's walking back to the car as Dr Akhtar answers the door. She notices him, as she beckons me in.

In her shed come office, I take my shoes off and tuck my feet onto the sofa. I tell her about what's happened and where I am. She asks me who Seth is, I explain. She nods.

When I finish talking, she looks at me and says, 'I think, you and Jason having a break from each other is a good thing. But I think having Seth looking after you isn't. You have a history of thinking you owe sex to people who care for you. This would make your current situation explode. Similarly, you are both drug addicts, together is usually worse than separately. Once your feet have improved, I should take a break from Seth as well. From all men. You mentioned visiting your friends and family in Worcester. That would make a lot of sense. Reconnecting with your roots. How's it being back in the flat, you haven't mentioned it?'

'Overwhelming. My memories of Charlie are everywhere, it's hard.'

I repeat what I said to Jason about taking drugs if it weren't for the baby.

'For some addicts, a baby wouldn't stop them. This is good Emma, you are making headway, even if it doesn't feel like it.'

'Thank you. I have a question. Why did Jason put up with

so much from me for all these years? It's like I've kept him on a hook dangling. I don't think I knew I was doing it, but now, looking back it's dreadful.'

Dr Akhtar looks down and shakes her head slightly, 'Maybe you did, maybe you didn't. Every person is good and bad, no one is perfect. Jason made his own choices, you didn't make him do or say anything, he's an adult and you're an adult and he tried to have other relationships. You're making yourself out to be the villain in your own story, but are you? He didn't have to stay close to you when you got together with Charlie, he didn't have to look after you after Charlie died, regardless of the promise he made. He didn't have to paint those pictures of you. Love and friendship are powerful forces, but they still allow for choice.

You haven't been the best friend you could be, but you haven't been the worst. Before and during the time you were with Charlie, you repeatedly told Jason, that you didn't find him attractive. The fact he continued to patiently wait for you was his choice. Yours and Jason's story is all about the choices you made as individuals. When you get back together, maybe you can make some choices together?'

I feel a lot better. I hear the ting. Dr Akhtar smiles, 'Let me know if you need to postpone a couple of your sessions to go to Worcester.'

'I will and thank you.'

When I leave, it's like I'm lighter. I open the passenger door of the car and get in.

'How was it?'

'Good.'

PATTERNS

Over the next week or so Seth comes every day, picks up shopping, takes me to my session with Dr Akhtar. He keeps his distance more and more as my feet improve. He's withdrawing again. He knows I don't really need him to visit daily.

Eventually, I sit him down.

'I'm going to go up to Worcester next week for a few days.'

'Right,'

He can't look at me.

'What about the scan?'

The appointment had come through this morning for the Monday of the week after next.

'I'll be back on Sunday.'

'I'll miss you. I suppose I'll need to look for a proper job now you don't need me anymore.'

'I suppose. But only until September.'

'Yeah. Just to tide me over.'

'Shall we watch a film, I brought popcorn?'

'Sure. When are you going to tell Jason about the appointment?'

'Later.'

'Are you going to tell him I'm coming too?'

'Yes. Can we stop talking about that, help me make the popcorn.'

'OK, I just need to nip to the loo.'

The popcorn is popping in the microwave, I try not to think about that conversation with Jason. We've had a couple more late-night talks. The mood has started to lift as we talk about shared memories and laugh more. Wounds are starting to heal. I don't want to ruin it.

Seth has gone to sit down. I sense him watching me as I push the videotape into the machine. He's on the sofa his long legs crossed at the ankle in front of him. When I turn around, I return to the corner of the sofa and curl my knees up, his eyes are still following me.

'What?'

'Nothing.'

'You're staring.'

'Sorry, you look nice today. Have you been doing more exercise?'

'Yeah, I went to ballet yesterday and started jogging last week.'

'Ah. Ballet.'

'Ah?'

'That'll be it.'

'Hm.'

I press play on the video. The bowl of popcorn is between us, we both are dipping our hands in and grabbing handfuls as the film starts.

'Em.'

The opening music is playing. I keep watching the TV.

'Mm.'

He's moving, putting the popcorn on the floor. Moving up the sofa.

'You look really good today.'

'Mm. OK. What're you doing?'

One hand is on the back of the sofa, the other on the arm in front of me, he has encircled me.

'I can't stop thinking about those photos.'

His hand has moved onto my leg and he has edged closer, the hand on the arm of the sofa is suddenly on my waist. He's hauling me towards him.

'Seth, stop it.'

Grabbing a leg and an arm he's dragged me down the sofa so I'm underneath him, how has he done this so quickly?

'I've really missed you, your body, your mouth.'

His breath is on my face, his pupils are dilated. My hands are pushing against his chest.

'I need to touch you.' He leans forward to kiss me as I turn away.

'Stop it, Seth. SETH!'

I'm shouting, his mouth is on my neck, a hand has moved to my top and is undoing the buttons, slowly and deliberately as I'm pushing him. I can feel his erection pushing against my leg, his hips are moving. Bobby Turner flashes into my mind. I try to calm my breathing.

'Please Seth. Please stop. I don't want this.'

His hand has reached inside my top, cupping my breast, his mouth goes to it, I'm useless and weak. Nothing is stopping him, my arms are trapped under his body weight, as he pushes my legs apart with his knees.

He tries to kiss me again; this time I bite his lip, blood starts to come from his mouth as he grimaces at me, 'Bitch.'

Leaning back, he slaps me around the face, then lifts me pushing me onto my stomach lifting my hips, yanking my joggers down. This can't happen again. I'm screaming, 'Seth, please. Stop. STOP. STOP.'

My head is pushed into a cushion, he puts a hand over my mouth, I bite it. He jerks it away. I start to scream again. When did he get so strong? I twist and manage to turn on my side, one arm is free, I elbow him. He recoils and loosens his grip on me, I scuttle back into a curled position away from him on the sofa. He stands up and staggers slightly.

'Shit. SHIT!'

He turns and punches the wall. He is looking everywhere but me, is he...?

'Seth, what are you on?'

Crouching down, he puts his hands on the back of his head so he's facing the floor. I straighten my clothes; I've started to shake. I'm going into shock. I've felt this before. Moving to the kitchen, I'm hyper-aware. I take a knife from the knife block and hold it as I boil the kettle. My hands are still shaking. My heart pounding in my chest. I hear him coming and turn around, knife towards him.

His hands are up, he has come to his senses. I put the knife back in the block and go back to what I was doing. Nearly all of the three teaspoons of sugar make it into the cup, although there is a dusting around the base. I spoon in coffee and add the water before pouring in some milk. The teaspoon rattles in my unsteady hands. Behind me I hear the scrape of the kitchen chair as he sits down, I sit down opposite with my coffee and look at him.

'What the fuck?'

'I know. I am beyond sorry, I'm a fucking idiot.'

'Yeah, no shit. How long have you been using again?'

'I don't know, a week or so, when you stopped needing me, I could feel you slipping away. I thought I had it under control, just a quick snort of coke before I got here. But then I started having it here. Coke and me... it turns me into...'

'Yeah, I know, I saw, I felt it.' My cheek smarts, 'Why didn't you talk to me? Tell me how you were feeling, I might've been able to help?'

'You've too much of your own shit going on...' His eyes lift, 'Fuck, I nearly fucking raped you. Who does that?'

'You have a problem; I get it more than you know. I tried

all sorts to get Jason to have sex with me when I was off my head.'

'And he didn't?'

'No.'

'He must have a vast amount of self-control, you are ridiculously fuckable.'

'That's not always a good thing.'

We're silent for a minute, I sip the coffee and taste the sweetness cloy in the back of my throat, my heart is slowing. Seth isn't a threat anymore. I ask him. 'When do you see your counsellor?'

'Tomorrow.'

'Good.'

'I don't want to do rehab again.'

'Can you stop without it?'

'Maybe. I don't know. I'll try. I could be a parent; I don't want to be a loser. I'd like to make something of myself.'

He pushes his hands through his hair, there's wetness on his cheeks.

'You can do this. Honestly, if it weren't for this baby, I swear I would have gone off the rails. Being sober is shit. It's boring. I'd much rather get twisted and party.'

I should be angrier but it feels like karma, I'm sorry for him, I understand him, better than most people could.

'Yeah, the trouble is that's how I am all the time. I just want my next hit.'

'Have you got your stash on you?'

'Yeah?'

'Show me.'

He takes his wallet out and brings out a carefully folded bit of paper that looks like a tiny envelope. He opens it and we both look. God I could snort half of that right now. He's watching me.

'Shit, no.'

He gets up from the table and empties the envelope into

the sink, then runs the tap over the bit of paper. A flash of memory bursts in my head, I'm licking a piece of paper just like that. Shaking my head, I try to shift that image from my mind. When he sits back down, his hands are trembling.

I say, 'We're OK. You're OK. This was just a wake-up call. That's all.'

'Em. I nearly raped you. I definitely sexually assaulted you. You could have me arrested.'

'You need help, not a prison sentence.'

'You're a better person than me, if this was the other way around, I don't know...'

'If this were the other way around, we would both be smoking a cigarette, having had awesome drug-induced sex.'

'Don't.'

His head is down again as he fingers the grains of wood on the kitchen table.

'Sorry.'

'So, what now?'

'You go to your counsellor tomorrow, ask for more than once weekly sessions, open up, talk. You know it helps. I'll go to Worcester and then we'll go and see what this baby is doing a week on Monday. Maybe they'll have the paternity test results there or they'll have arrived by then and we can sort this whole mess out and get on with our lives.'

'Simple?'

'No, but better than what just happened, yeah?'

'Yeah.'

After Seth goes, I call Jason, 'I've got the appointment, it's at Kingston Hospital.'

'What time?'

'Ten thirty.'

'Do you want me to come and get you?'

'No, I'll meet you outside the Maternity Unit.'

'OK. About ten fifteen?'

'Yeah... Seth's going to come as well.'

'Right.'

I can sense his jaw clenching.

'He has a right to be there.'

'Hm. Fine.'

'I haven't heard about the paternity thing yet. I'm going to Worcester for a week, I'll be back on Sunday, maybe by then...'

'Yeah. That's good, that you're going home. Say, hi to everyone for me.'

'I will. Right, I better go, I'll see you soon.'

'Yeah. I love you Em.'

'Love you too.'

HOME, HOME

The drive up to Worcester seems faster than I remember. It's not long before I'm passing landmarks I recognise and seeing green fields. I crack the window open a little, it smells like home. It is completely different to the multitude of aromas London gives off. I've arranged to stay at my parents' house. When I arrive, the familiarity of it all is overwhelming, it smells and looks exactly the same. I haven't been home for over a year.

My parents hug me tightly in turns. I grin at them and hug them back. I have decided to wait to tell them I'm pregnant until I know who the father is, there's no need to drag them down into this mess, they've been through the mill enough. It's normal to wait to tell people until you're twelve weeks, so it shouldn't raise questions later.

It turns out that being a drug addict thing is a great excuse for not drinking when I'm out with them later for a meal. Although explaining giving up smoking as well was harder, 'I'm trying to live a healthier lifestyle; I may even give up caffeine next.'

'OK, where is my daughter and what have you done with her?' My dad says smiling at me.

'Yeah, you're probably right. One step too far. So, tell me what's been happening here?'

They tell me all the village gossip, some of it I know already from Kaz, but I don't tell them and just let them talk. Neither of them asks me about Jason or rehab. I don't know whether they are waiting for me to open up or whether they don't want to discuss it. I'm happy to leave it but it sits like a big heavy elephant in the corner of the room.

Sleeping back in my old bed is weird, my mum and dad haven't changed my room at all, although there are a few boxes in there that mum says she didn't have room for anywhere else. I snoop inside the boxes, they're photographs of my gran and grandad, old albums, some letters. I read a few and put them back. I stare at the wall opposite me as I climb into bed, Adam Ant is staring back and the Dulux dog poster is on the wall next to him, I briefly wonder what happened to Adam and the Ants, Adam was my first ever crush. I'm thinking about this as I turn the light out and fall into a long exhausted dreamless sleep.

The next day I visit Kaz in the nice three-bedroom semi she used to share with Dave. She's on her own, Gracie is at school and Arthur at playgroup. She has work for the rest of the week so this is my only chance to see her without the kids.

She makes us coffee and gives me a slice of cake. She asks how everything is going. I say what happened with Seth. She's furious and surprised by my attitude. I explain that I understood why he did what he did. She says it's no excuse and mutters stuff about it being unforgivable. If Seth ever had a chance of dating Kaz, I think I may have just blown it. I tell her he's going to get the extra help and is looking for work. She isn't convinced.

'On the upside, I have only projectile vomited three out of the last seven days and just have mild nausea the rest of the time.'

'Oh, that's good.'

Kaz asks if I have a date for the scan, so I tell her all that as well. Then she says, Matt was asking after me.

'Oh yeah, how is he.'

'Good, his wife didn't adjust to living here very well, she's gone back to Abu Dhabi, he plans to join her and the kids in the next couple of weeks, once he's sorted out the house and work.'

'That's a shame, but I suppose if that's what it takes for them to be happy, that's what he has to do.'

'Yeah, I'll miss him and so will the kids. Gracie and Arthur dote on him and love Aaban and Raya.'

'I wish I'd got to meet them.'

'Well, you're here now, how are you in pubs?'

'Fine.'

'The White Hart at seven? I'll let Matt know.'

'Yeah, sounds good. Has Dave got the kids tonight?'

'Yes, they're staying over for the first time in his new flat.'

'Oh, so this isn't about catching up with Matt, it's about taking your mind off the kids being away.'

'Maybe.'

'It'll be fine.'

'What if they don't miss me and like his place better?'

'They won't. He's rubbish at house stuff, they'll have bedrooms with a bed and that's it, they'll be bored in five minutes.'

I hug her.

'Thanks, mate.'

———

When Kaz and I walk into the pub, Matt's already there, he's sitting at the table we always used to sit at. I grin as he gathers me in my arms for a big hug. He lets go and puts his hands on my shoulders as we both give the other the once over. The familiarity of him and his newly acquired laughter lines are reassuring. He's the only man I had an uncomplicated relationship with. I often wonder why I let this one get away.

'You still look like you. A little older, maybe?'

'Oi.' I punch him gently in the arm.

'Still prone to violence, nothing changes.'

He's grinning at me. I grin back as we sit down.

Kaz interrupts our grinning,

'So, I'll get the drinks in then and leave you two to gurn at each other, what're you having?'

Matt says, 'A pint of lager please.'

I say, 'A double gin and tonic, with a chaser of tequila. Oh, and some coke if Dozzer, over there, is still dealing. Just a snifter.'

'So, a pint of orange juice and lemonade.' Kaz says, looking at me, unamused.

'Yeah, I s'pose,' I sigh.

Kaz goes to the bar and Matt says, 'So, how's that going, the whole being sober thing.'

'It's going, I'm doing it.'

'And what about the other thing.' He glances at my stomach, Kaz has a big mouth, I wonder how much he knows.

'I'm less vomit-y. Which is nice.'

'And this Seth fella. How's he doing, you met him at rehab, yeah.'

Jesus Christ, everything. He knows frigging everything.

'Yeah, this place hasn't changed, just don't say anything to my mum and dad we're doing a paternity test. It all needs to be sorted before I tell them. And it's still really early.'

'Hey. Hey, it's me, it's OK. My lips are sealed. Kaz needed to talk to someone she's been worried sick, we all have. Jason has kept us in the loop this past year but said he was dealing with it.'

'He was, he did. And then this happened and it all went to

shit, but we're working on it. We're just giving each other some air to breathe.'

'That's good, having a baby is a big deal. You need to be mentally and physically strong, they really take it out of you. You look well.'

'I've been dancing and jogging, it helps keep my mind off... other things.'

'That's good Em.'

As Kaz comes back with the drinks, I have just asked Matt how he feels about moving back to Abu Dhabi.

'It wasn't what I necessarily wanted, but Tabitha tried to make a go of it here, but people were just...'

'Insanely racist and ignorant?'

'Yeah.'

I rub his arm and take a sip of my orange juice and lemonade. It's very sweet. I eye up Kaz's gin and tonic but try not to think about it.

We chat until last orders. I get another massive hug from Matt before we leave.

Kaz and I go our separate ways to walk home. It's a clear night with a full moon.

I can't help thinking people are still treating me like I'm fragile and high maintenance. Do they constantly worry they'll find me dead from an overdose? This thought causes me to involuntarily shudder, I wrap my arms around me as I walk. Maybe I'm the jinx, the bad omen, the cause of all the problems with Charlie. Briefly, panic fills my chest. I take a big breath in and blow it out as I pass the oak tree on the corner. I rub the worn patch on the bark that we touched every day on the way to school for luck. I'm being ridiculous.

Then I'm thinking about another night just before we got to the Oak tree. I was with Matt walking home and we saw a fox screeching and he joined in. After we got stoned before running up to Top Field. I have a lot of happy memories in this village and only a few I wish I could forget.

It feels good, getting involved and participating in other people's lives instead of just being wrapped up in my own feelings and thoughts. I was so bundled up in my grief that I couldn't see beyond that. Now I'm starting to glimpse light through it, like a ray of sun through a window.

My sleep is infiltrated with ghosts from my past, Matt and Charlie intermingle becoming one unrecognisable thing. I wake up sweating and need to throw up.

My mum looks worried when I come downstairs, I mutter something about Kaz's dreadful cooking and apologise to Kaz, silently in my head.

After breakfast, I set off for a jog. My mum makes it clear she finds it curious that one minute I'm throwing up, the next stuffing my face, then jogging. I ignore her and make light of it.

When I reach Top Field. I'm surprised to see a familiar shape leaning against the gate.

'Hello you.'

'Hello.'

'What're you doing up here?'

'Same as you, I suspect. Reminiscing.'

'Hm,'

I lean up against the gate looking out at the field and down into the town below. He puts his arm around me and kisses me on the top of the head.

'I've missed you.'

He squeezes me a little tighter and we slip into silence as we watch birds peck at the field, it rained earlier and the worms are near the surface. The sky is amber as the sun makes its way up through the clouds. Eventually, he says, 'We thought we were going to lose you.'

'I did lose me.'

'I'm so sorry I wasn't around to help, after Charlie, we'd just had Raya... it was a difficult time.'

'It's fine, I don't think you could have done any more than Jason and family comes first.'

'You're my family.'

I turn into him and hug him. He says, 'I think a lot about when we were together. It felt perfect. I could have stayed with you forever.'

'Like I said to you at the time, it wasn't realistic.'

'And then you got together with Charlie and you were so happy. I was happy for you, so I married Tabitha. We have a good life.'

'Are you happy?'

'Happy enough.'

I'm leaning back as his arms stay around me. He looks sad. He moves a loose hair behind my ear and leans towards me. I step back, as his arms release me and hang loose by his sides.

It's like I've kicked a puppy. We have too much history, it wouldn't be fair, 'That was a terrible idea.'

'Yeah, stupid I just wanted to step back in time.'

'Yeah. I've thought about that too.'

He looks older, tired.

'You know it was always going to be you and Jason. He told me, years ago. When we got together, I felt terrible for him, me then Charlie. But he's waited patiently for you, for so long.'

'Charlie said, before he knew us properly, that Jason was my loyal dog. I keep hearing him say it, it seems so cruel now.'

'Jason knew who you were from the get-go. He knew that you would come to him eventually. He knew he was who you needed. I'm sure he didn't expect or want Charlie to die, but I think he would have waited until you were both ancient and wrinkly if he had to. He loves you in a way I've never experienced and I loved... love you a lot.'

'I love you too, Matt. I'm sorry we never worked out.'

'When you go home, say hi to Jason for me and be kinder to yourself. Charlie dying like he did when he was so young, would have sent anyone over the edge. And this Seth fella... he's not one of us, is he?'

'Neither was Charlie.'

'Yeah, but he made sure he became part of us. Part of our family.'

'Yeah.'

We both squint out at the sun coming up over the field for a moment, the birds are twittering and a breeze moves the grass making it look like waves. Nature continues regardless of feelings and people. Eventually, I turn back to Matt and say, 'When I have this baby and you come back with the kids, can we get together and do kids and family things? I'm not entirely sure what that entails yet but you do, so I am hoping you and Kaz can show me.'

'Of course, we can.'

'Thanks.' I nudge him with my elbow and I hear him laugh.

'Come on are you, jogging or walking?'

'Jogging.'

We jog back down the hill; I kiss him on the cheek as we say goodbye outside his house. He kisses me on the lips, softly, quickly and then disappears inside.

I run back to Mum and Dad's deep in thought. Matt would have been the easy choice. The simple choice, but I didn't choose him. I need to talk to Jason about what Matt told me he said. It can wait. This is time apart, time to think.

By Sunday I'm relaxed and ready to go home. My mum does a Sunday lunch, she has persistently ignored my vegetarianism all my life, and nothing has changed, but she does loads of vegetables which I pile high on my plate.

I smirk when she says, 'You'll get fat if you continue eating like that.'

They'll be brilliant grandparents. It'll be nice to share

some good news. Over the last few days, I've managed to find out that my cousin, Kevin, is currently jobless, living in a flat in town with a girl who has a kid with another man. Dad has hinted at an alcohol problem. They're clueless as to why the children they brought up have turned out this way. I wonder if telling them everything would hurt them more than not. I'll talk to Dr Akhtar about it at my next session.

As I drive off with them waving in my rear-view mirror, I think how lucky I am to have them and Kaz and Matt. I'm relaxed, but as I drive back towards London, the thoughts that I have kept at bay return and by the time I reach the flat I'm feeling nervous about tomorrow.

I open the door; Jason has put all my post on the hallway table and fed Harold Lloyd in my absence. I pick up the mail, scanning the fronts and discarding the junk, until I come to a formal-looking manila envelope. Jason has put a note on the front – *This arrived at my place, I thought you should see it first J X* – The return address is for the clinic that performed the paternity test. My stomach jumps.

Bringing it to the kitchen table, I make a coffee, then sit with it unopened as I sip my drink. It's shrieking, "OPEN ME! OPEN ME!" Patting it, then holding it up to the light, I shake my head. No.

I move into the living room, I don't want to be in the same room as it, the temptation to open it is too great. I'll bring it with me tomorrow. We'll open it together after the scan. They've as much right as me to know what's in that letter. It wouldn't be fair to look first.

After a fitful night's sleep, I try to switch off with a quick jog in the morning. It doesn't work. I choose to take the bus to Kingston Hospital and get there early. I wander up and down outside the entrance to the maternity wing waiting for Jason and Seth to arrive. Jason is there just after me.

He comes towards me gathering me into his arms. Holding me tightly. As we come apart, I notice he looks tired.

'How was home?'

'Good, Matt was there, it was nice to see him.'

'What about Tabitha and the kids?'

'They've gone back to Abu Dhabi, he's sorting some stuff out then going back too, I'll tell you everything later.'

'Have you opened the env...'

Seth is approaching, Jason takes my hand. I say, 'Hey.'

'Hey, are we going in?'

Seth is looking at me and avoiding eye contact with Jason.

'Yeah.'

Jason scowls as his anger encircles us.

We walk into the maternity unit and wait to be called in, when they call me in, I get up onto the bed, Jason takes my hand. Seth stands at the end. I can't look at either of them.

I uncover my flat belly and the man who's doing the scan pours the clear gel on it. Then the pressing down thing again. Swooshing sounds, clicking and a black and white blob appears on the screen.

'That's an arm.'

All three of us look, we are struggling to make out an arm, 'And this is the head.'

The head is much clearer although it does look a bit like Skeletor.

'Everything looks good you have a healthy baby in there, Mrs...'

I shake my head at the man, then he looks from Jason to Seth. He puts two and two together and makes five, which makes me laugh inside. I don't think either of them would be amused to realise he thought they were a couple and I was their surrogate.

'Would you like to know your estimated due date.'

'Yes please.'

'Based on the size etcetera, I would say about the twenty-first of September.'

Jason looks at me and says, 'The day before you.'

'Yeah.'

Seth looks uncomfortable; I don't know when his birthday is either.

The man hands me some of the blue paper they use to cover the bed to wipe the goo off my belly, which is his way of telling us we are done.

As we leave, Seth says, 'OK, well I suppose I better be off.'

'No. Hang on, there's something else.'

Both of them watch me as I rummage in my bag.

'I have the paternity test results. Shall we find the restaurant and have a coffee?'

Jason says, 'Yeah, come on.'

He takes my hand and we start walking. Behind us, Seth shrugs and follows.

We move through the corridors, past unconscious people being pushed on gurneys by orderlies, past old people walking slowly as they go to visit a relative. It seems like the corridors go on for days. Jason is gripping me tightly my hand feels numb in his.

When we finally get to the restaurant the smell or maybe what we are just about to do makes me feel nauseous. It still smells like rehab, maybe they have the same caterers? I'm relieved when we sit down. Jason stands up, mumbles something about coffee and goes to the queue.

I say to Seth, 'Are you OK?'

'Been better, but if you mean am I taking drugs, the answer's no. Not since last...'

'Good, that's good. However, this turns out, can we be friends.'

'I don't know if I can do that. I see him,' He nods towards Jason, 'and what friendship with you can do. You send us a bit mental.'

'Us?'

'Men.'

'That's what Charlie said, but a bit more kindly.'

'Hm.'

Jason is coming back and Seth has returned to staring at the table with his shoulders rolled forwards. He looks beaten.

I take the envelope out of my bag and put it on the table as Jason puts three coffees there as well.

'Who wants to open it?'

I'm looking at them both, neither look at me.

'OK then. I'll do it.'

I calm my breathing then rip the envelope open, taking out the letter and unfolding it.

I read it, slowly, making sure I understand and get this right, then hand it to Jason. The relief he is feeling seems tangible, like a colour or smell, Seth sees it and says,

'It's his, isn't it.'

He doesn't wait for an answer, but gets up and walks away.

'Give me a sec.' I say to Jason, touching his arm, before I run after Seth.

He is already out of the canteen and halfway down the corridor when I catch up to him. He's crying. I move around to the front of him, putting my arms around him so he has to stop walking. He returns the hug. His head bending to be on top of mine, his shoulders shaking as he sobs. Eventually, it subsides, and when it does, I let go and step back to look at him, holding his hands with mine.

'Seth, it's OK. It's for the best.'

'I know. It's just I liked the idea. I could see us together, the three of us.'

'Look, we really can still be friends.'

'No. I don't think so. I need to make a clean break. I need to lead a healthy life, otherwise, I'll be fucked. I'm not sure I could do that having you as my friend.'

I let my hands drop out of his.

'OK, but if you ever...'

'I won't. I'm sorry.'

He kisses me on the cheek and walks past me. I watch him walk away, he doesn't look back.

When I'm back in the canteen, Jason is where I left him, the letter still in his hand. He's staring at it. When I sit down opposite him, he looks at me.

'I'm going to be a dad.'

'Yes, yes you are.' I smile at him.

He grins back.

'Shall we go?'

'Yeah.'

As we leave, he takes my hand again, this time it is gentler and more relaxed as all his anger disappears. When we get to the car park, I say I'll catch the bus home.

'I thought we could maybe celebrate, go for a meal?'

I'm not in the mood for eating out or celebrating. I'm weary. I take his other hand.

'That sounds lovely, but I'm knackered. I just want to go home and put my feet up.'

'That's OK, I'll cook something.'

He thinks I'm coming back to his, but I still need to find myself again. I'm nearly there and going home really helped, but I don't think I'm ready. I say as much to him and watch his shoulders sag.

'Em, please. Come home.'

'My flat is home; your flat is your home. When I do come home, maybe we should look for somewhere new together?'

'But someone should be with you, to look after you.'

'I'm pregnant, not sick.'

'You're a recovering addict who's pregnant.'

'I am, I'm also grieving, I need to work through all of it before we meet our little person.'

He leans down and kisses me. It would be easy just to let him look after me, but our dynamic needs to change.

'You have to stop looking after me and treat me like an equal.'

'I think of you that way, I just want to help.'

'I know, and you have and you do. Matt said something to me.'

'Oh?'

'Yeah, he said years and years ago that you knew we would end up together and you'd wait forever if you had to. Is that true?'

'I said a lot of things, but yeah, that sounds like drunk stoned me.'

I kiss him again. He puts his hand on the base of my spine and moves me closer. I put my hands between us and push him away.

'You could come back to mine, just for a little while.' I know what he wants and it isn't food.

'I could but wouldn't that just confuse us.'

'I'm not confused.'

I would be lying if I said I didn't want to, I could go to his first, then go home.

'Fine.'

He grabs my hands and opens the passenger-side door for me.

When we arrive at the flat, nothing's changed. The smell of Jason mixed with the background scent of turps, drifts up from his studio. As I walk through the door, he's behind me, kissing my neck, removing my coat, letting it drop to the floor, we step over it as his hands move to my breasts, we keep moving towards the bedroom. By the time we get there, we're both naked, he's still been working out, his muscles even more defined. I brush my hand down his stomach, it's hard. His eyes are pouring over my body.

'Your nipples are darker.' He says before putting his lips around them. My hands are in his hair, then moving to his back, he feels broad, strong.

Afterwards, he holds me and whispers, 'You got your body back and then some, being pregnant suits you.'

'You haven't been slacking either.'

I put my hand on his six-pack. A little less hard when he's relaxed but still impressive.

'I couldn't work, think. So, I went to the gym. It was better than getting drunk, which is what I did to begin with.'

'I get that, jogging and ballet switch my head off and I get a nice little rush of endorphins after which is nice.'

He squeezes my arse, 'Naughty.'

I sneak a peek at his alarm clock on the bedside table. It's six o'clock.

'I should go.'

'Please stay.'

'Don't make this harder than it is, I need to go and feed Harold Lloyd.'

'Let me drive you, at least.'

'OK.'

As we get dressed Jason says, 'Maybe we could go on dates? We kinda missed a whole load of relationship steps. Would that help? Take it slow?'

'Yeah. Dates would be nice.'

'Cool. Dates.' He grins and leans down to kiss me as I put my shoes back on after he found them somewhere near the front door. I put my hands in his hair and let my fingers run through it. I've missed him a ridiculous amount and leaving is taking every ounce of my willpower.

As he drives me back to Barnes, I chat about my visit home.

Suddenly, Jason says, 'Do you think Seth will be OK?'

I'm surprised. Jason has seen him as a threat from day one. Now he knows the baby is his, I suppose the threat is gone.

'I don't know, he started using again not so long ago, he had it at the flat with me there.' Jason's knuckles go white as he grips the steering wheel, 'He threw it away. He has increased his time with his counsellor and is trying to find work. Boredom is not the drug addicts' friend.'

'Are you going to keep seeing him?' His jaw is clenching as rays of the setting sun streak across his face.

'No. He doesn't think I'm good for him,'

'Ah. And what are you going to do to fill your days?'

'Jog, ballet classes, read, write, see Dr Akhtar and go on dates with you.'

A smile twitches on Jason's lips.

'Sounds like a plan.'

'Yeah.'

When we get to the flat, I say a long goodbye in the car, I don't want him in the flat, I can't imagine having sex with Jason in the flat I shared with Charlie, it would be too weird.

I open the door to a meowing Harold Lloyd. I say hello, pick him up and we both wave at Jason, who waves back and drives off. I'm exhausted, but at least there's one less thing to worry about.

NORMAL?

Over the coming weeks, I meet up with Jason once or twice a week, he's painting again and I'm writing. It's good, balanced.

I've developed a small bump and have started to feel little flickers when the baby moves. I'm due to go for my twenty-week scan in a couple of weeks. The nausea has gone and I'm healthier than I've been for over a year. Working on my novel is giving me a focus that I never expected, some days I lose track of time completely.

Our dates have varied from going to the theatre, art exhibitions to a romantic meal. They all end in the same way. Neither of us can keep our hands off each other and we end up having sex either back at his flat or discreetly against a wall somewhere. I'm convinced my hormones have affected my libido; it's almost the only thing I think about. Some of my writing is bordering on pornographic.

We go for brunch with Ken and John one Sunday morning, they're thrilled we are back together. Ken offers to photograph me and the baby. He says he can do some lovely ones of me pregnant. He says he would start with something similar to the Annie Leibovitz cover for Vanity Fair with

Demi Moore. Jason is thrilled, I agree, it's worth it just to see Jason happy. They ask us both what we're working on. Jason says he's doing a whole Madonna, Whore, Madonna and Child thing. I wasn't aware of this and raised an eyebrow.

'I'll show you. Next time you're over.'

'Fine.'

'What about you my beautiful girl?' John says.

'I'm writing a novel about a drug addict, a girl who's grieving the death of her husband.'

Jason frowns briefly, he wasn't aware of this either. Somehow, we've managed to talk about a lot of things, but not our work.

'So, autobiographical?'

'Sort of. I'm fictionalising it.'

'Ooh, are we in it?' Ken is grinning at me.

'Maybe, you'll have to read it, if I get it published.'

John claps his hands, 'Exciting.'

It's lovely to catch up. John tells us he's been commissioned to paint the portrait of a well-known politician, whilst Ken is working on a series of portraits for the National Theatre. We congratulate them, we all know how hard it is to find work for artists, but since Jason's exhibition all three of them have been inundated with offers.

That afternoon we're lying next to one another breathing heavily in Jason's bed. I'm enjoying having my stamina back.

Curling into him and throwing my leg over his, I say, 'We should make the most of this, after the baby comes, things will change.'

He turns his head to me, 'Babies sleep.'

He puts his hand on my bump.

'Holy shit what was that?'

'I don't know a leg or an arm, they're moving.'

He's welling up as he puts his hand on my cheek, keeping his other hand on my bump.

'You can feel it?'

'Yeah, every time.'

'That's amazing.'

'Yeah.'

'What do you think it is, boy or girl?'

'I don't know. I know you'll be fucked if it's a girl, she'll have you wrapped around her little finger.'

'Hm, probably.' He grins at me, the tears still wet.

'Shall we find out at the next scan?'

'Yes. I'd rather know, so I would like to think about names and stop calling it, it and start calling him or her something.'

'OK. Have you thought of names?'

'Not yet, what about you?'

We spend the rest of the day discussing and vetoing names – Jason's grandma's name was Lucinda, I tell him it's too close to Lucy, but could be a middle name. I mention Thomas, after my dad, he likes that for a boy. Then I suggest Fern or Honey.

'Hippie.'

'Fuck off.'

'The potty mouth will have to stop.' Jason is starting to smirk.

'Ha, that's rich coming from you.'

'Still, I do like your mouth.'

I glance at the clock.

'Stop it.'

'What?'

'Clockwatching.'

'I'm not.'

'You are. Stay.'

This is an ongoing argument. I'm still refusing to stay over as it feels too soon. I don't want to mess this up.

'Fine, but you can stay a little longer.' His hand gently parts my legs as thoughts of leaving disappear.

———

At the twenty-week scan, we are told everything's fine. We ask for the gender. They tell us it's not one hundred percent accurate but based on what they can see they think it's a little girl. I grin at Jason and mouth "fucked" at him. He grins back.

After the hospital, we're in the car driving back to Jason's for lunch, he says, 'We need to start looking for a place together. I don't want to bring up our child in two houses.'

I know this is the right thing, but the idea of giving up Charlie and my flat seems massive. He glances across at me as he drives.

'Look, I know you don't want to give up your flat just yet. I made a load of money from those paintings, I've enough to buy us somewhere, big enough to have a studio and an office for you and three bedrooms.'

'Three bedrooms?'

'Little Maya might want a brother or sister?'

'Might she? And we were going to talk about this when?'

'Now seems a good time?'

'Hm. I don't know. Maybe she would be better off as an only child.'

'As an only child, speaking for my people, I wouldn't recommend it.'

'Well, speaking of someone who sort of had a cousin sibling, I wouldn't recommend that, either.'

As we're speaking, I notice we're not going the normal way home. Jason keeps driving, he pulls up outside a tall Victorian terrace in Putney Heath, it reminds me immediately of the flat I shared with Charlie and Jason at college. There's a for sale sign outside.

'Come on, I've got us a viewing.'

Giving a frown I still follow him out of the car. We're let in by an estate agent. Whoever's home it is has decided to leave potential buyers to view it in peace. The agent says if we have any questions just ask, but she'll leave us to look.

I hold Jason's hand as we walk into the extended kitchen at the bottom of the house. Patio doors open out onto a smallish garden with a large tree in its centre. There are skylights in the ceiling of the extension, bathing the kitchen table in natural light. Upstairs there's a large room with big windows and great light, it would be perfect for Jason's studio, next to it a smaller one which would do as an office, and then a third with an ensuite which is the master bedroom.

We go to the converted attic, it feels so like our flat it makes my heart pump a little harder, Jason squeezes my hand. This has been converted to have two bedrooms and a bathroom, there are skylights in the roof of each room so it feels considerably lighter than where we used to live.

'What do you think?'

'I like it. Can you really afford this?'

'You'd be surprised what people will pay for paintings of you.'

'Hm.'

I'm still not sure how I feel about those paintings in other people's houses, together they tell a story, individually, some of them are incredibly tragic. Are they still me once Jason sold them? Or are they just a girl in a painting. Am I just a girl in a painting, is the girl in the painting even real? I'm none of those girls he painted anymore.

Staring out of the window of the smaller room looking down at the tree in the garden, the view feels almost identical to my room in the flat at college, I wonder if it is a magnolia tree. I'm snapped out of my reverie by Jason's voice.

'So, shall I put in an offer?'

'Yes, go on then.'

He kisses me, the smile still on his lips. This is the Jason I remember. This is my friend.

As we drive away from the house.

'But what about my flat, I can't just leave it empty.'

'You could rent it out, maybe?'

'Maybe. I need to think about it.'

'Take your time. But once this baby is born, promise me you'll sleep all night in a bed with me.'

'I promise.'

PAINTINGS

I wake up in Jason's bed, the evening light flooding through the bedroom window. Being pregnant is all-consuming, sapping my energy as I head towards thirty weeks. Jason is sitting on the floor at the side of the bed, naked. He's drawing in a sketch pad. A small crease has formed between his eyebrows from concentrating. Before I yawn and stretch, I watch him for a moment.

'What time is it?'

'Later than you'd like.'

He continues to draw.

'Let me see.'

'It's not finished.'

'Don't care.'

'Hm.'

He passes me the pad, getting in the bed behind me so he can look over my shoulder. It's beautiful. I'm asleep, my stomach covered loosely with a sheet, but that's all it covers, I have one arm above my head, my hair tumbles over the pillow, my arm and some of my face. My other hand is caressing the base of my bump. My legs are loose and parted.

'Show me how you're getting on with the rest of them.'

'I hate this, they're not finished.'

'You promised.'

'Fine.'

We get out of bed, he throws on some boxers, I wrap the sheet around me like a towel, tucking it in above my breasts.

He holds my hand as I walk down the stairs to his studio, there's no bannister and he's concerned I may fall.

All of his paintings have stayed in the same style as his exhibition. In the first one, I'm standing in a doorway, holding Harold Lloyd. My clothes seem ill-fitting, but when you look closely you can see the buttons are done up incorrectly on my blouse and my short skirt doesn't cover the tops of my stockings. There's a ladder in one of them. My mouth is pink and looks wet, there's mascara running down my cheeks. I appear dirty.

The next is of the three-month scan, two faceless men are watching a screen as the nurse puts the ultrasound thing on my stomach. The tip of my thumb is in my mouth, my stomach exposed. One man is squeezing my breast, the other has his hand clutching my thigh. It looks like we are all just about to have sex, even the nurse has a finger on my stomach next to the device he's holding.

The third painting is of the new house, I'm at the bedroom window looking down at the tree, my arms loose by side, the beginnings of a bump showing. I look like I'm thinking of something else. I'm astounded at the beauty of this one and how well he's captured the moment.

I know he hasn't started any more paintings yet and suspect the next one will be based on the sketch he's just done. Jason's still observing me.

'What do you think?'

'I like the third one, the other two I don't hate. They don't exactly cast me in a positive light.'

'They aren't real, real. They're my interpretation of what I was seeing at the time. It's hard to explain.'

'I get it, but you make me look like a slut. Is that how you see me?'

He puts his arms around me.

'No. Never. You're sensual, sexy. Someone who knows their own body. I'm also trying to show the thing that makes men want you. You're almost naïve, sometimes the way you move... you're oblivious to how it affects us. God, this is hard to explain.'

On tiptoe, I kiss him.

'It's OK, it's art. Do your thing. You're talented and brilliant. But surely you must get bored of painting me.'

'I do the other commissions and stuff, but you're an ever-changing thing. Now is a great example, each time we make love your body has changed. Your boobs are outstanding right now.' He grins at me.

'Make the most of them, who knows what they'll be like after birth and breastfeeding.'

'They'll always be beautiful to me.'

'Aw. Sweet.'

'So, when're you going to let me read your novel?'

'I'm just editing it. Then I'll let you read it.'

'OK.' He leans forward to kiss me as his hands undo my sheet. It's cold in his studio. I shiver as he draws me closer to him. I should be going, but his fingers are slowly moving down my back.

————

Professional photographer Ken is very different to the Ken I know and love, he's all business.

As I'm getting undressed in his studio in the garden, I can't help but think of when Charlie took my photos. I shake my head and try not to think about it. I have only just managed to walk past the picture of Charlie and Jason in John and Ken's kitchen without bawling.

Ken was very clear. When I come to the studio, don't wear underwear and wear something loose fitting, he doesn't want to spend an age editing out indentations on my skin from bras and pants.

He has set up a black background and has a black sheet to wrap around me. Initially, I'm a bit shy in front of him, but then his professionalism stops me worrying. Soon, I'm naked as he tells me to move a fraction of an inch here, a tip of my head there, move my hair, lift my arm. I'm a puppet. He fetches a chair and tells me he wants me to do the Flash Dance pose from the end of her dance with the shower. I lie with my neck on the top of the back of the chair, my arse on the very edge of the seat, my back straight along with my right leg, my left bent at the knee, my foot on its toes. My arms are relaxed as my fingers graze the floor.

'Perfect. Jesus, that looks amazing Em. Hold it, and turn your head, look at me, right down the lens. Relax your mouth.'

Relax your mouth, Charlie used to say the same thing, over and over again.

The tears are coming and I have no power to stop them, the flash is still going. I come out of the pose and sit on the chair, wrapping the sheet back around myself.

'Please, can we stop for a sec.'

'Darling. Shit, what happened.'

'Over sensitive, pregnancy hormones. Charlie used to say that when he was taking my photo, relax your mouth. Stupid.' I'm sniffling.

Ken produces a clean tissue from his pocket and gathers me into a hug.

'I'm so sorry.'

'You weren't to know. I'm fine, I was just having a moment it will pass. I'm doing so much better, but occasionally I have a blip, something catches me out. Grief is a bastard.'

'I know. We've lost a lot of people we loved these last few years.'

Jesus, I'm insensitive. I've been so wrapped up in my stuff that the AIDS pandemic has completely passed me by. It has devastated the Gay community and only now is there any sign of something close to the medicine that they need.

'I'm sorry; I've been so busy with my selfish shit.'

'Hey, we know what you breeders are like.' He's grinning at me.

'Yeah, quite literally a breeder.'

'But an aesthetically beautiful one. Your breasts are magnificent right now. And how is it you don't have stretch marks?'

'Good genes?'

'So, how're you doing? Shall we carry on?'

'Yeah.'

'I'll get Jason, some of you together now.'

'Should I get dressed?'

'No, definitely not.' There's a twinkle in Ken's eye. Now I know why Jason was drinking wine and wearing joggers instead of jeans.

When Jason comes in, he's about two large glasses of wine in. He's smiley and very touchy-feely.

Ken goes back into professional mode and tells Jason to get undressed. Jason kind of salutes him and strips. He has nothing on under his tracksuit bottoms.

Ken has moved the chair and asks us to stand together in the middle of his studio, my back against his stomach. Ken is appraising Jason's hard body. A twitch of jealousy slips into my psyche. It passes quickly as Ken tells Jason to put his arm around me so his hand is on one breast and his arm covers the other. His warmth slips over me as I place my hand on his hip. Our fingers are to join around the bump. We do as Ken says. Ken tells Jason to relax, maybe kiss my neck, which he does as I stretch my head back so he can get in there. His fingers move to pinch my nipple. He has forgotten we're being photographed, he's getting hard, as the flashes from the camera continue. Jason's other hand starts to move off my bump and head towards between my legs I put my hand over his.

'Jason. Stop.'

His hips are moving and he's manoeuvring me closer.

'Jason, look at me.' Jason looks at the camera, there are a couple of flashes.

'Shit.'

I look down as Jason remembers where we are and what we're doing, His erection softens against me.

Ken moves the chair into the centre of the shot and asks me to sit on Jason's lap. He wants me to bend backwards so my arms and legs are on the floor. Jason places his hand under my back to help me lower myself down. I built up my flexibility and strength at the beginning of the pregnancy but now I'm starting to lose it and my balance is off with the extra weight in my tummy.

'Beautiful, can you put your feet en pointe for me Em.'

I do as Ken says as the blood rushes to my head.

'And lift her up and kiss her.'

Jason does as he's told.

'Let your arm fall to your side Em. Let me see that bump. Keep kissing, good. Good.'

Jason's tongue flicks into my mouth.

I pull away and say, 'Later.'

He moves his fingers up onto my neck into my hair. His lips are back on mine.

'And that's a wrap.'

We kiss for a second longer. Then stop, then both look at Ken.

'Well, you two are damned sexy together. If it weren't for my lovely John, I would serve myself on a platter to you two.'

I grin at him.

'Even though we're breeders?'

'Sexy is sexy is sexy, my darlings. Now I'll leave you two to get dressed.'

Ken winks, then leaves us alone. Jason still has that look in his eye. He kisses me again. I move so I'm astride him across the chair, the bump is between us but not in the way.

When we're finished, we get dressed and return to Ken and John's kitchen. I'm flushed. They say nothing but everyone in the room knows what we've just been doing.

'So, Ken thinks he has some amazing shots, he tells me you've been working out. Someone has a six-pack?'

John leans forward, rubs Jason's stomach and makes an Ooh face at Ken,

'Don't, these two together are ridiculously hot, imagine what they are like when this one isn't pregnant. Can I take some photos of you then?'

Jason nods, 'Sure. Why not.'

'Excellent. I get why you need to paint her all the time. She has something... special.'

I laugh, 'She's in the room. But thank you, I'm sure the pictures will be amazing, because of your talent.'

'Ah, it helps to work with pretty people. Some of my commissions with the more characterful are challenging. Actually, do you want to see? I have some proofs. Top secret, of course.' Ken looks mischievous.

'Of course.' I say as Ken runs off to his office to fetch them.

The rest of the day is spent laughing, eating and for the three of them drinking wine, I've said I'll drive, so Jason can relax. I rarely see him drink; I think this is out of respect for me. There's a tiny part of me that hopes when this baby comes that I can have the occasional drink without it being an issue, but that's a pipe dream. I just want to feel normal. Like everyone else. We'll see. Who knows how it will be? I'm both excited and terrified. The only thing I'm sure of is that babies change things.

———

The nurse moves the ultrasound wand around my tummy and we hear the familiar swooshing sound. At thirty-six weeks, the baby looks like a baby and both Jason and I are grinning as we see it very clearly on the screen. The nurse is frowning.

'Could you wait here for a moment, please.'

The nurse closes the door and disappears. Jason takes my hand and says, 'Is there something wrong?'

'There can't be, we heard the heart. She's fine.'

We wait in silence, watching the door. Eventually, the nurse comes back with someone else.

'Hello, Mr and Mrs… Richards?' We don't bother correcting her. 'I'm Dr Kane, one of the maternity doctors here at Kingston, I just want to have a little look at your scan and listen to baby's heartbeat, OK.'

We both nod at her, too worried to say anything.

As she observes all the readouts, she frowns like the nurse did. Jason is watching the doctor's expression.

'OK, we need to keep you in for twenty-four hours just to monitor you and give you some steroids.'

Jason gives my hand a squeeze.

'What's the problem doctor?'

'Well, looking at the scan, it appears there isn't quite as much amniotic fluid as we would like at this stage in the pregnancy and baby's heartbeat is slightly slower than it should be. The steroids are to encourage the baby's lungs to develop, just in case we need to get this baby out a little early. There's nothing to worry about, thirty-six weeks is long enough to still have a perfectly healthy baby. This is just a precaution. And it'll do you no harm to do nothing for a while.'

She taps my hand with hers, 'Now, I'm just going to find you a bed,' and she's gone.

Oh God, fuck, this is retribution for all the bad things I've done, I knew it was too good to last. Fuck.

Jason says, 'It's fine, Maya is fine. It's just a precaution. Come here.'

He pulls me into a hug, ignoring all the gel all over my stomach.

When I'm in a bed with a heart monitor wrapped around me, Jason is told to leave me and come back at visiting time a couple of hours later. He says he'll fetch me some things.

In bed the beeps from the monitor as Maya's heartbeats are constant. I need to stay calm and try to relax. I try to rest, using the breathing they taught us at rehab. A few minutes later a nurse arrives and gives me a gown that does up at the back. She tells me to undress apart from my pants. She closes the curtains around the bed and I do as she says trying not to disturb the monitor on my belly. When she comes back in, she puts an IV in my arm which contains a mixture of fluids and steroids.

Jason returns a little later, he sees me in the gown, attached to the monitor and the IV and panic flips across his face before he has time to stop it.

'I'm OK, it's just the steroids.'

He gets a seat and sits next to me.

'I brought your book, a magazine and your wash stuff.'

His attention briefly shifts to my stomach then back to my eyes.

'We're OK, Maya is OK.'

He puts his hand on my bump.

'I know. It's just scary.'

'We'll be fine.'

'Oh, when I got home, this had come from the solicitor,' He's holding a letter in his hand it is thick vellum, 'We exchange on the eleventh of September. We can move in before this one arrives.'

'Hopefully.'

'Yeah, hopefully.'

He leans in close to my stomach and whispers, 'Just stay put a little bit longer so I can sort out your room.'

I grin at Jason, 'You're going to be a great dad.'

He leans in and kisses my bump and then me.

'You make me incredibly happy and we're going to be a great family.'

After Jason goes, I try and settle down for the evening. Reading turns out to be pointless, there is too much going on. A lady next to me has just given birth and there is a tiny baby in a crib next to her. She looks exhausted but every time the baby makes a noise, she shifts towards the crib. In the end, she gets up and starts to walk with the baby.

'Hi. Can I see? Are they a he or a she?' I ask as she comes past my bed.

'She's a she. This is Grace.'

'Oh, my Goddaughter is called Grace, great name.'

'I'm Caroline.'

'Hi, Em, Emma.'

'Are you OK?' She is looking at the monitor and IV.

'Yeah, I think so, just a precaution. I should be going home tomorrow. How was the birth?'

'Do you really want to know?'

'Yeah? We've been going to the prenatal classes but I haven't really got a feel for what it's really like.'

'OK, you asked for it,' a bit of a smile, a glance at Grace, 'the pain is unbelievable. Forget your birth plan, music, all that shit. You can't hear the music; you're just in so much pain and it goes on forever. My labour was only twelve hours. I'm told that's short for a first baby. Felt like a lifetime. And this one didn't want to come out, however hard I pushed. It felt like I was on fire between my legs and not in a good way.'

Grimacing, I cross my legs in the bed.

'In the end, they dragged her out using the Ventouse, you know the suction cap thingy they talk about in your classes. But and this is a big but, as soon as she's in your arms you forget it all because it was all worth it, I mean look at her.'

Caroline is beaming at her baby, and then as an afterthought she says, 'If they offer you drugs. Take them, forget natural birth it's bullshit.'

Shit, I can't have the drugs, pain killers are not allowed. I need to talk to my midwife. I haven't even thought about this. Fuck.

I don't sleep well; women are moaning and screaming. The babies are crying in the ward all night. By the morning I just want to go home. How long until morning visiting time? The clock on the wall in the ward says eight o'clock. Shit. We are brought breakfast in bed. It reminds me of the mush from rehab, I think the yellow mush is scrambled eggs. I push it around the plate. Caroline's family arrive, her partner and parents. There's much cooing over the baby. She's exhausted, I feel for her. I try to read again with slightly more success, until a doctor comes and says they want to do another scan to see how things look. It's been nearly twenty-four hours. Jason should be there, but that doesn't seem to be an option.

The doctor moves the device around. After what feels like forever the doctor turns to me.

'A marked improvement. You can go home Mrs Richards, just take it easy for the next few weeks.'

'Thank you.'

I need to tell Jason. When they wheel me back to the ward to get dressed, he's there with a bunch of flowers looking worried.

'We can go home.'

'But she has to take it easy.' The doctor says this to Jason who nods.

'Not a problem, doctor.' He's grinning.

The doctor puts the curtains around the bed. My IV was taken out last night. Jason comes and gives me a hug, kissing my neck.

'Let's go home and yes, you're staying at mine. No arguments. I'll get Harold Lloyd in a bit.'

'OK.'

I just want to go. When we're in the car, I tell him what Caroline said about the birth and the drugs.

'So, you can't have any painkillers, what about the epidural?'

'I don't know. I can't believe I haven't thought of this.'

'I didn't either. At least you're strong and fit. You should be able to handle it.'

'You're not the one pushing a football out of your vagina.'

Jason smiles slightly. I punch him in the arm, 'This is not funny.'

'No, sorry. We'll call your midwife when we get home.'

When we speak to the midwife, she tells us that although the epidural is largely an analgesic there are opiates in it as well to relax the patient. She says that if I have to have an epidural regardless of my addiction problem I should, because there is no other choice.

Fuck.

I decide I don't want to think about it, I tell Jason to leave it as he starts asking about natural alternatives. He realises I need some space and says he'll go and get Harold Lloyd.

By the time he comes back, I've had a nap and feel a little better. Women have been giving birth since the dawn of time. It'll be fine. I'll be fine.

As we're sitting at the table having a vegetarian spaghetti bolognaise Jason looks over at me with a frown.

'Did you leave your fridge door open when you left your flat?'

'No, I don't think so. I've been a bit forgetful lately though.'

'Hm, just wondering, the flat felt weird.'

'Weird?'

'Yeah, I can't put my finger on it. I turned the heating down and put it to only come on once a day now you'll be here for a while and I picked up some clothes and things.'

'Thanks.'

Harold Lloyd has jumped onto the table.

'Jesus, I forgot he has no discipline, get down Harold Lloyd.'

The cat ignores Jason and sniffs his food instead, which makes me giggle.

In bed later, Jason comes in all smiles.

'What?'

'Your first sleepover since, well everything.'

He stands behind me putting his arm around me so his hand is on the bump. He kisses my neck as his hand moves from my bump to my breast.

'Still fucking sexy.'

His hips have started to move.

Later, as he curls around me, sleepily he says, 'I look forward to seeing your face when we make love.'

———

The day of the house move comes around in no time. I'm leaving most of my furniture at my flat, but Jason has to empty his as it was a rental. We've hired a white van and have enlisted the help of John and Ken. When Jason's flat is empty, we both stand there looking at the bare space, already it feels like it isn't his anymore. As he takes a last look around, he seems sad, I take his hand.

I say, 'It's a big step.'

'Yeah, but a good one, I'm looking forward to our space, Em and Jason's.'

'Me too.'

He gives it one last look before we leave. We're following Ken and John in the car.

When we get to the new house, they start unloading, this is the third van load so they already have a system. I try and help Ken and have my hands around a box of kitchen stuff when he taps me on the shoulder and shakes his head.

'Your job, my darling, is making tea and looking beautiful. You need to keep that baby in for a little longer.'

I look at him and flounce towards the kitchen, I hate feeling like I'm no help, but the bump is huge and shifts and shoves me intermittently throughout the day and night. She's squashing my bladder, I need to pee every five minutes. Having a baby is not a glamorous affair.

When everything is unpacked from the van and boxes are put in the appropriate rooms, the three of them return to the kitchen, I've made a pot of tea (in Jason's pot, I refused to buy one) as Ken and John prefer it to coffee. I have told them they are worshipers of the devil's juice but they don't seem to care. Jason will drink either. I've put the pot on the table with a jug of milk and some cups. My hands are wrapped around my mug of coffee trying to keep them warm. We're still trying to work out how to get the heating to come on.

Jason is glowing with a sheen of sweat, he looks amazing, his muscles are literally rippling as he moves towards me. My libido has refused to settle down. If Ken and John weren't there... the things I would do to that man. I notice him looking at me, he's grinning. He comes over and whispers in my ear.

'We'll christen every room.' His hand moves over my arse slowly. I get wet just from his touch.

'OK, stop it you two, you have guests and we have a

housewarming present for you.' Ken and John are smiling at us and are holding a massive, framed picture.

They turn it around and we see a photograph of us. Jason's beautiful body is twisted around me, he's kissing my neck, the muscles in his back are defined as he curves over me. I'm looking down the lens of the camera, my lips apart, my hand on Jason's hip. Somehow Ken has managed to only show a small part of my nipple the rest of us is covered by each other, so it's sensual rather than pornographic.

'Wow. It's amazing.'

Jason is next to me, he seems speechless. With tears in his eyes he goes and hugs Ken. Who runs his hand down Jason's back and squeezes his arse, which makes me giggle.

John hands me a folder with the rest of the photos they're all incredible. I love the Flash Dance one, but I look sad. I show Jason as we all sit down to talk and have our drinks, I get some biscuits out. The perpetual hunger of the pregnant lady. Everyone digs in. Eventually, John and Ken say they have to leave. We thank them again for the pictures and wave them off from our new front door.

After they've driven off, Jason makes me step outside the house and then lifts me up to bring me in. Kissing me as he walks.

'Now which room would you like to start this christening business.'

I grin at him and then kiss him hard.

In the early hours of the morning, I wake up with a sharp pain in my side. Jason is asleep next to me. I leave him where he is and start waddling downstairs, thinking I'll get a glass of water. Halfway down I get another cramp. This time it doubles me up and I nearly fall. As I turn to go back upstairs, my waters break and leaks down the dark wood on the stairs in a stream. Another pain. These are coming too fast. Jason. I need Jason.

I scream his name as the next pain takes me, still trying to stumble up the stairs. I'm clutching the door frame moaning when Jason wakes up.

He's wide awake in seconds.

'Em. What do you need?'

'Ambulance, they're coming too quick, too close...Aaaaahhhhh'

I felt some twinges over the last twenty-four hours, but put it down to Braxton Hicks and ignored it. In a moment of clarity, I realise I've probably been in the first stage of labour for over thirty-six hours.

Jason puts on his joggers and runs downstairs, I hear him on the phone, answering questions. Then I'm screaming again. He runs back up.

'Can you walk, we need to get you downstairs.'

'Yes....NO. FUCK.'

Jason swoops me up in his arms and takes me downstairs as I scream in his ear.

'Lying down or standing up. What's best?'

'Up, hold me up.'

I'm bent over again; One of his hands is holding my arm and another rubbing my back.

'Jas, I'm scared... They're not gonna... FUCK!!!'

I manoeuvre to the end of the sofa to brace myself using the arm. Jason is facing me, half kneeling on the sofa cushion, his eyes on mine. His hands over my hands.

'Breathe Em. Remember your breathing.'

I start to do the panting we were taught between contractions; it helps a little and seems to slow things down slightly.

I've no idea how long I stand there breathing then screaming, until the pain is rocketing through me, my whole-body hurts from the top of my head to the tips of my toes. I'm screaming again.

'Towels, Jas, Get TOWELS.'

There's something between my legs, I'm yelling and squatting. Jason is behind me, he has spread a towel under my feet.

He draws me down slowly so I'm sitting, my back against his stomach, I put my hands between my legs and feel the head.

'FUCK...Ahhh.' I'm pushing and then there is a sense of release, the pain is gone and my hands feel for the baby.

Jason passes another towel too me, I wrap her up, she's still attached by the umbilical cord. I'm crying, Jason is crying, Maya is crying.

'Ah, we may be a bit late, Mike.'

A paramedic has come through the door that Jason had the good sense to leave on the snib. He kneels next to us and opens his case getting out a pair of surgical scissors.

'Dad, do you want to do the honours?'

The paramedic has quickly and efficiently put butterfly clips above and below where he needs to cut. Jason wipes the tears off his face with the back of his hand and nods. He snips the cord.

'Now, maybe a blanket for your lady?' The other paramedic is covering me up, I'm completely naked and covered in blood as I hold Maya to my breast, she latches on. Jason starts crying again. All I feel is pure joy.

'Right, you're not quite done, I just need to give you this. An injection goes in my leg.'

'What was that?' I fear he has given me some kind of painkiller.

His blue gloved hands are up, 'It's OK, it's OK. It's just a little something to encourage the placenta to come out.'

Almost immediately my stomach starts cramping.

He says, 'Is it OK, if I just...'

I nod as he lifts the blanket and massages my stomach until something else come out of me. He puts it into a bag.

'We need a doctor to check that all of it has come away. It's a problem if it hasn't. Now, we need to get you to the hospital to be checked out by a doctor, but based on how you both look, I reckon you'll be home in a couple of hours. You've done really well...'

'Em. Emma.'

'And you too,' He says nodding at Jason, 'Most men we find curled up in a corner rocking in this sort of situation.'

I put my bloody hand to Jason's cheek.

'Can I go in the ambulance with them?'

'Of course, VIP for your family, my friend.'

Jason lets me go and runs upstairs to get a shirt and some clothes for me. When we're ready to go, the paramedics insist on putting me on a stretcher to take me out. Curtains are twitching in the houses nearby. The new neighbours having an ambulance outside their home at three in the morning is gossipworthy.

As I get dressed, I pass Maya to Jason for the first time. He gently touches his little finger to her lips as he cradles her in his arms. She looks like a dot next to his bulk. I fall in love with Jason all over again at that moment and as for Maya, I have never felt anything like it.

At the hospital, I'm examined, Maya is examined. Jason refuses to leave our side at any point, much to the vexation of the doctor on call. We're told Maya weighs a healthy seven pounds eight ounces and that from what they can see I've managed to give birth without any rips or tears, apparently, I'm extremely lucky. The doctor checks the placenta, weighs it and says that yes, it's all there. We're free to go home. We catch a taxi outside the hospital.

When we get home, we realise we're far from ready, I've a few nappies and baby clothes but we've nowhere set up for her to sleep. I vaguely remember babies going into open drawers in the old days. I get Jason to clear out one from our chest of drawers, drawers and put towels and blankets along the bottom and sides to make it soft. When she falls asleep, we put her in and cover her with a soft blanket.

'Go and have a shower, I'll watch her.'

Jason sits next to her; he isn't going anywhere. When I shower, the water turns pink as it goes down the plug hole, the last time I saw blood in the shower like this it was about death. Today is all about being alive. When I return to the bedroom, Jason is leaning against the bed, his head lolling to one side as he sleeps cross-legged next to our baby. Maya is wide awake gurgling at me. I pick her up, nudging Jason with my foot before I climb into bed. It's seven in the morning. He comes and joins me.

'You were incredible today. I haven't the words for how much I love you. And her, Jesus who knew you could love such a tiny thing so much.'

'I know, it's mad. I would kill to keep her safe, she's everything. I'm sorry to say it but you have taken second place in my affections.'

'Same. Sorry.'

He leans in and kisses my head as I start to feed Maya.

'And that will never get old. You look amazing.'

'I look tired and drained and all sorts.'

'No, you look like a gorgeous Mama.'

When I've finished feeding Maya, Jason takes her from me and puts her back in the drawer. My adrenaline has well and truly run out, exhausted, I sleep for a couple of hours before I wake up to check on her, her little chest is going up and down. I climb back into bed and sleep for another hour before I hear her. Jason has her in his arms. He hands her to me.

'I suppose I should make some phone calls. We're not in the least bit ready for visitors but I suspect we are going to get some.'

By the next day, Kaz and both sets of parents are in our kitchen. My Mum is holding Maya, cooing at her, whilst Jason's mum looks on smiling.

My Dad is talking to Jason, there's a lot of back-slapping going on. I've made an excuse and gone outside with Kaz to show her the garden.

'So, tell me all the gory details, spare me nothing and by

the way, I know we're here to see Maya, but your new house is fucking gorgeous, who knew art could be so lucrative. And has Jason been working out, he looks fit and I mean fit, fit.'

'I'm knackered and that was a lot, Kaz.'

'Sorry, excited, my bestie had a baby.'

'Yes, Jason has been working out. There's a photo we had done when I was pregnant, Ken took it. It's not one for the parents though, it's leaning against the wall in our bedroom, go and take a sneaky peak. Yes, the house is gorgeous and I had Maya on the living room floor, just before the paramedics arrived.'

'Fuck, that's hardcore. That's a great birth story, how's downstairs, rips, tears stitches? Any piles popped out.'

'Ew...No. Is that really a thing?'

'Yes, I had stitches and piles. Still do. The joy of childbirth. You're one lucky lady.'

'That's what the paramedic said.'

'Well, I'm proud of you.'

'Thanks, we have a favour to ask, I know Jas won't mind me asking you without him. Will you be Godmother to Maya?'

'Yes. Get in. I was thinking no one was going to ask me.'

We grin at each other, then hug.

When we go back in Mum passes me Maya saying she thinks she's hungry. I move to the living room to breastfeed her. I don't want to embarrass the dads. I notice Kaz sneak upstairs. As the mums start hunting around in our cupboards to make something for lunch, Jason breaks away and comes and sits down next to us.

'Are you OK?'

'Yeah, you?'

'Yeah.'

He's watching Maya feed like it's a miracle.

'Is it wrong that I'm a bit jealous of her, there.'

'Yes. It's definitely wrong.'

'Just checking.'

Kaz comes back down the stairs in front of us, she stops halfway down and mouths the words "Fucking Hell" with a grin and two thumbs up. Jason looks up and sees her, she winks at him and then casually goes into the kitchen.

'What was she doing up there?'

'Looking at the picture.'

'Ah. I see.'

Everyone leaves the next day, until the evening, when John and Ken come around bringing with them a Moses basket with some beautifully embroidered handmade blankets with Maya's name on. We're extremely touched. We'd already agreed to ask them to be joint Godfathers to Maya. After tears and hugging they open the champagne and there's a toast. Jason hands me a glass.

I only have a mouthful for the toast and I tell Jason to drink the rest of mine. I'm terrified of doing something stupid now I have Maya.

HAPPY

As we settle into a routine, we start to unpack and sort out the house. Jason spends most of his time upstairs in Maya's room painting a beautiful mural on the wall with animals and insects in a jungle setting. When it's finished, he takes the cot up and we buy her a chest of drawers. For now, she needs to be in our room as she is still feeding every few hours, but in a couple of months, she'll grow out of the Moses basket and go into the cot. It will be strange having our bedroom to ourselves again.

I've been trying to set up my office, I only have a few more edits to do on my novel. I've found an agent who suggested a few minor changes before she sends my manuscript to several publishing houses. I work as much as I can while Maya sleeps. We are grateful that she seems to be a fairly happy baby, with few grumbles.

I amble around the house with a baby monitor tucked into the top of my leggings. Jason does as much as he can but feeding falls to me. I tried expressing milk, but it just made me feel like a cow, so I plan to keep her on the breast until six months when we will start weaning and give her formula. I'll be happy not to have engorged breasts for much longer, they feel twice the size they once were.

Maya is sleeping, so I wander upstairs with a cup of coffee for Jason who's in his studio. He's working on the painting of me in bed when I was pregnant. I like how it looks. He's concentrating when I walk in and jumps when I speak.

'Hey.'

'Fuck. You've got very quiet lately.'

'I'm in mummy stealth mode.'

'That's what it must be. Is that for me?'

'Yep. I was going to try and work while she's sleeping.'

Jason lays his paintbrush down and takes the coffee, putting it on a table before kissing me. We haven't made love since Maya was born. I kiss him back.

'I've missed you.'

His hands move down my back.

'God, I've missed this. You look amazing Em. No one would guess you just had a baby.'

'I think the breastfeeding helps.'

He's kissing my neck, 'Mm breastfeeding. Your body tastes of milk'

'Maya's a messy eater.'

'Just like her Mama. Now can we not talk babies, just for a little while.'

I couldn't talk if I wanted to.

———

I need to pick up some notes I've left in my old flat. I've brought Maya with me; in case she needs a feed. Releasing the car seat gently, I lift the handle to bring her with me, she's fast asleep. As I let myself in, I notice some photographs on the floor in the hall. They're the ones of me that Charlie took for his finals. I wonder if they got knocked when we were moving stuff to the house. Placing Maya down in the hall, I pick up the photos, there's a trail of them all the way into the living room. There's a socked foot sticking out over the armrest of the sofa. Stopping in my tracks. My pulse quickens, behind me Maya is still sleeping. My senses heighten and I notice the flat smells different, I recognise it but can't place it. I take another quiet step forward. Who's on my sofa? I freeze as the foot twitches slightly. Are they awake? They would have heard me come in; they must be asleep. Another step and then another. Crunch. Shit. I'm standing on an empty packet of crisps. Whoever's here has made themselves at home. The foot is still, one more step. There's a rucksack leaning against the wall, clothes are spewing out of it. What is that smell? Cigarettes, an aftershave I recognise... reaching the end of the sofa I see the owner of the foot. Thank fuck, my heart starts to return to a more relaxed beat.

I pinch his toe, at the same time seeing the state of the coffee table. The ashtray looks full, a half-empty glass of red wine and an empty bottle on the table. I can't see any drugs. He doesn't stir.

'Seth. Seth, wake up.'

He wakes up slowly, 'Ugh, wha' time is it?'

'I don't know, midday maybe,' He's pushing himself onto his elbows. I've kneeled down next to him.

'Are you OK?'

He sits up and stretches out his long legs, I'd forgotten how lanky he is.

Moving to the kitchen, I put the kettle on.

Seth comes and sits at the kitchen table still looking blurry-eyed, 'I'm sorry. I've been kinda squatting here.'

'Yeah, you could've just asked.'

'Hm.'

I put a black coffee in front of him.

'Have you started your course?'

'Yeah, but they can't get me into student accommodation until next week, some kind of administrative fuck up about mature students or something.' He looks at me properly for the first time, 'You look good.'

I hear Maya, 'Thanks, hang on.' I return to the hall and unclip her from the car seat her lips are suckling.

'Oh. You had the baby then.'

I briefly wonder what he thought happened to the baby, then sit down and take off my jacket one-handed and lift my shirt, pulling my bra down.

Seth, looks down quickly, 'Shit.'

'Yes, I had the baby. I'm breastfeeding, stop being such a dick. It's not like you haven't seen my tits before.'

He still tries to avoid looking at Maya feeding, 'Yeah, but that's different to this.'

I ignore him, 'So, why the wine, you know we're not supposed to.'

He rubs his forehead before he looks at me, 'Yeah, lesser of two evils I suppose. It was wine or drug, drugs, I went with wine. I was pissed off about the accommodation thing, I had to move out of my halfway house and I thought I was going to have to live rough until they sorted it. I'd been to your flat one other time when I needed a break from the halfway house, sorry,' He glances up at me, 'and I thought you weren't using it so...Do you have any paracetamol, my head's throbbing?'

'Yeah, medicine cabinet.' That explains the open fridge that time. Jason probably surprised him and he did a runner. Maya's eyes are closing and milk is dribbling from her mouth and my breast. I rummage in the pocket of my jacket trying to find a tissue.

'Here,' Seth is back, handing me kitchen roll. He's contemplating my dripping breast, 'Hmm... So, you're living at Jason's?'

'No, he brought a place in Putney Heath.' I wipe the milk away and cover myself up.

'Oh, fancy. So, you're a kept woman now?' A smirk forms

and an eyebrow is raised as Seth puts the paracetamol in his mouth and swallows, before taking a slurp of coffee.

I hadn't thought of myself that way. I frown. 'No, I...'

'Mm.'

Time to put Maya back in her car seat. When I've sat back down, I say, 'You can stay here as long as you want. But don't go rummaging in my stuff. My photos were all over the floor.'

He looks down, some colour rises on his cheeks.

'Sorry, they...er... I like them.'

'Yeah, well they were never for what you were using them for.'

'Hey, I wasn't wanking over them. I was just looking.'

He's pissed me off, putting doubt in my mind about my dynamic with Jason, I consider asking for the key back but notice the stubble on his chin and the tiredness in his eyes. He's watching me like a caged animal, unsure whether to attack or hide. I put my head down and sigh.

'I'm sorry. It's just, they're personal.'

'No, it's my fault, I shouldn't have looked at your stuff... What're you going to do with this place?'

'I don't know. I should sell it I suppose. It just... Charlie and I were...yeah. I'm not ready.'

'Even now. New starts and all that.' Seth nods towards Maya.

'Even now. It would seem disloyal. I thought about renting it, but I don't like the idea of strangers being here. Maybe I should get over that, contribute and be less of a "kept woman," I don't know.'

Seth changes the subject, 'So, what's the baby's name?'

'Maya.'

'Nice, a little girl, she's beautiful like her mum.'

'Thanks.' I hear a key in the lock and frown.

'Hey, you forgot nappies.' Jason says from the hallway.

He walks into the kitchen and sees Seth at the kitchen table. I hadn't realised quite how much Jason filled a room these days. He's looking from me to Seth, 'What's he doing here?'

'He needed a place to stay. A cock up with his accommodation.'

'You said you weren't in touch anymore.'

Seth is standing up, 'We're not, mate. I let myself in, I had a key from before.'

I wince, that sounds bad.

'Kaz gave him a key when my feet were bad.'

Jason must think it sounds like excuse after excuse. Shit.

Jason picks up the car seat and looks at me, 'I'll take our daughter home. Sort this mess out Em.' He's glaring at me. He doesn't bother saying anything else, walking out of the house. I put my head in my hands.

'Em.'

'Wait, I need to think.'

Seth moves and I hear the rustle of clothes being shoved back into his rucksack.

'No, Seth. Stop. It's OK. Stay as long as you need, but less wine, yeah?'

'Yeah, OK. Thanks.'

'I should go home.'

I leave him standing there with a t-shirt in one hand and his rucksack in the other. I need to speak to Jason.

Driving back to the house, my heart is racing. As soon as I walk through the door he stands up, he's waiting for me. 'What the fuck, Em?'

'I didn't know. I found him there.'

'He has a key?'

'I completely forgot; it was from ages ago, honestly.' I step towards him and watch as he turns his back on me, putting one hand through his hair. I put my hand on his arm, but he shrugs it off.

'Please Jason, I know it looks bad. But I'm telling you the truth.'

He rounds on me then, 'How could you "forget" you gave a man a key to your flat? You never let me stay there. Never. Is this why? Have I been a complete idiot? Are you playing house with Seth and me?'

'No. I let him stay because we weren't having sex. I didn't want anyone...Me and Charlie...that place is all about. Shit. Please believe me.' I hear the monitor; Maya is waking up. I walk past him to go upstairs to see to her. She's in the Moses basket by the bed. I lift her and cradle her in my arms seeing her beautiful face. I don't want to mess this up with Jason. I want us to be a family.

When I turn, Jason is watching us. He walks towards us and puts his arms around me and Maya drawing us close. I lean my head on his chest.

'I'm sorry Jas, I just found him there today.'

'I believe you. I wish you'd told me about the key thing.'

'I honestly forgot, with the pregnancy and everything else happening. It was a lot.'

We sit on the bed, putting Maya down to play with her feet and gurgle next to me, she tugs off a sock like a pro. As I'm putting the sock back on, I ask Jason, 'Am I a kept woman?'

'No, why would you say that?'

'Because I don't pay for anything.'

'You're the mother of my child, you don't have to pay for anything.'

'Yeah, but surely that's the whole point, you're the father of my child. Surely, we should be contributing the same.'

'If it hadn't been for you, I wouldn't have painted the pictures that paid for this house.'

'But what about bills and things, they're all in your name. I don't know how much the electricity is or anything. I still have money from Charlie. I might make some money from my book. I can afford to pay half.'

'But you don't need to.'

'I want to. Don't you see, we've fallen into typical male and female roles, except you do more with Maya than most dads?'

'What are you saying?' Jason has sat down on the other side of the bed and is putting on Maya's other sock as she chortles at him.

'I want us to be equals in everything, including our finances. I know it's boring but my name should be on our bills and I'll pay my half. I need to be a good example to Maya. I should show her I'm independent and that you can be in a loving relationship without being "kept." With Charlie it was the same, he had the money from his work and I was looked after. I don't want to do that anymore. I want us to be different. Better.'

Jason looks down and smiles.

'What?'

'I never imagined I would ever hear you say something could be better than your relationship with Charlie. I've always felt like second fiddle.'

'Oh, Jas. My gorgeous man.' I crawl across the bed being careful not to dislodge Maya and kiss him. He helps me onto his lap whilst keeping a hand on Maya's tummy.

He says, 'We can do all of that. You can keep me if you want. I just want us to be happy.'

'I am.'

EPILOGUE – 22ND SEPTEMBER 1995

Jason has been acting weird for weeks. He won't tell me what's going on but just says it's a birthday surprise.

On the morning of my birthday, he wakes me before Maya so we can make love. Then says he has to go, but my real present will be later. As he gets dressed, he grins to himself. Before he leaves, he comes back upstairs with a coffee for me and kisses me. I hold onto him, I'm not done. He's practically naked again when we finish. He's still grinning and refusing to tell me anything as he gets dressed again. I hear Maya, on the monitor, 'Mama? Mama?'

Jason runs upstairs, collects her from her cot and places her on the bed before kissing us both. 'I really must go, I'm already late.'

He leaves us as I say to Maya, 'Where's Daddy going? I shake my head at her. She giggles. Her dark hair is like mine and has started to curl around her ears and down her neck. She has Jason's light brown eyes that turn dark when she's upset.

I put her on the floor onto her feet, she's started taking some tentative steps, so we have put stair gates up. She holds onto the bed as I go through my clothes. Jason said smart casual. I have no idea what that means.

Maya and I go and wash. I'm trying to show her how to clean her two little front teeth that have just come through when I hear the doorbell.

'Who's that coming around at this time in the morning?'

We go to the front door and see John and Ken smiling at us, 'Hello? Everything OK?'

'Yes, it certainly is.'

Maya is already straining to get out of my arms, 'Ka Ka.' Her hands wiggle to get to Ken, who takes her, kissing her cheek.

'And how is my beautiful girl today?'

'She's good, still teething so a bit grisly when she's tired.'

'My goddaughter grisly? I don't think so. No.' He's rubbing noses with her as she giggles.

John looks at me in my dressing gown, 'Aren't you ready yet? You need to go. We're babysitting.'

'You are?'

'Yes, under strict instructions from Jason. Go and get dressed, you need to get going. You don't want to keep him waiting. You need to meet him in Leicester Square at eleven.'

'I do?'

'You do.'

Shit, it's already nine. It will take at least an hour to get from here to Leicester Square.

I put a little bit of make-up on and return to my wardrobe. Smart casual. I still have no clue what that means. In the end, I choose tight black PVC jeans, a black lacy camisole over a black bra and a big grey cowl-necked jumper over the top, which makes the PVC jeans look less full on. Feet, what to wear on my feet. I know I want to look taller but I need to be able to walk. I find some black wedge ankle boots and look in the mirror. Hm. OK, for a mum of a one-year-old. My hair hangs in large messy waves down over my shoulders.

When I get downstairs John and Ken are sitting on the floor at opposite ends of the rug in front of the sofa. Maya is taking it in turns to toddle from one to the other.

'How do I look?'

Ken stands up and gives me a once-up and down.

'Hm. Hang on.'

He grabs a pencil off the table and twists my hair into a loose bun on top of my head, with a few strands still falling around my face. He shoves the pencil in to hold it.

'Perfect.'

John has picked up Maya, 'Now kiss mummy, she's going to see daddy. You get to spend today with us.'

Maya grins at him, I lean in and kiss Maya, then kiss both John and Ken as I grab my bag and leave. It's a mild September day, my feet crunch in the first of the fallen leaves as I walk to the station. I've got butterflies. John and Ken have babysat a few times so Jason and I could have some alone time. This is the first time we've left her for the whole day, but I'm not nervous about that, I'm excited to see what Jason has planned.

The trains seem to be on a go slow, I travel from Putney to Waterloo and then catch a tube to Leicester Square. I'm ten minutes late. Jason is sitting on a bench waiting for me. He stands up when he sees me, gathering me to him for a kiss.

'You made it. I was getting worried.'

'I did, the train was so slow.'

He lets his hand slip under my jumper to my arse, feeling the warm PVC against my skin, 'You look good.'

'Thanks.'

He leans in to kiss me again and we stay like that for a while, snogging like teenagers in the middle of Leicester

Square. Eventually, he leans away from me, 'We need to stop. I've a plan. We're going to be tourists today.'

'Hang on.' I remember this, 'we're going to retrace our steps?'

'Uh huh, only this time, I'm going to do and say all the things I wanted to that time around.' He's holding my hands looking down at me.

'Oh, like a do-over.'

'Yeah, more or less.'

'Excellent, let's do it.'

He takes my hand and says, 'Trocadero. Come on.'

We go in through the crowds of tourists filling the Trocadero, bumping into people with bum bags as they suddenly stop in front of us to take photos. One couple asks us to take their picture in front of one of the shops.

When we get to the photograph place where I'd dressed as a saloon girl and Jason as a cowboy, Jason tells me to put on the same thing. This time we go in together. Standing on a small stage with a stagecoach painted on the background. He wraps himself around me as the photographer takes the shots. He's kissing me, his hand moving up my leg that I have wrapped around his back, he feels the garter on my leg putting his thumb under it, squeezing my thigh. I lean back so he can kiss my neck. The photographer carries on clicking. Until we hear him say, 'Times up.' Jason squeezes my arse as he releases me.

'Is that really what was going on in your mind all that time ago?'

'That's been going on in my mind since the day I met you.'

'You two can pick up your photo or photos on the way out.'

We leave the stage, going around the back to change into our normal clothes. When we go to the booth to pick up the photos, we choose one where he's kissing my neck and another when he first took hold of me. The woman's expression doesn't change, I imagine she sees all sorts; it makes me giggle. I nudge Jason and look from his face to hers as she takes the payment. His shoulders start to shake, as she hands him the changes, he manages a 'Thanks,' before we run out holding the photos laughing.

'So, now where?'

'Chinatown.' Of course, lunch.

We go into the same restaurant and order. This time I'm more proficient with the chopsticks than I was, managing not to spill food all over myself. As we eat, we talk about when I was first in London trying to find my place in the world. Jason had been in London for just over a year. When I finish my bowl of noodles, Jason orders green tea and I order water. He nods and we tap the small China handle-less cups. He leans forward and kisses me over the table. I can taste the tea on his lips, as he whispers, 'To us.'

'To us.'

As we leave Chinatown, we walk holding hands. Comfortable in our silence. Watching people running and walking around us, pushing past in a rush to be somewhere. I smell food, cigarettes and diesel. When we get to the banks of the Thames the scent of mildew and dirty water is added to the mix. Jason puts his arm around me as we continue to walk towards the South Bank.

I remember bouncing around in front of him asking him questions as he patiently answered me. As we walk across Waterloo Bridge we stop in the middle and look at the city. There's something beautiful in the oldness and newness of it all. Cranes tower over everything, building upwards as there is no more room on the ground. Big Ben stands majestically across from us. We kiss, then continue to walk.

When we get to the Southbank, we wander slowly through, until we reach The Hayward Gallery. This time

Jason doesn't feel the need to explain the paintings we see, we just slowly move around observing, until I see myself.

'Jason, why didn't you tell me?'

'I wanted to surprise you.'

'But this is massive. Isn't it?'

He grins at me, 'Yeah, kind of.'

'When did this go up?'

'This morning, that's where I was, there was press and stuff, I didn't think you'd want...'

'No. I wouldn't.' It's the Weeping Widow. I still look strong. It was before I completely broke apart. My face is the picture of grief.'

An American comes up to us, 'Oh my God. That's you, isn't it? Can I take a photo?'

'No.' Jason looks at the man in the tropical shirt like he's ready to kill him. The man scuttles away.

Jason is bristling next to me, I put my hand on his waiting for him to look at me and say, 'I'm so proud of you.' He leans down to kiss me.

'I'm proud of you, look how far you've come.'

'Thank you.'

We stand holding hands, looking at the picture for a while longer. I remember that me. I was a different person. After a while, it feels time to move on.

'Come on, let's keep looking at everything else.'

'OK.'

He squeezes my hand.

When we leave The Hayward Gallery, we go back across the river taking our time as we go, when we pass The National Portrait Gallery, I say to Jason, 'One day, your work will be in there.'

'Maybe when I'm dead.' He grimaces at me.

'I think, before that.'

'We'll see.'

Then we're in Soho, I expect us to go to the pub we

ended up in, talking all night, instead Jason takes a different turn.

'Are we not going to the pub?'

'Nah, it's closed. So, I thought we could do a little better these days.'

As we go in, there are Michelin stars above the door. We're taken to a corner table out of the way. The waiters are efficient and seem to be aware of our every need. We order and wait for our first course. I take off my jumper, my camisole can pass as evening wear, my scars are still a light pink on my arms but have faded.

'So, have you done everything you wanted to on that day?'

'Nearly. There are some things I hadn't even thought of then that we are still going to do.'

I raise an eyebrow. He runs his thumb along my lip. I poke my tongue out to lick it as he pushes it into my mouth. The waiter arrives with her eyes cast down. Jason takes his time pulling his thumb out, his face shadowed in the candlelight.

We eat our starters and move quickly on to our main courses. It's delicious and I'm relishing it. I could eat twice as much as what's on my plate. Jason is watching me. I ask him if we're staying for dessert. He shakes his head, 'No, I need to get you to the hotel.'

'We're not going home?'

'Maya will be fine. Ken and John have got this. We can call them when we are... settled.'

'OK.'

We leave and Jason walks us quickly to a small boutique hotel nearby, he's already booked it, we tumble into the room in each other's arms.

As we reach the bed, he takes the pencil from my hair and it falls down my back, 'I've wanted to do that all day.'

He pushes me onto the bed, coming forward to kiss my

shoulders as I undo the buttons on his shirt. Then he's tugging off my PVC jeans.

We are facing each other afterwards in bed, 'Happy birthday, Em.'

'It's been an amazing day.'

We are both out of breath. He slowly unwraps himself from me to get out of bed. I frown at him as he rummages in the pocket of his jacket then climbs back next to me and hands over a small black square box. He says, 'Open it.'

He's nervous, his eyes dart from my face to the box and back again. Inside is a white gold ring with a sapphire, surrounded by tiny diamonds embedded into it.

'Will you? In a completely equal, sharing everything kind of way?'

I still wear my wedding band from Charlie. I take the wedding ring off and put it on the fourth finger of my right hand. Then hold out my hand for Jason to put the engagement ring on.

When it's on my finger, we kiss and hug and then I gaze at the ring again. We're both crying and smiling. I say, 'I'm going to sell the flat. I need to let go.'

'You don't have to Em.'

'I know, but I want to, it's time.'

'Oh Em, I love you so much.'

'I love you.'

We check in with Ken and John, then fall asleep holding each other tight.

———

When we get home, we find an exhausted Ken and John sitting on the sofa as Maya runs rings around them. They stand up as we arrive.

'Let's see it then.' John says looking at me. I grin at him and hold out my hand.

'We helped him choose it and made sure he got the right size; he didn't have a clue.' Ken says taking my hand and looking at it, then bringing me into a hug, 'Congratulations.'

'Thank you and thank you for babysitting. How was she?'

John pulls a face, 'A bit grisly as you said, but then we let her have a gin and play with knives.'

'Excellent. Just what we would have done. But seriously, thank you.'

'Our pleasure, now we need to go home and have a rest. How you do this twenty-four-seven is a mystery.'

Jason gives them both a hug before they leave.

'Coffee?' I'm already in the kitchen.

'Yes please, oh look what's come in the post.'

It's a box from my publisher, I have spent the last year, between changing nappies, weaning Maya and going through the whole business of getting my book published. It's a much longer and drawn-out process than I imagined. I open the box and smile taking out a first edition hard copy.

'Look Maya, here's mummy's book.' Maya runs towards me.

'Mama, boo.'

'Yes, Mama boo.' I pick her up and walk towards Jason in the kitchen who has put the coffees on the table.

'Let's see then.' I hand him the book, 'Clever Mummy.'

He flicks through the pages, then looks up and grins at me, before giving both of us a hug.

The End

ACKNOWLEDGMENTS

Writing a novel is no easy thing. This isn't the first nor, I hope will it be the last, but it is the first one that I am close to comfortable sharing.

In my meagre opinion, novels take time, effort and a fair amount of emotional input and support so, there are several people I would like to thank.

Firstly, Ruth, my very talented partner in crime at Castle Priory Press, my beta reader and editor. She has read this novel in its many forms, many times and she has been nothing but patient, positive and supportive. I will always be grateful that we get to work together.

My writing groups, both Novel Club and the 20/20 Writing Group – thank you to all those who read drafts of various chapters and who offered vital constructive feedback. All of your thoughts and feedback, I hope, have made this a more rounded novel.

My family have put up with me whilst I daydream and mither over characters, plots and worldbuilding whilst missing important information about their lives. Thank you, Paul, Heather and Lola – I love you.

I would also like to thank my Girlymers, who are my fellow adventurers, my girl-gang, my people. I have known you the longest and snippets of you all form parts of my many ideas.

My Dad taught me to love the written word, he read or invented stories constantly. His first novel was published when he was eighty-one, proving that it is never too late. He was, and always will be an inspiration.

And finally, you. If you have made it to here and read to the end, thank you. I hope you enjoyed Em's story, I know she wasn't always easy to love – but hopefully, you warmed to her by the end.

ABOUT THE AUTHOR

JM Langan was brought up in Shropshire and now lives in Birmingham. She has been published in various online journals and anthologies including, The Cabinet of Heed, The Drabble, 50-Word Stories, Poetic Sun and The Crowstep Journal. She has published a short story collection and two collections of poetry and has an MA in creative writing. She is working on her next novel.

You can find her on social media @MuddyNoSugar

ALSO BY J M LANGAN

<u>Poetry Collections</u>

Blood Kisses

Love & Being

<u>Short Story Collections</u>

The Solstice Baby

Printed in Great Britain
by Amazon